MISERCORDIAS
Carson McKenna

BOOK 1

To Haley F., my queen of July, and muse.

Dear Reader,

Thank you so much for picking up my book!

This book contains a small universe of characters. For your convenience, I've included a character index in the back. This could help you to keep all those darn Foleys and Walshes straight. Plus, there are bonus tidbits which could help to color your experience.

Ta, and thanks again!

Carson

Table of Contents

Title Page

Dedication

Note From the Author

Table of Contents

A Soldier's Brief Manifesto

Chapter 1

Chapter 2

Chapter 3

Chapter 4

Chapter 5

Chapter 6

Chapter 7

Chapter 8

Chapter 9

Chapter 10

An Afterword

"Greetings from the Hawkeye State"

In the Sun King's Dark Shadow

Character Index

Book 2: Domini

Acknowledgements

A Soldier's Brief Manifesto

You already know parts of this story.

You've probably seen a billboard of her posing with her bourbon like a sultry perfume ad, knees locked together, gem-like eyes unfocused below the ubiquitous FOLEY logo, an emblem of Americana as classic as Coke or Cadillac.

You've heard about the half-century-long dispute between the Foleys and the Walshes, two dynastic Irish-American families that merged in the 1920s and diverged in the '60s. *Vanity Fair* called them "the Kennedys of Kentucky," writing in an article: *"instead of senate seats, the Foleys and Walshes have bourbon barrels, and blue-eyed Irishmen embattled in stubbornness and cirrhosis."* Most articles written about the Foleys and Walshes have been titled some variation of, 'Blood and Bourbon.' The blood, of course, refers to both their dovetailing lineage (Sully Foley and Wilkie Walsh were second cousins) and the violence between them in the 1970s. If you think that hatred is journalistic puffery, you need only to visit their distilleries—located right next door to each other 15 miles outside of Louisville, Kentucky—and ask. You'll see. Those blue eyes don't lie.

If someone has ever given you a gift of Foley bourbon, you probably wrote them a thank you note, as you might for cashmere or crystal. When Kentucky women are done with the bottle of Foley, they often reuse it as a flower vase, careful to let the logo face outward.

If you went to college in the South, you drank Walsh bourbon from plastic jugs poured into red solo cups. Walsh is the unofficial sponsor of frat parties, the progenitor of good times. If your last name is Walsh in Kentucky, then you're a fortunate son, an heir to the boozy bloodline, and your dominion spans from Lexington to Louisville—all the way up to the twelve-foot hedges of Foley. You cross the property line with the last name Walsh, Mr. Foley fires his rifle at you. Even if you gave a ring to the Foley heiress, and she has every intention of marrying you.

Even then.

The red-haired girl on the bourbon billboard is not a model, she is an heiress. She is the Foley heiress. That is how she was referred to on University of Louisville campus—"the Foley heiress"—in hushed tones of intrigue and jealousy. Her name is actually Blaise.

Blaise Foley. The sun of our solar system, the blood in our veins, boyhood crush turned manhood obsession.

She was Blaise at dusk for our interviews, the shawl of Kentucky sun slung over her freckled shoulders.

She was Kelly Rhiannon on her birth certificate. Her mother chose Rhiannon because she was born on Halloween, and Mrs. Foley felt a witchy name was in order ("And Johnny didn't like Kelly Morticia!"). At her First Holy Communion in '96, she took the name Blaise. No one but her Uncle Duffy was allowed to call her Kelly, ever again.

She was "Foley" to Patrick Walsh—and while his tone would vary depending on what she was doing, his blue eyes were sotted with affection most times they fell on her.

She was a writer's wet dream. When I interviewed her, I could not believe that the most extreme versions of spoiled, beautiful, charming, generous, plotting and passionate could exist within a single person's 140-pound body.

I call her all the names, but principally she is my muse. She was a tonic of Metamucil and prune juice for my literary constipation. She was God and I was Adam, coming into being from the graze of her hand. The meaning of my life is to convey the meaning of hers, through the conduit of written word. If I am successful in this, if I am true to her, then I can go in peace and honor to a soldier's death, never again fearing the eternal blight of the unmarked grave.

-James Branagh
2015

Chapter 1

Every American soldier born after 1945 has read Black-Jack's war memoir, *Kilkenny-Kentucky*. So have many people of Ireland, where Jack was born in 1893 and died in 1948. The years in between were spent in Kentucky, where Black-Jack achieved nationwide notoriety as the greatest bootlegger that America ever saw. For this, you would also be hard-pressed to find a Kentuckian who doesn't own a copy of his famous book.

There's an old joke that if you ask a Louisville librarian to bring you the bible, she'll respond,

"Which version—the King James or the King Jack?"

I am an Irish boy from Kentucky, born in 1986, who served in the US Army from 2005-2009. I can tell you in absolute terms that Black-Jack is the reason I wanted to be a soldier, and a writer. His memoir is my soul's parable; the blueprint for my own postbellum scrawls. From memory, I could fill this Word Document with Jack's first three pages, but I'm thinking now of the opening words:

"Writing and fighting, those are the only two things I ever wanted to do."

Me too, Jack. What a miracle that everything you want from this world can be packaged up into one sentence. If I hadn't read it, I may have spent forty years wandering the earth trying on identities that fit like poorly tailored suits.

Patrick Walsh, my oldest friend, whose wedding I was to wear a Best Man suit for this December, has told me that I'm a soldier before all else. No, that's too poetic. What Pat actually said was that I couldn't get two minutes into a conversation without bringing up the Army. His blue eyes crinkled, so I knew not to go all disgruntled grunt on him.

"You're like a bad game of Taboo," he informed me. "Where *Army* is always your secret word, but no one asked to play."

Pat is wont to make stupid jokes like this. When telling a story from college, he'll say to me, "Oh, this was when you were in

Baghdad, working on your tan." I think it's a privilege of our bond that he can lampoon my service like that. Even my closest cousins don't say much, apart from "Happy Veterans Day" in November.

I told Pat that he was living in his own game of Taboo, but his secret word is *Accounting*. Pat is a CPA with an MBA, and all of his friends—except me—have gone to work at the Big Four accounting firms. He claims to hate his auditing job at KPMG, but it's a lie. No one truly hates the thing which gives them their identity. He and his suit buddies grumble about SEC filing and audits in the same way my vet buddies grumble about military pay and hero worship.

Pat laughed, "That's because KPMG is the Iraq of my life!"

His real Taboo word in this game would of course be Blaise Foley, his indescribably coveted fiancée. Blaise is the kind of girl who makes a selfish libertine like myself fantasize about becoming a dad someday. I don't consider it a big deal that I'm in love with her, too. Pat got shot for her, and wears a scar for her, so I guess he deserves her in his bed. I'm a man of honor, after all—I'm a soldier first.

Before I left for France in June, Pat began a good fifty percent of his sentences with "*Foley wants*" and "*Foley thinks.*" You could tell from his eyes that Pat was proud to be in the know of what Foley wanted or thought. This was all back before their love soured like a bowl of cereal left on your desk overnight.

Like milk, love is a fickle and fragile substance.

Yesterday, Pat told me that he doesn't want to hear Blaise's name spoken. She will be an extended round of Taboo for us, with associative terms like *bourbon heiress* and *girl-next-door* also verboten. He made me promise not to ask questions for now, just to help him get away.

I was slurping a Bomb Pop and reading *Catch-22* on our porch when he told me all this. The ice cream truck guy was the only person I'd spoken to so far that day. It was a fatally hot August afternoon and, when Pat came outside, I expected him to ask if I wanted to go jump in Deebo's pool.

"Did she break it off with you?" I asked, cramming his suitcase into the back of his Jeep Cherokee.

Pat dropped an armful of lacrosse sticks into his trunk, his stony face growing defiant. "You don't think I'd break it off with her?"

"No," I said. Because that would be madness, and we both knew it.

"Well, you never know. A man has his limits…"

"A man does. *You* don't. Not for her."

He leaned heavily against the car, wiping his sweaty forehead with his sleeve. His black lab, Shadow, pawed lazily at our ankles. Neither of us knelt down to scratch him.

"Is this about her dad?" I pointed to the scar veining his chiseled cheek. Blaise's father was the one who shot Pat, years before she ever agreed to go out with him. Though she eventually changed her mind about him, Mr. Foley never did.

"I don't want to talk about it," Pat said curtly, checking his oil gauge. "Anyway, she's coming home tomorrow."

"From New York?"

"Yeah. I want to be gone when she gets here."

"And—where are you going?"

"I think I'll go and see Crummy for a little while," Pat said, naming his lax buddy who lived in Bowling Green. "Then, who knows?"

"When will you be back?" I said, getting impatient with his Man of Mystery act. Really, how far could he roam when he had to be to work on Monday?

"I'm taking some time off," Pat grumbled. "*Fuck* KPMG."

Now, I was scared.

"And whatever you do," Pat turned his ignition, looked me square in the face. "On your honor as my Best Man, *don't* tell her where I'm headed. *Please*."

I swore it. What else could I say?

His phone started vibrating, the screen lit up with *Foleyyyy* and a string of heart-eyed emoji. Except for a tendon flexed in his neck, he ignored her call.

"So, are you not speaking to her…?" I asked, trying to keep up.

"You promised not to ask questions, James," he said with pretend reproach and, for a second, his eyes were not just blue stones on dull earth. Ordinarily, his eyes *shimmer*. A middle school girl would call them "dreamy." A writer might draw comparisons to Neptune, both the sea king and the misty blue planet. I won't, because Pat would enjoy it too much.

"And I'm getting rid of this phone, *ugh*." He brought the screen two inches from his face and grimaced as *Foleyyyy* flashed again. "It's the root of all my problems."

"You're not gonna have a *phone?*"

"Well, not this one." Casually, he frisbeed his iPhone into the street. The screen shattered into a spider web.

Finally, I understood that this was really happening: Patrick Walsh was going off the rails in a 2012 Jeep Cherokee.

"*Wait!*" Desperately, I signaled for him to hang on a minute, and ran into our house. In my room, I tore the thing off the mirror, where it hung like a talisman.

As I came down the driveway, Pat was busy grinding his tires over his poor phone. He glanced up gloomily, his expression sharpening when he saw what I had in my hand.

"Are you sure?" he asked in surprise.

"Try it on." Instinctively, I knew he was the only other person in America whom it would fit. "Just don't let it show. It's never supposed to show."

Pat obeyed, admiring himself in his rearview mirror with a crescent moon smile.

"Now you'll have to come back," I added, trying to make my tone menacing.

"Thanks, I'll take care of it." He swatted my hand. "I'm gonna get going." He whistled, and Shadow jumped obediently in the front seat, his big tongue lolling around his mouth.

Pat paused for a moment, looking like he had something else to tell me. But then, he waved limply and revved down our tree-lined street, away from the house we lived in for two years together.

Most of them with Blaise Foley.

Black-Jack Walsh came to Kentucky from Ireland when he was twenty-eight. By then, he had been fighting in the IRA for years, and wanted to try out his luck in America. He celebrated his twenty-eighth birthday on the steamer that brought him over with his wife,

Clara, and newborn son, Wilkie. It was the second to last day of January, and they were probably somewhere near Newfoundland.

I am twenty-eight now. This is my Jack year—it has to be. Twenty-eight is the year that a soldier stops fighting and regenerates with the lessons of his service. At least, that is how *my* Scripture will go.

My plan was always fight, school, write. I finished my degree in May and vowed to start my war memoirs.

Not that many people have asked.

I remember at Pat Walsh's graduation party, years ago, there were throngs of avuncular smiles, hands cuffing his shoulder, everyone asking what Pat would do next.

At my grad party in May, the future seemed to be a disease I was dying from that people thought it impolite to speak of. When I said I got my degree in English Literature, they asked me what would I do with that—teach?

"I'm going to write my war memoirs," I replied with dignity. My aunt widened her eyes and asked where she could reserve her autographed copy. My mom said that sounded lovely, and could I go outside and tell the children the cake was served?

I got the vibe that my family expected little else of me. This was very unusual for a Southern son raised on stout Catholic values. Maybe my Veteran status exempted me from the abysmal sacraments of marriage and children. As long as I didn't hatch an assassination plot against my president with a copy of *Catcher in the Rye* in my pocket, I was okay, all things considered.

My short-term plan after graduation was to return to France, where I lived when I was nineteen. That I did, spending five weeks bobbing around the Aquitaine region, misting through sea towns like Arcachon and St. Jean-de-Luz. I grew needy for the ocean, craving only its fruit for meals and licking my brackish arms after swims. Kentucky has no ocean, no shrimp that fresh. I stopped asking the cafés if they had bourbon, ordering instead two Aperol Spritzes at a time. The only time I spoke English was to text Pat and Foley on WhatsApp, or at the moment of *petite mort* with whatever Chloe or Lou I'd met at the beach. A few rosé-soaked nights, it was a Chloe and Lou and me all together in my €50/night bed.

Books and bourbon, girls and guns. Those are my four food groups. I had plenty of girls and books this summer, now it was back to Kenfucky for guns and bourbon. Plus, the balance in my checking account was shrinking at an alarming rate. My financial advisor and accountant (Patrick A. Walsh) warned me that, if I stayed in Francine, I'd soon be broke.

On the beaches of *l'Aquitaine*, the idea of bankruptcy sounded kind of sexy. I could write my novel on fish heads and dumpster dives, naked but for my words. However, I knew that girls are a lot less friendly buying their own drinks, so I sobered up and did the responsible thing, buying a very cheap ticket back to Louisville with a twelve-hour layover in Reykjavik.

On the other side of the Atlantic, my best buddy Pat was there at the airport to greet me, smiling with his fully dimensional eyes. There was nothing to suggest that he would soon pack up and leave town, leaving whispers of scandal in his wake.

The morning after Pat left, I woke up to a skull-fuck hangover through both temples. *I only had four drinks,* I thought indignantly, opening my eyes to the black box of my room. It wasn't anything that scrambled eggs and 500 milligrams of acetaminophen couldn't cure, but when my feet first hit the floor, the whole day felt unlikely.

I felt the familiar chapping of my lips and loins and realized that I had rutted on a girl last night. As usual, my bed was left vacant, so I had no idea who she was. I stumbled upstairs towards the sunlight, which punished my eyes for sin. I reside in the basement; Pat and Blaise sleep on the second floor. The mezzanine level is our shared space, where the three of us hang out together doing absolutely nothing and everything.

In my fridge sat a tin of leftover jalapeño brisket. One cold, gluey bite triggered my memory like Proust's madeleine. My conquest last night was a waitress at Johnny Jake's, the hipster BBQ joint where I ate dinner alone at the bar. I recalled being transfixed by the way she shook her dark ringlets free of a ponytail. Afterwards, I did not invite her to spend the night.

I fired up my dead phone, hoping Pat had texted me from Crummy's phone to say he made it there okay. Negative, but there was a text from 502-423-9988 at 2:12 a.m., *"heyyy it's Alissa. Wanted to let you know I made it home. :-* :-*"*

I texted her back something sweet, hoping she would not ask me to take her to get Plan B later. I wanted to get some writing done.

I opened my MacBook. The document 'Untitled 2' had been minimized at the bottom of my computer for weeks:

These Are My War Memoirs
by James Branagh
Title subject to change

1.) It was fucking hot
2.) K.C
3.) those mini cans of Rip It Energy

"Idiot," I muttered, hating it so much.

As I reread my words into retardation, I began to notice the mortuary silence of my house. It did not comfort me to see Blaise's stray heels kicked into a corner; Pat's gym ID on the counter. To me, they already felt like mementos of abandonment.

Pat and Blaise were the clamor of my life; the heavenly bodies around which I orbited. Now they were gone, and the silence they left behind was deafening.

I didn't realize I was waiting for her call until it came. I lunged, knocking over a full glass of protein shake. *Her*, the hypotenuse of our right triangle; our *rara avis*—half-swan, half-stingray.

"Is this Kelly Blaise Foley?" I yelped into the phone.

Her bubbly laughter poured into my ear. *"Yes,* and is this my priest? 'Cause usually he's the only one allowed to call me by my Christian name."

I almost said, *And what sins have you to confess, my child?* thinking of Pat's flat eyes. But knowing she could get mad, I just laughed, "It sho' is. How are ya? *Where* are you?" There was weird background blabber on her end, loudspeakers and distant voices. "Are you still in New York?"

"I'm at the airport—*JFK*," Foley sighed in her despairing way. "My dad is letting me come home, but he's making me fly commercial."

"Well, I hope you're in first-class," I said solemnly. I knew at once Mr. Foley's decree had nothing to do with dearth or thriftiness. The Foleys had a whole field designated for their private aircrafts, and at least three pilots on call 24/7. (If McCullers, Blaise's little brother, had flown the Airbus to Switzerland to sky for the week, then her cousin Zabana could take the Jabiru home to Tucson).

Denying Blaise the luxury pleasures of her birthright was her father's favorite way of controlling her. Usually, Mr. Foley's tactics worked: Blaise's strong will corroded under his iron heel, and she sulkily returned to his 24-karat castle. But over time, I began to notice a push-back from the heiress. The plates of Foley Bourbon were shifting, and it seemed like someone would wind up swallowed into the earth.

When Blaise got engaged to Pat last spring, Mr. Foley essentially kicked his daughter out of the house ("the house" being the twenty-nine-room manor abutting their distillery, known as Foley Bourbon). He warned her not to come back with Pat's ring on her finger. Blaise drifted to NYC to crash with her bougie friend Agnessa, while Pat sweated it out in Kentucky.

Now Mr. Foley was booking Blaise a ticket home. It didn't look good for my Best Man suit.

"So, have you talked to Pat?" I asked her, forcing a casual tone.

Blaise sighed deeply. "He isn't answering his phone."

"Well, his phone is busted. Like, actually busted."

She sniffed, "He told me he was going to take an axe to it. No wonder all my texts are going through as green."

I winced. My best friend wasn't the type to threaten to go Paul Bunyan on his phone. He just *wasn't.* "Can I ask what happened with you guys?"

"You can ask," she answered stiffly. "But I don't feel like discussing it."

"That's cool," I said quickly. "You don't have to."

"Did he leave?" Foley murmured. "He told me he was skipping town."

"Last night."

There was a considerable pause on her end. "Well, I'm glad *you* answered my call," she cooed, sounding like the chorus of a country song that you roll your eyes at while your heart explodes. "I wasn't entirely sure you would…"

"You never have to worry about that," I said curtly. She went, "*Aww*," so I added swiftly, "Do I seem like the judgmental type to you? I worked at a brothel in Paris when I was eighteen."

"I know, dolly," she giggled, "and it made you into the lay of a lifetime, at least according to all my sorority sisters."

"Don't exaggerate. I haven't slept with *all* of them."

"Well the lion's share. My entire pledge class is in love with you, you goddamn heartbreaker."

My cheeks flushed. *Even you?*

I coughed, proffering a sophisticated segue, "So, do you need a ride from the airport, or what?"

I pictured her sitting on a plastic seat in an airport, her mirror ball eyes lit up. I knew her face as well as you know your country's flag. I could see her biting her nails bloody and jiggling her impossibly long legs, impatient, but not really for her plane's arrival. Even hungover and heartbroken, she still collected furtive glances from hurried dads, businessmen, women who felt their curiosity flicker over to her. *Who is she?* they wondered. *Where is she going?* Whether she inspired envy, lust, affection, joy, or disgust in her beholder, it was impossible to pass by Blaise Foley unaffected.

She sighed hugely. "That would be great, thank you. This pigeon coop should arrive at 2:45." Another sigh. "But who even knows how reliable these things are?"

I agreed, nonetheless promising to be there at 2:45. When I hung up, my heart thrummed with tender anguish.

My best friend said that he didn't want to hear her name. He hadn't asked *me* not to see her.

By now, the news of Pat Walsh's departure was disseminating through his wedding guest list.

At McGettigan's, the Walsh bar on Zzyzyx Road, (other than North Korea, it was the one place in the world where Foley bourbon wasn't sold) a few of Pat's second cousins were gathered for their daily drink. Talk turned away from pensions and potholes and over to Patrick, the Runaway Groom.

"What did he expect, getting involved with a Foley?" Meath Walsh remarked coldly, from under his Vietnam Veteran hat. He and his eight brothers were sons of the late Kilkenny Walsh, whose 1943 Navy picture watched them somberly from above the bar, beside their grandfather Black-Jack's Alcatraz mugshot. Their father Kilkenny was assassinated by car bombing in 1971, a probable casualty of the Foleys' wrath during the Dark Ages of Zzyzyx Road. In the opinion of his nine sons, there was no "probably" about it—the Foleys had done it, or paid someone else to.

"Dad coulda told Paddy how a Happy Ending with a Foley looks," Kildare said darkly, signaling to the bartender for another drink.

"She *is* a beautiful girl, though," Tyrone volunteered, prepared to show some clemency. He liked young Patrick—they all did. As a boy, they taught him how to fly fish and grill with charcoal. As an adult, Pato did their taxes and gave them advice on retirement ("Little Paddy taught us that the IRA stood for something other than Grampy Jack's army," they would say). Pat was only twenty-eight, but because of his fancy job and MBA, they believed in him like they believed in fish on Fridays.

"His girl is beautiful," Kildare agreed wryly. "Classic case of the little head giving orders to the big head."

"Maybe that was the problem," Meath muttered, raising his bushy brows meaningfully. "Another fella in New York was finding her pretty, too."

In downtown Louisville, the two youngest Walsh wives, Maura and Allie, were having coffee and fierce conversation at Starbucks. After their mother-in-law texted them the alarming news about their brother-in-law Pat, the girls exchanged a quick look and jetted out of ballet barre class as quickly as their yoga pants could carry them.

"So, that's all Pat said in his note?" Maura whispered, absently rocking her baby's carrier. "That he and Blaise were having some *problems* with their engagement?"

Intently, Allie reread the message. She was married to Pat's oldest brother Killian, the Master Distiller for Walsh Bourbon (Mr.

and Mrs. Walsh referred to Killian as their son, "the Master Distiller" in the same proud tone that parents referred to their son, "the doctor").

"I don't know. I keep asking Killian to send a picture of the note, but he's trying to calm his mother down."

"Poor Mrs. Walsh," Maura murmured. Then, after a respectful moment, she added quietly, "Do you think Blaise was cheating on him in New York?"

"I don't think she would," Allie replied, shaking her blonde head firmly. "I mean, her dad was always threatening to cut her off if she went ahead and married Pat. Maybe he finally made good on that."

"Yeah," Maura agreed, nodding fiercely. "Maybe he, like, met with an attorney to take away her trust fund."

"Or he was gonna fire her from Foley Bourbon," Allie added, frowning gravely.

"Wait, the wedding isn't off yet—right?" Maura clarified.

"No, thank *God*. But we're supposed to go get our bridesmaids' gowns sized next week."

"Should we *text* Blaise?" Maura asked gingerly. She was only just starting to like her. After all, Maura was Conor Walsh's wife. Blaise and Conor had arguably the strongest and most notorious rivalry in Foley-Walsh history.

"I think so," Allie replied heartily, "Just to ask how she's doing."

And from the tiny coal-mining town of Paw Paw, West Virginia, up through the tony Chicago suburb of Lake Forest, down to the adobe plains of Tucson, and over to the ultra-luxe hauteur of a twenty-eighth story Manhattan penthouse, the other bridesmaids were clucking in mayhem over the text Blaise had sent to their group. Tactfully, one of them (probably Lauren) had temporarily removed Blaise from the group text, because fervent speculation was afoot. All of Blaise's bridesmaids texted her separately to ask just what the *hell* was going on.

Blaise texted them each a slew of sad emoji and heart emoji. Nothing could soften the blow of the original message:

Wedding may be off, girlies. Please keep 12/21 open in case of a miracle. Love you all </3

I suppose the reason that the Foleys always felt superior to the Walshes boils down to age. The Foleys are one of the oldest families under Betsy Ross's flag. They are the Rothschilds of America. Even during America's industrial era, when "Irish" and "Catholic" were synonyms for dirty and poor, the Foleys were covering their communion wafers with caviar. Their name was being made as America was being made. For this, Foley Bourbon resides high in the pantheon of American antiquity, alongside the ivy-wreathed colleges, within the crack of the Liberty Bell, under the ruins of the Santa Maria, and in the splinters of the Mayflower.

Most historians agree that the Foleys were the first millionaires in this country. Besides the bourbon, the family has enjoyed empires in many of America's industries over the years, including fur-trading, the railroads, steel, oil, and even entertainment.

The Foleys first made their mint back in Ireland in the 1760s, selling their original whiskey distillery, Bunratty Gold, to a wealthy Scottish Lord. As the story goes, Angus Foley convinced the Lord to overpay for his distillery with the fatal Foley charm ("I couldn't bear to part with my family's prized business to anyone less worthy, my Lord,"). The reality was that the Foleys wanted to escape the Catholic persecution that was endemic to Ireland at the time. Their land was owned by a stern British landlord who came in on horseback once a week to collect forty percent of their whiskey earnings.

After the family sealed the deal with Lord Nitwit, they packed up and fled for America in the dead of night. According to legend, when the landlord rode in that Wednesday, he found only a note on the kitchen table: *"Distillery's sold and we're off to the Isles of the Blessed. You can have your 40p if you are clever enough to find us, a feat which we very much doubt. May the Devil keep you in the crook of his grin, and may we never meet again."*

To this day, there is a tax lien on the abandoned Foley Corners in County Mayo, Ireland. An engraving proudly reads,

"FOLEY is a name meaning plunderer or pirate. Here in 1761, one unfortunate Brit learned why."

I remember our sixth grade Social Studies teacher Mr. Card telling us this story. He was a total history nerd, often referring to

President Lincoln as a "hometown hero" because Old Abe was born in Kentucky.

Pat's cousin Brendan Walsh, sitting in the back row, hollered out, "*Fuck the Foleys!*" Everyone laughed, and Brendan had to sit out the class trip to Lincoln's birthplace as punishment. Upon hearing the story, his father Marty Walsh, a hard-boiled lawyer, famously deadpanned, "That'll teach you to curse in school, Brenny. And you also shouldn't say *fuck.*"

At 2:15, I gunned it for the Louisville Regional Airport. I found "Strange Fruit" by Billie Holiday on YouTube and played it over and over, even when my phone alerted me that I had used fifty percent of my monthly data allowance, then seventy-five percent. Parking my Biscayne in Arrivals, I thought how odd it was that I had just been here a week ago, when Pat picked me up after my France trip.

It was another August day with dog-breath heat, but even in the air-conditioned airport, my sweat remained. I could have kicked myself in the shins for forgetting my fish flask in the car (twenty-seventh-birthday present from Blaise, her blue eyes lit up spectacularly: "I got you a fish flask 'cause you're a Pisces!").

In the gift shop, I was lazily asking the Indian cashier if I could get a Veteran Discount on a keychain when my phone vibrated.

Blaise: *hey doll! I just touched down in Arrivals! Are you here??*

I texted her that I was walking over now. She responded that she couldn't wait to see me with a couple of kiss-face emoji.

Girls who will never kiss you shouldn't be allowed to send those.

I did not just see her coming, I sensed her coming. Heard the giddy thwacking of her sandals on linoleum, felt her strawberry silk tendrils against my arm, smelled the ghost of bourbon on her breath. Blaise Foley, of the bright blue eyes crystallized with mischief and mystery, the checkpoint for anyone who slobbered too closely. Lips like petals, shoulders and cheekbones dusted with freckles, legs as long as January to July. And her radiant, capped-tooth, strand-of-pearl smile. That smile upheld all the expectations one had for her: an heiress raised in America's heartland, daughter of a bourbon baron and Miss America 1981. Spoiled? *Absolutely.* But not beyond self-awareness.

Blaise threw her arms around my neck. I pretended, there in her dorsal warmth, that I was the one she came home to.

"Hi, doll," she purred, touching my back in a way that was both sexy and maternal. She leaned back to grin in my face. "Lord, am I glad to see you."

"Welcome the fuck home," I growled, handing her the new keychain. It said, *GETTIN' LUCKY IN KENTUCKY.* She gave a tinkering laugh, because we both knew she would never allow something so homely near the keys to her Jag.

"How are ya, Foley?"

"Honestly? A little drunk." Blaise wrenched her sleek little suitcase by the handle, grinning naughtily. "But it's not my fault, it's those TSA fucker's faults!" she nodded earnestly. "They *tried* to get me to *pour* out my flask!"

I laughed at her spoiled brattiness. Remember, the girl had never flown commercial before. "Well, Foles, you're not supposed to bring liquids over three ounces on a plane—"

"*Yes*, but I had 24-year-old bourbon in there! And it was the last of the barrel!" she wailed. "I told them I'd *walk* back to Kentucky before I poured good bourbon down the drain, and they didn't seem to care!" Blaise lowered her voice derisively. "They probably drink Canadian Mist."

I laughed from a well of deep fondness. Blaise considered this to be her prickliest insult, to say that someone looked like a cheap whiskey drinker.

"So I had to *chug* a 24-year-old bourbon right there on the spot—"

"I can't believe what you've been through!" I cried, feeling myself relax as I grabbed her suitcase. "Where's all your luggage, Foley?" Glancing around her shoulder, I half-expected some poor bellhop of Peter Dinklage stature to be wheeling her Vuitton crates over.

She waved a hand aristocratically, "I had it all shipped to the compound, doll! I told Agnessa to take whatever she wanted from what I left behind." She met my eyes somberly, "I'm done with New York."

"Good," I said heartily. *Now you won't leave me again.*

Blaise looped her arm through mine, navigating her tennis skirt towards the airport Starbucks, "Let's get us a Venti quick—what do you think?" she whispered, as if proposing something naughty that could very well get us expelled from life.

"Oh, yes—let's." I never said no to a drug that had such a profound effect on my nervous system.

Plus, I could go for a coffee.

If you think for one goddamned second that I wasn't as curious as all the Walsh wives and the bridesmaids and the crusty old men at McGettigan's about Pat and Blaise's fight, then you're about as wrong as a margarita on St. Paddy's Day.

My money was on infidelity. A man doesn't leave town with a deadened soul just because his fiancée shrunk his laundry in the dryer. Pat's eyes came to me again in their mortuary stillness; molecules made in the same factory as my night terrors.

In the car, I glanced at her alabaster legs, imagining them parted, her heavenly mound-of-Venus arched to a stranger. The swelter of August ran helter-skelter through my body.

Beside me, Blaise jibbled about how nice it was to be back in Kentucky, how good the wind felt from my sunroof. Her head of burnished blond whipped my face, sending another electric jolt to my loins.

She smiled at me behind her cat-eyed sunglasses and asked, "Could you go for a Hot Brown right now, honey? I don't feel like I'm home until I have one."

"Sure," I agreed, thrilled that she wasn't asking to be driven straight home. After all, I was in the groom's camp, so I had no real claim to her without Pat. I realized with a great thud of dismay that, if Pat and Blaise's engagement were called off, I would be forced to side with Pat and let her fade out of my life. That's 500+ nights of movies and takeout and drinking together just zapped into non-existence. *What in God's name was the point?*

"Stella's?" I managed to ask, naming the diner that was SOP for our Sunday mornings.

"*Ooh*, yes!" Blaise clapped her hands giddily. I could have cried.

From outside, Stella's looked like a 1970s airstream trailer. Inside, the '70s theme continued with wood-paneled walls and orange Formica tables. It was staggeringly ugly, and we were home here.

The host, a ghastly little man who wore no name tag, guided us to a booth and slapped down oversized menus. From tiny speakers overhead, bluegrass music twanged to the empty dining room. Kentucky is home to bluegrass music, and Stella's was one of those "My Old Kentucky Home"-type places. You could buy sun-bleached postcards of famous horses like Seabiscuit and American Pharaoh off the rack beside the cash register. Mr. Card probably took his wife here on date-night.

"I think the host secretly died in '72," I muttered to Blaise, watching him stoop over to refill the dish of pastel mints.

Blaise nodded absently and glanced around. "I'm glad no one's here," she whispered. "That was the good thing about New York—anonymity." She twirled a champagne lock. "I mean, if anyone asked me about my wedding right now, I'd cry. *Seriously*."

"You could tell 'em to fuck off," I said, cocking a gun with my pointer finger and thumb and making machine-gun noises. "*Seriously*."

Our server came over, a mountain of a woman who I thought would look very at-home in lederhosen and braids. She stared disapprovingly at Foley, who had dared bring her Starbucks into Stella's.

My date seemed unfazed. "Can we have two Hot Brown sandwiches with French fries, please?" she ordered for us sweetly. "Mine with extra bacon? Oh—and can I have a strawberry shake *and* a Diet Pepsi?"

Frau scribbled on her pad. "And for you to drink?" she nodded at me curtly.

"Sweet tea." After she left, I gave Foley a wolf whistle. "Nice order, champ. The fat kid from *Stand by Me* would be jealous."

Blaise put three fingers to her collar bone. "Do you think I'm fat?" she whispered.

No, I think you're heaven, and if you weren't Pat's girl, I would fuck you until I died.

"Shut up," I grunted. "You know you're skinny."

Looking doubtful, she sipped her coffee. "In any event, it doesn't matter if I eat bacon or celery seven days a week. Foleys don't live past the age of sixty-one."

"Why's this again? That Indian curse?"

"Yup. Dates back to the Trail of Tears," Blaise nodded dogmatically. "An Indian chief put a curse on our heads saying that no one born into our land would live to be a day older than our founder, Angus Foley. He died at age sixty-one in 1795."

"No one lived past sixty-one in those days. Haven't you ever played *Oregon Trail*?"

"But it's been true for every Foley since him!" Blaise insisted, jabbing our table with her finger.

"Just look at my poor Uncle Duffy, gone last month!" Her pretty face was clouding over. "Only a few months before his sixty-first birthday."

"I know, I know—sorry" I mumbled guiltily. Her Uncle died while I was in France doing my sea, sex, and sun tour. I never met Duffy Foley, a formidable lawyer of great wealth, but Conor Walsh admitted to me once that Duffy was the only person he ever feared. That's saying something, considering Conor is a sadistic cop who would Taser a pedestrian for jaywalking.

Pat was not allowed at Duffy's funeral in July, per Mr. Foley's edict. He went anyway, like any good man in love, concealing himself behind the rows of elegant mourners. He watched as Blaise's back trembled with tears of grief, then as her brother McCullers and cousin Jericho shouldered their uncle's casket and carried him out of the church. Mr. Foley followed, his auburn head bowed.

Pat told me how upset Blaise was. She curled up on our couch like a potato bug poked with a stick, bawling, "Duffy was my one phone call from jail!" He stroked her red hair and promised he would be her one phone call now, but Blaise didn't even hear him. She *adored* her Uncle Duffy. Their mutual loyalty was as boundless as it was mysterious to me.

A tear dribbled now from Blaise's eye. If Pat were here, he would brush it away with the tenderness of a lost era.

I sat on my stupid hands and felt the moment age. Finally, she dabbed her cheek with a napkin.

"So, are these the sorts of snake oil tales you spew on your bourbon tours, Pocahontas?" I asked, in a mock grumble.

Her rosy lips parted in a giggle, and I thought with deep pleasure that it was like watching a baby chick poke its beak through a shell.

Until I died, Mrs. Branagh. Until I died.

After our drinks arrived, the heiress asked me, no hedging about, where Pat had gone off to.

"I'm sorry, Foley," I told her dolefully, "I'm only authorized to say that Patrick made it to Location X between Coordinates Y and Z safely."

"So you *are* in touch with him?" Blaise said fiercely. "I thought his phone was smashed."

"Well, he called from a payphone to tell me to let all interested parties know that he's okay."

A bell dinged from the kitchen. Adolpha brought our food on aluminum dishes, cautioning that they were very hot.

"Kentucky's finest," I said in satisfied tones, blowing on the sandwich of turkey, bacon, and Mornay sauce.

"Patrick has the wrong idea about me," Blaise said suddenly, shining her blue orbs on me. Her face was as open as the earth when viewed from space. You knew there were wars raging beneath that cerulean serenity, but it didn't deflect from the beauty of the whole.

To put it simply, I believed her. Whatever version of the truth was hers.

I nodded encouragingly. "You can tell me about it."

"I'm sorry," she exhaled into her milkshake, "I don't feel much like discussing it."

"That's cool," I said swiftly. "And you know, I'm still here, so, I'm not, like, not gonna be…"

"Wow, James," Blaise smiled up at me. "From an Irishman, that's like an '*I love you.*'"

We grinned in opposite directions. I tried not to feel so damn giddy.

"So, what's new with you, doll?" Blaise asked, cutting into her Hot Brown sandwich with her utensils. "Pat mentioned that you're working on your war memoirs?"

"Yeah," I said evasively. "They're not done yet." Our waitress emerged from the kitchen, and I signaled to her for an ashtray by double-tapping my lips with two fingers. Joe fucking Cool. She didn't look over.

"Oh, but you've made some headway?"

"Sure. So far it's the best six words ever written."

"Maybe it's too soon," Blaise opined, her big eyes bleeding pity. "You're still having night terrors."

My hand wilted reaching for the pack of Marb Reds in my pocket. *You're still having night terrors.* I realized then in horror that Foley must hear me howling at night from the basement. *Patrick, is it a robber?* she would ask, sitting up in her lacy nightgown. *Nah, it's just James having a night terror,* Pat would say, kissing her forehead. *That's why I keep him in the basement. Don't worry, babe, we'll chuck him out after we're married.*

"What I meant is," Blaise said briskly, sensing my shame. "*Obviously* you're a brilliant writer—"

"How would you know?" I sulked, "You've never read my shit."

"I can just tell," she said simply. "But I remember that one night you called me drunk this summer." *Shit.* "You were saying how even if you were stranded on a desert island with your computer, you could still come up with excuses not to write."

"Fucking Campari."

"Maybe you just don't *want* to write about Iraq."

"But I went off to war so I'd have something to write about," I said loudly. From behind the counter, the waitress glanced up from her phone with one eyebrow raised. Again I signaled for an ashtray, but her eyes were back the next moment to *Candy Crush.*

"I'm going outside to smoke," I stood up stiffly. "Brb."

"*Wait,*" Blaise grabbed my wrist and yanked me back into the booth. "I want to help you." She tucked her hair behind her ears, looking all cute and earnest. "Or, I want you to help me."

"*How?*" I demanded. In an alternate universe, I winked and purred that I always knew we would answer each other's prayers someday.

"I want you to write my story instead."

I sighed, "I told you I'd update your LinkedIn, Foley, I've just been busy—"

"*No,* I mean my whole story," she said, "The story about the Foleys and the Walshes, and how Pat and I came together."

Too bad you guys are on the fritz now, I thought nastily. The *schadenfreude* seeped into my stomach, nearly as delicious as the Hot Brown.

"You could start with Black-Jack," Blaise said charmingly. "You *love* Black-Jack."

"He's the reason I wanted to be a soldier," I said with dignity. "But he was way before your time." I paused, allowing it to trickle into my mind. "Are you saying, write in the present with flashbacks to the past? To Black-Jack?"

"*Love* that," Blaise breathed, swatting my wrist. "Look at you, the think-tank's already flowing."

I felt my face redden. Charm was a natural Foley trait, that's what people always said. Blaise was about to do to me what Angus Foley did to the Scottish Lord, and I didn't even see it coming.

"If we were gonna tell it, we'd have to tell the whole story," I went on slowly. "Not *just* about you and Pat and your little millennial Romeo and Juliet saga."

"Exactly," she agreed, her blue eyes bright.

"We'd have to talk about how the Foleys and Walshes became enemies—"

"Right."

"Maybe even take it back to Prohibition—"

"Love it."

"Definitely touch on the trial of '68 and the building of the Twelve-Foot Wall—"

"*Absolutely,*" Blaise clapped her hands giddily. "See, there's a story here, I knew you would see it!"

I paused, zoning out on the cuckoo clock above her head. "I dunno how much of a biographer I really am though, B." I realized that I wanted her to reassure me some more. I could already feel my quill going erect for her.

"But I wouldn't want it to read like a biography!" Blaise insisted, clutching my grubby palms. "I see it more like an abstract family portrait done by a talented, zany artist."

I pointed at my chest, mouthing, "*Moi*?"

She bopped her head sincerely, "You're the only one who I would want to do this. *I'm serious.*"

It's important to note that this moment is hallowed in my memory. The divider between Before and After. I assure you that, as long as I'm still drawing breath, I haven't gone an hour without thinking about her. Before, she was known to me as Pat's Girl. After, she would be known to me by the dedication that I gave her in my first novel, *Misercordias*. The one in your hands right now.

"For Blaise, My Muse."

Zzyzyx Road
15 minutes outside of Louisville, KY
Foley Bourbon
Later that Night...

Chapter 2

I dropped Blaise off at the iron gates of Foley Bourbon, a twenty-nine-room Beaux Arts-style mansion at the end of Zzyzyx Road. The official address was Old State Road 434, but not even the governor called it that. To us Kentuckians, Zzyzyx Road is the four-mile stretch of land fifteen miles outside of Louisville, and home of the two most notorious distilleries to ever be nemeses, Walsh and Foley Bourbon.

Though Foley Bourbon looked like a Southern plantation house thriving under the Buchanan administration, something about its absurdly manicured hedges always reminded me of Versailles. Incidentally, Mr. Foley was known as the Sun King by his friends and foes. Blaise's childhood home had been a historical landmark since the 1930s. Schoolchildren from Frankfort to Lexington are shuttled there for field trips to learn how bourbon is made.

Outside the gates, the Foley name and logo, a shamrock set in a horseshoe, was cut into the stone facade above the, 'EST. 1788.' At close range, I could see their eroded Latin motto, MISERCORDIAS DOMINI CANTABO IN AETERNUM. Pat and I used to draw chalk weiners on this spot as kids, bolting when Mr. Foley yelled at us over his intercom. I couldn't help but grin at the skidmarks, a relic of all the times Blaise raced Conor Walsh down Zzyzyx, eluding a speeding ticket and car crash by inches.

"Bye, doll," Blaise said, fingering the keypad out front. As the iron gates opened, I noticed Pat's ring was off her finger. *Mr. Foley'll be so stoked.*

In my rearview mirror, the twelve-foot tall hedges loomed, reminding me of my task.

The Walsh side of the hedges was far more familiar to me. I grew up playing lightsabers and Nerf guns with Pat on that lawn.

Sometimes, Mrs. Walsh let us dig holes, not to China, but to look for Black-Jack Walsh's treasure.

Whenever our class took the field trip to Foley Bourbon, I always stayed behind with Pat. Walshes have been banned on Foley property since 1968, and the fatwa applies to Walsh kids, too. Pat's cousins got away with sneaking on the field trip, but Mr. Foley recognized Pat and his brothers as the brats next door. The blitzkrieg of baseballs and lacrosse balls we lobbed over the hedges, not to mention the processional of ding-dong-ditching, Chinese food delivery pranks, dog doo at the gate, and chalk weiners drawn everywhere, did nothing to ease Mr. Foley's grudge.

"I think you'd be brilliant at writing my family's story."

At home, I lay in bed and closed my eyes, letting myself be consumed by her warmth. How could Pat up and walk away from it?

I did not sleep beside women, I slept beside books. Currently snarled in my sheets were *Dutch Courage* (London); *The Long Day Wanes* (Burgess)*; Best European Short Fiction 2012;* (miscellaneous) *Pnin* (Nabokov) *Tropic of Capricorn* (Miller) and, kicked way down at the foot of my bed, *Kilkenny-Kentucky* (Walsh).

Pat's great-grandfather, and the twentieth century's most revered gangster, Black-Jack Walsh, was offered a book deal in 1946 to write of his adventures in Prohibition-era Kentucky. Jack wrote chronologically, documenting first his boyhood in Kilkenny, and his move to Dublin to participate in the Irish Rebellion of 1916. He only got ninety pages in before he was killed.

I mentioned before that I own his book in six editions, including this rare first edition from 1949 with Jack's St. Michael's medal on the cover.

In this version, like all copies of Kilkenny-Kentucky, his dedication is the same:

For Ulysses, who saved me.

This was for James Joyce's *Ulysses,* the book Jack carried with him everywhere, even to court. He stored the key to his treasure in a secret compartment cut into the back pages.

I flipped to the first page:

Writing and fighting, that's all I ever wanted to do. I type these words in a state of welcome exile in my native Kilkenny, 120 miles from Dublin, where much of my fighting took place, and 3600 miles from Kentucky, where the battlefields were more clandestine.

My sons are not sons of Ireland, they are sons of America. When my Clara and I left the United States in March, our first and second born sons, Wilkie and Kilkenny, were still laying down their lives for President Roosevelt and his Allies. I admired President Roosevelt, and not merely for his Ulster blood. We disagreed on the sanctity of banks, but were in accord on many matters of social reform. It brought me tremendous pride that my boys should enlist in this war, for I have told them that a man does not become a man until he stands up for his country. My nephew Sullivan Foley laid down his life as well, as a fighter pilot over France. The view from where I type is a deceptive mirage of viridian peace, for truthfully I cannot know any peace until the boys are called home.

When my boys close their eyes to wipe their minds free of the malignant spirits of war, it is of Kentucky they dream. Kentucky is the patron state of race horses and bourbon. Kentucky was admitted to the union in 1792, four years after the founding of Foley, purveyor of the bourbon that has become America's blood. Foley is the idyllic land to which my sons were born. My firstborn, Wilkie, arrived at Foley a mere two months after he arrived here on earth.

As I pen these words, in the year of our Lord 1945, Jodl is waving the white flag of surrender to Eisenhower, and the Russians have extracted the cremated remains of Hitler and his bride from the Führerbunker. The break of war comes over Europe like a watery and hesitant sun. For my son Wilkie, whom I pray is still alive, the end of war means that he can finally return to Kentucky and be reunited with his bourbon. My nephew Sullivan, meanwhile, phoned today to lament that his twenty-fifth birthday will be spent at a tavern in rural France instead of at the Kentucky Derby.

Foley Bourbon has a proud tradition of employing none but their own sons to make their elixir. Historically, the firstborn son is the "heir," managing the business aspects of the distillery, and the second-born son becomes the Master Distiller. Then they came to their eighth generation of bourbon-making. Unto the Foleys was born a son, the bright-eyed, Sullivan, and a kind and pious daughter, christened Lucretia. The incumbent Master Distiller, Andrew Foley, attempted to teach young Sullivan the fine art of bourbon-making, but he found it to be a chore. My son Wilkie, however, was beguiled by the bourbon for reasons that none but his Creator could explain. From the age of seven, Wilkie began making the bourbon for Foley and, by fifteen, he was making all of it. Wilkie's biggest woe during wartime is being separated from his bourbon. He laments over its well-being, wonders how much longer it must age in its charred barrels before he may be discharged from his patriotic duty…

"Hmm," I murmured, reaching for my laptop and pulling up "Black-Jack Walsh" on Wikipedia. Up came Jack's Alcatraz mugshot from 1929, a picture more familiar to me than my parents' wedding photo. Every kid in America had either owned this mugshot poster, or at least seen it hanging it in someone's dorm in college: Jack with a cigarette lit, gingerly holding the sign that announced his height (6'3") and his weight (160), looking away from the camera in disdainful boredom.

"I knew the risks were great…but the rewards were impossibly greater," read his quote.

It was the universal line of total badassery. Jack's poster was as iconic as Farrah in her red bathing suit, or John Lennon in his shades. Maybe even more so, because Jack never went out of style.

Like any normal, Irish boy from Kentucky, I of course have Jack's poster on my wall. At my and Pat's housewarming party, his three brothers and twelve male cousins were there, and someone (probably Kiki) went in my room and drew a talk bubble coming out of Jack's mouth: *"Please tell that Branagh lad to stop spanking to me, as I can no longer see out of my left eye."*

The Walsh men know how much I revere their great-grandfather. I keep it a secret that I believe that I've been incarnated with Jack's soul, because I know just what they'd say: "then where the hell's his treasure, dingus?"

I read on:

John "Black-Jack" Walsh (January 30, 1893—March 31, 1948)
Born: Kilkenny City, Co. Kilkenny, Republic of Ireland.
Died: Kilkenny City, Co. Kilkenny, Republic of Ireland
Spouse: Clara Walsh (née: Clara Sullivan)

Other Names: Jack-the-Saint, the Saint, Blacko-Jacko, the Irish Ripper (for his national origin and his propensity to use an army bayonet on enemies)

John "Black-Jack" Walsh was a member of the Irish Republican Brotherhood who rose to massive fame and notoriety in America during the Prohibition Era. From 1921-1933, he trafficked an estimated $20-35 million annually in alcohol, most of which was Foley Bourbon. Based in Kentucky, Walsh worked alongside his cousin-by-marriage Ulysses Foley to transport barrels of bourbon whiskey from Foley's famed distillery up through Chicago and across America.

Walsh often drove a big rig truck from Kentucky to Chicago or New York. If stopped, Walsh had a permit claiming that the bourbon in tow was "medicinal," and plenty of fake order forms from various apothecaries to vouch for him. He also used cargo trains to transport barrels, capitalizing on the privatized system of the day to pay off the conductors.

Black-Jack's record for illegally transporting alcohol is unsurpassed by any other bootlegger of his time. Many of his ways of operating are still mysterious, though much credit is owed to the Foleys, the wealthy bourbon family who sponsored him as a cherished family member and employee. It has been said that the Foley's powerful ties to both politics and the underworld were used

*to ward away the menace of Prohibition agents and the newly
formed FBI.*

*Walsh became involved in the gambling and prostitution circuit of
Chicago and Louisville. He controlled all the brothels in Louisville's
Green Street district in the years before his 1945 deportation to
Ireland. He earned the nickname "the Saint" because, although he
conducted much business in brothels, he was alleged to be faithful
to his wife Clara. In 1929, when testifying before a grand jury, the
D.A. asked Jack if he considered himself to be a good Catholic.
Walsh answered yes. The D.A. pressed him, "Even though, if half
the papers are to be believed, you've routinely committed the
cardinal sin of murder?" Jack famously replied, "To me, the cardinal
sin is infidelity to one's wife. On that score, my conscience is clear."*

*Walsh was considered the prime suspect in the disappearance of
his nemesis, Jimmy "the Wall" Fleming, Sr., who was pronounced
dead in absentia in 1974. The matter of where Black-Jack buried
Fleming's body has been the source of much media speculation
over the years. In 1946, when a reporter from the* New York Times
*called Walsh at his home in Kilkenny to inquire about Fleming's
whereabouts, Jack deadpanned, "He's buried in the same place as
me treasure is, isn't he?" (see: Black-Jack's lost treasure)*

I clicked here, which lead me to a section between "Later Years"
and "Death:"

Black-Jack's Lost Treasure:

*Records show that Black-Jack never had a bank account in the
U.S. He used only the Western Union Company as a means to
transfer money, and never more than $500 at a time. Walsh was
vocal about his distrust of banks, fearing that if prosecuted for his
crimes, his bank accounts would be frozen and his fortune lost.
Walsh lived conservatively, and it is believed that most of his illegal
earnings went into his secret vault. He made frequent allusions to*

his fortune being "buried" somewhere "between Kilkenny and Kentucky," seeming to enjoy the feverish speculation this inspired.

After being robbed at gunpoint once, Walsh carried very little cash on him. His friend and business associate, Walter "Egghead" Zimmerman, advised Walsh to seek out gold, silver, and stocks instead because of their appreciation factor. Operating under a series of aliases, so as not to leave a paper trail, Walsh exchanged cash for gold and silver bullion for years with great regularity. In 1933, when President Franklin D. Roosevelt ordered all gold to be surrendered to the Federal Reserve, Walsh ran an underground practice of paying cash for gold, offering 15% more than the government's price of $20.35 per ounce. His gold trade was untraceable, another point of great irritation for authorities. Walsh devotes a chapter in his memoir, Kilkenny-Kentucky, to this practice, explaining his firm belief that Roosevelt's gold seizure was unconstitutional, and a violation of American liberties (his views are frequently referenced by left-libertarians and capitalists of today).

In his book, Walsh chides President Roosevelt, whom he considered to be the cat to his mouse, writing: "Although President Roosevelt was weighty in talent, I remained weighty in Talent, and my walls of Troy were never scaled." This is a reference to the heft of his treasure in 'Trojan gold ounces,' and the fact that his illegal gold trade was never raided. In another passage, Walsh brags, "Roosevelt said that Kentucky is home to America's biggest gold reserve. He was right, only you wouldn't find it at Fort Knox."

Walsh's treasure was intended for his three sons, Wilkie, Kilkenny, and Pearse. Though he had no will, he wrote of this in his memoir, referring to the fruits of his earnings as "My boys' inheritance." There is much speculation as to what lies in Jack's treasure, which has been lost since his 1948 murder. There are receipts showing that he purchased Coca-Cola and General Electric stock after the crash of 1929. If the dividends were continually reinvested, as believed they were, these stocks would be each worth a quarter of a billion dollars. According to urban legend, the Irish Crown Jewels, stolen from Dublin Castle in 1907, can be found in Black-Jack's vault.

The treasure is considered lost because only Jack and his wife Clara knew of its location. When Jack served a nine-month sentence in Alcatraz in 1929, Clara wore the key to the treasure around her neck, telling people it was the key to his heart. Otherwise, Walsh hid the key in a secret compartment cut into the back of the novel Ulysses, *by James Joyce. Walsh promised to reveal the location to his eldest son Wilkie, but was murdered before he could do so. The treasure is valued at anywhere from $300-900 million in 2013 dollars."*

I skipped the section "Death" because it always depressed the hell out of me. He and Clara were killed in a botched robbery while enjoying their retirement (*see:* deportation) in Ireland. The killers, Al Meehan and Peter Dyer, were petty crooks, nowhere near deserving of Jack's legend. If he had to be killed, I wished it had at least been by Jimmy Fleming, Jr., or some other enemy seeking vengeance. (Worth noting: The killers were both sentenced to life in prison, but didn't make it a month. Al was beaten to death by a prison mob, and Peter hung himself before he could meet the same fate).

Next, I searched "Foley Bourbon."

Up popped the ubiquitous Foley logo of the shamrock set in a horseshoe. Foley Bourbon was founded in 1788, only twelve years younger than America, and exactly 200 years older than the heiress I'd just shared diner food with. According to Wiki, Foley Bourbon had $4.4 Billion in revenue in 2013, and $735 million in operating income. (And that wasn't counting the family's *private* trust, which had been marinating since the 1760s. By some accounts, it was up to eleven digits). Their Master Distiller was John W. Foley, the man who had given Blaise everything, except for his blessing to marry Patrick Walsh.

I skimmed the history of the company, which contained stuff I vaguely knew. Foley had been the official bourbon of the Kentucky Derby since the first Run for the Roses in 1875. Its mash bill (bourbon formula) was one of the few to remain a secret, though the recipe had reportedly not changed since 1790. During the Civil War, the Union Army torched and raided Foley Bourbon, but the family still took in General Ulysses S. Grant when he showed up later with his injured men. (Worth Noting: in 1875, when Ulysses Grant was President, Foley was the only distillery in America not implicated during the Whiskey Ring scandal.)

There was a whole section dedicated to the Foley and Walsh feud.

"The Foleys and Walshes have entered the American lexicon as a metonym for any bitterly feuding rival parties."

Image 3.1 showed Wilkie Walsh (Pat's grandfather) hollering on the court steps into the microphones of about twenty reporters, his gaunt frame and ebony hair recalling a young Abe Lincoln. Image 3.4 showed Sullivan Foley (Blaise's grandpa) frozen in time as he sidled into the passenger's seat of a Cadillac, shooing away the reporters with his Stetson hat.

Wikipedia gave the CliffsNotes version of their quarrel:

"In 1968, Wilkie Walsh, the Master Distiller for Foley Bourbon, sued his second cousin Sullivan Foley for refusing to release equity shares to him. Walsh claimed that Foley's father had recruited his father, Black-Jack Walsh, from Ireland in 1920 on the premise of a joint partnership in his bourbon distillery, but never honored their agreement. He additionally claimed that his work as Master Distiller for Foley Bourbon for forty years entitled him to equity in the family-owned company.
The 100- Day Trial was a media circus, attracting nationwide attention. The involvement of a household name alcohol like Foley, in addition to the public fascination with bootlegger Black-Jack Walsh, added to the frenzy. The trial was filled with the colorful courtroom antics of the Walsh brothers, an Irish mob presence, and a bizarre, week-long armistice after Robert F. Kennedy was shot, in which Wilkie Walsh and Sully Foley had Judge Willets over to the

distillery for an extended "Irish wake." At the time, Senator Walter Huddleston (D-Kentucky) joked that coverage of the trial was, "more entertaining than Bonanza."

On Day 98 of the trial, Kilkenny Walsh threatened to give testimony that would implicate the Foleys in decades worth of criminal activity, including "bootlegging during Prohibition, profiteering during wartime, selling via the Irish Mob channel to avoid taxation…and far worse." Judge Willets subpoenaed members of the Fleming crime family, Terry "Python" Collins, and James Fleming, Jr. (Jimmy) to testify against Foley. Before they could testify, Foley announced that he was ready to settle. The dueling parties reached an undisclosed agreement.

Wilkie, alongside his brother Kilkenny, founded Walsh Bourbon in 1969, next to the very land upon which Foley Bourbon stood. Walsh had purchased the land years earlier from Sullivan Foley when they were still friends. When asked why he would want to found a distillery next to his cousin/enemy, Walsh half-quoted Woody Guthrie, saying, "this land was made for he and me." Foley had twelve-foot-high hedges planted to block his view of Walsh.

The Irish Mob was displeased that the Walshes used their names in court. They sent threatening letters to the Walsh family via the Kentucky Herald for years afterwards. Jimmy Fleming, Jr., the son of Black-Jack's missing nemesis, was the prime suspect in the car-bombing murder of Kilkenny Walsh in 1971. The Walshes' belief that the Foleys were accomplices to Kilkenny's murder has helped to intensify the Foley-Walsh feud.

In 1977, Wilkie Walsh burned down the Foley's main rickhouse, claiming it to be an act of vengeance for his brother's murder. According to the Foleys, upon seeing the bourbon go up in flames, Sullivan suffered a fatal heart attack. Furious, his son, John Foley, publicly announced that any Walsh caught on Foley property from then on would be shot.

I scrolled down to the section, "Foleys and Walshes in Modern Times:"

Both the Foleys and Walshes take credit for Black-Jack Walsh, the Irish gangster who trafficked $25-30 million worth of Foley Bourbon annually during Prohibition. Though the Foleys do not publicly admit to operating illegally during that time, John Foley commented in 2009 to Bourbon Spectator, *"Ol' Black-Jack was helpful to us during the Dark Ages of our nation's history, or Prohibition, as it's called in history class...when the Eighteenth Amendment came along, my Granddaddy was said to be at the end of his rope...then Black-Jack came over and helped to keep spirits up, pun intended...that's all I'll say about the matter!"*

In January of 2014, Blaise Foley became engaged to Patrick Walsh. It is unclear if the engagement has signaled an armistice between the two families."

"Got that right," I muttered.

And then something happened.

I took my laptop and began writing with ejaculatory force.

Ab ovo seemed to be way the story wanted to be told, from the very beginning. Black-Jack and Clara surfaced easily; my masculine ideal and his feminine paradigm. I wrote of them back in Ireland, living as modest newlyweds before the whole Prohibition racket ever hit them.

Hours passed. My basement windows became draped in tapestries of night. Allie-the-server texted, asking if she could come get the hair tie she left in my bed, but even that couldn't distract me.

At some point, I messaged Blaise: "*Yes I said yes I will Yes.*" This was me agreeing to write her book, in the most symbolic and meaningful way possible.

She wrote back: *Lol what??*

I sighed, replying patiently: *It's the last line of James Joyce's Ulysses...who Black-Jack dedicated his book to...??*

No he didn't, Blaise answered.

I sent her a pic of Jack's dedication page: *"For Ulysses, who saved me."*

Foley called me up right away. "Oh, you poor, sweet, confused little lamb!" she laughed. I could hear the seven-year-aged bourbon in her voice. "Black-Jack wasn't talking about *Ulysses*, the book!"

"Then who was he talking about?" I said impatiently. "President fucking Grant?"

"*No!*" Blaise laughed again, "It was for my great-granddaddy, Ulysses Foley! He's the one who brought Jack over to Kentucky, ya know!"

I settled into my flannel sheets, letting her tell me more. I had been to Jack's Ireland many times before, but never with a Foley as my guide.

Chapter 3

Kilkenny, 1920

Black-Jack had never heard of bourbon when his American cousin came to visit him in Kilkenny.

"You wouldn't find it here in Ireland, not yet," Ulysses Foley explained, leaning forward in his seat at Jack's kitchen table. "You're a whiskey man, aren't you?"

Jack took a long drag off his Carrol, confirmed that yes he was. In the Army, they called him Black-Jack because of his raven hair that stood out against the droves of milk and honey. He had married a girl who was dark too, Clara Sullivan. The child, nearly fully formed in her belly, would probably come out looking like an Arab. They ought to call him Ali Baba Walsh.

Ulysses Foley had taken only a polite sip of the tea that Jack's wife Clara set before him. Now, the steam rising from the cup had fully extinguished in the November dampness of their flat. Someone had told Jack that Americans didn't like tea. Then what the hell did they all drink? This bourbon?

Ulysses chuckled easily. He wasn't Jack's blood cousin, he had married Clara's favorite cousin, Deirdre Sullivan. Unlike Jack, Ulysses was milk and honey Irish. He had earnest blue eyes and tawny hair, which he slicked back with pomade that he was stowing beside Jack's razor in the washroom. Ulysses had a portliness about him that seemed to match his hearty demeanor. The man was a stranger to Jack last week, but he had been hearing about this American cousin of Clara's forever. The first time Clara came 'round his mother's for tea, she mentioned visiting Mr. Foley on a huge horse farm in the American South and getting crustless sandwiches brought to her in bed. Such familial ties were a thing Jack liked about Clara. He told his brothers in the Army that Clara was kin to American royals, and had once had stepdanced at the White House.

"I bet I can make a believer out of you," Ulysses stood up with a wink. From his gleaming caramel suitcase, he unearthed a glass decanter and brought it into the kitchen. The swishing sound of the amber bottle made Jack's mouth water.

"It won't be whiskey as you know it, son, as it's half corn," Ulysses said expertly, "And my little brother ages it in charred barrels for a minimum of five years. This is the first breath of air this stuff has caught since 1915. Consider it a wedding present to you and my lovely cousin." With this, he raised his tea cup to Clara outside. She was hanging linens with a clothespin in her mouth, dark brows furrowed. Her pregnant belly looked like she had a pillow stuffed under her pinafore dress. Ulysses had already gifted them with a box of spiced rum cake and two cartons of Gauloises, picked up on his week-long stay in Paris (which he pronounced as "Paree").

Jack drank. The bourbon went down like fire that dulled to an exquisite warmth in his gullet. He coughed, trying to pretend like he was clearing his throat. "That stuff's stronger'n whiskey!"

Ulysses laughed gayly, "It's a baptismal from the Devil, isn't it? Anyway," he tipped a stream of amber into his tea, "This bourbon is the blood in my veins. *Truly.*"

"Is it?" Jack took refuge from laughter in his cigarette. The American had such an odd manner of speaking.

"Absolutely!" Ulysses boomed, "The Foleys are on our eighth generation of whiskey-making. We started here in Ireland with Bunratty Gold."

"Did you?" Jack wasn't laughing anymore. Bunratty Gold was good stuff. When he used to tend bar in Dublin, the white-collared lads called Bunratty "payday whiskey."

"Yessir!" Ulysses cried. "Then we made our way over to the States. Been brewing it in Kentucky since beaver skin was still legal tender." Again, the American went to his suitcase, this time bringing a pile of pictures. He handed them to Jack.

"This is Kentucky," he boomed. "Here's our card going out this Christmas," And he pointed to a crisp card of a sprawling home that Jack would have guessed housed an important American statesman. There were a friendly looking Coupe and Speedster parked in the endless driveway, and a beautiful horse on the front lawn. Ulysses and his wife, Deirdre, stood beside the horse, just as dark and pretty as Clara, holding her baby with a sense of adamant belonging. The text said, *"Blessings for a Merry Christmas and prosperous 1921 from the Foleys and Exterminator, this year's winning horse at the Kentucky Derby."*

"You didn't want to give your boy your name?" Jack asked the American. "'Tis Latin for Odysseus, Ulysses." He kept it a secret for now, the reason he knew this. The name *Ulysses* had been ringing in Jack's head even longer than *Clara Sullivan*, dating back to his dreary days as a prisoner at Frognoch.

Ulysses chuckled, "I figured we'd spare Sullivan that particular handicap. My mother, of course, was hissing in my ear that only Protestants give kids the mother's maiden name." He shuddered, which Jack was proud to see. "But we were breaking with tradition, no doubt. Foley men are always named for war generals. There's my brother Andrew, he's our Master Distiller—Momma named him for Andy Jackson, a proud Anglophobe like yourself." He raised his teacup admiringly to Jack. "I'm named for Ulysses S. Grant, a war general who went on to be President. I had an Uncle Zebulon named for a War of 1812 hero—"

"And what was your father's name?" Jack asked.

Ulysses' joyful expression wilted. "Actually Jack, I wish I knew his name, but I do not. I never knew him." He explained that his hard-knuckled mother, Blaise, refused to reveal his father's identity, a fact that nearly drove him mad as a boy.

"I never knew my father, either," Jack said instantly.

"See, I must have had an inkling," Ulysses replied, nodding, "Usually, when someone asks, I give some myth about Daddy never coming home from the Spanish War of '98."

"If ye have full artistic license over your father's image, why not make him a soldier?" Jack murmured. He explained about the London police executing his own father, a Fenian brother, when Jack was but two years old.

"Ah, so you're a soldier with a score to settle," Ulysses said wisely, sipping his tea.

Jack shrugged, "Just trying to do what's best for my country."

"So am I," Ulysses said stoutly, knocking his teacup against Jack's. "So, down with Home Rule, and may the Eighteenth Amendment rot in hell."

"*Sláinte,*" Jack murmured, then he paused with the teacup midway to his mouth. "The Eighteenth would be who now, slavery?"

"Prohibition!" Ulysses roared, as if spotting Lucifer himself out in the yard.

"Aye," Jack nodded; he knew of this from the news. "Can't be good for bourbon sales, that one."

Ulysses sighed despondently, "My brother thinks the solution is to focus on selling internationally. This is really an ambassadorial trip that I'm on. Trying to wean the French off their wine and get them over to," he tapped his flagon, "bourbon."

The two men drank in pensive silence. They both knew things about each other, by way of their wives. Clara wrote to her cousin Deirdre that her new husband Jack Walsh had the bravery of 100 leading men. He left school at Trinity to fight in the War of Independence, and had been imprisoned twice, most recently in Wales, where he was placed in solitary confinement and fed only bread and water. Jack wrote excellent articles for the rebel newspaper, *The Irish People*, and had even been paid by *Sinn Féin* to write speeches to keep up morale as the fight drudged on. Whenever Clara prayed, she asked God to bring Jack peace and make him forget about all the fight for Ireland. Jack's mother was fond of commenting on her knee pain from saying prayers for her radical son. "Tell him he's done enough," Mrs. Walsh implored Clara, "Jackie only listens to you."

Deirdre wrote to Clara that her husband Ulysses was a silver-tongued salesman who could've convinced Padraic Pearse to sing "God Save the Queen." Ulysses Foley loved horses, tobacco, and of course, her. He was coming over to Ireland soon to buy Deirdre a house because, though life in America was a holiday in Heaven, she missed Kilkenny so. Three weeks later, this jolly millionaire was sitting in the Walshes' flat, talking in a crispy accent that sounded nothing like the King's English as Jack knew it.

Clara came inside, the wicker basket of linens perched on her hip. She hovered above Jack to admire Ulysses' pictures, then sniffed the air. "Is that the blood of Christ on your breath?" she asked him.

"It's American liquor," Jack explained. Clara made an "oh" of acceptance, a face that grew into shining approval as she examined

Ulysses' pictures. She loved how Deirdre wore her hair, parted severely and in short, flowing waves. Sifting through all the pretty horses, she identified each one by their kooky names, and cooed over Baby Sullivan, so cute and fat and happy in Deirdre's arms.

"He's named after our maiden name," Clara told Jack, with the girlish boastfulness that reminded him at once how young she still was. It was as though she sought to claim her small piece of this Camelot spread before them.

"I know your maiden name, *macushla*," Jack told his wife, and his curt tone was at odds with his pet name for her—*my darling*. "I'm the reason it's changed."

At dinner, Ulysses effusively praised Clara's cooking. "Deirdre's notion of a recipe is phoning the reservations line at the Salty Pigeon," he said wryly, helping himself to seconds of the buttery potatoes. He had a proposal for them: "Tomorrow, after church, would you two like to come see about a house with me? The clerk at the Gresham said it was about thirty miles from your flat."

Jack and Clara said yes, though neither of them knew how far away thirty miles was.

In church the next morning, Ulysses did not seem to notice that everyone was staring at him, casting suspicious eyes over his lush suit and leather shoes. He had not needed to attend Confession the day before because, as he told them with a wink, his conscious was clear.

After church, he asked Jack if he minded that they stop off at home, so he could change out of his "Sunday dandies," as he called them. He hung up his Battistoni, changing into a far more modest pair of slacks.

"It pains me to admit it," he told Jack in grave tones, in his well-filled-out undershirt, "But the Italians *do* have it all over on us Irish in the art of suit-making."

They hustled out into the street, Ulysses apologizing to Clara for causing a holdup. Jack decided then that he liked this cousin. There was sincerity, not snobbery, in the root of all his theatrical gestures and phrases.

The party drove out to the countryside in a Coupe that Ulysses had borrowed from his in-laws. "My momma and daddy from the dowry," he called the Sullivans, with a good-natured growl, rolling his eyes at Jack in a fraternal sort of way. He didn't mention that he had bought the car for them in the first place, that it was the first car in the Sullivan's piss-poor neighborhood.

Jack and Ulysses passed a flask between them, Jack directing his American cousin through the winding dirt roads, roads he used to walk for hours as a telegram boy. The drink emboldened Jack, made him admit that he had never driven before. At this, Mr. Foley pulled over immediately and insisted he try.

Heeding Ulysses's instructions, Jack stepped on the gas pedal and cranked the gears, sending the car into jaunty motion down the country road. He felt at ease, from the bourbon and its owner's confidence. Even if the Brits were to catch him up and accuse him of not having a driving permit, he was sure Mr. Foley could chuckle the matter away, forcing them to feel their own ignorance. *Maybe Mr. Foley will buy us a car too,* he thought vaguely. So much of the fighting was happening in Cork and Galway lately. He could drive there at a moment's notice, give his bayonet a few more notches.

The house they were touring was situated atop a great hill, the foot of which was toothpicked with a sign, "Castlecomer Road." They drove over an endless cobblestone driveway before reaching an iron gate, barnacled with rust and woven with ivy.

Smartly, Mr. Foley instructed Jack to park the car behind one of the brick columns that twinned the gate—"The 'P' lever, son, then take the keys out, there you are." Then he swiftly removed the gold watch from his wrist, and hustled out of the car to open the door for Clara, cawing, "I declare, usually when I get the door for a Sullivan woman, she's screeching at me to hustle my step!"

A man was waiting for them at the end of the walkway, visibly tapping his toe. This did nothing to hasten Ulysses' step.

"This is the *one,*" he hissed to Jack and Clara, slinging an arm around each of them. "But this sonuvabitch, excuse me, Clara—he's askin' for $75,000. Deirdre said she'd cry like Alabama rain if I didn't come home with the deed to this place, but we can't let ourselves get chiseled, now."

Mr. Foley sobered up when he shook hands with the owner, a slight man with a golden toothbrush moustache, who revealed himself to be a Mr. Aloysius Flynn.

"Foley? 'Tis a Mayo name, isn't it?" Flynn demanded.

"That's where we came from. Correct, sir," Mr. Foley said, and his beefy accent made it apparent that the Mayo exodus hadn't been two Tuesdays ago. *Deaf men could hear the amber waves of grain in his voice*, thought Jack.

"You don't sound the part, forgive me for saying so." Flynn squinted at him as though he was a Protestant in masquerade.

Feeling annoyed, Jack intervened, "'Foley is his name, America is his nation, Kentucky is his dwelling place, and Heaven is his expectation.'" He was quoting Stephen Dedalus, the antihero of his favorite writer, James Joyce.

Foley grinned swiftly at him, and Jack wondered (again) if the American knew Joyce. He imagined (again) telling Foley how Joyce's *Ulysses* had saved him in prison, keeping him buoyed against the darkest currents of heart and mind.

Flynn seemed satisfied by his Kilkenny accent. At least, he unlocked the oak door and bade them enter.

The home was beautiful and equipped with all the makings of modernity, sending Clara into trills of delight. ("Jackie look, the kitchen has an electric stove!") Jack, himself, nodded his cool appreciation for the four-meter-high ceilings, the stone fireplace that buttressed a mahogany dining room. It did not occur to him to long for such for such a home. The way he saw it, Ulysses was rich and he, Jack, was a soldier. He could no sooner aspire to be a swami or a squire or a saint. It just wasn't how his tea cup looked, as his Mam would have put it, with no small dollop of resigned cheer. His Mam worked as a dressmaker, and her gaze didn't fall too far beyond the window of Seagreen Seams.

Clara felt differently. "I cannot believe that Deedee gets that *whole* house!" she pouted in the car as Jack drove home, his foot fluttering anxiously between the gas and brake pedals.

He noted the petulance in her voice, and wished again that he had waited a good two years to marry her. Then she could have danced more and flowered into a woman, and he could have seen out the resistance front in Dublin. He tried to tell himself that the babe being born was the thing he was so impatient to happen, but the truth lay inside him, hard and half-awakened.

"Aw," Ulysses rotated in his seat to deal her an avuncular smile. "First of all, my dear, we have to wait and see if Flynn accepts our offer—" here Ulysses' voice grew contemplative. "Though he seemed a greedy sort to me. I'll bet we'll come home to his telegraph demanding $75,000 or nothing. And *secondly,*" He resumed his kind boom, "This isn't just for Deedee—it'll be a family home! We'll come in from Kentucky at Christmastime, and we can all spend the holidays there, if you like. It shall be a new tradition, with Baby Sullivan and his cousin you've got in there." Ulysses made a coochy-coo sign at her stomach. He was a man who could carry it off well, same as how his addressing Jack as "son" felt like a warm hand cuffing his shoulder.

"Christmas could be nice," Clara conceded, in tones of watery hope.

"Let us first see how we do with the offer," Ulysses said comfortably, settling into his seat, trusting Jack to drive, trusting God to deliver for him.

"Uli," Clara said, leaning forward with sudden inspiration, "Who will live in the house apart from Christmastime? You'll be all the way in Kentucky, not needing it much."

Her innuendo was endearingly clear, but Ulysses chuckled to himself. He did not foresee these cousins of his remaining in Kilkenny much longer, so there needn't be any talks of them setting up house on Castlecomer Road.

"We shall see, Clara, we shall see."

Jack and Clara's landlady, Mrs. Finucaine, was a lonesome widow with excellent furnishings. Indeed, her willingness to share her comfortable parlor was the big selling point when they toured her flat. She had a big piano, cozy chaises, and subscribed to no fewer than seven world newspapers, all of which Jack devoured each night. After nine (or Jameson o'clock, as Jack termed it), Mrs. Finucaine often took to her piano, warbling old tunes like "Take Me

Home Again, Kathleen" and "The Bloom is on the Rye." Sometimes, Clara danced along sportively, her coltish legs flying and inevitably knocking over a vase or an end table.

An unspoken term of lessorship was that Jack be on-call for any of Mrs. Finucaine's many household needs. The landlady requested more spiders be executed and jam jars opened than Jack's mother had in eighteen years. These tasks were drawn out by the landlady's insistence on rewarding Jack with a cup of tea afterwards. Clara often returned home to a note from her husband: *Hi Mrs. Walsh, I am downstairs serving my mistress. I will quickly resolve this "leaky sink" issue and accept your compliments on how clever my subterfuges are. Kiss, J.*

Mrs. Finucaine made a fuss over Ulysses, trotting out a dusty pouf to rest his feet on, and insisting he smoke the late Mr. Finucaine's pipe. Ulysses sidestepped out of this by saying that as much as he would love a puff, Kentucky tobacco had ruined him for any other chaw.

Tonight, *The Irish Independent* reported that there was another bombing at the British naval port in Dublin. In retaliation, thirteen brothers had been shot dead by the RICs. Jack both craved and dreaded to know the names.

"Are you, ah, still active in this uprising?" Ulysses asked Jack formally, reclined in the tufted armchair. There was a cigar hole that Jack liked to put his finger in while he read; ordinarily this was his seat.

Jack drank, feeling his guilt smothered by the bourbon's warmth. "Not as much, lately."

Clara, sipping daintily from a sherry glass in her rocker, patted her belly. "He's trying to live to see his babe be born." And Ulysses went "ah" in Jack's chair.

Tuesday night, Ulysses and Jack went downstairs to have a pint. Clara stayed in to clean their flat. When she wiped the dust off the mantle, she was careful to move the envelope bearing Ulysses' first-class return ticket on the RMS *Menelaus*, so as not to dirty it.

At the pub, Jack told his American guest: "You know, there is a new novel called *Ulysses*." It took him two drinks to excavate this heavy stone from his chest. He did not know why.

"No kidding?" Ulysses yelped, slapping the bar with his gold-ringed hand.

"Or there will be," Jack muttered, "If Joyce can ever finish it."

Ulysses gave a serenely puzzled look, so Jack had to explain: James Joyce's new book was genius, a modern day parallel of Homer's *Odyssey,* but because of its illicit themes, only a small American magazine would take it on. *Ulysses* was being published in serial format, a chapter every month or so. When Jack was at Frognoch, his friend Peter mailed him the monthly installments of *Ulysses,* but only the first twelve chapters had been completed so far.

In prison, Jack composed angry letters to the editors-in-chief of said magazine, *The Little Review.* There he was, suffering a bread and water diet for Ireland, and Joyce couldn't be bothered to finish his novel. He may have written more in the letters, it was hard to recall. Hunger and hatred had rendered him quite delirious in there.

"You wrote angry letters?" Ulysses' mustache quivered with mirth.

"I did." Jack refrained from telling him that, when he heard Mr. Foley was called Ulysses, he felt this same desperate expectation, as though the American man would be his deliverance instead.

"Have you read Joyce?" he asked instead.

"I plead American ignorance" Ulysses replied, putting a hand to his velvet lapel. "But I do like a lot of the new Irish playwrights," he sipped and smiled, "You know, the first time I saw Deirdre, she was acting in a Synge play."

"At the Abbey, was it?" Jack murmured. Everyone heard when Deirdre Sullivan made it to the Abbey. Old bats called it a sin, and girleens idolized her. When word got round that some American millionaire saw her perform and was pushed to propose, her story became *Cinderella* legend. Jack had overheard more than one girleen in his mother's shop swooning her hope that the same fate would befall her one day.

"Yes," Ulysses laughed with a dab of sheepishness. "My mother was after me to marry an Irish girl. I was well past thirty, and all that happy horseshit."

"My mother's favorite homily," Jack agreed. "She stopped only when I was halfway down the aisle to Clara at St. Ann's."

"Remind me how you met Clara?" Ulysses requested. He sipped his Guinness in the same pinched, unpracticed way he did his tea. "You saw her Irish dance?"

"Aye," Jack said. "She had a reputation for being a bit of a prize in the town. Talented, pretty." He pictured Clara on stage, legs flying like a marionette. There were other dancers onstage, but the spotlight only seemed to follow his Clara.

"She is certainly both things, Miss Clara," Ulysses murmured approvingly.
"When she came to visit, we took her to see a Synge play in Chicago." Ulysses paused, "You know where that is, right Jack?"

"Er, Chicago would be in the middle?"

Ulysses laughed, producing a bullet-like pen from the breast pocket of his suit. He began to sketch a map of the US on his cocktail napkin, drawing key-shaped Kentucky first and filling in the states around it like moons in lazy orbit (as a result of this map, Jack regarded Kentucky as America's nucleus until the day he died). Without looking up, Ulysses said, "Our cousins in Chicago have been helping us this past year to stay in business. Moving bourbon across the country without the wrong people knowing."

"Is it stewing the poteen in the bathtub you are now?" Jack asked, picturing Foley rowing crew in amber waters.

"Well, our stills never really closed." Ulysses' voice nearly flickered out, "We brought a doctor in who will swear on a stack of Bibles that we're brewing it for medicinal purposes. Because, you know, the inspectors come in to check up on us with some kind of regularity." Mr. Foley paused. He did not yet tell Jack the fate that had befallen Hornsby, the Prohibition agent who came nosing around Foley one too many times.

"The fact is, Jack, I'm sitting on about $3 million worth of bourbon right now," he leaned in so closely that Jack could smell his minty breath. "People will pay a premium for our stuff because they know the name, and they know it's good. The swill they're peddling in the blind tigers, it's no good. Every other day you hear of some poor bastard drinking moonshine, taking ten paces out the bar, and keeling over from methanol poisoning." His blue eyes were ablaze now, but no less earnest. "People want Foley, we just have to figure out how to get it to them."

"What about a ship?" Jack suggested. "In '16, that's how we stowed our weapons for Easter Week. 'Course the limey RICs intercepted it before the fight."

Ulysses shook his head despondently, "Kentucky is landlocked. No seaboard." He cocked his slick head. "Now, if we can get our barrels to Chicago, we can make some good money selling there."

"If you get it on cargo trains, as well," Jack mused, "You could make stops to unload in all the major cities."

Ulysses snapped his fingers, looking delighted, "See, now your wheels are turning." He took a plug of his Guinness, wearing the face of a man playing chess. "I am short, however, on men that I can trust. I need a man that I can trust like family. Hell, a man who *is* my family…"

Jack finally registered the strain of innuendo in his cousin's voice. "Is it asking me to be your guy you are?" His tone suggested little more than if Ulysses was telling him to lobby for Prohibition here in Ireland.

Ulysses didn't say yes or no. Instead, he flagged down the barman for a light. Using the second to last match in the book, he lit the cigarillo that he pulled from his pocket. After a long moment, Ulysses asked from behind the wall of bluish smoke between them, "John, may I ask what your plans are? For your life, I mean."

Jack nettled a bit. Perhaps this nosiness was an American thing. His mother did not ask him about life plans, even as he finished school at Kilcooley. Still, Jack did not deal Ulysses the vague lie he gave Clara.

"Once the babe is born," he said quietly, "I'll be off to Dublin or Tipperary, wherever the fighting is at."

"I could have guessed that," Ulysses murmured.

"Everything else feels meaningless."

"Even being a husband and father?"

"Clara *knew* I was a soldier from the first day she met me."

"Clara writes a letter to my wife every week, scared to death that you're going to leave her and rejoin the fight." Ulysses said, leaning out of the smoke like a holy apparition, "You might want to give your son a chance to know his father."

Jack felt a strong need to make him understand, "No. I am trying to make Ireland a better place for my son. If I am to die in service of that task, then he will grow up knowing that it was so he would be free." Emphatically, he pounded his glass against the bar. Jack's policy was to keep his cool at all costs, but sometimes when he started in on Ireland, the octopus living in his chest squeezed its tentacles around his heart, staining his blood with ink.

Ulysses was listening. Listening was what made him an excellent salesman. He understood what this young man before him with the ebony hair and St. Michael pendant wanted most: He wanted to matter. Jack Walsh thought he had to spill the blood in his veins to do it, as though the Irish Republican Brotherhood held the monopoly on making men matter.

"Here's how I see it," Ulysses said finally. "You did your time for Ireland. You wrote speeches that made dull men sound eloquent. You took out as many British bastards as you could before they locked you up in internment. I have nothing but respect for what you've done for your country."

Jack inclined his dark head in curt thanks.

Ulysses leaned forward, "Now, I'm asking you to be a soldier for a different cause." He took a steeling sip of his stout, "A year ago, my president decreed that the bourbon that has been my family's lifeline since 1788 was all of a sudden illegal. I *can't* accept that—and I'm thinking of my son when I say so. What success are we as men if we can't leave something for our sons?"

"None at all," Jack murmured. And this line of Ulysses' would become the chord around which he tuned his life. "But what am I to do?" he asked baldly, "Become the bourbon prophet for Ireland?"

"*No.* Come to America."

"Is it codding me you are?"

"I would not offer a man and his family passageway to America as a joke," Ulysses said solemnly, "Not to mention, a job at my company."

Jack had not truly believed it was a joke. Though the octopus in his chest jolted, it was not angry or even surprised. He felt its tentacles unfurl, reaching desperately, surging and surfacing. With a schoolmaster's fear of disorder, he kicked it back down.

"AMERICA!" said a drunk at the bar, to whom Jack sometimes gave his spare pence, bolting upright on his stool. "Where the streets are paved with gold, and the hole is *free*!"

Ulysses glanced over at the drunk, chuckling indulgently. "Well, I can't make that a part of my recruitment speech. That would be sheer entrapment."

"And you want me to move your bourbon for you?" Jack said, still concentrating on buttoning up his chest.

"Every drop," Ulysses agreed.

"I don't drive, me," Jack argued.

"And what do you suppose you've been doing in the Coupe?"

"Alright, so I'm Henry Ford. But you know that apart from my wee holiday in Wales," he thumbed over his shoulder towards Frognoch, "I have never left Ireland."

"I know that, Jack," Ulysses said lightly. "And I'm thinking the time has really come for you to travel more."

The drunk ambled off his stool. "I want to go to America!" he bawled, wringing his cap in his hands. Ulysses snapped his fingers at the bartender, smartly peeling a note from his billfold. The barman nodded sagely, fixing a round for all three of them.

"You're a slippery one, Foley," Jack told him gruffly, hunching his shoulders over the drink. "You know that when I go to my wife with these tidings, she'll be on both knees, and it won't be for saying prayers, either."

Ulysses nodded wisely. "Of course. And across the pond, Deirdre's having her tea, sitting on tacks to get my telegram. She's sent me two already asking if I popped the question yet."

"So, Deirdre was an accomplice to this scheme, too," Jack murmured. Her face came to him, not from Ulysses' holiday card, but from a backdrop of verdant hills in the early Kilkenny morning.

Deirdre, a few grades behind Jack, walked a few paces ahead of the boys to school, casting playful looks over her shoulder until they finally caught her up. Anyone could tell from her tied-on shoes that she paid the reduced tuition of fifty pence, but you forgot about that when you saw the blue ribbon tied in her raven curls, heard her elegant voice, like spoonfuls of sweet plums.

"The Black Beauty herself," Ulysses said, his eyes growing unfocused with admiration. "It would be good on our girls, to be together again. Our sons could grow up playing together. We could build y'uns a house next to the rickhouses, for easy access." Ulysses began to sketch out his land for Jack. This time he used two cocktail napkins to express its longitude. He lamented his inability to draw, but his beautiful words made up for the handicap: Kentucky was a Elysium of horses, health, wealth, and happiness. And bourbon—barrels and barrels of it.

In Jack's head, a cool calmness was descending. "May I ask what the penalty is, being caught trafficking alcohol in the US?"

"Well, let's talk risks and rewards," Ulysses said readily. "For an average Joe, the penalty for crossing state lines with mass quantities of liquor is something like ten years at Alcatraz. But with our lawyer, you'd get off with a prayer of contrition."

"He's that good, aye?"

"The best," Ulysses growled. With a pointed glance at the drunk, who was openly goggling them, he added in his lowest voice yet, "If you worked for me, I'd protect you like my brother."

Jack heard him. "And rewards?"

"Well, I'll give you a percentage of every barrel sold," Ulysses explained. "Typically, a barrel goes for about this much." And he wrote down a number that was about half the salary of a laborer for a year.

Jack blinked hard. "And you say this job is only for as long as Prohibition lasts?"

"Prohibition won't last another year or two," Ulysses said confidently. "But this could make more of a permanent career change for you, Jack. Maybe we can make it a partnership. We Foleys, historically, only work with family but you *are* family now."

His eyes shone with divine luminosity, "And I know the Army is great and all, but it doesn't come with stock options."

Jack felt all the seduction that Ulysses intended. But mainly what reverberated now was his American's cousin's initial pitch: *Now, I'm asking you to be a soldier for a different cause.*

"Och, I will be needing to speak to Clara," he said finally. "We can do nothing until the babe is born."

Ulysses smiled. With flushed cheeks, he asked the barman to switch him to Bunratty Gold, "And one for my friend here!" he yelled, wrapping an arm around Jack. The drunk joined their huddle, helping himself to Ulysses' discarded ale. At some point, the grandfather clock chimed, but Jack was not mindful of the hour. Ulysses was in his ear, saying things that hummed like the end of a good book, planting seeds for his mind to sow: "We men without fathers go through life without a compass. We have to know for ourselves when something is right—just like when you saw Clara and I saw Deirdre. Otherwise, we are always wandering, forever lost."

That night, out of his dreamless sleep, there arose for the first time the question of life beyond dying for Ireland.

The next morning at eight, Mrs. Finucaine rang the door and breathily told Jack there was a telegram for Mr. Foley. It was all in Irish, and signed by Mr. Aloysius Flynn. Jack translated it for Ulysses while Clara fried up some doxy bread. To everyone's surprise, Flynn had decided to accept Ulysses' offer on the house.

Ulysses hastened to telephone his father-in-law, telling him he wanted to get the inspection done right away. ("Hi, Uncle Tommy!" Clara trilled in the background). After he hung up, Ulysses murmured to himself, "And while we're there, we can drive over to Waterford for Deirdre's crystal. She said she'd rather those goblets come back than me."

Alone with Clara, Jack told her that Mr. Foley had offered him a job. His words were still hanging in the air when Clara gave a jubilant whoop and began jigging about the flat, as much as her belly would allow.

"Oh, Jackie, *please* can we go to America? 'Tis truly as wonderful as they say, you'll see—you will *love* it there, truly you will."

Jack lit one of his Egyptian cigarettes that Clara hated for the stench of them. "The parlor smells like half a harem," she would say. This time, however, she kept quiet, leveling her hazel eyes at him.

"Another Irish family fleeing like the Israelites," Jack griped, putting his boot on the windowsill and peering down into Patrick Street. In prison, he dreamed of those brightly painted shops.

"But Jackie, half the people of America are Irish nowadays!" Clara burbled, "You'll find more Walshes over there than here!"

"I am not sure if the time is right," Jack murmured, gesturing vaguely to her midsection.

Clara patted her belly, "The babe may come before Christmastime, and that's but a fortnight away! When has Uli said we might come? Shall we go over on the Wednesday steamer with him?"

Jack stared. "Is it wanting to give birth over the North Atlantic you are, girleen? These talks are for after the New Year!"

"Oh, yes!" Clara breathed, clasping her hands together in rapture, "1921 will be the best year of our lives, Jackie! You know how I adore Deirdre. If we could raise our babies together in America, oh, Jackie, I would be so happy. *Please,* Jackie!"

Jack Walsh had a streak of defiance in him that his new wife had yet to discover. Her begging and carrying on was more likely to make him want to stay firmly planted in Ireland. Still, he could feel his cells multiplying and vibrating, as though he too had new life inside him.

"I'll be needing to discuss it with my Mam," Jack said, to get the matter tabled.

Clara looked stricken. "Is there anything I can do to help you decide?"

"Just let me think, *acushla,*" Jack said, giving her one of his fractional smiles. Future journalists, courtroom reporters, and historians would observe that stoic Black-Jack Walsh's smiles were reserved only for his Clara, and sometimes her elegant cousin, Deirdre Sullivan-Foley.

Over the next few weeks, Jack thought ceaselessly about America. He did not mention it to the lads at the bar, nor at the mill. They would gurgle at him to go to America and never look back. Those men were all living pint to pint on gristles of soap, with only a marginal allegiance to God and country.

Jack was different. He studied letters at Trinity. He was sworn into the Irish Republican Brotherhood when he was but nineteen. He had gone to jail twice, marinating for months in his cold hatred for Britain and his savage love for Ireland. He had been so dogmatic about his fate as a soldier that he was experiencing now a full-on crisis of faith. He knew this happened to priests, and wished that he could get a trip to Africa to pray over negro children until he saw the burning bush, or whatever happened at the moment of epiphany.

On December fourteenth, four members of the Second Ballylooby Brigade were killed by RIC gunfire, including Timmy Hogan. Hogan was an old friend of Jack's from Dublin, and a regular on the WANTED posters. The story going around was that a young British soldier had collected 1,000 pounds for his head.

That week, Jack took the train up to Tipperary, writing fond eulogy notes for Hogan in his journal. After the funeral, Jack and his brothers raised their pints in the pub and murmured Hogan's name. Then they repeated their fraternal oath in a voice like prayer.

"In the presence of God, I do solemnly swear that I will do my utmost to establish the independence of Ireland, and that I will bear true allegiance to the Supreme Council of the Irish Republican Brotherhood and the Government of the Irish Republic and implicitly obey the constitution of the Irish Republican Brotherhood and all my superior officers."

That settles it, Jack thought, drunk on a mixture of pride and grief. Ulysses and his bourbon utopia had no home in his life. He knew there, in the arms of his brothers, that they were in the hands of God, and there could be no greater glory than winning independence for Ireland together.

A few days after Christmas, the babe was born, a boy with feathery black hair. Jack thought they might name him Pearse, after

Padraic, his mentor who was executed after the Uprising of '16. When the nurse at St. Erasmus brought out the sleeping bundle, however, she cheerfully announced that Clara had named him Wilkie.

"It sounds like the names I heard down South," Clara explained happily, sitting up and cradling Wilkie in her starched white cot. "We want him to fit in, no?"

Jack said nothing. Clara had been steadfastly keeping the Kentucky dream alive since Ulysses left them. She told Mrs. Finucaine that they were likely moving "down South" in the new year. The next time the landlady saw him, she asked Jack if he had found work in Cork.

Jack did not wish to upset his Clara, so he let her talk. At night, she steered him towards the Land of Nod with her blissful recollections of Kentucky. Jack felt the leaden vest of vengeance lift as his consciousness eroded, and he joined Clara in the blond fields of bourbon dreams.

Ulysses' voice revisited Jack often. *I would protect you like my brother.* Jack trusted this man. He knew, somehow, that no one could move Ulysses' bourbon as well as he could. When he thought of telegraphing Ulysses to say that he accepted, Jack felt fiercely wracked by the honor of it. Then Ireland would wave from outside his window and Jack would be tugged back to her.

It was impossible.

A few days into 1921, Jack received a letter postmarked from Paris. It was addressed to John Walsh at Frognoch Prison in Wales, and had gotten very scuffed up on its forwarding journey to Kilkenny City.

The letter turned out to a grand surprise, one in league with Ulysses' bourbon proposal.

John,   17 Septembre MCMXX
                                         Paris, France

In departing the capital of our *chère* Hibernia, I have installed myself in the Gallic capital, where Dadaism and debauchery serve to flavor and texturize one's writing well. Paris is an excellent prescription for a young Irishman with a "flair!" or "knack!" for writing, such as ourselves. The Bible ought not be the Alpha and Omega of literary utility; the character's paternity ought not be attributed to Jesus alone. I think (*ergo sum*) that if I re-read *meine* oeuvre someday from a pristine, dusted shelf and envisioned only the faces of Dublin priests and Dublin martyrs, I would cremate said oeuvre (incidentally, I have no fewer than six obscenity cases budding right now—maybe the books shall be kindling yet!)

You wrote my American publisher from prison to express your disgust that *Ulysses* was taking me so long. Blame it on the serial format, blame it on Irish sensitivity, just do not blame the madman. I have been told that someone mailed you *The Little Review* in prison because you were a fan of *Dubliners* and *Portrait* (Cheers to fandom! 'Tis like playing for Manchester United, only with no hole to be had!). It may gratify you to know that I have received word from New York that the 13th chapter, *Nausicaa* will be published in *The Little Review* this December. If you like, I can request that it be mailed to you. Though by account of your letter to my publisher, you were being punished in prison for recent insubordination, on a bread and water diet, with incoming and outgoing letters restricted. Thus I may await your confirmed receipt of this letter before sending my 13th, for fear that arborists might otherwise condemn us for the waste (might I ask what your crime of insubordination was? I will tender a secret for a secret)....

My *Ulysses* is not a completed manuscript. I cannot proffer any reading material beyond my latest chapter. I wish I could feed you beyond the provisional bread and water that is the prison library (I imagine devotional books and the dreadful biography of Cecil Rhodes). I can tell you that I am in the habit of composing the last line of my schizophrenic symphonies before even the first.

Dear sir, as a compatriot and an admirer, I will now furnish you with what shall be the last words of my 'Ulysses':

"his heart going like mad and yes I said Yes I will yes..."

-Ulysses (page ? of ?)

Is it customary to thank an IRA member for his service? Just don't die in there, it would give the Brits a great cockstand.

Ta,
Jim Joyce

(PS: Send me none of your writing. I am busy composing brilliance, with no time to read and condemn it.)

Jack stood there outside Mrs. Finucaine's parlor with the letter in his shaking hands. His idol Joyce was an arrogant fecker, but that was okay. The last words of Ulysses would be, *yes I said Yes I will yes*. That yes was so good it took all the no out of the universe. It was about as close to a burning bush as a soldier could get.

Suddenly, Jack knew just what to do. He jetted upstairs and reached euphorically for his typewriter.


```
    Jim,

        Thank you for deviating from your busy
    schedule of writing and tipping your hat to the
    whores of Pigalle to drop a soldier a line. Your
    name was the last one I expected to see in my post
    today, though admittedly it did take the edge off
    a gas bill.
        Those are fine last words for your Ulysses. I
    cannot know which character is affirming to what,
    but if the question makes one's heart beat so,
    what answer could there be but yes?
        I have been released from prison. Like you, I
    have decided to depart the land of Brian Boru and
```

Buck Mulligan in pursuit of new opportunities.
I'll be moving to America soon.

   Have your 13th chapter sent to me right away.
These cliffhangers are best left to Dickens.

   My new address is—

(Here, Jack snatched Deirdre's latest letter off the nightstand,
learning his new address for the first time):

Foley Bourbon
Old State Road 434
Louisville, Kentucky

Sincerely Yours,

Jack Walsh

(P.S: I refused to salute the British flag. God
hang the Queen)

(P.P.S: Think your publisher could get me a book
deal when I am done with my Prohibition adventures
in America? Fret not, I shan't be sending you any
drafts).

"Jackie? Where are you going?" Clara asked, entering the bedroom
with baby Wilkie in her arms.
   But Jack grabbed some pence and bolted, blowing on his letter to
dry the ink, his own heart going like mad. It was 8:45 now, the post
office opened at 9:00. First he would mail this letter to Joyce, Yes he
would yes, then send Ulysses a telegram. Jack knew exactly what
he would say:

Ulysses,

Yes I say Yes I will yes. How soon can the wee family come over?

The Home of Patrick Walsh and James Branagh
Six miles from Zzyzyx Road
Ten miles outside of Louisville, KY
Labor Day, 2014

Chapter 4

In the fall of 1993, Pat Walsh and I started third grade. We had different teachers; he, Miss Pepper, and I, Mrs. Marcus-Link, though we were in band together. Pat played the sax; I, the trombone. Pat was never really into his sax, but his father told him that they'd spent $300 on it, so he better hear his nightly thirty minutes of honking. There was an entire year where if you got the Walshes' answering machine, you heard Pat playing "Louie Louie" and his brother Killian laughing that the Walshes weren't in right now, but to leave a message. Finally, Conor Walsh changed it to a single burp, which deeply offended Mrs. Walsh's mother when she phoned long-distance from Dalkey.

Anyway, the fact that he played the saxophone is a footnote in Pat's biography, except that he stored his most prized possessions in his sax case. Inside, you would find a Red Hot Chili Peppers album signed by Anthony Kiedis; a picture of Pat and his high school girlfriend, Axel, cheesing at Prom 2004 ("Rhapsody in Blue"); a handwritten note from Killian in 2007, asking Pat to be the Best Man at his wedding; his CPA scores (cumulative 93% across all four sections); the cool, contrite note that Blaise Foley wrote him after her daddy shot him on Halloween 2009; the receipt from Karina Jewelers for Blaise's engagement ring, purchased in January; and an iconic picture of all fifteen of Wilkie's grandsons at Conor's wedding (where even Paytah the Montana shaman is wearing a tuxedo).

He also kept the ultimate Walsh heirloom in the sax case, given to him by Grandpa Wilkie in 1994 (yes, the grandfather who was a newborn baby in the chapter you just read). Wilkie gave each of his fifteen grandsons a small treasure for their First Holy Communion. At age seven, it made the Walsh boy a Show and Tell rockstar. Now that everyone was grown, Pat's cousins privately coveted his treasure above anyone else's.

After Pat left town, I snooped in his room to see if he brought said heirloom with him. He had, of course, but he left behind the gold-lettered card it came with: *to my Grandson, on the Day of his First Holy Communion…*

Inside Wilkie wrote:

Dearest Patrick,
May 22, 1994

For the boy whose namesake is the patron saint of Ireland himself, I give you my blessing on your First Eucharist. You are a true joy to all who know you. You have good judgment and, dare I say, a certain business savvy?

I was very impressed when you chose the gift I offered you. Eight of my older grandsons chose the flashier option with very little hesitation. (Except your cousin who calls himself "Falco," who took a whole day to decide. You should go into business together when you grow up!)

At eight, you seem to understand better than most men of fifty about the true nature of value. Money is fleeting. Family is eternal. Now you have a small piece of immortality to pass along to your son. I gambled everything I had to get it, so if anyone tells you it's worthless, you tell them exactly what it's worth.

You will always have a job with our family bourbon, should you need one. I hope you never stray far from your old Kentucky home.

With Great Fondness,

Grampy Wilkie

His grandfather's greatest gamble wasn't all Pat took with him: somewhere between last Monday and 1920, I noticed the spot atop the fridge where we kept our bourbon bottles was empty. Apparently, Pat swiped our entire *fucking* collection on his way out of town: the Seafarer's Quenchen, (a small batch aged on the North Atlantic); the Clara's Nightcap (aged three years in a sherry cask); the Ruby Jubilee Fortieth Anniversary bottle with Black-Jack's IRA mugshot; the half-gallon of Diablo's Death, and even the unlabeled jug of Moon Juice that Killian gave me after he made it for a bachelor party last month. (Moon Juice is distilled with kava and South American mushrooms. It's a Walsh "Friends and Family only" product that will make you trip like George and John circa '67.)

When I called Pat on his shitty new track phone, he said remorselessly that where he was going, Walsh Bourbon wasn't sold. "You can always go get more from Killian. He won't charge you."

It's been a week since Pat left, and two days since I sent Blaise my Kilkenny pages. I have been checking my phone every two minutes. Finally, my muse texted me about an hour ago: "*heyy love! Sorry, been busy. Can I come see you this afternoon??*"

I wrote back, "*yes you can yes you can yes*" with a prayer emoji. That was a prayer that she would like my writing enough to let me proceed with her story.

Just then, I heard the back door open.

"*Doll!*" Blaise's voice rang out musically. "Are you home?"

"Yeah!" I called back, hastily shoving all Pat's junk back into the sax case. A moment later, she appeared in the doorway to his bedroom.

"Aww. Do you miss him?" Blaise asked, her head tilting in sympathy.

I cringed, picturing the scene through her eyes: it was five p.m., and I was sitting at the foot of Pat's bed, staring at his bedroom walls like a dog with a dead master.

"You know," I shrugged, jumping to my feet. "How are you? Did you read the pages I sent you?"

"You do miss him!" she laughed.

"No, I don't! *Do you*?"

Blaise sighed, collapsing dramatically onto Pat's bed. Her bare legs glowed like freckled moonlight. "I had to get out of Foley. My Dad is up my ass."

"About what?"

"He's like, manically happy because he thinks Pat and I are broken up. He keeps talking about us going away together."

I paused, letting this Donald and Ivanka *soupçon* wash over me. "But *aren't* you and Pat broken up?"

She sat up, fixing me with eyes like fiery comets. "We're not broken up, honey, we're *on pause*. Do you think I would jeopardize my relationship with my father if I wasn't sure about this boy?"

"Okay, okay!" I threw up my hands in mock surrender. "I'm sorry!"

Blaise stared at me a moment, her cheekbones burned fuschia. Then she turned away and said primly, "I'm sorry, too."

I mashed my toe into Pat's dresser, adding gruffly, "Did you read the pages I sent you?"

She examined her ringless hand. "Did you send them to my louisville.edu address, doll?" she asked carelessly. "'Cause I'm sorry, I seldom check that one."

"*Liar*. You forwarded me an article about homeless vets, like, two days ago."

"*Okay,*" she sat up with a comically arrested face. "I haven't read your pages yet, doll. I'm *sorry!*"

"Alright," I forced myself to grin at her. "Can you read them now?"

Blaise laughed, jumping off the bed and heading downstairs. I followed her, a needy human question mark.

Ours is a bright yellow Sears and Roebuck-style house with a front porch that could stand to be repainted, and a back deck where we grill year-round. When we first toured it, Pat and I made our cute realtor giggle as we envisioned our plans for the yard, promising to invite her to our many barbecues and bourbon pong games.

I wasn't desperate to buy a house, but Pat talked me into it. He said that I could qualify for a Veterans Assistance loan and wind up putting 0% down.

"When one of us gets married, we'll buy the other out," he concluded reasonably. He was single then, but looking towards the future. It is a truth universally acknowledged that a man in possession of an MBA must be in want of a wife.

For the first few months of our lordship, it was a total bachelor pad. The only furniture we owned were the tattered, tufted, scuffed-up pieces that Pat inherited from the lacrosse house. The walls were a gallery of our dream-girls: Pat had Carrie Underwood's poster from the *Some Hearts* album taped up, while I displayed Sharon Tate in a leather catsuit clutching an M7.

Then Pat got his true dream-girl to love him back, Blaise Foley. Framed pictures of them as a couple began adorning our walls. Pat's Carrie Underwood poster came down, after a few snippy remarks from Blaise. ("*I'm* the lady of the house now, honey," she purred, scratching Carrie's airbrushed cheek). Blaise began sneaking rococo-style furniture from Foley over to our house— gilded cabinets and tables with fleurettes and foliage carvings, and chairs upholstered in burgundy velvet. Now, our living room now looked like something out of a Guy de Maupassant novel, where you would expect to see a dapper young swain seducing an aging madame, rather than a pile of twentysomethings arguing over what to watch on Netflix.

"Do you have anything to drink?" Blaise murmured, perching on a saffron silk loveseat patterned with Foley horseshoes. She examined her ringless hand again, looking pouty with ennui. "If I'm going to have to read, I'd *really* love a drink."

"Your fiancé made off with all my bourbon," I said flatly. "But do you *need* a sedative before you read my writing?"

"*No,*" Blaise gave me a scandalized look. "It will just add to the overall enjoyment of it. *Jesus,* doll."

"Sorry," I grunted, swallowing past the stick of dynamite in my throat. *I thought you came over to talk about the book. Your casual indifference is killing me. Seriously, it's like looking at a sonogram and seeing a half-digested hot dog instead of a heartbeat. You got me excited about writing this book, and now I have to write it. Don't you get that?*

She was still staring at me distrustfully. I had a strong need to make her understand how I felt. I took a couple of deep breaths. When I spoke again, it wasn't from my mind.

"I *need* to write this story, Foley. I *know* this is the thing I've been waiting for my whole life; I just didn't know what to look for before. Even if no one else ever read our book, if it cost me everything I owned, if my house got repossessed and I wound up another homeless, panhandling Veteran in the street, I would *still* need to write your story." I looked straight at her. "And I need you around me to write it, because the energy you give me is limitless. Through you, I've entered a room with no ceiling, where I've never been able to get before."

Blaise stared at me with the whole Earth of her eyes. "Jesus," she whispered, knuckling away a tear. "I don't think I've ever been so devastated."

I couldn't watch her read it, not when my whole life was on the line.

"I'll be in my lair," I called from the backdoor, "Where only nightshade plants grow."

Blaise said she was running to the store to get us Jameson. "*Not* because I need a sedative" she gave me a look, "But I just read better when I'm a little slushied. Helps get me out of my own head."

An hour later, I was halfway through *Full Metal Jacket* and she was still gone. *Are you coming back?* I wrote her, backspacing a bunch of question marks.

Yes!! Blaise replied, *Almost done! :-D*

A few minutes later, I heard the Jag zip down my driveway, and closed my computer on Gomer Pyle. Her footsteps bounded through the backdoor with an especially frenetic timbre. She called my name, and I was at the top step to greet her in a second.

"I *love* it," Blaise said to me. Her big eyes shone with the fluorescence of a superstore at 3 AM.

"You read it?"

"In the parking lot of the Liquor Barn" she breathed, grabbing my forearms, her whole being dancing with erotic admiration (for me— *ME!*).

I will omit the transcripts from the next twenty or so minutes, because we were annoyingly high off each other. It's hard to remember what was said. Things that make a guy blush into his pillow when they return to him.

One thing Blaise said was this: "I feel like you get us." Her soul shone abashedly through her eyes, how I imagine Ulysses' had when he told Jack he never knew his father, "You can see us Foleys from all angles, even the ones we try to hide."

We plunked down at the dining room table.

"What do you think should come next?" I asked excitedly, plunging on without waiting for her answer, "What if I write about Jack in the throes of the Easter Uprising?" I spread my palms through the air, "Just as Padraic Pearse is waving the white flag of surrender, Black-Jack shows up with some of his Cheka buddies. They free all the condemned Irish rebels *just* before they're executed, and they shove the British officers into spiked barrels and roll them through Dublin—"

"But doll, that didn't happen!" Blaise laughed.

"Or," I inclined my head generously, "We could focus on *your* Grandpa. Take it back to World War II. Young Sully Foley, only twenty or twenty-one, watches the attack on Pearl Harbor unfold. He spends two years mastering the art of aviation here in Kentucky, so he can combat the Luftwaffe in France."

Blaise stood up to pour us some Jami. "Those are some very good ideas," she said, her voice taking on a cubic zirconium gleam. "But speaking of twenty-one, I think we should cover the first time Pat and I met."

"Ah," I said wisely, reclining in my chair. "Your twenty-first birthday."

Blaise nodded, sipping her amber, "We have to explain how we got into this mess in the first place."

Come reader, pile into the DeLorean with Foley and me, as we journey from 1920 to 2009. The genesis of Pat and Blaise, the single cell from which our whole mad universe generated, the reason for the ring and runaway groom, is all traceable back to Mr. Foley's primal bullet.

Year 21
Fall 2009-Spring 2010
Zzyzyx Road/University of Louisville campus
('A Season of Obsession' or
'How Patrick Walsh Got His Scar')

Chapter 5

Every year, about seventy-five invitations went out for the Foleys' Halloween Bash, which Mr. Foley lavishly threw in honor of his daughter's birthday. This year was extra special because, as the invitation trumpeted under the embossed Foley logo, *Our Blaise is turning 21!*

In the weeks leading up to the party, plenty of arguments broke out between father and daughter. They fundamentally disagreed on the vision for the party. If Mr. Foley had his way, the invitees would be the same Kentucky Royals they always hosted, the distillers and horse-breeders and heirs to tobacco farms. Everyone would sip his bourbon and bob for apples, and the big hoot of the night would come when kooky Aunt Kennedy did the "Thriller" dance with Mrs. Barnaby.

Blaise, however, craved more fun and intrigue. Since being crowned president of her sorority, she and her friends had garnered a reputation for throwing the wildest parties on campus. They had a very Kate Moss approach to rumors, refusing to deny any of them. "Everything you've heard is true," was what they liked say whenever anyone asked. And there was *a lot* to inspire curiosity.

The story currently going around campus was that Blaise had choppered herself and a few friends to Chicago during a party, because Sammi was craving Giordano's pizza (true). Last week, people talked about a Turkish exchange student doing MDMA at the house, stripping naked, and breakdancing to 'I'm a Slave 4 U' (true). Another one was that the girls performed a seance in which Blaise became possessed by Marilyn Monroe and talked breathily about which Kennedy brother was better in bed (only half-true: it was a stunt to scare the pledges).

Blaise accessorized her sorority house with as many fun amenities as she and her friends could think of. There was an eighteen-person hot tub in the backyard, and nobody was allowed in unless buck naked. Blaise also had an Olympic swimming pool installed. Now that the weather was getting cooler, she had the pool drained, and converted it into a giant ball-pit. The rumors of drugs were often true: "sexy" uppers like Adderall and coke were passed around to guests at parties like trays of hors d'oeuvres.

Blaise kept the bourbon flowing by the barrel, feeling as though she were doing a charity to her young guests by awakening their palates to sophistication. Kids all over America were cutting their teeth on cheap, flavored vodka, but not at University of Louisville, and not under President Blaise (her daddy approved: "You're makin' lifelong Foley drinkers out of 'em, angel.")

"The best of everything," was their party slogan. The other one was, "if you're not on the list, you don't exist." Blaise's friend Sammi G. spent all week carefully crafting the list. If you weren't on the list, you *did* exist, but you had to wait in line and pay $10 at the door.

This was precisely how Blaise wanted her twenty-first birthday to go, like an episode of *Gossip Girl* mixed with exquisite bourbon, hot guys, and maybe a Day-Glo paint station.

"Hot guys?" Mr. Foley said impatiently, when she shared her vision. "You've got the Barnaby boys coming."

Blaise rolled her eyes. The Barnabys were the second wealthiest family on the Bourbon Trail, and the Foleys' best friends. She and Loyce Barnaby, Jr. were the same age. Everyone was always saying she and LJ would wind up married, which made Loyce blush and Blaise cringe.

"What about LJ?" Mr. Foley prodded her, raising his russet brows.

"He's like my brother." Blaise protested as usual. And she couldn't count on Loyce, in his argyle vest and penny loafers, to supply the sex appeal for her party. "I want *real* boys there, Daddy— or else my friends are gonna order me some Chippendales dancers." At this, her father choked on his double-oaked bourbon.

On Halloween morning, a brawl broke out in the Foleys' elegant dining room.

Mr. Foley yawned behind his newspaper in his pinstripe pajamas. Beside him, his younger sister Kennedy serenely sipped a cup of hot water with lemon. She flew in from Tucson last night with her son Jericho.

"I feel like a kid coming home from college when I'm here," Kennedy burbled, smiling at the crimson walls.

Blaise's nineteen-year-old brother McCullers strolled into the room, rubbing his strawberry blonde bedhead and yawning. "Happy birthday, sis," he poured himself a champagne flute of OJ and raised his glass to her.

"Thanks Cully," Blaise smiled from her phone, where birthday texts were flying in from her sorority house and beyond. "Just *wait* 'til y'all see my costume!" She told the room that she was going as Uma Thurman in *Pulp Fiction,* specifically the overdose scene. "I just have to find a way to get the needle to stick in my chest."

"I love that scene," her cousin Jericho said reverently, earbuds dangling from his ears. He was eighteen, and at the age where Tarantino is God.

"Like hell you are!" Mr. Foley squawked at Blaise, tossing aside his *Kentucky Herald.*

"Like hell I'm not!" Blaise fired back. She was already at her limit with Daddy for telling her the basketball team couldn't come. "I'm twenty-one I can do whatever I want!"

"There are seventy-five people coming to our home tonight, and not one of 'em wants to see you with a heroin needle in your chest!" Mr. Foley bellowed, his face turning the color of a bad sunburn. "You have to represent our bourbon, now." His voice downshifted to a gentle purr; this was his angel he was speaking to. "Why don't you get mommy's Beauty Queen sash out and go as Miss America?"

"Because I do that every year!" Blaise screeched. "It's so *homely*! I want to do something with *edge*!" She downed her drink and ran out of the room. She heard Aunt Kennedy starting to argue her point in her 'cool big sister" voice, which was nearly as annoying as Daddy's sauce.

"If I die, tell the coroner there's no need for an autopsy," Blaise heard her father bellow, "'Cause it's *that* girl gonna be the death of me."

In her room, Blaise stewed and hugged her knees. She thought about going into the bathroom to press her Sonicare against her PJs' crotch to make herself feel better, but she didn't want to feel better yet.

Happy Birthday, Bam-Bam!! her cousin Zabana texted her. *I love you!! I wish I could be there tonight, I hope you have a blast!!*

Thanks Zaza, Blaise replied, adding glumly, *My Dad is a penis.*

That morning, two events occurred that were standard for Blaise's birthday. Mr. Tuttle came by, knocking formally at her door and handing her the envelope sealed in wax. He had managed the Foley's trust since before she was born. Every year, her father gave her shares to Foley Bourbon, to express his love and remind her of what she would one day inherit. Blaise kissed Mr. Tuttle's taut, freshly shaved cheek, motioning to the phone cradled against her ear. Her other birthday chore was in progress.

"I'm well, Uncle Jimmy, how are you!"

Jimmy Fleming, Jr. rasped over the phone that he was doing A-ok. The seventy-year-old was not Blaise's blood uncle, he was a semi-retired mobster out in Chicago whose family had been connected to the Foleys since the 1920s. He was the only person who hated the Walshes as much as they did, because Black-Jack had murdered his father Jimmy, Sr. and buried him with his long-lost treasure. This was why every year on Blaise's birthday, he called her up to make her renew an old promise.

"So, when you inherit your distillery, duckling, you'll let Uncle Jimmy look for his dad's bones?" he wheezed in her ear, "You know I just want to give him a proper funeral."

"Of course, Uncle Jim!" Blaise chirped automatically. She promised to call if she ever came to Chicago, (neglecting to mention her recent pizza chopper ride) or if any boy was mistreating her. This was why she liked keeping him around. Whenever Jake Abramo took longer than twenty minutes to text back, she threatened to sic Uncle Jimmy on him with a <3. It was a fun kind of power.

But she couldn't yap on the phone with the aging mobster forever—her three best friends were arriving to help set up. They hugged her, shrieking greetings of "*Happy Birthday, B!*" into her red hair. Lauren clutched a bottle of nice champagne, which made Blaise melt—she knew she probably spent an entire paycheck on it.

"Thanks ladies," Blaise smiled bravely, "I'm *so* pissed at my dad."

The girls gasped, ready to dole out attention and sympathy, suture supplies for any male-based wound.

Sammi Goldstein, Elliot Appleton, Lauren Taylor, and she, Blaise Foley were known on campus as the Untouchables, a nickname they only pretended to hate. One fraternity hazed its pledges by ordering them to approach an Untouchable and attempt a cheesy pick-up line. Otherwise, the wisdom of the Greek community held that you shouldn't bother approaching those girls unless you had a job offer from Goldman, or Kanye West levels of confidence.

"What makes them so *Untouchable*?" was the rhetorical sneer of girls outside the sorority. No one could verbalize it, but they knew the answer had to do with beauty, wealth, freedom, and the affordability of recklessness. Behind any scoff of, "*Blaise Foley buys her friends,*" was an aching envy to be invited to the Foleys' Swiss chateau for skiing, or on the private yacht Blaise rented in Acapulco over spring break, or to watch the Kentucky Derby from her family's luxury suite at Churchill Downs.

Blaise and her friends had an extra layer of Untouchability for a particular subset of boy on campus. The school was crawling with Walshes and, as Blaise warned her bouncer, Mohammed, who worked the door for her parties: "I just want you to BOLO, Momo." Sure enough, freshman Mickey Walsh tried to attend a recent Hell-Heaven party, not bothering to put devil horns over his black curls. Mohammed blocked Mickey, reading aloud Blaise's prissy edict from his clipboard, "*Absolutely no Walshes allowed, unless it's Black-Jack's ghost coming to tell me where his treasure's buried.*"

"Why don't you just be Mia *before* the heroin scene?" Elliott suggested gayly, after hearing the saga about Blaise and her dad. Elliott had a face like a sunflower and a mealy little cheerleader bod. Guys loved her, and she worked the ditzy blonde angle to her full advantage. She didn't care much about grades, which meant she had tons of freedom, and was always available for Blaise's imaginative plans. On Tuesday, for instance, they got all decked out in Blaise's great-grandma Deirdre's best fur and priceless jewelry and went out to dinner at Succotash, the Michelin starred restaurant next to Foley Bourbon.

Lauren agreed, nodding her straightened chestnut locks. "Yeah, just wear the Cleopatra wig we bought and a white button-down shirt. You can be Mia in the dancing scene."

Sammi was on the phone with the DJ, bossily making sure he had the song list for tonight's party. She winked a light brown eye, covering the mouthpiece, "You have to go barefoot. Uma Thurman is barefoot there." Blaise smiled.

Lauren and Sammi grew up together in Lake Forest, a tony suburb of Chicago. Lauren had a soccer scholarship to U of L, and Sammi followed her oldest friend to a school where she knew no one else. They had an intimacy that made Blaise a little wistful, like when Sammi would snap at Lauren and then ask to borrow her dry shampoo in the same breath. Lauren was sturdy and competent, Blaise's VP, with a smile so dazzling that her orthodontist had put her on his marketing brochure. At 5'1" and 100 pounds, Sammi appeared waifish and doe-like, but that was above layers of feminine steel. On Sunday mornings, when Sammi sat crocheting and calling her mom in her floral bandana, it was hard to believe that any of the stories from last night could be true.

Sammi wanted to marry a nice, successful Jewish boy and Lauren wanted to become a State Supreme Court justice like her mom. Neither of them had ever fooled around with a girl or an ethnic guy. Mr. Foley felt like the girls were a positive influence on his Blaisey.

Unlike Elliott, who was raised by her grandparents in a tiny coal-mining town in West Virginia, Lauren and Sammi had grown up in cul-de-sac neighborhoods with a BMW in every driveway. Growing up, both girls had closets full of Limited Too clothing, and a family vacation to a resort in the Dominican Republic every year. They believed they were raised "upper-class" until they turned eighteen, came to school, and befriended Blaise Foley. They couldn't compete with the Foley's leviathan wealth and influence, so they gave themselves over to it. Blaise wanted it this way, for her precious friends to assimilate into the Foleys' sterling Derby Crowd, become adoptive sisters to her brother, drink her father's bourbon and nothing *but* her father's bourbon. They were all on her tab because she was investing in friendships that would last for generations. That's how the Foleys' were—nothing in their estate was younger than 100 years old, not even their friends.

"I fucking love you guys," Blaise bawled. They put on Gaga, popped the champagne, and had an impromptu dance party.

At two p.m., the girls bounded downstairs, yanking Patagonia fleeces over their heads, grabbing for car keys. They went out front, past the buzz-cut hedges draped in fake cobwebs for Halloween, flinging carefree goodbyes at Mr. Foley.

Blaise's father stood in his corduroy trousers, talking to George, his live-in valet. Beside him, the fountain gurgled water from the stone angel's mouth. At the base of the fountain, an inch of green patina was visible, not yet noticed by Mr. Foley. Had it been noticed, he would have asked George to expunge it with a toothbrush.

"Blaisey?" Mr. Foley called his daughter over, in his slow caw. "Where y'all going?"

"To Liquor Barn," Blaise answered impatiently, jogging over. She was still feeling a little tender from their fight. "I want to make my first legal purchase, remember?"

The corners of Mr. Foley's auburn mustache sank down. "There's no need for you to *purchase* anything, honey. I opened up a barrel of the 21-Year for tonight." His voice shone with plaintive pride, "I barreled it the week after my angel was born, you know."

"Thanks Daddy, but I've never had anything *but* bourbon," Blaise whinnied, "It's my twenty-first birthday, I want to try tequila or vodka!"

"The proud piss of Mexico and Russia." Mr. Foley took a bitter sip from his coffee. The wind blew its steam over, and Blaise could smell the 21-year-old bourbon in there. "So ol' Flemmy called you up, huh? What did he have to say for himself?" Mr. Foley didn't object to Blaisey keeping time with Uncle Jimmy. You never knew when he would come in handy, especially with the Walshes around, acting like damned animals all the time.

"The usual," Blaise rolled her eyes, "Happy birthday, and the same business about his daddy's bones."

"I suppose he thanks we're running a catacombs here," Mr. Foley muttered. "Never heard a man make more fuss about his father's bones in my life. I'd lend him *my* daddy's bones if that would shut him up. Sorry, Daddy!" he called affably towards the family cemetery, where his father, Sullivan Foley (1920-1977) was buried. He sipped again, his voice going moony, "Of course, you probably told ol' Flemmy that you can't wait to be rid of me. Have the place to yourself."

"Oh, Daddy, stop," Blaise sighed.

"You did," Mr. Foley insisted petulantly. "You told him you hoped the Indian curse cleaned me out well before sixty-one."

"Daddy, *stop*. You know I want you to be the first Foley to make it to a hundred."

Mr. Foley pretended to purse his lips while sneaking an arm around her, which she snuggled into. This was their ritual for making up. Father and daughter were twins in stubbornness, and the words "I'm sorry" seldom visited their mouths. A bourbon shared on the terrace could also cancel out their anger, and restore the cool dignity to the halls of Foley. Sometimes at night, if they were particularly drunk, their savage adoration for one another led Blaise to crawl into her father's lap, and he would murmur history into her hair like he did when she was little. *Our distillery down there's older than our country, baby. They grew one alongside the other, like twins.* Sometimes he would talk about meeting her mother. *Your momma was the sun in my universe—until you were born, baby.* Night after night, this oration of love and pride formed her world growing up. When he finished—*Someday, it will all be yours*—she always shivered, even now that she was fully grown.

"I love you, baby," he murmured in his voice of sincere sterling. He broke away and said more loudly, "Well, if you girls have been drankin,' maybe George ought to drive yins." George smiled obligingly up at Blaise as he set down the leaf-blower, his dark face sheeny with sweat.

"No, it's okay! We can drive!" she skipped off, sliding into the shotgun seat of Elliott's old Mustang. Lauren waited behind them in her Toyota, her sunglasses down and Adele crooning robustly. They elected to drive separately, in case they actually bought a keg or something big. Sammi stayed behind to show the DJ where to set up, and to bake gluten-free cookies for McCullers.

Watching Blaise lean over her friend's lap to finger the keypad that opened the front gate, Mr. Foley muttered to himself, "$15,000 barrel of ambrosia, and my daughter wants a tequila shot. Do you believe that Georgie-boy?"

George turned off the leaf-blower, politely asking Mr. Foley if he had said something. Johnny just waved a hand, shuffling back inside his castle, grumbling more things that only he could hear.

As she and Elliott parked at the Liquor Barn, Blaise admired a pair of tall, black-haired guys sauntering in. Being in the 99th percentile of height had trained Blaise to be able to spot a boy over six feet tall from 100 yards away.

"Ooh, who are *those* hotties?" Blaise said in her horny housewife voice.

"They're cute!" Elliott agreed, peering above her dusty dashboard. "We should invite them to your party."

"We *should!*" Blaise agreed, absently fluffing her hair in the rearview mirror.

Inside, every phylum and genus of alcohol was on display in neat pyramids. Blaise blanched somewhat under the bright lights. She realized with a blip of panic that she had *no* idea how to buy alcohol.

"Didn't you say you wanted vodka, B?" Elliott indicated a display of Burnett's. "That's what we used to drink in high school."

Blaise frowned. Her sweet, bumpkin friend, pushing for the Walsh equivalent of vodka. Quoting her Auntie Cricket, Blaise quipped, "That's N-O-T-D: Not Our Type, Dear." She smiled to soften the phrase. "C'mon, I was born this tall to reach the top shelf, baby! How do we know what the good stuff is?"

"From rap music!" Elliott said cheerfully. Deferring to the wisdom of Jamie Foxx, whose song "Blame It" serenaded them on the way over, Elliot stood on her tippy-toes to reach a bottle of Patrón, then a few handles of Grey Goose. They noticed Lauren up towards the front, scrutinizing shot glasses.

Blaise pushed their bitsy shopping cart on towards the aisle of her family's bourbon. Seeing it anywhere outside of her home suffused her with deep pride. She grabbed a bottle of the sacred tonic, letting the light exult the gilded lettering of her name, **FOLEY**, aged six years. Her daddy had barreled it himself, before she could drive, before she had even been properly kissed by a boy.

"Here's where the *good* bourbon's hiding!" Blaise trumpeted.

But then—

"You call that *good* bourbon?"

She whipped around. The tall, identically tall, identically black-haired boys from out front were there, arms folded across their chests, smirking with identical cockiness.

Blaise felt dread and thrill clang in her stomach. The area of her brain which signaled danger was searing red. These faces were foes.

Faces with sparkling blue eyes and chiseled jaws. Very, very *cute* foes. Oh—*and so tall.*

The name surfaced in her brain like a piece of flotsam, just as her eyes linked up with the shelves of bourbon above their dark heads, stamped with Black-Jack's face.

Blaise had never been this close to Walsh bourbon before.

Five minutes ago, if someone had asked Blaise about the Walshes next door, she would have spoke of them like a litter of stray cats in a neighborhood, exaggerating their number, referring to them only as "they." It was true that there were scores of Walshes around Louisville, but Blaise knew that the house next door now belonged to Sean, Wilkie Walsh's oldest son. If someone *really* plied Blaise, she could tell them the Walshes next door had four kids: "Killian, the youngest Master Distiller on the bourbon trail" (her daddy would say it was fitting, because his bourbon was also the youngest); "Conor, the cop from hell"; and— "I dunno, didn't they have twin boys close to my age?" She had been bred not to be curious about them; was never taught their names.

"I'm Seamus, this is my brother Patrick." The twin with diamond gauges in his ears grinned at Elliott, extending a hand to her. His arms were veined with tattoos. As part of their tacit social code, he did not address Foley directly. "You have a thick accent!" Seamus said, and Elliott giggled. "Where the hell are you from, the city where the Devil goes to steal souls?"

"No, she's from West Virginia," Twin Patrick replied for Elliott. He wore a crisp Polo with the top button undone, as though to allow the golden Jesus on the chain around his neck room to breathe. He shrugged at Blaise bashfully, "I noticed the license plate on that Mustang y'all rolled up in."

"Oh."

Patrick kept his dreamy blue eyes on Blaise. Seamus looked at her too, but his eyes roved continually over Elliot, the cart, and Patrick, all fulcrumed on a crocodile smile. Blaise had never seen a more perfect asymmetry than in their identical faces. Seamus's eyes were the same color and shape as Pat's, but what glowed behind them was like harbor lights in a foggy marina. They were so much dreamy as undefined, and at some angles there shone a glint of delirium. Blaise understood the twins' duality as girls had understood it since fourth grade—Pat was sweet, Seamus was sexy.

When Blaise accidentally looked into Pat's eyes, she felt plates shift inside her. She dwelled on his chiseled jaw, imagining fleetingly what his collarbones looked like, his bare chest. She felt vines shooting from the cracks he created, and for one swift moment the whole flashy comedy of her life was made earnest by his eyes.

Patrick's smile was on her now, the gentle pluck of a harpsichord. "*You* have a pretty strong accent, too."

"Do I?" Blaise's trembling fingers flew to her neck. "Well, my momma's from Tennessee.."

Elliott bandied her smile between the boys and Blaise, the red checker in this game of Connect Four. "Wait, do you guys know each other?"

Blaise felt horror at the largeness of the question, but Seamus only chuckled.

"We're old family friends of Foley's here," he winked with a dime's worth of malice.

Shame and anger arrived at her in waves, as though someone pushed a big red button in her brain. This must be her body's emergency protocol for when she met a Walsh boy and felt something other than disgust. She forced herself to glare at Pat, stomping the fecund green vines back into her floorboards.

"I'm going to find Lauren," she told Elliott, her brows raised pointedly. Elliott, still tipsy from the champagne and male attention, said sure but stayed put.

Blaise felt Patrick's eyes follow her, touching her back and legs with an odd warmth. Whatever it was, she wanted to shove it back at him.

"Who are *those* boys?" Lauren asked Blaise with great intrigue, while the cashier wrapped up a box of pink shot glasses that said, *You're 21!* "They're really cute. Are they twins?"

"They're *Walshes,*" Blaise hissed into her ear, with such force that it rippled her hair. "They're trying to work their voodoo on our sweet baby Elliott."

"So, are you girls having a party?" Patrick asked Elliott, just as Seamus asked her what she was being for Halloween. If in a triangle, they often asked the girl questions at the same time, to compete for her attention.

"I'm going as a dead cheerleader!" Elliott answered Seamus, then turned fairly to Pat. "Yeah, it's a Halloween birthday party for Blaise! She's twenty-one today!"

"Really," they purred.

"I didn't realize we had a blackjack birthday in the house," Pat added, craning his neck to have seconds of Blaise's legs. Meanwhile, Seamus amused himself by placing bottles of Walsh in the girls' shopping cart.

"Yeah. Omigosh, you guys should come by. Come to the Foleys' tonight!" Elliott lowered her voice conspiratorially, "She said she thinks you're cute."

"Whoa." At this, the boys grew very serious. "Which one of us did she say was cute?" Pat asked Elliott, as though this were a matter of cutting the blue wire or red wire to disarm a bomb.

"Aren't you identical?" Elliott laughed. Her pocket vibrated; Blaise was calling her. "Oops, I think I'm being summoned. Happy Halloween, guys," her voice dropped coyly as she grabbed the cart. "Come to the Foleys' later—if you know what's good for you."

At the checkout counter, Blaise stared straight ahead. Two people behind her, the Walsh twins clamored into line like wolf cubs, clutching the sherry their mom had requested.

The balding cashier asked to see Blaise's ID, which he held up to the light.

"What's wrong, Foley?" one of Walshes called in mock concern, "Did your card get declined?"

Blaise turned her nose into the air.

Dubiously, the old cashier pulled the bottles of Walsh bourbon from their cart. He had seen the name Foley on her driver's license. "Is this yours, Miss?"

Fury bloomed scarlet on Blaise's face. She rounded on Patrick and Seamus, whose smirks and remarks of, "*Oh, hey, she's got good taste,*" and "*Shit, Foley, if you wanted to try it so bad, you could just come over,*" were enough to make her want to crack the bottles over their heads.

"You can leave these out," she said loudly.

Pat did not realize it then, but his brain was shooting its own Zapruder film. He would replay   this scene of Blaise at the liquor store over and over for years, even when she wore his ring.

Frame 170 was Blaise accepting help in transporting her box of liquor to the car—"Yes, *please!*" she nodded, and the rivulets of burnished blonde down her back jerked up and down.

Frame 173 was Blaise beckoning the teenaged stock boy to come, flicking two fingers in his direction, making him spring to the soles of his Converses without even looking at him. (Pat thought if Blaise made that lazy "C'mere" signal at him, he would get on his knees and crawl to her).

Frame 175 was Blaise slipping on red sunglasses and striding to the door, her friends bopping behind her, the boy with their box of alcohol shuffling behind them.

And in Frame 175.5, the bullet came that blew the filmstrip apart.

"Happy birthday!" Pat heard himself crow, with all the cheery homeliness of an office secretary. Seamus groaned.

Blaise glanced back. Her shades slipped, and the blue of her orbs came like sunlight between blinds. She did not *not* smile at him as she mouthed back *"Thanks,"* using only the tip of her pink tongue.

"So, that's Blaise Foley," Seamus murmured appreciatively, "She's kind of a bitch."

Pat was thinking that if Blaise had actually said he was cute, he would be okay with dying, okay with losing 35% of his paycheck to taxes, okay with picking up dog-shit and waking up at 6:15 for work five days a week. All the shittiness of life could just cease to be shitty.

"She is," Pat agreed. He watched Blaise boss the stock boy into loading her friend's Mustang. "I think I'm in love."

That night, Blaise's spread of birthday gifts was slightly above the average twenty-one-year-old's.

Willie Cooper, President of the National Jockey Club, came to the Foleys' party dressed as Abe Lincoln, and brought her a Jockey Charm in 14-karat yellow gold.

"Thanks, Coop" Blaise purred, kissing his faux-bearded cheek. Her thin ankle was wreathed in the horse-charm he gave her on her sixteenth birthday.

Roscoe Robbie, boardman of Churchill Downs by day, but Zorro for the evening, brought Blaise a jar of bottle of spicy Scotch from his recent sail of the Highlands (Blaise's father pretended to purse his lips in objection to another brown water in his palace).

Mr. and Mrs. Brubakker from Hermitage Farms came dressed as Bonnie and Clyde. They bequeathed Blaise with a full Kentucky bison-worth of meat, proudly telling her that he was milling around their pasture just yesterday morning ("*Brutal!*" Blaise muttered to her friends).

The Barnaby boys wheeled a full barrel of Old Barnaby into the ballroom, nearly breaking the old elevator in the process.

"From my personal vault," Loyce Barnaby, Jr. told Blaise quietly, "My dad barreled it the year we were born."

"*Thanks!*" Blaise drawled, kissing his cheek in front of the crowd. "I always drink your bourbon when I'm mad at my daddy!" Even for Halloween, Loyce hadn't forsaken his usual corduroys and argyle sweater vest. He did, however, permit Blaise to paint his face, probably because she straddled him while she worked, politely ignoring his erection.

Uncle Duffy brought a suitcase full of Honduran cigars that he believed would complement the 21-Year well. He also gave Blaise a few tins of albino caviar—her favorite (it was the most impressive, so she *made* it her favorite). Duffy came dressed as a lawyer, a wry joke because he was one (JD, Vanderbilt University, 1982). He got stuck talking to the CEO of Kentucky Coal Mining Corp. about some dispute he was having over an easement but rolled his eyes liberally at Blaise over his shoulder. Duffy was unmarried; he had no kids. Blaise's father said it was because the trial with Walsh in the '60s had scarred him deeply, making him avoid contracts signed with emotion. Blaise thought Duffy's bare ring finger had more to do with firstborn prudence: as the heir to the Foley's eleven-digit trust, Duffy was too cautious to gamble fifty percent of it on an enterprise that had a fifty percent shot of working out.

Her favorite present of the evening came from the Forsyth's, a distinguished couple whose horse farm had been around for two centuries. The Forsyths showed up late in a carriage drawn by two beautiful horses, then announced to Blaise they would be leaving the white one, Schneeball, with her. When Blaise and her friends ran outside to take kissy-face pictures with Schneeball, Mr. Foley tried to insist on paying for at least half of him.

"You can write me a check, John-boy," Mr. Forsyth said somberly. "After all, I'll be needing a coaster for that 20-Year you're gonna give me."

Blaise's father shook Mrs. Forsyth's gnarly hands and said how wonderful the horse was, that Blaisey hadn't ridden much since her mother's accident. Someone made a joke about Blaise finally getting back on the saddle. Everyone laughed except for Blaise's mother, frozen in her wheelchair with cat ears on her head, unable to laugh or move.

"I'm so jeal that you got a pony for your birthday!" Elliott slurred to Blaise. Her saffron hair was mussed and sweaty from dancing, and patches of tan ebbed through her dead cheerleader makeup. "All these people love you so much, B!"

Blaise scratched her black wig. How to explain the plutocratic orgy of this room to her sweet friend? "I don't think they truly love *me*. They just know that whoever gives the best present will be rewarded," she sipped from her julep cup. "My dad will gift them with a barrel of his 20-Year bourbon, which he sells only once a year. *Or* they'll get to invited to our suite on Derby Day."

"Well, *I* love you" Elliot went on briskly. "And I have the *best* gift for you yet!" she clasped a clammy hand over Blaise's ear. "Guess who has a crush on you, who I invited out for your birthday?"

"Who?" Blaise was instantly giddy. "Jake?"

"*No,* it's—"

Lauren sprinted over in her velour pants and tinted glasses, dressed as Gloria Steinem for the night. "Omigod, I just met Mitch McConnell and he offered to help get me an internship," she said in a fierce whisper. "But do you think it has to be with a Republican office?"

From across the room, the old senator woozily raised his julep cup to the girls, stumbling as though it were a thirty-pound weight.

"When I told him I was Gloria Steinem," Lauren went on, giving him a professional little wave, "he said he loved her in the Charlie Chaplin movies, but thought she went downhill after she got into talkies."

Blaise couldn't answer, because she noticed their friend Alex needed rescuing. Her dad, upon hearing that Alex was a history major, had decided to entreat her with a sermon on Foley history. Ten minutes later, Alex was still nodding, looking over her shoulder for an exit.

"Now you see, Miss Alex, this is the new house that we're standing in," Blaise heard Johnny moo, in his drunk-but-trying-to-hide-it voice. "It had to be rebuilt in '63, you see, because of the war."

"1963?" Alex asked politely.

"*1863*" Mr. Foley yowled. "Lord girl, did you think I was talkin' 'bout the Cold War? See, General Ulysses Grant had taken Kentucky by then, but after the Battle of Shiloh, he and the Army showed up at Foley demanding food and shelter—"

"1863, good year!" Blaise interrupted, gliding over. "Did the Foleys get invited to Scarlett O'Hara's Sweet Sixteen that year?" She touched Johnny's arm. "Daddy, I think the Senator needs some water, and not the brown kind."

Once her father slunk off, Blaise asked Alex if she was getting bored of the old man convention.

Alex was too polite to say yes, but Lauren swooped in to announce that Mike was texting her, wanting to know what time the girls were headed downtown. Blaise surveyed the room. She had flirted sufficiently with everyone, made all the powerful men blush and melt, then chatted charmingly to their wives. Scott from *Bourbon Review* took her picture with the barrel of 21-Year before it got her too sloppy. Hildy had already wheeled Momma off to bed; Blaise would need to go and kiss her cheek before they left.

"Let's round everyone up," Blaise murmured to her cadre, "And get the feck out of here."

Across the twelve-foot-high hedge, the Walshes home next door, styled in Irish Country, was lit up like a friendly jack-o'-lantern. If Blaise ever cared to look, her bedroom provided a view of Mrs. Walsh's cherished pergola, vined with lilacs and filled with comfy cushions. It was a darling oasis in a huge yard that actually doubled as a distillery. Killian Walsh, the distiller, could wave to his mother from one of his rickhouses as she sat outside with her tea.

Inside, the house's pale green walls were adorned with countless family pictures and Irish proverbs. These cheerful rhymes in ABAB scheme were what the Walshes lived their lives by, what they wrote in countless baptismal, wedding, and birthday cards to children and nieces and cousins and nephews. The gilded plate above the back door told all who left, "*May your troubles be less, may your blessings be more, may nothing but happiness come through your door.*" The Walshes agreed that their troubles (the Foleys, and other manifestations of the Devil) far outweighed their blessings (four sons, one granddaughter, and many more to come, God willing).

Their wedding vows hung too, in Celtic font and framed, with Mr. Walsh promising his wife that she would always have Christmas with her family ("Every year since 1980," Sean Walsh would tell you stoutly, "We've either gone over to Dublin or they've come over here"). They promised each other that they would never name their son Patrick, a joke that became one of the favorite stories of their marriage. Mrs. Walsh had a bad taste for the name, because growing up in Ireland, there were always six or seven Patricks in her class. Before 1986, Patrick was a blacklisted name in Walsh World: Black-Jack wrote contemptuously in his memoir that 'Paddy' was what the prison guards called them at Frognoch. But then Mr. and Mrs. Walsh had twin boys born on St. Paddy's Day '86, and everyone said it would be a scandal not to name one Patrick. It was the only vow they would ever break.

The third vow, *I promise to never stop loving you,* was the unquestioned principle that ruled the home. Even when Conor Walsh shattered his mother's prized chest of Waterford crystal with a rugby ball in '95, she did not leave her men and go back to Ireland, as she threatened to from behind the locked bathroom door.

Presently, the Walsh twins sat on the couch in the TV room, their mother's crystal chandelier set on the lowest dimmer. Patrick was plotting his visit to Foley Bourbon. He came over to his parents' house early, under the guise of seeing his toddler niece Fiona dressed in her Tinkerbell costume. His big brother Killian was there, along with his perky wife, Allie. They were taking Fiona trick-or-treating in the Peter Pan and Wendy costumes Allie sewed herself.

"Looking good, Tink!" Pat cooed, giving Fiona a high five. She grinned adorably.

Pat happily agreed to his mother's request for pictures. During snaps, he kept his smile intact like a ventriloquist, intoning to his bored twin, "We're going over to Foley later."

"*Fuck* no, dude," Seamus said ferociously, pointing Fiona's sequined wand at him. Both Killian and their father Sean glanced over curiously.

All of Pat's hopes and dreams for the night would bomb into rubble if his dad or Killian learned of his plans. They especially hated the Foleys: Dad, for the forty-plus years of neighborly grief; Killian, because snobby Mr. Foley openly looked down on his bourbon. Last month at the Bourbon Barons festival, when Mr. Foley made some loud crack comparing Killian's ambrosia to paint thinner, Killian had actually launched himself at Mr. Foley, getting himself barred from the Kentucky Colosseum for the year.

After Killian's family left for trick-or-treating and Dad went to the bar, the twins smoked, drank a quart or two of the bourbon Killian brought over, put on *The Shining,* and tore into the bag of fun-size Kit-Kats that Mom bought. By the time the trick-or-treaters came through, (most of whom were little cousins shuttled along in cars) the candy was all gone. The twins amused themselves by passing out cans of Dinty Moore and Spaghetti-O's to the kids instead, ignoring their confused faces with trills of, "Happy Halloween, little guy!"

They barely watched *The Shining*; it was really a blank projection screen for their thoughts on Blaise Foley. Every few minutes, they would recall some memory of her and dazedly, drunkenly, dreamily say it aloud.

Unlike Blaise, Pat and his brothers all grew up knowing her name. Killian was too old and too busy to grasp her legend; in his mind, Blaise was probably still a twelve-year-old brat. Conor got it, but he was too thick to realize that his obsession stemmed more from intrigue than hatred.

Pat and Seamus were both born liking girls, and Blaise was close to their age and close to their house. These factors, combined with the fact that she was forbidden fruit, upgraded Blaise Foley to an obsession unrivaled by any girl they had ever known.

Pat and Seamus were only four years old the first time their dad told them not to ever cross the property line, warning that there was an evil man living next door who might fire his gun at them. This made for a very scary and exciting childhood. The Power Rangers had Rita Repulsa, the Ninja Turtles had Shredder, and they had Mean Mr. Foley as the bad guy of their lives.

But the other bad guys did not have a daughter whose voice wafted over their twelve-foot hedge, all honeyed tones and garbled words. The girl whose marigold face held the mystique of every R-rated movie they weren't allowed to see, all the sharp objects they weren't allowed to touch. Spying on her from their treehouse was like trying to catch a butterfly: just as soon as you spotted it, it fluttered up and out of your grasp (or in her case, back inside Foley, slamming the screen door behind her).

When they got older, they searched for her MySpace but could never find her. In high school, her name occasionally gusted down their corridors. If they ever went to investigate further, it was already gone. The twins did not know any girls who hung out with her, or guy who hooked up with her. They automatically hated any dude who had so much as kissed her, with equal parts voyeur and big brother. If they heard even *one* account of Blaise Foley being nothing special or not that hot, it would have been ointment on their blistered hearts. Instead, the buzz words that reached them—words like *boarding school in Switzerland* and *mother's accident* and *equestrian;* later, *president of her sorority* and *wildest parties on campus*—only upheld the goddess archetype that they formed long ago. She was the girl of their most unattainable dreams. She wasn't just a golden apple, she was the entire orchard.

And now she was actually *real.*

Seamus was remembering a time from when they were probably fourteen. They were going fishing with Grandpa Wilkie, and he insisted on stopping at the bait and tackle shop about a half-mile from home. After a few minutes of waiting in the truck, Seamus hopped out to see what the hell was taking Grandpa so long. The door chimed, but Wilkie didn't even glance over at him. He was at the end of the aisle talking to a young girl.

"I knew it. I could tell from those eyes," Grandpa was telling her. The tender look on his gaunt face made Seamus feel like he was trespassing somehow. "You're Sullivan's girlie, aren't you?"

"He was my grandfather!" the girl replied. Seamus couldn't see her face, but the shiny hair down her back was like a July sunset. "I never met him though. He passed away before I was born."

"He departed in '77. I say a prayer for him every night," Grandpa uttered. He looked at Seamus and looked away, as if his grandson were a stranger.

"How did you know my Grandfather?" the girl asked intently.

But then—this part Seamus remembered best—the owner of the store interrupted them, his face grave. "Mr. Walsh," he said, swooping upon them, "is there a problem over here?"

The girl stiffened, slowly backed away. When she whipped around, she stunned Seamus with horrified eyes, the size of fifty-cent pieces and so blue. Seamus let her pass, understanding that he too was part of her horror. She jumped on a pink bike and peddled determinedly away, her glittery streamers blowing against the road.

Grandpa bought their bait, but the fishing trip was no fun. By the time they went to fry up their trout, Grandpa was rambling drunk. "You are twins," he told the boys. "Imagine if the one you called your twin had a girl who looked at you like an escaped convict." He told the fire in a yowl that he had only made their bourbon for forty years, just for the girl to look at him like he was a killer.

Seamus kept this to himself now, as Pat texted his lax buddy Matt Crummy, demanding he come over for a *sick* party next door.

"What party?" Matt demanded, showing up twenty minutes later in a *Friday the 13th* mask. He pushed up the mask to shove a forgotten Kit-Kat in his mouth. "Hi, Mom!" he greeted Mrs. Walsh, as she trudged into the kitchen with a thumb in her novel, her petite frame blanketed in a fisherman's sweater.

She looked wanly at them with her gooseberry eyes, as she so often did her men. When they stood around like this, she expected them to demand food or confess to breaking something.

"Hi, Jason," Mrs. Walsh deadpanned, touching Matt's ski mask with vague affinity. To her actual sons she asked, "Did you savages eat up all the candy I put out?" Her Dublin accent, an odd contrast to all the Kentucky twang around her, made even her deadliest accusations sound like a wry melody.

"A Yeti came in and ate it all," Seamus told her regretfully. "Mom, Matt came here because he wanted to see the pictures you took of Fifi in her costume."

"I'll see them," Matt said nobly, looking around.

"Oh, I'm sure." Unbated, the twin's mother rolled her eyes, pouring herself a centimeter of sherry from her crystal decanter.

"What are you guys watching, *The Shining?*" Matt craned his furry neck to see into the dim living room. "Do you like *The Shining,* Mrs. Walsh?"

"Oh, yes," Mrs. Walsh replied, "I only gave birth to the twins from it." And she retreated upstairs to be at peace with her novel.

"What party next door?" Matt asked again, pointing his thumb towards Foley, incredulously. "Walsh, you're not seriously tryna go over there?"

"Pat is desperate to fuck Blaise Foley. It's pathetic," Seamus announced, and Pat shushed him, fearing their mom would overhear.

Crummy shook his bristly head. "If we're playing the *Aladdin* game, Walsh, why don't you just wish for your own NFL team?"

"Ouch!" Pat pretended to wince. "Crumms, you think she's out of my league?"

"Do I think the president of the hottest sorority on campus is out of your league? Not necessarily. But do I think *Blaise Foley* is out of your league?" Crummy paused. Pat was watching him hopefully, so he tried a different angle. "I mean, last week my Grandpa in Florida called to say your family was the answer to a crossword. The hint was, 'Foe of Foley, five letters.'"

"So? We could be like Romeo and Juliet. It's sweet," Pat sighed, belly-flopping onto the couch.

Seamus took a dubious swig of bourbon from the bottle, "What, a one-night stand and a suicide pact?"

Crummy accepted the bottle Seamus passed him, but poured it in a glass and added ice. "I thought you guys were banned from Foley Bourbon?" In reasonable tones, he reminded them how, whenever the lacrosse team did the Kentucky Bourbon Trail, Pat remained on the party bus as it stopped off at Foley. Though Seamus wasn't at college with them, he came along for the last trip in May before graduation, and acted as Pat did.

Seamus objected to this. "Excuse me Crummy, but *I* stayed on the bus to finger Jackie Healy."

Pat was unpleasantly reminded of hamsterly shrieks from the seat behind his. "God. I wish Mr. Foley shot me so I didn't have to listen to that."

Seamus snapped his fingers. "There you have it. You go over there, you get sniped in the head. Dingus."

"Yeah, but," Pat looked appealingly at Crummy, "We got invited to Blaise Foley's birthday party there today, so I think the ban doesn't matter. It's *gotta* be rescinded if the heiress says so."

"But if her dad's there?" Seamus said, lighting a cigarillo. "Dude, there's a better chance of them serving pruno tomorrow than of us getting in." He wasn't used to being the voice of reason so, when Pat's placid expression didn't crack, he yelled sweatily, "Even Fiona knew better than to trick-or-treat there, and she's like *one!*"

"Yeah but," Pat smiled a fool's smile. "I don't know how to explain it, guys, but I can't stop thinking about her." Because the cables between his heart and brain were soaked in bourbon, he told the truth, "I feel like if I don't marry her, I'll kill myself."

Crummy grabbed at his chest. "Walsh, that's sweet." And after a respectful minute, he added, "Think her whole pledge class is gonna be there?"

Seamus studied his twin's profile. He hadn't seen Pat this resolved to lovestruck idiocy since the summer of 2006, when he had dragged Seamus to two concerts on Carrie Underwood's *Some Hearts* tour—one of which was at a fucking Windmill Festival in deep Mississippi.

"Well, sounds like you're gonna die either way, *mein Bruder.*" Seamus expelled a plume of smoke from his nostrils like a dragon. "I say we snort some Adderall and rip a few shots, then we'll march to our deaths like gentlemen."

"Via the Underground Railroad?" Pat said, making a diabolique steeple with his fingers, Evil Genius style.

"Our deaths?" Crummy said, his glazed smile flickering. "What?"

Seamus ignored him, reaching across the coffee table to slap Pat's hand, "You be my Harriet Tubman, my brother," he affected his idea of a slave's accent, "And I will follow you into hell."

When Blaise gave a tour of Foley, she liked to point out a giant slab in the grass. "*This* was the entrance to a tunnel on the Underground Railroad," she told her small crowd importantly. Then she fed them some corn chowder about how her great-great-uncle Zebulon Foley would put out sandwiches and milk for the slaves below as they pushed on towards Lexington. "But we had to seal the tunnel up."

"Why's that?" someone usually asked, looking up from jotting notes in their Kentucky Bourbon Trail passport. Or (pointing keenly towards Walsh next door) "Does it have to do with, you know…"

"Well," Blaise had to tread carefully here. The truth was that Wilkie Walsh had used this secret passageway to infiltrate Foley camp and burn down their big rickhouse in 1977. The next week, two policies went into effect. One was that a Walsh was not to step foot onto Foley property, under penalty of death by her father's rifle. The second was that the ingress and egress of the secret, fifty-foot tunnel between Foley and Walsh must be sealed up.

She could not tell this whole story, though. Marty Walsh took her father to court for slander in 1987, saying that their portrayal of his father Wilkie during their bourbon tours was unjust. Marty alleged that customers came to Walsh after touring Foley with shifty eyes, as if expecting black-haired savages in loincloths to set fire to their cars. The verdict they reached was: Don't taint the customer's opinion of me, and I'll do you the same courtesy.

But people came from sea to shining sea to taste her bourbon, *and* to inquire after the Foley-Walsh scandal. Blaise understood that. After all, you wouldn't visit Verona without asking the Capulets about the Montagues. So, she would throw her guests a big bone dripping with tendons. "Let's just say it's sealed up because *somebody* wasn't being so neighborly a few years back."

Our Blaise was wrong about something: the tunnel was no longer sealed on the Walsh side. A family with four sons and scads of mischievous cousins couldn't go through boyhood without opening an underground tunnel in their yard. Killian smoked one joint down there in eighth grade, and promptly told on himself. Seamus and Patrick used to reenact scenes from *The Goonies* down there, their throats rasping as they did Sloth's "HEY, YOU GUYS!" over and over. Conor formed the Skull & Crossbones club in fifth grade, and potential members had to run down the fifty-foot length the tunnel, without a flashlight, and touch the Foley side to be in (naturally, once the kid was in deep, Conor would bellow, "SHIT, I HEAR OLD MAN FOLEY COMING WITH HIS SHOTGUN! *EVERYONE RUN!*")

One weekend in summer 2006, when the Foleys were away in Nashville, Conor got dared to crack open the Foley side. The idea was that it be done without their knowledge, so the Walshes could play tricks on their unwitting neighbors (i.e., let a cage of gophers free in their yard or feed their dog sausages filled with Ex-Lax). Conor recruited his friend John-the-contractor, and after a few sweaty hours with a circular saw, the crypt of neighborly discord was cracked open. It slid open like the lid of a jewelry box, and when it closed, the seams bled imperceptibly into the grass. Even the Foleys' master gardener never noticed when she got on her knees to prune the bushels of goldenrods around the entrance once a week.

"This is creepy as *fuck*," Matt Crummy muttered, shining his phone on the slimy tunnel ceiling.

"Perfect, it's Halloween," Pat said sportingly, his shoes crackling against the rocks.

Crummy viciously brushed a dirt clod off his arm. "Walsh, I hope you're glad that the hottest girls at Lou are going to see us looking like gravediggers."

"Perfect, it's Halloween," Seamus, traipsing behind them, parroted his brother.

Pat's head felt like the surface of Jupiter. He kept forgetting to pick up his feet higher to not trip over sticks. They were getting closer to the place where Blaise Foley was real again. Pat was going to hear her voice, be close enough to her to smell a butterscotch candy in her mouth. He didn't dare imagine touching her, because he knew real life wasn't designed for reaching such euphoric heights, *right?*

At the end of the tunnel, a staircase crumbling with rust led to a set of old Bosco doors. Pat tugged their rusty latch open with some difficulty. As it screeched agony in their ears, he noticed his heart doing boxing drills against his rib cage. It surprised him—usually when he drank, the bourbon simmered all nervous feelings into a bland bisque in his stomach.

Seamus shone his phone over Pat. "Your face is all red, brah."

"Walsh, are you pussin' out?" Matt asked incredulously.

"'Course not" Pat scoffed. "Crumms, give me a hand here." With the calm methodology that had earned them the nickname the Two Horsemen of Midfield, the boys slid open the block of stone and grass. Seamus held up the flashlight for them, squawking as clods of moss rained on his head. Finally, the flashlight's small orb was eaten up by the full moon above. They had broken ground on Foley Bourbon.

"Crumms, take your mask off, for fuck's sake," Pat hissed. "The girls are gonna think they're getting murdered."

"Not a bad set up you got here, John-boy," groaned Loyce Barnaby, Sr., eyeing the twenty-one-year-old girls scattered across the Foley's ballroom.

"Not bad at all," Mr. Foley agreed. He looked theatrically over his shoulder, adding with mock concern, "My wife's gone, right?"

Mr. Barnaby guffawed, stroking his graying lion's mane of a beard.

The DJ shut off his gothic tunes, and someone switched on the overhead light. Blaise's friends were chugging water, calling for cars, grabbing purses. Sammi G., dressed in a nude bodysuit and cheetah ears, was looking for the heels she had kicked off to dance.

Blaise swept barefoot across the ballroom, calling, "Sammi-boo, you can't find your shoes?"

"What are you looking for, sweetheart?" Mrs. Cooper asked Blaise, elegantly sipping from her China cup of coffee.

"Sammi's shoes," Blaise replied, shooting a quick smile. "It's okay! We'll find them." Loyce was on all fours, groping frantically underneath the cocktail tables.

"Blaisey, why don't you lend Sammi a pair of your shoes?" John asked his daughter.

"*Because,* Daddy, I would need to do *years* of foot-binding to wear the same shoe size as Sammi!" Blaise whinnied, flexing her size-eleven foot. She could fit into Jake Abramo's Nike Shocks, but none of her sorority sisters' teensy heels.

Ultimately, it was decided that a car would stop off at the sorority house to pick up shoes for Sammi. Elliot promised she had a pair of black heels in a size six that would perfectly compliment the cheetah outfit.

Blaise's cousin Jericho and Loyce left with the girls, bobbing behind them like shepherds. Blaise murkily hoped to be freed from Loyce at the bar, so she could cozy up with Jake Abramo in peace. All night long, even when she posed for *Bourbon Spectator* magazine, she had worn a coke mustache as part of her Uma costume ("It's baking soda!" she assured Daddy—*it wasn't*). Her fantasy was to have Jake lick the coke off her face and then ravage her in his bed all night long. *Maybe I could nudge some cute pledge girl Loyce's way so that everyone goes home happy.* She could even feign huffiness over such an event later on, if Loyce tried to get her alone. "After you broke my poor sorority sister's heart, Barnaby?" Her flirting style was strategic, modeled after Catherine the Great's, cozying up to everyone, but choosing no one. She could never say never on Loyce, because she may have to marry him someday.

Her father used barrels of 20-year-aged bourbon to wield his influence. Blaise used a force all her own.

She was not faking anything, however. She *did* love anyone who loved her bourbon, or played a part in its history. Even the Walshes had their worth, Blaise supposed, (and she willed away Pat and Seamus's faces as they bloomed in her brain) because every great story needed a villain.

The party ended soon after the girl's departure. Without their lithe bodies and squealing voices, the Foleys' ballroom took on a sad, deforested look.

Mr. Foley cawed at Cressida and the other kitchen girls to stop cleaning up, leave it for tomorrow, "And have some god-dang cake, for Chrissakes!"

His maids beamed timorously, but did not pause in their stacking of dirty cups and plates. They wanted to sleep in tomorrow, not have to race back to Foley to finish cleaning up.

"Let's go out on the big terrace," Johnny growled at Mr. Barnaby, jerking his head upstairs. Barnaby nodded, refilling their julep cups with a small plink of ice.

The Foley's ballroom had four sets of French doors, each leading to their own private piazza. Before the sun set and Blaise's party got underway, Johnny went outside with his brother Duffy and Loyce, Sr. to smoke one of the Hondurans. Their terrace was awfully tight for three men, but Duffy asked what the alternative was—each of them stand on his own ledge like snipers guarding the president?

John guffawed at his brother's wit, then his gaze steeled as he noticed some motion across the hedges. His view of the Walshes below was slight, but he caught a glimpse of Sean's son, Kinahan or Kilhooley or whatever he was called, all trussed up in a felt costume, leaving the house with his wife and toddler.

"Get a load of Walsh in tights," John hooted to his pals, and they leaned over the stone balustrades, waving aside their gauzy cigar smoke to see. "Dear Lord—his little daughter there is older than his bourbon!"

The men cackled with relish, not bothering to keep their voices down. Young Walsh glanced up, casting them a furious look and clutching his daughter's hand with dignity. He had heard them, or at least inferred that he was the butt of their joke. The three men puffed their cigars righteously. It was Walsh's own damn fault, they thought, for having the nerve to install his trashy dud of a distillery right beside the palace of Foley. His family deserved all the flack they dished out. Mind you, they flung their share of shit over the hedge too.

Now, as John led Loyce onto the terrace, he said dubiously, "I hope Walsh brought his little daughter home." It was late now, after midnight. The crisp air of new November felt wonderful against their flushed skin. The stillness was an emollient on their ears, which rung with the noise of the party.

Loyce nodded. "Speaking of daughters, LJ and Blaisey were pretty close tonight, huh?"

John grunted. "Tell him to stay away," he forced a joking tone.

"What?" Loyce Senior said innocently, "It'd be sweet, wouldn't it?"

John puffed and shrugged. It brought him no joy whatsoever to imagine a boy with his baby. He never pictured her wedding day, with LJ or any other squirt. He liked to imagine them still having breakfast together at Foley when she was thirty, before they kissed goodbye and embarked on their days, cozily united in keeping their distillery at Number One.

This picture was still warming John when he noticed three figures traipsing out of the darkness below. John could hear them whispering and snickering together as they slowly approached the back entrance of Foley. *Walsh,* something whispered inside him. His hackles rose like a junkyard Doberman.

"What are y'all doing down there?" Mr. Foley bellowed. He switched on the exterior lights, casting a halo over three swarthy heads. *They must have snuck around the hedges*, he thought furiously, though why the alarm didn't go off was beyond him.

"Thought y'all would have some fun, did ya?"

"No, Mr. Foley!" one called back, shielding his eyes from the light. "We're just here for the party?"

"*The party?*"

"Blaise's party," another insisted, with a sneer in his voice. "She invited us."

Hearing Blaise's name lassoed out by a Walsh triggered something within John Foley. He stood here on this very spot before, some thirty years ago, watching in horror as a Walsh sank his world into total disaster...

John-boy stubbed his cigarette into his loafer and, with a final glare down below, ran off the terrace to tell his father what he just witnessed.

Downstairs in the parlor room, his whole family was assembled: his parents, Sullivan and Sabina, his big brother Duffy, little sister Kennedy, his Aunt Lucretia, and Nana Deirdre. Everyone was in high spirits because today Duffy got the news that he scored 170 on his LSATS. Thirteen-year-old Kennedy played show-tunes on the piano while the family sang along. Nana Deirdre winked and promised them a bit of Irish dance later, though at eighty, she wasn't as spry as she had been in the halls of Kilkenny.

"Dad!"

"John-boy, your sister's playing," Sully glanced up from his teacup with vast blue eyes that mirrored his son's. Johnny also had Dad's tawny hair, a middle shade between Duffy's blond and Kennedy's copper.

"No, Dad, come look," Johnny insisted, "Walsh is outside, he's up to no good. I can tell."

Frowning, Sully followed his son upstairs and out on the terrace, where Johnny emphatically pointed down below. Wilkie Walsh was walking the length of the Foleys' big rickhouse. He stared up at it, then expanded his arms as if trying to measure it. Walsh didn't seem to notice them.

Sully stared down at Wilkie a long moment.

"Leave him alone, Johnny," he murmured.

"But Dad—"

"C'mon son. Let's go inside." Sully gestured for him calmly.

John-boy stayed anchored to the terrace, still feeling like a ship's watchman who has spotted an iceberg.

"He's plotting to do something to my bourbon," he said stubbornly, "I can tell.

"Oh, it's your bourbon, is it?" Sully took a step forward.

"Well, I made most of it," Johnny said adamantly. "I don't want him around it. He's not supposed to be on our property anyway. He quit us ten years ago, Daddy. Remember?"

"Johnny," his father clamped a hand on his shoulder. "Let's go."

Sulkily, John followed. Downstairs, he chewed on the edge of his tie and did not join in the singing. His mind spun with all the possibilities of what Walsh could be doing out there. He didn't like seeing him, and he especially didn't like seeing him around his bourbon. At the center of his anger was an old wound with the stitches suddenly busted wide open. Ten years ago, that man was his Uncle Wilkie, patiently showing him how to make the bourbon, giving him words of encouragement and pats on the back. Then, he betrayed the Foleys by taking them to court and dragging their name through the mud. He left Johnny in the middle of his education, forcing him to walk the rest of the way alone. Now Johnny was twenty-two, and getting better and better each day. Someday, he would surpass Uncle Wilkie as the greatest bourbon-maker this country ever saw. That would show him…

You should have fired a warning shot, *came a reproachful voice in his mind.* Go check to see if he's gone.

Johnny waited a few more minutes to be sure his father had forgotten about him. Then he got up, haphazardly excusing himself, and made for the third-floor terrace. This time, a strange orange light suffused the glass doors. Ensnared, Johnny crept closer. The orange came from a giant fireball down below. At first, Johnny honestly thought Armageddon had come. Then he saw Wilkie Walsh running pell-mell across the yard, and he understood: Walsh had set fire to his biggest rickhouse.

"NO!"

The flames grew bigger, as if to taunt his horror. "Bourbon's an accelerant," *Wilkie told Johnny himself, when he was a little boy following his every step.* "That's why Uncle Wilkie always goes outside to smoke."

Johnny remembered his shotgun, his rage ripened to kill. He stumbled to get it, but there was his father stopping him again, his hands weighing on Johnny's shoulders.

"NO!" Sully's howl echoed his son's. "Oh, Walshie. Oh, no. Oh, God."

This horrified Johnny immeasurably more than the fire, because his father was an even-tempered man who carried himself with dignity and grace. He did not even swear in front of his kids.

To Johnny's ensuing terror, Sully sunk to his knees, still grasping at him, his eyes bulging out of their handsome serenity. The rest of the family rushed in, his mother Sabina cursing in French and grabbing fistfuls of Sully's slacks.

"I think he's having a heart attack!" Duffy shouted, running off to call an ambulance.

Aunt Lucretia, a nurse and a nun, stood above her brother tremulously saying the Lord's Prayer.

Nana Deirdre slapped her clean across the face, "To hell with prayers, Lucy!" she screeched, "Give him mouth to mouth!"

"Regard-moi, chèri!" Johnny's mother screamed. "Je suis là!"

But Sully's gaze stayed unblinkingly upon his son. Johnny lowered himself to the ground, staying eye to eye with him, whispering "Please, Dad. Daddy, please." Kennedy was sobbing in the hall, and no one consoled her. Then, Johnny felt his father's grasp slacken, watched his eyes go unseeing. The spirit that made him a beloved father, son, brother, and husband to the people in the room simply slid away, and he became a stone.

"Johnny?" Mr. Barnaby called questioningly, as his friend tore from the piazza.

Mr. Foley returned a minute later, clutching his Beretta. He crouched down on the terrace and angled his gun like the sniper Duffy joked about earlier. The Walsh boys below clearly could not see him, because they were still hanging around and laughing.

"Y'all better clear out now!" Mr. Barnaby called to them. "You weren't invited here!"

"Yeah, we were!" one called back. Then, with sneering innuendo, "My brother wants to give Blaise her birthday present."

Scum. Mr. Foley angled his gun straight at him. Through his haze of rage, he registered that the two were twins. The third looked like reluctant triplet. *Sean's boys,* he thought.

"Johnny, what the hell are you doin'!" Barnaby hissed.

"Relax," Mr. Foley breathed. "I ain't gonna *kill* him."

Barnaby didn't relax. Leaning over the balcony, he yelled in his most menacing voice, "You're best advised to get on home. *Now.* 'Fore it's too late. Put Miss Foley out your minds."

The first guy called back swooningly, "Sir, I couldn't do that if I tried."

John swiveled his gun towards this twin instead. He pulled the trigger with thirty-five years' worth of loathing.

Sunday Morning

Pat always caught a terrible hangover when he smoked weed and drank. Today's bout of Irish Influenza (as Grampy Wilkie called it) was about ten times worse than usual. The left side of his face felt as though it had been punched out by Mike Tyson circa '97, and he had all the plummeted serotonin levels of a loser to match.

He and Seamus got in from the ER at four a.m., and Pat crashed in his childhood bed on Zzyxz Road. All through the morning, no fewer than ten family members had popped in to ogle him. His orange-haired cousin Eems came in and whistled gravely, "That's gonna leave a mark!" and snapped a picture. "Why would you idiots try to infiltrate Foley?"

Pat could only roll over miserably onto his unbandaged cheek.

A little later, he heard his father screaming on the phone to Mr. Foley. They spoke about five times a year, always hotly and bypassing hellos. Pat tried to muffle the humiliating conversation with his pillow, but he could still hear his father's thunder:

"You're a sonuvabitch who thinks it's okay to just…what's that? *Warning shot*? You call that a goddamned warning shot? My son's layin' up in bed with six stitches and two molars missing!…Oh, send you the dental bill, real funny, Foley."

The longer he stayed in bed, the better off he was. Dad would turn his wrath on him as soon as the gun smoke cleared. Pat had violated Rule #1 of Walsh World: he crossed the Foley's property line. He knew, just as well as his father did, that they had no case here. Pat was lucky that he or Seamus or even Crummy weren't dead today.

Luckily, the misstep happened to coincide with Halloween. Pat would say he had been a drunken idiot, and say they had some foolish plot to toilet paper the Foleys' rickhouse. He would admit nothing about the heiress who beguiled him to the point of tempting death.

When he woke up again, his phone told him it was 11:37 a.m. No texts, not from Crummy, not even a two a.m. "*R U out?*" from that laxtitute Ryan who refused to give him his jersey back. The house was now completely empty, because Father Tim had suggested everyone attend mass to calm down. Seamus eluded this by claiming that he could feel Pat's face pain. He furthered his identical twin privileges by bringing Pat's Oxycontin prescription to Walgreens, so he could get it filled and enjoy a "'lude nooner," as he termed it.

"Shay?" Pat called out. He felt chagrined when he didn't hear his sarcastic echo. "Ow," he spat out a tooth crumble, tonguing the bloody spot where his molars had been. At the ER, the nurse told Pat that smiling would be painful, and that he should try to curb it for a while. He wanted to tell her that he couldn't imagine being in the mood to smile again.

He heard tentative footsteps coming down the front walk, padding the plush carpet of damp leaves that needed to be raked up. Girl's feet, Pat could tell by their delicate timbre. His curiosity clinked higher inside him like keys on a piano.

Pat slugged out of bed, cursing the phantom brass knuckles that pounded his face. His bedroom sat directly above the front porch, and he heard the lips of the mailbox click shut just as he arrived at his window. Below—a girl, he was right. *The* girl, he realized with a stomach full of swamp. Her hair camouflaged perfectly against the red and yellow leaves as she sprinted away, legs bare, along the fence that divided them, all the way up to the state road. Then, she vanished into the hedges of Foley.

Pat went to the mailbox to see what Blaise left behind. *It's probably a summons for violating the restraining order,* he thought, though his heart fluttered on hopeful wings.

She had written him a letter. His name was even on the envelope:

Dear Patrick,   November 1, 2009

I'm so sorry about what happened to you last night. If I were home, I would never have let that happen. I really hope you're alright.

Blaise

He returned to his twin bed with a head full of helium. His cheek throbbed because he was violating doctor's orders and smiling like a jack-o-lantern.

Dear Patrick…

The thought of Blaise even knowing his name just thrilled him. He wondered how she knew it was him who was shot, not his identical twin. He decided to chalk it up to her goddess magic.

Pat laid down, welcoming Blaise up through the blankness of his brain, her clacking in in sexy heels, straddling his shamrock boxers, her milk breath on his neck, "*Is there anything I can do to make you feel better?*" Onto his mangled face he placed her letter, imagining with ruby lust that it was the exquisite wet musk between her legs…his mouth making her wetter and wetter…

Seamus came about twenty minutes after Pat did.

"I've been on Yahoo Answers trying to figure this out," he hollered torpidly into Pat's room, kicking off his duck boots in the middle of the dark hallway. "I took two of your Oxycotins…wanna punch me in the face, see if I can feel it?"

When Pat didn't respond, Seamus went in and found his twin with the letter over his face, his breath making it flutter up and down imperceptibly.

"What are you doing?" Seamus asked.

Pat groaned into her signature. The ink left a smudge on his stout nose when he finally sat up. "Making Blaise Foley sit on my face."

St. Patrick, the Patron Saint of Ireland, was in love with St. Blaise, the Patron Saint of Knit-Wear.

Her name chimed continually in his head like a meditative Om: *Blaise Foley, Blaise Foley, Blaise Foley*. When Mrs. Walsh sent him to Ave Maria Catholic Gifts to pick up a First Communion Crucifix for his little cousin, Pat bought a nickel pendant of St. Blaise as well. He kept it chainless in his coat pocket and ran his thumb over it often.

He was pretty sure the human Blaise still hated him though.

"Why?" asked Crummy and Seamus.

"I sent her a friend request on FB," Pat told them. "She didn't accept me."

He checked often, indulging in a very masochistic new ritual. Blaise's profile had a moat of privacy around it, the dreaded banner that shooed away all her social media Peeping Toms: "to see what Blaise Foley shares with her friends, add her on Facebook." *I fucking tried,* he wanted to yell out, into the mortuary quiet of his Intermediate Accounting III lecture.

Another part of the ritual was to admire her profile picture ("Hi baby," he murmured, running his knuckles over his computer screen). The picture was from the night Blaise was elected president of her sorority: Blaise is on her knees at the foot of a grand staircase in a spangly black dress, her sun-peppered thighs bulging healthily under her weight. Her long torso is draped in her mother's yellowing 'Miss America 1981' sash. Her fingertips are pressed to her florid cheekbones, mouth an O of delight. Elliot stands above Blaise, beaming in a polka-dot dress, while Lauren places a rhinestone tiara on her head.

A platinum blonde girl named Whitney Elizabeth commented on December 4, 2009: "*All hail our President, Queen Bee! Haha pun intended! :)*" Michaela Rae commented, "*omggg such a great sophomore year mem! Literally love you more than anything, B!!!*" (Editor's Note: if you visit these girl's profiles today, you'll see that Michaela is working as Senior Brand Manager at Foley Bourbon, while Whitney is employed at Foley as a Systems Chain Analyst. Not bad for being 26). Elliott's comment was: "*if I drank a gallon of bourbon a day and played tennis in Loubontins would I be this gorgeous??*"

The heels were another thing that drove Pat bananas. In the picture, he noticed that Blaise's feet were bare and oblong. He thought he'd give five years off his life to take them in his mouth just once.

Crummy was the social for the lacrosse team, and he was cyber friends with everyone, including Blaise Foley. Whenever Crummy and Pat got drunk, Pat asked to look at Blaise's Facebook. His descent into love with her was like tripping into the Grand Canyon. He imbibed the slides from Blaise's life: playing tennis, brushing Schneeball's mane, kissing McCullers' cheek while he looked away in angst. Pat particularly liked the photo-shoot Blaise and Elliott did in matching platform heels covered in gold spikes. In one picture, Blaise is perched on a white leather chaise with Elliott kneeling before her, one of Blaise's freckled shins propped on her shoulder, and Elliott mimes kissing the golden thorns of her heel. Pat looked and felt drugged with desire. *I want, I want, I want,* he thought, as though stuck conjugating the verb.

Patrick turned 24 on the holiday that gave him his name. He had returned to the University of Louisville for his MBA, mostly because he hated his first year working at KPMG. Whenever people asked him what he would do next, he would laugh too heartily and say, "Oh, I'll probably just wind up working at Walsh." Whatever family member was asking would robustly assure Pat that there was nothing wrong with that, *nothing at all*. People came to tell one another that Pat Walsh would do the books for the distillery. At McGettigan's pub, his old man cousins sang "Tax Man" whenever Pat came by.

Except for Crummy, also getting his MBA, all of his friends had graduated. Pat felt like a creepy dad now when he hung out at the lax house. But school still brought him a big thrill: Blaise Foley was ubiquitous on campus (possibly because he had learned all her paths). Around ten a.m. on MWF, she stopped at the Fine Arts cafe to buy a snack (Diet Coke and a spotty banana). She bought the *Kentucky Herald* just to get herself over the $3 credit minimum, because, as she laughed to the student cashier, she never carried cash. Blaise always seemed to have shiny coins to drop in the styrofoam tip cup though, which clanged with such piggy-bank satisfaction. None of Pat's classes were in the Fine Arts building.

If Blaise caught him staring over the brim of his laptop, she gave him a semi-colon of a smile. Pat wondered what prejudices lurked beneath that smile. Once he got to know her better, he would understand: Blaise, who had the pride of five lions, was terribly ashamed. Thanks to Matt Crummy, the story about her dad's Halloween shooting had been widely circulated. Girls with letters on their shirts talked about it at parties. Boys teased Blaise about it. Jake Abramo texted her that she was pretty cute but: "*I don't want your dad to shoot me haha.*" Blaise felt an awkward guilt over Pat Walsh and his big scar. It tethered him to her like Voldemort to

Harry Potter, and she did *not* want to be Voldemort. Each time Pat smiled and waved, that ugly pink cicatrice leered down at her. She steeled her heart to his nice guy act. What the hell was he even driving at? They weren't friends. He was either a sub 75 IQ idiot, or he was mocking her.

She couldn't have guessed that he watched her. That a Blaise sighting to him was what a golden eagle is to a birder. When Pat noticed her outside the window of his lecture hall, sitting alone and pouring her flask into her coffee, his heart turned to pulpy tenderness in the breast of his Polo. Any guy had a better chance than he did of approaching Blaise, even the Asian kid who wore high-water jeans and drew Manga during lecture. Because he was a Walsh, because she was a Foley, because the bourbon she poured into her Venti coffee was at odds with his own, he could not talk to her. It was just *fucked*.

But crushes are nourished by hope. Pat's departures from the world around him were with Fantasy Blaise as his guide. He pictured them sitting in a field under a silo, or on jetties lapped by the sea, passing a bottle of bourbon back and forth. The bourbon had no label, just like dreams have no plot. He imagined telling Blaise things. *I'm studying so hard to be a CPA, but I'm pretty sure I hate it. I just don't know what else I would do. My brother Killian knows his purpose: He's the Master Distiller, and even on bad days at work, he feels like the one who's pulled the sword from the stone. Is that what accounting is to me? I don't think so.* He pictured her mermaid face nodding with all the understanding in the world. Pat would tell her, on the jetty, in her gingham bikini, that he felt sure Tom Petty had written all of his good songs about her.

That semester, Matt Crummy was a frequent guest at Blaise's sorority house. He was enjoying a tryst with a sophomore named Sarah whose meetings were rarely scheduled in terms of sobriety or before sunset. Crummy was verified by many social circles, and it was okay for him to slum about the house, chatting up the girls as he waited for Sarah.

Like Pat Walsh, Matt Crummy was a proud son of Kentucky. He drank bourbon well and goodly, calling Killian's 120-proof his personal supply of mother's milk. (Of course, when Blaise invited him to drink with her, he was happy to forgo his mother's milk for a Foley 7-Year).

One weeknight, while Blaise's sisters watched *Notting Hill,* she and Crummy sat talking and drinking in the kitchen. She told him that he and the Walsh twins were idiots to attempt a visit on Halloween.

"Why do you think we did?" Crummy asked, with the gentle prod of a psychologist.

"To prank me!" Blaise huffed. "The Walshes *hate* me, Matt. You don't know the half."

Crummy was amused, "Walshie opposite of hates you, Foley." He could not tell Blaise that she had usurped Carrie Underwood as Pat's #1 Fantasy Dream Wife, so he just said, "Maybe you guys should make peace. It would be good publicity, if nothing else."

Blaise knew that peace between the Foleys and Walshes was about as likely as her daddy switching to vodka, but she didn't want to seem like a warmongering bitch. After all, the Halloween shooting was barely in her rearview mirror. So she nodded, "Yeah, maybe we should."

Crummy brought Pat this report, who felt buoyant with new hope.

Suspiciously, Seamus asked Crummy what stake he had in bringing Pat and Blaise together. Crummy told Seamus with exclamation points in his eyes that it would be "fucking *sick,*" to be the one who ended the Foley-Walsh feud. "If I do nothing else with my life," Crummy said, "I'll have this for a legacy. I'd probably get a Wikipedia page."

Also, Crummy was being well compensated for his work as a mole. Pat let him bring empty flagons to Walsh and siphon from any barrel of his choosing. When Crummy revealed that Blaise and Jake Abramo had yet to go all the way, (a truth Sammi G giggled tipsily in his ear during a hot-tub soak) he got to drink Killian's 12-Year double barrel when it was only a 10-Year.

Blaise's sorority was throwing an end of the year luau party ("Come get LEI'D with your favorite Kappa Kweens!!" said the Facebook event). Crummy told Pat he *had* to go: He was graduating, and this was his last chance to be in a room with Blaise Foley.

"I live next door to her," Pat countered weakly.

Crummy gave him the whole *Varsity Blues* speech, saying that he had to go out there and leave it all on the field, because if he made half-ass excuses and didn't try, he would always wonder *what if.* (Truly the Gettysburg Address for any guy under 30 caught at a crossroads between going for glory or just staying home).

Pat told Crummy, "I'll pray on it."

At ten p.m. on the night of the luau, Pat decided that there was something very final about this party. In a month, he would be back to work for KPMG. This party was his last chance to see Blaise Foley at close-range, without the hedges separating them. Pat Walsh was a reasonable man. One does not study accounting for five years without having their brain shaped for reason. He realized that his obsession with Blaise was affecting his pursuit of other girls. He drunkenly confessed to Seamus that all of his orgasms were self-induced over the past three months. Seamus told him that his record was shameful. That he would expect that from the Asian who wore high-waters to lecture, but not from a 6'3 bourbon heir who was described as "classically handsome," by his aunts and *"really cute!"* by millennial girls the world over.

Pat agreed to go as Crummy's Plus 1 to this luau party. They stopped at the Alaska Mart to pick up a couple 12 packs of beer.

"Anything to win favor," Pat murmured to Crummy, forking over his ID to the Indian cashier.

"Are you Walsh, as in the bourbon?" the clerk asked, looking excitedly up from his ID. When Pat nodded, the clerk gestured to the pyramid display of his bourbon in plastic jugs. "We have plenty of it, if you need."

"Walshie doesn't *pay* for his bourbon," Crummy replied, with the dignity of a king's steward.

Pat laughed admittedly, trying not to let his gaze linger on the Foley displayed adjacent to the Walsh. Every liquor store owner in Kentucky knew better than to put the Foley and Walsh side-by-side.

The clerk's smile lingered on him, and as Crummy and Pat each slung a case of beer onto their shoulders like boom-boxes, he called eagerly, "Hey...did you guys ever find Black Jack's treasure?"

Pat only half turned, "Sir, if we had found it, then I wouldn't be paying for beer either."

"Classic," tittered Crummy. Pat made his customary salute to the label that bore Black-Jack's silhouette.

At Blaise's sorority house, the party was in full rollicking swing. Kids streamed in the front and back doors, slapping each other on the back with the joy of being done for the year. Boys came dressed in Hawaiian print shirts, leaving three buttons undone to showcase their pecs. Girls were equally as chest showy; many wore just bras in neon colors. The blue cellophane taped over the windows cast an underwater light over the scene, making the partiers look like a school of mermaids and mermen.

Earlier, Blaise's friends tried to hollow out coconuts to drink from, a task that proved too arduous for their short attention spans. Jake Abramo was dispatched to Party City an hour ago to fetch plastic cups and toy ukuleles.

Elliott passed out leis and smiles at the door like a flight attendant for Hawaiian Airlines. Then she got some rum punch in her and put all the leis around her own neck. Running around the party in her straw skirt, she was belting "I GOT LEI'D!" into the faces of random partygoers.

"She wishes," Blaise giggled, watching her fondly as she sipped from her glass of amber. Self-conscious of her B-cup chest, Blaise tied a glittery bolero over her own seashell bra.

"What about you, B?" asked her friend Alex, through a mouthful of punch. Her sisters all turned their pointed smiles from Blaise, to basketballer Jake Abramo, who across the room was heckling the DJ to put on some Lil Wayne instead of the steel-drum music he had going.

Everyone knew that she snuck into his hotel suite on Final Four weekend. Some people knew that she had invited him over to Foley Bourbon for a "private tour" last weekend. But only Lauren, Elliott, Sammi and her gyno knew that Blaise was still a virgin.

Yes, she wanted Abramo, all six feet, four inches of him, but this was her *virginity*. "It's like…opening up a barrel of 24-Year," she emoted to Lauren and Elliott, who didn't fully grasp the metaphor, but still bobbed their heads solemnly.

"Maybe," Blaise allowed, twirling her own lei and eyeing Jake with sultry appraisal. "After all, I can only pretend to be a good Catholic for so long…"

The girls whooped with laughter and fondness for their cosmopolitan queen. Someone suggested they take all take a picture of them doing a "Cheers!" with their punch goblets.

"B, go get some of the punch!" Lauren pouted, a slave to symmetry in pictures. "You can take a night off from bourbon, can't you?"

Blaise sipped her bourbon skeptically. *Like I want to drink a bunch of rotten fruit juice rather than a nice ambrosia aged eight years.* Fortunately, her phone rang just then: Matt Crummy was calling her.

"I have to get this, it's Matt Crummy," she rolled her eyes at her friends to disguise her thrill that an older lax boy was ringing her. "Hi Matty! Why aren't you at my party?" This, she said loudly, gravitating towards Jake, who was now talking to some Sigma girl with tits popping from her coconuts. *Maybe I could run off to France to get implants, make a Euro trip out of it with Elliott,* she thought. Mr. Tuttle wouldn't see the credit card statement right away; her dad couldn't yell at her until it was too late.

"Aloha, I'm here," came Matt's gruff voice on the other line.

Blaise smiled. "Well come the fuck on in, boy! I need my drinking buddy, they're all trying to force rum down my throat," she dribbled honey into her voice, two people behind Jake, "Can you be my partner in bourbon pong? No one else here knows how to shoot whiskey."

Jake Abramo finally turned around, eyeing her with drunk defiance. "Hey, I can shoot whiskey."

"You can shoot baskets, Abramo," Blaise quipped. "I'm not sure you can properly shoot whiskey."

She didn't realize that she was on speakerphone, and that her lilting voice was being drank up by Pat Walsh, sitting next to

Crummy in his Jeep. He thought dreamily, *Blaise and I could obliterate anyone else in bourbon pong…*

"Well I'm right outside," Crummy said bracingly, watching some shirtless guy hurl a stream of toilet-paper off the balcony of the house. "I'm not alone, though."

"Did you bring a girl? Don't worry, Sarah isn't here, she hightailed it back to Ohio after her last final—"

"No" Crummy cast a half glance at Walsh, who was nodding. He thought the call was a stupid idea, but Walshie had insisted. "A guy…"

"Well, the more the merrier!" Blaise babbled, slithering away from Jake as he tried to caress her bare torso. "Any friend of Matty's is a friend of—oh wait." Comprehension dawned on her. She saw in her mind's eye Crummy and Pat Walsh, trudging together across the lacrosse pitch, their dark heads matted from sweat. She had been about to beep and wave, but as Walsh's scarred profile came into focus, she just drove on. "You're with my neighbor, aren't you? The Welshman?"

In spite of the displeasure in her voice, Pat couldn't help a smile. *The Welshman, she calls me?*

Crummy also found this amusing, "Your neighbor, the Welshman…I feel like I'm on *the Sopranos* here…" Clearing his throat, he went on, "You know, I forgot Pat and I had plans to hang out, and I mentioned that I was planning on hitting up your party and—" Pat was nodding encouragingly; Blaise was giving him nothing—"It's the end of the year and all, no pressure, we just want to hang, uh, we brought drinks—"

"Does he think he's bringing *his* brown water into *my* house?" she yelped.

"No, no!" Crummy said hastily, "We brought beer!"

On Blaise's end, Jake thundered, "What's going on?" He grabbed her hand clumsily, but Blaise yanked it away like a child who's been properly warned about strangers.

"Beer?" she snorted, "Bourbon heirs don't drink beer…"

"You're right, you're so right," Crummy said, and Pat silently cracked up. "Watching him trying to tap a keg is like watching

Captain Hook play the piano, it's pathetic. Hey, Walsh plays beer pong with bourbon too, maybe he could be your partner?"

But Blaise wasn't listening. She muted the call and ran over to her friends. "Guess who's trying to crash our party?"

"Who?!" they asked eagerly.

"Pat Walsh! He's apparently waiting outside with Matt Crummy!"

"Aww," crowed Elliott, jumping up and down in her tangle of leis. "He likes you, B! Even after what happened on Halloween, he still wants to see you!"

"No he does not!" she said harshly, catching Alex glancing out the window with unmistakable interest. She *refused* to think it sweet that a Walsh boy try to attend her party. He was her enemy. In weeks, she would forget the formulas and terms she had memorized for finals, but she could never forget this fact. It was Condition #1 of keeping her life in order at Foley.

"Blaise?" she heard Crummy's voice. "Are you there?"

"Yes," Blaise rolled her eyes at her friends, creeping onto the porch to escape the party noise. "Can you put Pat on the phone, please, Matt?" Crummy agreed.

"Hi," Pat said.

"Hi," she said.

"I can see you," Pat told her quietly. He waved limply at Blaise, watched her scan the parking lot. Her eyes snagged on his Jeep and she jogged over, arms hugging her bare torso.

"Hi guys," Blaise breathed, peering into Pat's half rolled-down window. His passenger waved, but for all her friendly feelings towards Crummy, she barely noticed him. Pat's face was halved by angular shadows, obstructing his scar and one astral blue eye. She felt the old, uncomfortably itch that sprang up whenever she saw him. It flamed the walls of her body, ignorant to the dewy May night.

"How's your party going?" Pat asked. *You don't want me here.*

"Fine," Blaise glanced impassively at the house, which was beginning to look like a half-eaten wedding cake. "Patrick, I don't know *why* you'd want to come here tonight." And she raised her eyebrows pointedly at Crummy. He got the hint and jumped out of the car, muttering something about making a call.

"I—" Pat tried not to stare down at her bare feet, Mattel pink toenails. "I don't know—"

"Do I have to explain it to you?" Blaise said, getting revved up. "I mean, you have a scar on your face for the rest of your life now—"

"I—I don't mind" Pat replied earnestly, "Crummy's happy, he's the good-looking one now—"

"And your brother makes sure I get a parking ticket on campus *every single day*," Blaise said, her voice rising, "Because of what my last name is—"

"Listen, I'm sorry for that, Conor can be a troll—"

She stared him down, blue eyes on blue, face a topography of rage and hurt. He felt something growing rapidly in his chest. There was a force there in her eyes that he felt so oddly acquainted with— the only thing he could compare it to was how he knew everything Seamus ever thought or did or thought about doing.

"I'm sorry, but"—Blaise's pretty face hardened resolutely— "We're never going to be friends. Not in this lifetime."

"Okay," Pat said, not to agree, but to get her to stop before he fell down several more stories. In separate stillness they stood there, staring in different directions.

Elliott ran out of the house, waving cheerfully at Blaise and Pat. She greeted Crummy on the lawn by forcing a pink lei around his neck, "You got lei'd, Matty!" ("Whoa," he said in his droll way, "I didn't even have to go in the party.")

"Well, take some beer at least," Pat said finally, hauling it from the backseat. "For the party."

"Oh, I couldn't…"

"C'mon," He placed a 12 pack in her arms, avoiding her eyes, because if he looked in them, he would call bullshit on the whole farce she was forcing upon him, "Bourbon heirs don't drink beer."

"Well…thank you," Blaise said, giving him a respectful smile. *I knew I'd never speak to him again,* she imagined telling her friends later, in emphatic Carrie Bradshaw narration.

"Make sure my boy has fun tonight," Pat said, nodding at Crummy.

Blaise said something else, something fluttery and polite, but he pretended not to hear her over the revving of his engine. Crummy wouldn't mind that he split. The luau was his plan for the night, and Pat was just his charitable add-on.

Zzyzyx Road
A Brief Branalogue
September 2014

Chapter 6

At this juncture in the story, it seemed unlikely that Pat and Blaise would ever get together. I can envision throngs of angry girls picketing my book, saying they were promised a Romeo-Juliet story. All I can say is, keep your panties on. The Nicholas Sparks shit is coming.

I'll also say that the part about Pat getting shot is difficult for me to write. I was back from Iraq by then, where my good friend Kevin Carr was shot to death. I don't talk about him much; have never written those words before. I wrote the Best Man speech at Kev's wedding in '06, and three years later, the eulogy for his funeral. Five years after that, I drove to Verona, a little Kentucky village you've never so much as stopped in for gas. Kevin's widow, Katrina, is living there in a little beige ranch with her German shepherd. I made savage love to Katrina in that ranch, a whole night's worth. A week after *that*, Blaise Foley called me for a ride home from the airport.

I will not, I will *not* sleep with Pat's girl. I will not even think about it all that much.

Pat and I made a pact not to compete for girls in 9th grade. Our difference in taste was starting to really crystallize by then. Girls linked to Pat were Cheerio wholesome, smiling in their panoplied yearbook photos for sports and clubs. Girls linked to me were the type to go to rock shows in someone's dank basement; skip Math and Bio but show up for AP English with a fair-trade coffee in hand.

We both had a crush on Mademoiselle Joubert, our 23-year-old French teacher. She was only in her second year when Pat and I entered her classroom, and she was actually French (well, French-Canadian). I did not find Miss Joubert's *Quebequois* accent sexy, but *she* was sexy to me, with her whippet-like body and hawkish nose and curly hair the color of coffee with cream. Pat and I used to go into her office after school, when the only sound in the hallways was the janitorial droning of vacuum. We flirted with her, and watched the hesitation ebb from her grey eyes. We admitted that I did Pat's French homework for him, and her refrain from scolding us was our first act of bonding.

Anyway, I don't like to talk about Mademoiselle Joubert, for the same way I don't like to talk about Kevin. Fundamentally, I ruined both of their lives. I had read 100 books about love and war and wanted to experience them firsthand. I convinced Kevin to enlist in the army with me because I had never done anything alone before. I convinced Miss Joubert to sleep with me because Pat dared me that I couldn't, and I wanted to have something to write about.

Mlle Joubert is the reason I stayed in France after the senior trip to Grenoble in April, missing my senior prom and graduation. I couldn't stomach attending the schoolboard hearing I was due to testify at in May. By then, Miss Joubert had been placed on administrative leave. When *the Kentucky Herald* broke the story about us, the headline was: "Ooh La-Latourneau! Student, 17, gets private lessons from his French teacher!" *Please*. I was a man and she was a woman. She used to make me crepes with Nutella in the kitchen of the Tudor home she rented. We read Baudelaire naked in her bed. We only spoke in French; she calling me *Jacques,* me calling her *maitresse.* Our love was not a crime.

It was me who caused our downfall: Retardedly, one night on AIM, I made some explicit comments about Ms. Joubert to my friend Clyde Kanis. Double retardedly, Clyde left our AIM conversation up, and his mother, the president of the school board, read it and reported us to the Principal.

Maitresse had moved back to Montreal by the time I finally returned to Kentucky, after nearly a year in Paris. The first night I got home, I stood outside her Tudor house swilling a flask of Walsh. I had spent the entire plane ride home fantasizing about doing to her some of the things that the Rue Saint-Dennis girls had taught me at the brothel where I worked. But then, I saw her name had been scraped off the mailbox. Only half of the letter J remained, and an A from her first name, which I never knew. Sometimes I like to guess: *Alouette. Angelique. Azura...*

Egoically, Patrick getting shot was hard on me too. I don't belief the mythology of Mr. Foley's bourbon tours, where he claims to be the best shot in all of Kentucky. I was a squad designated marksman in the army from '06-'09. My M14 would love to go to blows against his Wogdon pistol.

Being on civilian soil, there was nothing I could do to settle the score for Pat on Halloween 2009. I had to be satisfied with firing paintballs in the shape of a dick at the Foley's rickhouse from the Walshes' treehouse. (B, you'll yell at me when you read these pages later—wholly deserved, baby cakes. I'm sorry for being such a savage <3).

Anyway, I decided to visit Kevin's grave today. I wanted to tell him about Katrina and me. First, I needed to stop off and see Killian Walsh.

"I'm going to visit Kevin," I texted Killian. 30 minutes later when I went around to Walsh Bourbon, I found Killian in his rickhouse in his dirty flannel and jeans. I've known Pat's big brother our whole lives, and nowhere was he more familiar to me than here beside his barrels. His Grandpa Wilkie had been teaching Killian the sacred alchemy of bourbon since before he could walk or talk.

On a barstool was a glass flask of what I knew to be Walsh brand Diablo's Death—120 Proof, Kev's favorite—that Killian had just siphoned from a new barrel. But he wasn't going to let me have it without payment.

"So," he said right away. "You know where Pat is hiding out?"

"Yeah, but I can't tell" I said. Killian's darkly-freckled face tightened with disapproval, so I added, "It would be a breach of Best Man confidentiality. But if you wanted to write him a letter, I could get it to him."

"*A letter*?" Killian scoffed. He has Pat's raven hair and bright eyes, but for some reason, there hasn't been as much fuss made over his looks. He's three inches shorter and, I don't know, he doesn't have that wink and dimples mastery that Pato does. "Actually, maybe I will write him a letter. I have some things I'd like to say."

"Like what?" I inquired, inhaling the familiar beer-y smell through my nostrils.

Killian rested one sneaker on a barrel. He told me in a voice of fatherly reproach that Mrs. Walsh was worried, that her brothers and sisters were all booked to fly in from Dublin for the wedding, and she hadn't told them yet that Pat was gone, everyone in Kentucky was asking what was going on, Dolfinger's had called Mrs. Walsh to pick up the 200 customized mint julep votives with *Patrick and Blaise* printed on them, and—"I can't believe Pat would just disappear like this, four months before his wedding." He shook his dark head with its comb tracks gelled into place. "I mean, what the hell is he thinking?"

"I don't know, Dad."

Killian's sigh was like a punctured kickball. "I guess you think it's funny. You know your friend Blaise is pretty upset. Allie and I invited her over for dinner. She said it was too hard to see us right now."

"I know," I deferred to this one. Last night, Blaise and I met up to review our pages. At one point, her bourbon became salted with tears as she told me that Pat's Great Aunt in Ireland had emailed her offering to bake their wedding cake: "*the best cake for a happy marriage is a whisky laced fruit-cake with almond paste! Love from Dalkey, dear, we can't wait to meet you!*"

Assuredly, I told Killian that Blaise and I were working on a collaboration that was helping to take her mind off her problems.

He looked at me stonily. "If you're sleeping with my brother's fiancé, I'll kill you. Ex-military or not."

"Jesus," I sputtered, feeling myself go red. "I didn't mean *that* kind of collaboration, sicko. I meant, we're writing a book together, about the Foley-Walsh history."

"*Really,*" Killian folded his arms over his flannel, looking interested. "Am I in it?"

"Maybe," I waggled my brows mysteriously. "On that note, thanks for the juice," I shook the bottle. "I'm sure Kevin appreciates it."

"Anytime," Killian replied, masterfully corking the open barrel.

I paused in the dusty doorway. "By the way, how do you think you could kill me?"

"Arsenic-laced bourbon," he replied casually, without turning around. "It's an old family recipe."

Kevin is buried in a military cemetery on Brownsboro Road, named for our 12th President Zachary Taylor, who was also a war general.

His grave is meticulously tended to. The flowers are always fresh, and if we're within 10 days of Easter or Christmas or his birthday, there is a floral wreath there tied with pretty ribbons. His mom and his sister's doing, I know, each of whom have one of his dog tags. Just knowing that Kev is that present in at least two other people's minds is another assignment of guilt.

"Hullo brotha," I said to Kev, finding his spot in Section E after about five minutes of meandering. "I heard you have flowers need a waterin,'" And, uncapping the Diablo, I drizzled it all over his mom's poppies.

"Remember when we got out of boot," I finally laughed, touching his white cross, "You had an allergic reaction to your tags?" Our instructor kept telling Kev to not let his dingle dangle dangle in the dirt, pick up your dingle dangle, tuck it in your shirt. Whenever Kev did, he'd get a rash on his skinny chest that looked like rubella. He'd take them out, seeking relief from an all-consuming itch, and I'd crow, "Who do you think you are, Maverick? Keep it in your shirt!" They made him do extra calisthenics for discipline, because military tags are never supposed to show, but then they realized that he was allergic to nickel, and he got a plastic casing for them.

"I don't know what made me think of that," I said, lying. It was because Katrina had asked me to wear my tags when I visited her. While I fucked her, she pulled on them and kissed me—hard.

"So I slept with Katrina," I said, a narration of the pictures in my brain—dim lighting, us thrashing on her mother's old waterbed, her German Shepherd watching curiously. "But you know bro, if you were still here, I'd die before I ever slept with your wife."

I could see Kev's furry eyebrows scrunched up, him frowning comically, just to hear me say "slept with." If we were out drinking or shooting together and talking about girls, I'd say *fucked*. Well I did the fucking; he did the listening. He was always in love with Katrina, since we were 16. "Isn't she kind of a bitch, bro?" I used to say, and it was the only time that Kevin ever got pissed at me. Now I kind of liked her—though I hadn't texted her since.

The cemetery was empty. I heard a ceaseless plowing of a lawn mower, but its operator was as disembodied as Kevin to me. I glanced over at Section B, where the World War II vets buried. Those guys were my favorite. Many of them had lived into their 80s, but there was one Medal of Honor winner who died in April of '44 in Anzio, Italy, at age 19. I was 19 when we went to Iraq, and Kev turned 19 that July. I was sure that anyone who went to his grave with a Medal of Honor wouldn't sleep with his best buddy's girl, even if his friend was gone. *Do you think he forgives me?* I wish I could ask that soldier. And I'm sure he would give some noble, GI answer: *He does, as long as you promise to take care of her where he cannot.* Meaning, move into the ranch with Katrina, eat her ziti, provide for her—I guess—and protect her. I just couldn't though. *You only lived to be 19,* I'd patronize him. *Just because you knew how to die doesn't make you an expert on how to live.*

My head was a sinkhole of fetal thoughts. One grew bigger and stronger until my mouth finally opened, "Even Pat wouldn't understand this, but it made me feel closer to you."

I didn't want Kev thinking that I only came here to treat his grave like a confession booth, so I told him what else was going on. That Blaise and I were writing a book together. That Pat had frozen his engagement and took off for parts unknown. That from the way he avoided saying her name on the phone, I wasn't sure there would be any wedding in December after all.

The thing that sucks about talking with your dead buddy is that you do all the talking. Your news is the only news; nothing is ever new with him.

"Love you, brother," I touched his cross and read what was tattooed for him there on my wrist: *He was going to live forever or die in the attempt.*

Catch-22.

On my other wrist, attached to the hand that I wrote with and shot with was something tattooed for someone else, someone dead long before Kevin ever was.

When dusk arrived, I went back to Walsh and climbed into my and Pat's abandoned treehouse. It was the perfect bell tower for spying on the two people currently on my mind, Killian and Blaise. Blaise's father had taken issue with this tree many times before, raising hell because its branches extended onto his property.

The warped floorboards of the treehouse groaned under my feet. I peeped through the tangle of branches down on Walsh, where Killian was rolling used barrels onto a truck.

From this vantage point, it was difficult to see much further beyond where Pat's brother and his men stood. Yet if I faced south, my view into the Foleys' heavily windowed manor was direct. The treehouse sat at the exact altitude of their second story, where my Muse lived.

I saw her there, in her bedroom of white plush, a taunt of red hair and moon glow skin. If I had binoculars, I would be able to draw her out of the dollhouse. Even with the handicap of distance, I could see Blaise wore one of those satin teddies that actresses wore in old movies.

I called her. She reached for her phone on the dresser and, seeing it was me, answered with some alacrity. *Thank God…*

"What are you doing?"

She exhaled with great force. "Tweezin' my eyebrows. Since Pat isn't around to look pretty for, I'm beginning to look like wolverine girl. Though you probably haven't noticed."

What I heard was, *I'm beginning to look pretty for you, Wolverine.* "Well, I wanted to tell you…I'm all caught up on Year 21. I was gonna start Year 22, but I may need you to help fill in the holes."

She gasped in starry delight, "James Branagh! Are you asking if you can interview me!?"

"Well shit girl, Lord knows you ain't got no date tonight…"

"Neither do you," she burbled. "Okay, I'll come over and play muse. Be at your place in twenty?"

"Sounds good" I chirped blissfully. Now I had to beat her there.

It was dark now, too dark for Killian to see me sprinting along the divisor hedges for my Biscayne. I could distantly hear his voice as he gave commands to his guys, his sharp tone belying nothing but concern for his bourbon. He told me once (drunk, natch) that he feels like Blaise is the only person who loves bourbon the way he does. "There's a mutual respect there," he said.

Now we go back to 2011, B's senior year at U of L, a time when, if Killian saw the Foley Heiress on fire in the street, he wouldn't douse her with the meanest thimble of moonshine.

After Blaise's sorority luau, the amount of time before she and Pat spoke again roughly spanned the length of the War of 1812. In history, that period was enough time to claim about 10,000 British and American lives, and see the White House get torched. On Zyzyx Road, where the horses roam, this period of Blaise's life is no less bellicose. Of course, Patrick was not the combatant in her life—his crush tempered; he had bowed out to the furthest periphery of her life—but another Walsh boy. His pursuit of her was no less ardent than Patrick's, but it ran on a demented petrol; love's mutated twin. Of all the Foleys and Walshes who have hated each other on this frenulum of incestuous land, no two hearts have beat blacker than Blaise and Conor Walsh's. Years later, when Killian Walsh gently suggested the two bury the hatchet, Blaise quipped that she'd bury it alright, in the same place where Black-Jack buried his lost treasure.

Hating Conor was Blaise's favorite hobby. Hunting Blaise was Conor's.

Year 22
2010-2011
The Breathalyzer Baron and the Heiress Immobilized
or
A Tale of Seductive Reasoning on Zzyzyx Road

Chapter 7

During Blaise's senior year at University of Louisville, the most apart she felt from everyone else was when talk of the future came up. She got bored listening to boys at parties telling her about jobs awaiting them at firms and offices across the country. Bored, because the boys seemed to all be mass-produced at a factory with U Louisville hoodies on.

Sometimes at the end of their monologue, the boys asked Blaise what her plans for next year were. She would just point handily to the bourbon in her cup. "Foley" was her short answer.

After she graduated, Blaise could work any job she wanted at Foley Bourbon, with some geographical restrictions. She wanted to get out of Kenfucky for a while, but her dad told her to forget it. "Can you imagine how our sales would drop if the heiress left Kentucky?' Mr. Foley dithered. "You're the face of my brand, baby. When you're CEO, you can buy a home in the Maldives."

When I'm CEO, you'll be sleeping in the backyard with Black-Jack, Blaise thought, smiling through her veneers. Foleys don't live past sixty-one, she reminded herself, and while Daddy seemed like Zeus to her, he was still mortal. Blaise resolved to make the most of living and working with him while she could.

If a job couldn't take her away, she dreamed that a boy might. It was only a fantasy; modern girls didn't sit around waiting for Prince Charming. Nevertheless, Blaise wore makeup when she did her bourbon tours, her expression open and searching. She always hoped that another Andrew would come her way. They could have really had something, if Conor fucking Walsh hadn't ruined it...

Blaise met Andrew last fall while giving a bourbon tasting to a bachelor party.

"This is Mike, he's the condemned," laughed one guy to Blaise, indicating a short, Italian-looking guy in a t-shirt that said "GROOM."

"Charmed, I'm sure," Blaise shook Groom's hand, her gaze snagging on his tall friend with the scruffy blond beard. As she carded them, she saw that Blondie was born in 1981, lived in New York, and didn't wear a ring.

Mike-the-Groom sputtered and choked on the Seasoned Oak. When his friends teased him, he glanced at Blaise, explaining defensively that they were already a little drunk from visiting Walsh. *That's your problem,* she thought, *you spoiled your appetite on fish sticks before sitting down to lobster.* But she beamed playfully and said, "You know, Walsh is a dirty word in this house. Be careful I don't scrub your mouth out."

"He can't finish his," Blondie informed Blaise, pointing reproachfully at the groom's shot-glasses. "Tell him he's not allowed to leave until his glasses are clean, Blaise!"

Mike-the-Groom groaned his refusal, so Blaise offered to help, draining his shots and beaming.

"Wow," the Groom said, as his friends cheered, "I just felt my testicles shrink up…"

Blondie was visibly impressed. He missed the tour of the grounds with his friends so he could keep talking to Blaise. As they leaned against the deck and towards the watery sunshine, he told her his name was Andrew, offering a crisp business card. Blaise judged from his card and snub-nosed leather shoes Andrew worked in *fin-ance.* The bourbon rose to her brain, applying a dewy lens to the camera that filmed her world. Maybe she and Andrew would fall in love and get married on Derby Day, ride Schneeball off into the sunset…

"So we're going to visit one of the craft distilleries next, Daisy something," he said. *Daisy Crown,* Blaise thought, resisting the urge to tell him that Foley owned that one too, "But why don't we meet up for a drink later?"

Smiling alluringly, she slipped his business card into the top of her chocolate riding boot. "You know, I have a weakness for boys born in '81," she purred, "That was the year my mother was Miss America."

"Really?"

"Yes. Well," she shrugged humbly, "She was Miss Tennessee first."

"Wow," Andrew said, leaning forward with intrigue. "So you're like…a bonafide Southern belle."

"Something like that," Blaise said demurely, burning to add, *and a future CEO to all that you see here...*

His friends were returning, a small fleet of leather shoes and fitted blazers. Andrew noticed them too. "So, a drink later?" he prompted her, "I want to see if I can keep up with you."

You can't. But she smiled and told him that *maybe* she'd text him.

"Well, maybe I'll answer!" Andrew laughed with a wink.

He was staying at the Louisville Doubletree, which slightly derailed Blaise's fantasy. She would have preferred to sip Manhattans with him under the dusky chandeliers of the Brown Hotel.

The Doubletree had a generic swankiness about it, though, she reasoned, as she texted Andrew throughout the afternoon. He reported that Foley was his favorite stop (*"aw…"* she wrote) and the second sample was his favorite (*"the Double Oaked? That means you have a mature palate* :-D") and that he had looked up Blaise's mother, Miss America 1981, and found her beautiful, but not as beautiful as Blaise (*"okay so you're at the Doubletree on Main? I can be there around 9"*).

Furiously rummaging through her closet, Blaise decided on white leather pants that fit her like a second skin, and red spike heels. She capped this with a mink fur cape. When she looked in the mirror, Blaise pronounced herself to be six feet of sex.

As she squeezed her vintage pump of L'Heure Bleue, a dreadful thought struck her. It was after eight p.m., which meant that Officer Walsh was probably on duty. Walsh claimed that he was stationed on Zzyzyx to help curtail the number of DWIs on the Bourbon Trail, but Blaise didn't buy it. Since her enemy got a badge, she felt like her life was a video game called "Escape the Castle." After she got past the crusty king (Dad) then she had to sidestep the troll under the bridge (Conor Walsh)

McCullers was away at a shooting competition in Biloxi. *I could take his truck—that would throw Walsh off the scent.* She jetted down the creaky staircase for her brother's room, finding the keys right there on his desk. For a moment, it occurred to her to snoop, maybe look for more *billet-doux* from the Frenchie who sent him a postcard from Biarritz, but she was already running late for Andrew.

On the other side of the house, Blaise heard Daddy's faint laughter and estimated that he was out on the piazza. She took the glass elevator rather than the stairs. This was a gamble, since the elevator sometimes got stuck, but it was a better to be stuck in there than out there, answering Daddy's questions and doing a smile and pirouette for whichever NRA member he was entertaining.

The elevator lowered her to the basement, which was full of enough dusty furniture for about ten antique shops. Blaise clacked her way through the cobwebs, her path to the Bosco doors memorized. She slid off her heels to run through the buzz-cut grass.

"Yesss!" she cried in triumph, firing up McCullers' truck. His stereo brayed country music at her. She opted to take Hazard Hill, the back road that ran parallel to Zzyzyx. Then it was just a straight 17 mile shot until Downtown Lou, and you'd best believe she wouldn't go above 45 the whole time. Not with Officer Fuckface cruising around.

Dammit Cully, why do you have to drive a shift? she thought, stalling out as she eased onto the back road. Blaise seized the opportunity to switch off the warbling cowboy channel and plug her Peaches playlist into the AUX cord, which would snap her into sexy mode—

"TURN OFF YOUR ENGINE!" a familiar voice boomed through a police amplifier. With dread, Blaise glanced in her rearview mirror and saw the red-and-blue lights show.

The Irish Gestapo had arrived.

Blaise obeyed, knowing the consequences would be worse if she ignored him. All she could do now was pray for patience, and that the lava running through her wouldn't spew out the top of her head...

Five minutes passed, then ten. She saw Walsh taking his sweet time in his car, drinking his coffee, making notes in his log. The lava gushed stronger and stronger. Blaise was verging on an eruption on par with Mount St. Helens by the time Walsh swaggered up to her car, mooing his usual greeting of—

"Blazin' saddles Foley…"

"I wasn't speeding," Blaise seethed, "I didn't do *anything.*"

Officer Walsh rested his leering grin atop her truck's window. Unlike Pat, she had always known Conor's name, because he had been bullying her for as long as she could remember. Now that he had a police badge, she was obligated sit there and take it. Conor had sandy hair, and green eyes that frequently narrowed like a serpent, or some other amphibian that belonged in a sewer. He had a hero-like jawline and chiseled cheekbones like Pat and Seamus, and was even taller and more built.

Not that she cared to check any of them out.

"Got a guilty conscious there, cuz?" he winked hideously.

Blaise ignored him. There were only two ways of dealing with Officer Walsh. One was to become a brick wall. This is what she used to do in 1st grade, when boys like Jimmy Tatro and the two Erics called her *Smelly Kelly.*

The better way of shaking him off was to embarrass him. It worked against her if she insulted his family's cheap bourbon, or the fact that didn't have a college degree. Once, when Conor suspected that she had been drinking, he asked her snidely if .08 meant anything to her. Blaise retorted, "What's that, your GPA?" and he wrote her a $150 ticket for verbally assaulting a police officer. But another time when he tried to breathalyze her, she quipped, "Sorry Walshie, I don't blow on a first date." Looking stiffly above her head, Conor let her off with just a warning.

Talking smut to him left Blaise feeling low, even when she knew she won the battle. She hoped that she wouldn't have to resort to such measures tonight.

"Nice wheels, Foley," Walsh gave a low whistle, laying a possessive hand on the roof. "Did you crash your Jag?"

"It's McCullers's truck'" she said stoically. As if he didn't know.

"*Whose?*"

"My brother's!"

"I'll need to see some registration on that."

Fuck you very much, she thought. Thankfully, McCullers had his registration right there in the glove compartment. His inspection was up to date and no taillights were out. So what could Walsh possibly think of to detain her?

"Hmm," Frowning, he held his flashlight above the paper. "Did your brother give you permission to drive his car tonight?"

"Of course he did," Blaise snapped.

"I think we'd better call him up and ask." Walsh said seriously.

"*What?*"

"Yeah. We've had a coupla GTAs across Jefferson County lately. You're probably lying," Lazily, Walsh nipped from his gas station coffee. "Get Prince Foley on the horn now."

"I can't call him right now," Blaise lied, her teeth grit like a junkyard dog, "He's on a plane."

"Where to?" Walsh demanded.

"M-I-S-S-I-S-S-I-P-P-I" Blaise simpered.

"This ain't no spelling bee," he grunted. She could tell that he was trying to drum up fuckery from another angle. "Have you been drinking tonight?"

"Just some Ovaltine with dinner," she mewed.

Walsh smirked, retreating for his car. He was going to breathalyze her. Well, she had only had two glasses of 90-proof with dinner. See if she cared.

"0.01" Conor read his radar dejectedly after she blew.

"Whoops," Blaise droned, "It must be picking up on that Listerine I gargled."

Her phone buzzed inside her clutch. *The boy!* Blaise opened her phone, ignoring Walsh's neaderthalic frown.

"HEY!" The cop shined his flashlight directly in her eyes and snatched the phone from her hands.

"Lookie here!" Conor whooped with glee. "Someone's hot to see you, Foley!"

"STOP!" she screeched, "That's unlawful search and seizure!"

He ignored her and read Andrew's text aloud in a dopey Special Ed voice, "'Hey Blaise...are you still coming? I ordered us some Foley on the rocks, but yours is starting to get watery - HAHA.'"

Walsh sneered, "Who the fuck's *this* clown? Sounds like an idiot with shit taste for bourbon."

It was rape by a different definition, this terrible toll she had to pay. Tears of loathing simmered in her eyes, but Blaise would rather get baptized by Walsh bourbon than let him see her cry. *Death before indignity,* she could hear her father preach. It was basically the credo under the Foley coat of arms.

Blaise pictured her mother in her crown and drew herself up.

"He's from New York. He works in *fin-ance.*" At this, she cast a highly disdainful look over Walsh's police suit.

"So?" he scowled.

"*Sooo*...I'm going to go sit on a barstool with him. Then I'm gonna sit on something else of his. So I'm *really* kind of in a hurry here, Walshie-poo," she smiled and snapped her fingers. "I'll have my phone back now."

Walsh coughed, but he couldn't hide the lust peeping out from behind his badge. "Well, don't let me stop you."

"Oh, I wouldn't," Blaise reached forward and grabbed her phone from his big hand. "Was there anything else?"

"Yeah" Walsh snarled, "You can't drive stick for *shit*. If I see you stall out again, I'm gonna call a state trooper and have your ass towed."

"*Fine,*" Blaise spat, but he had already clomped off. He gestured to her to drive away first, but her hands were trembling with such rage, she could barely turn the key.

Blaise cried her eyeliner off, didn't hear a word Peaches sang. She no longer cared if she saw Andrew tonight. Her run in with Walsh had been too much of an anti-aphrodisiac. Now, all she wanted to do was crawl into Elliott's bed and zone out on a Miss America show (maybe 1982 or '84).

What's more, Blaise knew she would pay for her sultry remark, if not in a ticket, then in torment. Seamus Walsh was on campus, even though he had to be like, twenty-five (Blaise didn't know why; she diagnosed him with generalized idiocy). Seamus always had some oblique comment to hurl her way on campus, with his tattoos and his wild eyes. Now she would see him at the Fine Arts Cafe, and he would say something puerile like, "Foley, all the chairs are taken…do you want to sit on my face?"

And she would see Pat, at the Derby Festival or wherever—he was always around. He would wave at her in his gloomy way that made her uncomfortable, all the way down to the bottoms of her feet…

She drafted a cancellation text for Andrew. With each version, the banshee voices in her head rose to a crescendo: *He only likes you because he wants free bourbon…he just wants to tell all his buddies that he copped a feel from the Foley heiress…what could YOU say to keep a Manhattan man interested, you only know about bourbon and beauty pageants…*

Blaise decided to send the one that was the biggest lie: that she had a boyfriend, and she was worried she might do something tonight that she would regret.

Then, she blocked his number.

It took Blaise a while to realize that Officer Walsh had her in his crosshairs. It started last year, when she began getting weekly parking tickets on campus. She figured that the school had just hired some aggressive meter-maid, maybe to make up for a low endowment year. Blaise let them go unpaid for months, passively protesting their existence.

Then, she got a notice in the mail at home saying that her fines had doubled. Her friends couldn't help but laugh: B would spend $1500 paying for Mohammed their bouncer's daughter's braces, but she refused to pay her parking tickets.

"I would have George chauffeur me everywhere," Blaise said regally, "But I wouldn't take him away from Foley Bourbon."

She finally stumbled into Student Accounts with her sunglasses on to pay, fearing they might withhold her diploma otherwise.

Then one day, Blaise parked for a fifty-minute lecture at two p.m. When she returned at 3:01, she had a ticket. The Corsica beside her sat in front of an expired meter, its windshield untouched. *Maybe I'm being targeted for having a nice car.* She reasoned that the Asian students who drove Maseratis had likely experienced such economic profiling.

It kept happening. If she slept at her sorority house, her Jag or Lincoln would have a ticket by 8:01 am. The other girls could sleep their hangovers off with immunity, but Blaise had to set her alarm for 7:45 to pay the damn meter. When she parked McCullers' dirt-splattered Porsche and still got a ticket, she began to suspect it was personal. She had a guardian devil on campus alright, one who knew the Foley's cars. Or, was watching her.

She had to catch him.

One day, with 10 minutes left to go in Women's Wellness, she asked Professor Jenn she could go to the health center. Professor Jenn gathered from Blaise's meaningful stare that she needed Plan B and/or Adderall, and let her go.

Blaise trooped across the parking lot, feeling like she was about to catch Jack-the-Ripper in the act. She had deliberately parked in the same spot as last week. Sure enough, at 2:56, she watched a University Police car roving slowly over the student lot. Very purposefully, a cop pulled up alongside her Jaguar, got out and assumed ticket-writing stance.

"*HEY!*" Blaise sprinted towards him. For some reason, she had expected to recognize him, but he was just some ruddy-face cop, looking no older than 30. "*Excuse me!*"

He straightened up, glaring at her. "You want to think twice before charging at a police officer like that."

"Sorry," Blaise said dismissively, "But you're writing me a ticket before my hour is up!"

"Oh" said the cop, squinting at the digital 0:03 on the meter. "So I am. My watch must be a little fast." And he got back in his car, leaving the ticket on the asphalt.

"*HEY!*" Blaise rapped on his window. "Haven't you been giving me tickets all over the place?"

A little desperately, she unfurled the ticket and pointed at his signature. "I have a car full of tickets with *your* name on them. You give *me* tickets even when you don't give them to other people." She felt her cheeks burning, "I mean, do you have a problem with me?"

"I have a problem with anyone who doesn't park right" the cop said gelidly.

Huh?

Then, Blaise had a brilliant idea. She reached into her backseat and brought out the bottle of Sweet Corn 1788, which she kept meaning to give to the librarian as a thank you for clearing all her late charges again.

"We seem to have gotten off to a rocky start, Officer, uh—" she strained to see his badge— "Sherpa."

"*Sherba*" he corrected her flatly.

"Right! Officer Sherba" Blaise switched into her velvety hostess voice, "I'm going to work harder to park better. In the meantime, why don't you accept this as a token of good will?" she held out the bottle, smiling benevolently, "From my family's *special* reserve."

The cop gave her a weird smile. "Yeah, I don't drink that."

What? Nobody turned their nose up at her family's bourbon. A guy on the baseball team once told her, "A bottle of Foley's as good as a blow job and a full gas tank." If they were trashy like Walsh, Blaise would've sent this on to the marketing department as a new ad slogan.

Nobody refused her bourbon. *Never.*

Officer Sherpa drove off, leaving her very confused and highly offended.

Blaise finally understood a few weeks later, when Officer Walsh stopped her on Zzyzyx. He ticketed for going 46 MPH in a 45, giving a satirical little lecture about how there were deer crossing these parts, and how would she feel if she ran over Bambi?

"So, I heard you ran into a buddy of mine on campus, Foles," Walsh added, rapping her window smugly.

Blaise scoffed, "Don't act like you have friends in college, Walsh. You're too old and too dumb." A few hundred meters beyond them, she saw Seamus Walsh tear-assing towards his distillery, doing 80 at a minimum.

"Isn't that your little brother?" Blaise pointed, "Now *he* looks like he's going pretty fast."

Lazily, Conor glanced over his shoulder. "Well, I didn't see it. Therefore, it didn't happen."

"Wow. Must be nice to have a PBA card," she said.

"Yeah, it is" Walsh grinned like a bonobo with a banana. "See, I'd bring you one, but I heard your dad's a fucking psycho who shoots people's faces off, so maybe not."

"He's no less psycho than your granddaddy who burned down our rickhouse."

"So? He got rid of some of your overpriced shit," Officer Walsh sneered, "As far as I'm concerned, Grampy did the world a favor."

As usual, Blaise longed to run him over, but then he would get a fucking parade and she would have to listen to the bagpipers from her jail-cell. She reached for the damn speeding ticket, but Walsh held it above her head, making an *ah-ah-ahh* sound.

"You've been getting a lot of tickets lately, Foles. On my street, on campus..."

Blaise stared up at him, comprehension kicking her stomach. "*You..?*

"Well, Sherba and me were in the academy together," Officer Walsh said, grinning proudly, "I told him to keep an eye on my little cuz on campus."

"So you're the reason I've been getting tickets?"

"No Foley—*you're* the reason you've been getting tickets," Walsh said, with maddening authority. "You need to stop offering bourbon bribes to cover your tracks." Walking back to his car, he called over his shoulder, "Sherba wouldn't drink your nasty-ass shit anyway. He only drinks Walsh."

So, the meter monster was actually a Walsh assassin in disguise. After two decades of tomfoolery, she ought to have known. All bloody Valentines of the Foley's lives were inevitably post-marked Walsh. Case in point, when a transsexual stripper showed up at Foley to give her dad a birthday lap-dance last year, he offered Chastity Hart $500 to go to McGettigan's and ask for Sean.

Uncle Duffy tried to temper Blaise's fury. Ever the dignified lawyer, Duffy told her to take videos of the campus cop ticketing her unfairly: "That's how you build a case, honey." But Blaise didn't *want* to build a case. Whenever the Walshes hurled bolts of menace onto

Foley turf, their response was always cool and dignified, sending over legal notices about breeches under a stern header. What match was dignity against a band of grinning monkey faces? There was no real satisfaction in continually fighting fire with ice.

Blaise desperately wanted to join her neighbor's league of dirty tricks.

"What if we went after the house in Kilkenny?" she asked her Uncle wildly. The mansion where Black-Jack and Clara were shot dead, now a historic monument of Kilkenny, did not belong to the Walshes in the perfectly legal sense. After Jack and Clara were deported to Ireland in 1945, Deirdre Sullivan-Foley had willed her cousins the Kilkenny house on a cocktail napkin, and notarized the deed with a lipstick kiss. Whenever the Walshes got too uproarious, John-boy would call up Sean-boy and threaten to go after the Kilkenny house. Usually this shut them up for a while.

Uncle Duffy shook his sterling head. "Just think of how bad the press would be on that. People love Black Jack; we'd come off looking like a greedy guts. It would be a shit-storm the likes of which Kentucky has never seen, if we tried to take Kilkenny."

Then Blaise remembered that she had a fatal weapon in her holster. Something Conor and his cop crony were no match against.

Actually, it was Elliott who reminded her. They sat in the living room of their sorority house one evening, watching Officer Sherba circle the house like a shark. It was 5:50, and at 5:59, Blaise planned on running out the house to stop him before he left another ticket.

"Let's seduce him!" Elliot said suddenly, if suggesting that they make fudge.

"Yeah? You think we could?" Blaise asked.

"*Duh!*" Elliot exclaimed, running upstairs. Blaise heard her exuberantly calling to the other girls that it was time for a study break.

"El? What are you doing?"

"Putting on my bikini!" she replied, popping her blonde head upside-down from the landing. "Go invite our boo in for a hot tub!"

Officer Sherba looked wary when Blaise invited him inside, "for a quick soak." Then Sister Brooke came outside in her cowgirl hat, and he put his car in park, smiling dopily. When Elliot cartwheeled outside in her neon pink bikini, cheering, "Rub-a-dub-dub, Sherba in the tub!!" he abandoned all pretense of holding back.

The next thing they knew, Officer Sherba was bobbing around in their sudsy 18-person hot tub, gruffly telling the girls that the President of the University better not hear about this.

Blaise ran to put on her own bikini, feeling like Math Hari preparing to seduce Prince Wilhelm. She took a fortifying shot of her bourbon.

"Let's do a shot, everyone!" Blaise cheeped, dancing her bottle out to the hot tub, "*OPEN WIDE!*"

Like a nest of baby chicks, the girls opened their mouths. "Ooh Elliot, what a good swallower you are..." Blaise giggled fakely, "C'mon Officer Sherba, you're next!"

"C'mon Officer Sherba!" cheered two freshmen girls, who blindly joined in at the words "hot tub."

"C'mon Officer Sherba!" Elliot cheered, "You're off-duty!"

"Alright, just one!" the cop relented, his florid cheeks even redder than usual. As he opened his mouth, Blaise grabbed her phone and filmed, zooming in on the FOLEY label, then him. Everyone cheered.

"Hey!" he sputtered at Blaise, his eyes back to beady, "Were you filming me?"

She put on her dippiest sorority girl voice, "No, I was filming Elliot because she's *so cute!*"

The sky spread periwinkle above their heads. Blaise climbed into the hot tub beside Sherba with her bikini top off and spent twenty minutes building his trust and lust, asking him things like, "Where do you like to hunt?" She realized that he was a plain and pure Kentucky boy, and felt a little bad knowing the damage she was about to do. *He's a Jihadi of the Walshes,* she reminded herself firmly, *I'll be doing him a favor by liberating him.*

"So Officer Sherba, now that we're *best* friends, does that mean you're gonna stop giving me tickets?" Blaise pouted like Shirley Temple hearing that there would be no lollipops in her dressing room.

The cop laughed shiftily. She knew it was impossible for him to say no with her eyes and areola bearing down on him. "I guess not," he winked, "but *shhh,* keep that to yourself."

"Officer Sherba, can I get you on video saying that?" her pout deepened.

"Uh—"

Elliot jumped in, draping her arms around his neck. "Please, Officer Sherba!" she moaned in his ear. Her bikini top was off and her bare breasts pressed into his chest.

"Alright, fine," Sherba cleared his throat and Blaise reached for her phone. On camera, he promised, "Never again will I give Blaise Foley a ticket, because she's my new best friend." His vow was met with a barrage of slippery hugs from all the girls.

Blaise waited a respectable 10 minutes before sighing that she *had* to get back to studying. Elliot agreed, lying that she had a big, scary test the next day, even though she was a Studio Arts major and didn't get tests.

"Isn't that great, B?" Elliot squealed, laying damply in Blaise's bed after they pushed the cop out the door. "I told you we could do it!"

"Yes, but we're not done yet. I want Walsh to see the vids I made!"

"That boy your daddy shot who likes you?"

"*No*" Blaise said, willing away Pat and the carbonated feeling he gave her stomach, "His brother, the cop! The one who put Sherba up to all this!"

Of course, she didn't have Conor Stalin Walsh's cell number. A search on Facebook brought him up, unmistakable on his snow-mobile in the woods behind his distillery. The idiot had his number up there all the world to see.

The following conversation ensued over text:

Blaise: Hi Walsh. I wanted to let you know that, while you may have won some battles, tonight you lost the war.
Conor: who is this
Blaise: I think you could guess…
Conor: who's U
Blaise: I'm the girl next door~**

Conor: Foley?

Blaise: <3

Conor: Ew

Conor: what do U want ?

Blaise: Remember when you told me that Sherba only drank your bourbon?

Conor: Ya

(Blaise attached the video of her pouring the bottle of Foley directly into Sherba's mouth)

Blaise: Correct me if I'm wrong, but that doesn't look like Black-Jack's face on the label :-\

Conor: Fuck

Blaise: Yeah :) He took a naked hottub with me and all my sorority sisters tonight lollllllz. Then he promised to never write me a ticket again. So glad he and I became friends :)

Conor did not respond.

Two things happened after that night: One was that Officer Sherba waved with gusto whenever he saw Blaise and her friends on campus. If he cornered Blaise, he asked in an offhand voice how Elliott was doing, and when the girl's next party was.

"It's been a slow season," Blaise lied. As she spoke, there was a 50/50 chance the maids were at the house, hosing puke and cum out of the hot tub.

Sherba nodded, "Alright, well even though I'm a *cop*," he put this in air quotes, "I can still party hardy with you guys, as long as we keep it quiet."

Blaise met this with laughter and lukewarm promises for future fun, thinking, *Dear Lord, I couldn't cringe harder than if I watched Daddy do the Macarena in a fruit hat.*

The second thing was that Conor Walsh ramped up his crusade against her.

The introduction of Sherba was for him, the incendiary match; the assassination of Franz Ferdinand; the invasion of Poland. Suddenly it wasn't kid stuff anymore. Blaise understood the Walshes' pathology. After all, they were sired from the same Sullivan DNA, through which Blaise believed a gene of dragon-fire ran. She knew Wilkie Walsh had to have it; setting the Foleys' biggest rickhouse aflame all those years ago. Lord knew her daddy, John W. Foley had it, and he had passed it down to her like blue eyes and Foley shares.

And she sensed in Conor that he too had magma in his veins. Blaise found it scary, because she knew that she had met her match in him. Other than her father, she knew no one else to rival her strength and stubbornness. Intimidation was as foreign to Blaise as the taste of tequila. What few doors her last name failed to open for her, her fatal charm and scalding prettiness had, blasting them clean off their hinges. She was taller than 90% of the men in any room and more confident than 98% of them (the 2% accounted for the times her father was present), so no man had ever dare try to make her his prey before. Until there was Conor.

He was not the least bit blinded by her supernova; she did not intimidate him one lick. She felt this from the first time he ticketed her, but after Sherba his evil smile was forever inverted. Conor Walsh *hated* her now.

Poor Uncle Duffy. He was the soul Blaise called to bail her out of jail all the times that Officer Walsh hauled her off, usually around 11 or 12 at night, on a charge of verbally abusing a police officer. Everyone at the police station knew that this was code for: Conor Walsh and Blaise Foley had got into a shouting match on Zzyzyx Road. It always ended with the cop cuffing the heiress, and her kicking her long legs out the window and screaming the whole way there.

At the station, Officer Walsh would cuff her, painfully, to a rail beside the vending machines. He did this at such an angle that the bill slot was *juuuust* out of reach, though the rows of candy and water were visible. Many times Blaise thought of pressing the B6 with her tongue for a Diet Pepsi.

"Wow Walsh, so this is what you're into? Handcuffs?" Blaise would crow, loud enough for all the senior detectives to hear. "I always saw you more as a sub. You know, in leather bondage with a ball gag in your mouth." To any officer who walked past, Blaise exclaimed, "Can you believe it? Officer Walsh is *still* holding a grudge because I wouldn't go to prom with him!"

"Keep talking, Foley," the cop would yell from the other room, "You're going in a cell next."

Fortunately, Uncle Duffy never took long to rescue her, trading his pin-striped pajamas for the tailored suit he'd worn that day. When he got there, he asked for Walsh directly, fixing him with a slew of threats that made the cop's face go even redder than when Blaise spoke of leather bondage. Then her uncle/lawyer/guardian angel took out a crisp billfold and bailed her out.

"We've got to get a hold of this thing, Kelly-girl" Uncle Duffy finally sighed, driving her home in his sleek Bugatti. He was the only person on Earth who was allowed to call her Kelly.

Blaise felt terrible, taking her uncle away from his nightcap and Lincoln memoir. Duffy liked a quiet life. "I'm sorry, Duff."

He gave her a Valentine One, a spiffy device that could detect a cop radar from the front, back, and sides of her car. It worked like a dream. Now when Blaise took the exit that lead to Zzyzyx Road, she could tell where Deputy Douche was and take the opposite road home. That's when he started to hate her even more than she loved bourbon, because he could never catch her. They would drag race, she on Zzyzyx or Hazard Hill, he opposite her, clocking her at 85, 90, muttering to himself, "Girl, you're just digging yourself a bigger hole."

Blaise sped up, waving her middle finger out her window at him, reaching for her clicker to open the massive iron gate at *EXACTLY* the moment when she reached Foley Bourbon. She cranked through the gate with such force that a series of skid marks were forever tattooed outside of Foley. An instant replay camera would show that she missed crashing into Walsh by centimeters.

Afterwards, Blaise loved to watch him on the security cameras in her dad's study. When Walsh kicked the gate and stood there huffing, she couldn't resist running to the intercom that they used to buzz in pizza boys.

"Welcome to Foley Bourbon," Blaise cheeped, in a Disney tour guide voice, "America's First *and best* bourbon, since 1788. Our next tour begins tomorrow at twelve p.m. Unless you're a Walsh, then you can get the fuck off our property before we release the hounds."

Walsh would growl stubbornly into the intercom, "I'm not on your property, the road is city property." Sometimes Blaise would play N'Sync songs into the intercom to annoy him, or Kids Bop. Or she might text him old pictures of Black-Jack looking especially somber, saying, *"Every time you do something annoying, you make Jack sad."*

It was a stormy spring, and not just because of the Walsh Wars. Blaise was blue at the thought of graduating and ending her reign as sorority president. All she could think was that there would be no more planning of themed parties, no more slinky dresses on a Tuesday, no more of her monthly newsletter that she wrote to applaud the successes and victories of her fellow sisters.

Her sisters were the inspiration for her final project for Consumer Research class. Foley Bourbon was ubiquitous, but it wasn't in glossy ads in *Cosmo* or *Vogue.* She realized that whiskey wasn't really being marketed to women. Blaise concluded in her research that while only about a fifth of bourbon-drinkers were female, that number could rise substantially with the help of a targeted market campaign. She surveyed her friends on what would make Foley bourbon more approachable for them. Some girls said prettier packaging. Some said that it could be livened up with fun flavoring. Most reported that their big hang-up about bourbon was how badly it burned their throats. Blaise's own gorge had evolved past the slightest scorch (unless she met a bourbon aged fifteen-plus years), but she listened sympathetically.

While Mr. Foley loved the idea of marketing more to women, he said making it without the burn would be damn near impossible.

"There isn't one of our barrels out there that's aged less than six years, honey," he said, proudly waving to his rickhouse down below from his study. "The older the bourbon, the greater the burn." Above the classical marble fireplace, an oil painting of McCullers and Blaise as big-eyed children peered somberly upon the scene.

Her daddy plowed on, "if we age it less, we compromise the *integrity* that we're known for. Then we become no better than Walsh," he thumbed next door, "He doesn't even say how long it's aged for, he's probably ashamed...either that, or they told him 'From January to June' wouldn't fit on the label."

Blaise sighed, recognizing this as just another idea she must table until she became CEO. She found herself making lists of potential names for her "girl bourbon" line. *Paloma, Georgiana, Demeter, Bluebell.* Each elegant name would correspond to an artisanal flavor: juniper and mandarin, dragon-fruit and hibiscus, English pear and lily. Blaise didn't dare broach the subject with her father, because the only flavors he considered acceptable for his bourbon were tobacco and tannery.

During Finals Week, Blaise went to the library to work on her final sorority newsletter:

My Sweet Ladies, As I remove my cap and gown from the wrapper, I realize that I have no idea how to leave you.

That's where she was stuck.

For inspiration, Blaise went to YouTube and pulled up "Miss America show 1982" (she couldn't do '81 right now, not sober in the middle of the day) and fast-forwarded to 33:53. There was Dru McCullers, gliding across the stage in her spangly white dress. The grainy 80s video couldn't diminish the high wattage of her mother's smile as she waved at the crowd, her ruby hair bouncing off her shoulder blades.

Chip Valentine, the spray-tanned Miss America host, swept his arm towards Dru and boomed, "As she takes her final walk and gives her last goodbye, your lovely Miss America 1981 would like to share a few of her favorite memories from this past year. Ladies and gentlemen, *Miss Dru McCullers!*"

Dru's voice-over came on as a photomontage began to play:

"Well, it's been one heck of a year!" Dru laughed, "And I feel so honored and blessed to have met so many of my fellow Americans, and to have heard your stories…" There she was, kissing a chubby-cheeked baby, hugging the freed Iranian hostages, grinning adorably on Johnny Carson's couch, shaking hands with Nancy Reagan.

Hearing that sweet, willowy voice, now forever buried in her throat, stuck thorns into Blaise's heart.

She was dimly aware of a sneaker nudging her side.

"What are you watching?"

Blaise gave a jolt. Towering above her was the face that always made her stomach go from weightless to leaden in about three seconds. *Pat Walsh,* she thought, then, *No...Seamus.* She could tell by the weird tattoos and wild eyes.

"Um," Blaise hugged her mother protectively. "It's a little movie called, 'None of Your Business' by this obscure director called, *Leave Me Alone*?"

"Ouch" Seamus grasped his chest, wincing. "Why so mean, Foley? Don't you know you're on my turf?"

"And what turf is that?"

Seamus gestured to the American Literature sign.

"What do you mean?" Blaise asked impatiently. "Are you an English major or something?"

Seamus nodded solemnly.

"Really?" Blaise didn't know any male English majors. It didn't seem to fit with his tatted-up, bad boy image. "That's...interesting."

"Yeah," Seamus wagged his brows at her lewdly, "Maybe I'll tell you about your book someday."

Before she could react to that, he went on, "Want to know something weird? I can always think of the book that corresponds to someone's life."

"What do you mean?" Blaise asked suspiciously.

"Like..." Seamus looked uncomfortable. Blaise observed again the veiled quality of his eyes, making her think of blue cataracts. *Haunted,* she thought. Not mean or menacing like Conor's.

"I think I know what you mean" Blaise amended, not unkindly. Like a casting director giving an actor ten seconds to audition, she added, "Okay, so what's your brother Pat's book?"

"Pat? Oh, he's a combo," Seamus cast his eyes upward, "He's like...that Tom Perotta book, *Election*...the earnest jock who gets tapped to run for School President...but I like the movie better...he's also a little Trip Fontaine, you know, *Virgin Suicides.* And, I read Dostoevsky this semester," Seamus sat avidly on the stool across from her, "I saw some shades of him in Alexey Karamazov, but I don't know if you've read that yet." All this he said without condescension, as if expecting Blaise to catch the references. "He's Mercury, God of Commerce. The Golden Boy statue of Manitoba. You know."

She actually did not, but she wasn't about to let him know. "Alright then…what would your brother Conor's book be? *Mein Kampf?*"

"No," Seamus said thoughtfully, "Conor doesn't have the stamina to be a dictator. He'll only ever be a troll."

Blaise giggled despite herself, and Seamus continued in his nasally voice, "I dunno if Conor has a book. He's more like the TV Trope of Annoying Big Brother. Like, a stock character until the sixth season, when he starts to grow a heart."

"Well," Blaise murmured, "I think our show's gonna get cancelled long before that."

Seamus let his veiled gaze slice through her. She felt a heartbeat in her panties and firmly crossed her legs. *This really was a genius trick of the Devil's*, she thought, *making my enemies handsome and tall, and with chiseled cheekbones and insane confidence.*

"Conor's not gonna stop chasing you until he nails you for a DWI," Seamus said finally, looking away.

"But…*why?*"

Seamus stared with his eyes like scratched lotto tickets. "Because, he's an Annoying Big Brother, and it would be a good story to tell at McGettigan's? What other reason."

Blaise sat up, seething, steeling herself to stupid Seamus Walsh and his 90s goth-boy tattoos. "Well, I really should get back to work."

Seamus saluted her, his intent gaze molting to indifference. He sashayed back down the aisle, crowing over his shoulder, ".08…don't blow it."

For the next few days, Blaise ruminated over what more she should have said to Seamus. *You know, the D.A drinks at our house. If your brother pulls me over one more time, I'll see that he's fired.* Or (more sinisterly): *Tell Conor that my Uncle Jimmy Fleming*

is very protective over me. If I mentioned the hard time he was
giving me, I suspect Uncle Jim would take care of it…

Sometimes, after the day yielded to night, Blaise thought about asking Seamus what her book would be.

"Isn't Foley Bourbon your *Bell Jar*?" he would say so succinctly (it was her favorite book from high school). Sometimes she got mad at him and sometimes she let him say it.

A winsome graduation season gave way to a carefree summer. All of Blaise's friends went back home, enjoying a few weeks of regressed adolescence before their new jobs began. Lauren admitted that she had done nothing for two weeks but lay by her family's pool rewatching *Dawson's Creek*. Elliot, back at her grandparent's in Paw Paw, was sleeping until noon, bartending in Daisy Dukes, and going off-roading with boys. Sammi was in Venice, enjoying a romp with an Italian boy named Santino who operated a water taxi.

Blaise sadly turned in the keys to her sorority house, which was being used to quarter new students for freshman orientation. She could no longer crash at the house if she had one too many drinks downtown. Blaise would be out late having fun, and Seamus's voice would come to her like a nasally wizard, "Conor isn't going to stop until he gets you with a DWI."

3:01 am, July 23rd, 2011:

Blaise went downtown with her cousin Jericho. She got so drunk, she made out with scuzzy Kenny Devine on the dance floor at Galaxy. His family also lived on Zzyzyx Road. Growing up, whenever his Dad came over to do contracting work, Kenny and Blaise used to play kissing games in hidden parts of Foley. She was pretty sure he had a kid now.

Kenny assured Jericho that he would get Blaisey home safely, and she hiccupped, "*yeah!*" so Coco left, looking tired but mollified.

Kenny bought her pizza at Pasquale's and slurred in her ear that she should come home with him.

"I'm not giving you *sex* for *pizza!*" Blaise screamed, so that two guys eating in a booth turned around.

"You're just a fucking cock-tease, Foley," Kenny sneered. "You always were."

"I was *three!*" she shrieked, though it was mostly middle school when they hung out. She tried to slap Kenny but he ducked. Blaise approached the cashier to get his money refunded, announcing haughtily, "I don't need *him* to buy my pizza," but he had already stormed out of Pasquale's.

To save face, she looked at the teenage pizza boys and said, "He was NOTD, boys." They offered tight smiles, but they were closing up.

Alone in the parking ramp, Blaise backed her car out, feeling victorious every time she didn't hear a crunch of metal. *I should not drive,* she realized plainly, but the thought of calling a cab was so overwhelming. She didn't call cabs, she called George, and George was fast asleep at Foley. *I have to drive,* she reasoned, *It's only twenty minutes to home.* For comfort, Blaise imagined Hildy bringing her eggs florentine in bed tomorrow morning, with the sun splashing her satin sheets.

As Blaise lurched off the exit for Zzyzyx, it did not occur to her to turn her Valentine on.

The flashing red-and-blue lights appeared in her mirror. Fear came to her slowly, as if the person in charge of dispensing her adrenaline was falling asleep at the controls. She saw Conor Walsh's cop car swiftly approaching, his python smile looming larger and stronger in her mirror. Blaise did not really pull over, she just kind of froze there in the shoulder of Zzyzyx Road.

"Well…well…well" Conor whistled 'Zip-a-Dee-Doo-Dah' as he did his slow march up to her window. "Impressive swerving there, Blazin' Saddles."

Blaise didn't answer. 500 yards away, bathed in the moonlight like a holy apparition, sat beautiful Foley Bourbon. If she gunned it—

"Cut your engine" Conor growled, following her gaze. "If you even *think* about pulling a fucking O.J, I'll shoot out your goddamn tires."

Listlessly, she obeyed, and Conor snatched the keys from her hand. He went to his car to get the breathalyzer.

"Blow," he droned, shoving the little tube to her lips.

"No thanks," Blaise turned away.

"Isn't that your nickname at the frat houses? Blowie Foley?" Knowing that he had her cornered seemed to make Conor manic with glee; his green eyes and smile were wider than Blaise had ever seen them before. "You don't blow, I take you to the station right now." He wagged a finger at her. "But the consequences of refusing can be even greater than a DWI. Didn't Uncle Duff teach you that?"

She leaned forward and did as told.

"1.1" Conor breathed, reading the little screen. "Can't pretend that I'm not gonna enjoy this, Foley."

The spigot of anger that ran richly through her had rusted over. Her insides were suddenly barren, except for fear, cold and dry as November grass. She imagined in a flash her name in the news, a slouchy-eyed mugshot, articles shared on Facebook, everyone whispering *"Blaise Foley got a DWI."*

The fear was awakening in her a deep survival instinct.

"Walsh," Blaise looked at him with all her might, forcing the corners of her lips up, "When you said you were going to really enjoy this, what did you mean?"

"I meant your ass was getting arrested."

"Ooh," Blaise pouted coquettishly. "Does that mean you're gonna use your handcuffs on me, Conor?"

He glanced over, and she saw something twitch behind his mask of steel.

"Don't talk like a whore, Foley."

She gasped in burlesque outrage, swatting his belt. "I'm *not!* And *Conor,* why don't you ever call me by my first name?" she gave him her most alluring smile, the one that finished with a nose scrunch. "Do you not know it?"

"Sure. *Kelly.*"

Playfully, she batted his arm, let her hand linger there, "Silly. I don't let a boy call me Kelly unless…" and she giggled, siphoning power from the grudging intrigue in his eyes.

"Unless what?" Officer Walsh growled. Blaise felt his bulging veins under her fingers and realized that her desire wasn't completely counterfeit.

"Come here," Blaise purred, unbuckling her seatbelt and hinging out the window. The air that greeted her was mild and warm, carrying a strengthening scent of Walsh's woodsy scent as he bent his neck closer to hers…

"Let's go to my house" Blaise panted. The clock on her dashboard said 3:57 a.m. Her eyes were sandy but her mouth was a pink grotto of desire.

Conor stopped caressing her legs, his sultry expression rippling with doubt. "Your house?" he squinted down the road, "You kidding?"

Blaise was suddenly excited by the challenge of it, "C'mon," she nibbled on his ear, making him groan aloud, "Haven't you fantasized about ravaging me in my bed at Foley Bourbon?"

"Of course," Conor whispered hoarsely, to her surprise. "But I'm not tryin' to get shot tonight."

She rolled her eyes as if he were being dramatic. "Well, isn't that the risk that every boy in blue takes when he wakes up each morning? I mean, you have your vest on." Blaise patted his unnaturally firm chest, "Don't tell me that this is all Walsh."

"But my parent's house is even closer," Conor reasoned. "Let's go there."

"Yeah, but at *your* house, isn't there only one way upstairs?" Blaise argued. "If your parents catch us, I mean, what would they do?"

"Disown me," Conor said matter-of-factly. "Tell me to change my name."

Blaise nodded, "*Exactly*, sweetums. At *my* house, we can take the elevator straight up to my suite." She cuffed his hammy upper leg, dropped words in his ear like pebbles in a creek, "There's no chance they'll even hear us."

Conor agreed. Gruffly, he told her that he was going to park his prowler in the driveway of his parent's house, and meet her at Black-Jack's grave, the Prime Meridian between Foley and Walsh. "If you're not there in ten minutes" he admonished, tapping her nose, "Any trust you may have built will be dead forever."

Blaise hastily agreed. A moment longer, and she would start to wonder what the hell she was doing, and he might remember the DWI. She parked her car inside the gate, disarmed the yard alarm, then raced up the embankment, past her almighty rickhouse and the mausoleums of dead Foleys, none of whose lives had gone a day beyond sixty-one years.

Apart from the feeble light of Hildie's bathroom, Foley Bourbon was dark. She had never admired the house from this angle at night, while it slept like an anchored yacht on a glassy ocean.

"Yo," Conor appeared, storming past Jack and Clara's graves and making the sign of the cross. He had traded the top part of his uniform for a T-shirt, and Blaise smelled nice cologne. Without sentimentality, Conor took her hand. She felt a spark in her panties as they illuminated their winding path with their phones.

"And here on your left is where we age our bourbon," Blaise chirped.

"Shut the fuck up," Conor scowled, grabbing her shoulders and kissing her with such ferocity that their teeth smashed together. He gave her house a Clint Eastwood glare, "You better be right about your goddamn dad. If he tries to take a shot at me, I've got my gun."

"Oh is that what that was?" Blaise said coyly, "I thought it was something for me…"

Conor gritted his teeth at her, his true smile, and she was alarmed at how sexy she felt.

"Don't talk," she breathed, leading him into the house and through the red Rococo parlor to the elevator.

In between the 1st and 2nd floors, the elevator stalled.

"I don't think that cable's been lubed up since World War I," Blaise sighed, "Give it a minute."

Conor was busy sliding his hands up her skirt and caressing her bare ass. "I may not be able to wait a minute," he groaned into her shoulder blades.

But then, the bizarre film they were starring in came to a pause. Above her head sounded the voice of the other Antichrist of her life, whose Dixie alto could affect her like warm milk or hot oil, depending on his words. *Daddy…*

"Blaisey?" her father calling unseeingly down the shaft, "Are you stuck, honey?"

She felt Conor's body stiffen, and saw him deftly take the safety off his gun. "Yes, Daddy, I've got Elliott in here with me!" she trilled, slamming her hand over Conor's mouth. "We took the elevator 'cause she was sick on herself; she didn't want anybody to see her."

"Aw no!" John dithered. Blaise could just see his monogrammed slippers just above their heads. "Is she okay, angel?"

"Well, she done learned her lesson about tequila, that's for sure," Blaise forced herself to chuckle, though her heart was beating so fast she thought it may explode. "Don't worry, I'll take care of her. Go back to bed, Daddy—I hear the gears moving."

Mr. Foley clucked that he hoped Elliott felt better. Blaise heard him pad away, muttering something about this being the reason that people should avoid any libation but bourbon.

Blaise exhaled. A moment later, the elevator lurched upward.

In bed, Conor was the sexiest boy she had ever been with. Ever sexier than Jake Abramo, whom she still fantasized about when she jilled off. Blaise got the feeling that anything could happen, a meteor could fall from the sky, her daddy could pound on the door, and he still would not stop. His body was perfect, a football gladiator whose muscles had never deflated from high school. After years of averting her eyes and shushing pangs, her hands and mouth were alive with compensatory greed.

"No sex though," Blaise panted, caressing his bulging biceps. Perhaps Walsh was well-acquainted with the Irish-Catholic girl's restraint, because he merely nodded.

They did everything else in Blaise's virgin manifesto, everything under her umbrella of *"passion without penetration."* The sun was coming up, and they still weren't tired. Blaise heard the front-gate creak open, knew it was Danny, the 9-year-old who delivered papers with his uncle. In about an hour, her dad would saunter outside in his silk smoking jacket to retrieve his *Kentucky Herald*.

She glanced over at Walsh, who was eyeing her, running his hands over her body's milky longitude.

"I'm so pale," she acknowledged, in case he was thinking it.

"Well don't go sunbathing on that front lawn," Conor said gruffly, "There'll be accidents for sure."

Blaise giggled, "Who knew you could be charming, Walsh! You're usually mean."

"'Cause you are first," he grumbled, tugging her hair.

"You are!" she laughed. As the sun brought its Midas touch to his chest-hair, reality set in. "My dad is an early riser," Blaise sighed. "I hate to be rude, but…"

"No, it's alright," Conor stood up. As he dressed, he kept glancing suspiciously at her, as though expecting Blaise to point and laugh and say, "*Psyche!*"

"Well, I have your number," Conor said awkwardly, standing there in his wife beater with the gun on his holster. He had placed it on her nightstand before ripping her panties clean off her hips.

She nodded, "Okay. Want me to walk you out?"

"Nah," Conor unlocked her door with the antique key, then tossed it to her with a grin. "If you don't hear shots fired, assume it went well."

Wrapped in her satin sheet, Blaise watched out the window as he jetted past her rickhouse. *Probably the last time a Walsh will be on our side of the hedges,* she thought. *How d'ya like them apples?*

Hours later, when Mr. Foley went to knock gently on Blaise's door to see if she wanted to come to church, he halted himself. He told the breakfast table that it would be a sin to wake his precious princess, no doubt exhausted from taking care of her sick friend all night, and everyone should let her rest.

"But Elliott wasn't out last night, Uncle John," Jericho said, frowning over his Belgian waffles.

Mr. Foley chuckled breezily, adjusting his tie in the mirror. "Coco baby, I think you musta been a little overserved yourself."

For weeks, Officer Walsh did not bother Blaise on the road. She did not do much to take advantage of this: Acting like a prisoner out on parole, she drove the speed limit and yielded to yellow lights.

Conor texted her once after 9 on a weeknight: *"What are you doing."*

Blaise did not respond. The two of them attempting to have normal conversation would be like forcing feral children down for tea.

Two days later, he wrote her again: *"K :-)"*

One September afternoon, as Blaise drove home from town, a 502-number called her. It was Conor Walsh. She had never saved his number.

"Are you alone?" he asked, bypassing any hellos.

"Yeah, but I'm driving…"

"I know" he grunted, "Pull over."

Seconds later, he came whizzing towards her in a sharp red motorcycle that she had seen on the road many times before, never realizing it was him. He was not in uniform, but in a bomber jacket and jeans.

"Hi," Blaise said, as he assumed his familiar stance outside her window. "Are you *allowed* to pull me over in civilian clothing?"

"Yup," Walsh said, "Cops have absolute authority to do whatever they want." He squinted into the sun for a moment. Then he looked at her with a frank, bothered expression, "You used me to get out of a DWI, didn't you?"

"I…" Blaise had not expected this. "No, that's not true," she could not believe her mouth was forming these words, "Conor, you seemed to fully *enjoy* yourself that night…"

"Yeah. *That* night."

Blaise felt herself getting defensive, "Well what more did you want to happen? You said yourself that if your parents knew about us, they'd disown you."

"Maybe if you answered my texts," he intoned, "You would know."

He squinted at the sun. His superman jawline and chiseled cheeks were a perfect twin of his brother Patrick's. Fleetingly, Blaise thought of her and Pat's conversation at the luau last year. Was this to be her life, sitting in or outside cars with a Walsh boy, trying to keep herself from cringing to death?

After a few more minutes of bizarre nothingness, they parted ways. As soon as Blaise got home, she started looking up job openings at Foley. She wanted something that would take her to a whole new city. She would become a shot-girl at a 2-star resort in Tahiti if she had to. She would get Uncle Duffy to help convince her dad to allow it.

The Walsh sludge was seeping into her soul. Life was getting too weird on Zzyzyx Road.

Death of James Branagh
Fall 2014
The Home of James Branagh and Patrick Walsh
Six miles from Zzyzyx Rd.

Chapter 8

Tonight Blaise asked me, "Are you going to publish as James Branagh?"

"I don't know," I replied shiftily. Lately I had been wondering that a lot. "Why?"

"*Because* I want to imagine how the cover of the best-selling book of the 21st century will look," Blaise said snazzily. "I think you should publish under your *real* name."

I scratched my raven hair. "Isn't there something to be said about making it on your own, without leaning on your family's last name?"

"Honey," she patted my hand, adopting her "Foley Knows Best" voice, "Every dollar I've ever spent or earned was tied to my last name. It's a brand. You *have* to own it."

"I have to own it," I echoed, reaching for a Marb Rouge, only to learn that I was out. "Hold that thought, Muser. I'm gonna run out and get cigs."

Waiting in line at the Red Rover station near my house, I let her words break against the jetties of my mind. They brought up a prickle of fear, and I wasn't sure why.

You're worried your writing isn't as good as Jack's, came a voice in my head. *And people will say you're riding your great-grandpa's coattails.*

"Just the Marbs?" the zit-faced cashier asked me in a townie accent. He was new. When I nodded, he asked to see some ID.

I slid my ID across the formica counter, counting to three. Sure enough, the glazed look in his eyes flickered to interest.

"As in—?"

"Yeah," I nodded, adding wisely, "You're new here, aren't you? It'll lose its novelty, I promise. You'll see my cousin Kiki coming in for lotto tickets about five times a day. My Uncle too."

"Oh..." the cashier said. But as I accepted my change and made for the door, he called after me eagerly, "Did you guys ever find Black-Jack's treasure?"

I half glanced over my shoulder, "Sir, if we had found the treasure, then I wouldn't be fetching my own cigarettes."

Few people know this, but when Jack Walsh was at Trinity, he used to write articles for a radical newspaper under the pen-name Sean Branagh. Sean being the Irish form of "John," and "Branagh" being a form of his surname, which means "Welshman."

I have never lied to you, dear Reader, but I have omitted a few details.

In 8th grade, I adopted James Branagh as my *nomme de plume*, writing it all over my Converses and my composition notebooks (which my brother Conor always managed to read). James Branagh is not the name on my birth certificate, which listed the number of babies born as 2, nor my dog tags, which say that I was born March 17, 1986, with type A-blood.

You can see why I gave one of my dog tags to Pat when he left: I mean, who else would that specific info fit but him?

Hours later, Foley and I were smoking on my front porch. Out of the misty twilight, courage came to me like a lost dog:

"I decided to tell our readers that I'm Seamus," I told her.

"Praise the Lord!" Blaise cheeped, enfolding me in a hug. "I was hoping all along you would, Shay. I didn't get why you wouldn't!"

Because, darling, what if it isn't good enough?

"I dunno," I said moodily, ashing onto the porch. "I didn't want my mom reading it and finding out I worked in a brothel when I was 18. She thinks I was giving tours of the Eiffel Tower."

Blaise eyed me a long moment, and ever so subtly, an eyebrow went up.

"What are we writing about next," I barreled on. "Should we take a break from the present?"

"I think so," she nodded, "I know you want to get back to revolutionary Ireland, but I think it's important to tell what happened after Jack arrived in Kentucky. Talk about how your grandpa started distilling for Foley at a young age…"

"Since he was 7," I said, because like any grandson of Wilkie Walsh, I could quote his legend. "Let's take it back to Prohibition era Kenfucky." I exhaled a lungful, "I'll get Pat to help me caulk any holes I may leave."

Her eyes grew big at the mention of my twin's name. It was nothing new: every time I came to the door, there was a millisecond before her brain registered that I wasn't Pat, and her inner-being swam out to greet me. Then she seemed to skin her nose against a shale bottom, and resurfaced with a distinctly leaner smile for me.

It was like getting knifed, but I invited her in every time.

Worth noting: My grandpa picked out the name Seamus for me, the Irish form of James. For my First Holy Communion gift, he gave me his father's copy of Ulysses, along with $250, and told me I was a writer before I even knew it myself. Of course, the book has a huge hole in it where Jack stored his key, so the last line is missing. This is probably the reason I had it tattooed down by right wrist:

"And his heart was going like mad and yes I said yes I will Yes."

Okay. Back to our story.

Chapter 9

Jack Walsh committed all of his and Ulysses' conversation in the Kilkenny pub indelibly to his memory. In the years to follow, the wild Kentucky years, he began to regard Ulysses as his long-lost father. He knew Uli felt the same way because whenever Jack returned to Kentucky after a long time away, Ulysses would say, "the prodigal son has returned!" and wave him into Foley to hear all about his latest run. Jack's loyalty to Foley was sealed with a dogma that none but the prophets of God could fathom. In a letter he wrote to his lawyer from Alcatraz, he admitted to putting Foley before God. *When the wills of my Heavenly Father and my Earthly Father were at odds,* he wrote, *I went with the latter.*

To Jack, the greatest fulfillment of Ulysses' prophecy was the closeness of their sons, Sullivan and Wilkie. Jack could not recall from his own boyhood having a friendship to rival theirs. It was odd to think that Sully and Wilkie were only second cousins. Little Sully had been calling Wilkie, "my twin" since his mouth could form words. Now everyone at Foley called Wilkie and Sully "the twins," except for Jack who called them the lads (or the Two Gallants when they got into mischief, but no one at Foley caught the Joyce reference). The seven months that spaced the lads' arrival on earth were seamlessly caulked after the Walshes first year, 1921, at Foley. Sullivan (born in May) was a slow walker, while Wilkie (born in December) was a quick talker. Carried along to daily teas and dinners with their mothers like treasured purses, the babies grew alongside each other, babbling and giggling in their secret language.

The house that Ulysses promised Jack took most of 1921 to build. It was a lofty three-story home with enough bedrooms that the young Irish family would have space to grow to the size Clara wanted, which was six healthy children. The biggest window that afforded the best view was in the master bedroom. Whenever Clara asked Jack to check on the boys, he need only to peep out this window and scan the verdant hills. The pinpricks of two heads, one golden and one ebony, were almost always within bounds. Out of bounds would have been the bar down the way, or the graveyard that morbidly buttressed the Foley's grounds. Usually, there was a third little head paces behind, frantically wailing for the other two.

"Wilkie!" Clara would holler from the kitchen, "*Sullivan!* Come get Kilkenny to play with you!"

If she were calling them to eat, they would have boomeranged home in three seconds. When Kilkenny was mentioned, the wee lads were suddenly deaf.

Of course, Wilkie and Sully hated whenever the little baby found them, usually by the crick or the stables. They had a plan that they worked on nearly every day, and they didn't want Wilkie's whiny little brother within 500 feet of it. It was actually more of a life objective than a plan, because the two of them had spent their whole entire lives trying to solve a mystery. That was seven years for Wilkie and nearly eight years for Sullivan.

The boys desperately wanted to know what happened inside the bar.

The bar was called the Dixie Stronghold. Wilkie and Sullivan knew this from eavesdropping on their mother's chat, their voices growing syrupy as the teacups laced with bourbon became empty. The mother's talk was often of the Dixie: "the Dixie this Friday," "Oh, let's do this at the Dixie." If Sully and Wilkie asked about the Dixie, the mothers mooed at them to be good boys. If they were ever caught at the Dixie, they were promised a clither on the gob.

Sully and Wilkie were allowed to do many things. Wilkie could sleepover on a weeknight. The boys could patrol the acres of Foley with Sully's rifles and shoot at any coyote they saw. They could go to the pictures with Uncle Andy and see one with kissing scenes and shooting gangsters.

The big rules of life were not to go by the bar, keep out of the cemetery, be nice to Kilkenny and Lucretia, and don't annoy your elders with questions about the bourbon.

Sullivan understood that bourbon was a health tonic that cured many diseases. His Daddy drank the miracle tonic every night, assuring Sully that bourbon was better for the body than even castor oil. He knew that his Uncle Andy made it, and his Uncle Jackie delivered it across America in his big truck.

Sully and Wilkie did not understand why they couldn't ask questions about the bourbon. Whatever the big secret was, everyone seemed to be in on it.

"Does bourbon cure polio, Da?" Wilkie asked Jack innocently one morning (he hoped not, because his dream was to be the scientist who discovered the cure).

"Drink your tay, son" came his father's gruff reply from behind his newspaper.

"Samuel!" Sully cornered his Uncle's worker as he ground corn inside the distilling room. "Why do we have to stop our sills whenever those cops come around?"

Samuel stopped whistling, wiping the yellow sawdust on his apron and smiling shiftily. "I think I heard your momma calling you, Little Man."

At school, Wilkie and Sully were often teased by the older kids, sons of soybean and tobacco farmers who walked miles to school every morning. These kids mocked them when Leon, Ulysses' valet, dropped them off in the shining Coupe and waved goodbye with a satin gloved hand.

"It's not that nice!" Sullivan yelled futilely, wishing he could trade his clothes and cars for suspenders and a jalopy.

"Yins are only rich because your daddies are crooks!" Floyd G called out. He was the meanest and smelliest of the bullies, but unfortunately, he was also the biggest. Sullivan went to charge at him like a bull, but Wilkie, more prudent by nature, grabbed Sully by the back of his collared shirt.

Other mornings, the big boys sang a song Sully and Wilkie didn't understand, but still loathed, for the implicit ridicule:

Sully's in the bathtub, stewing up the juice
Wilkie's keeping watch over cops on the loose,
Black-Jack's in Chicago, selling off the sauce
He'll kill anyone who says he has to listen to the law

When Sully asked his father what the song meant, Ulysses looked sadly from his son's face into the fire.

"Son, if I told you you'd understand later, would you trust me?"

"*Yeah* but—"

"Then trust me, Sully, and let this alone. Those boys covet the nice things you have, for they have nothing. You must look into your heart and find compassion for them. Do you think boys at school didn't make fun of Uncle Andy and me when we were your age?" he sipped his bourbon, leaned back in his leather armchair. "Someday, the bullies will come and ask if they can work for you, and you must forgive them and show them kindness— "

"*Yeah*, but—"

Ulysses sternly held up a finger to quiet him, "And I will be disappointed in you, Sully, if you fight any of them. You have to hold your head high and conduct yourself with *dignity*. Dignity always wins." His father's walrus mustache spread into a monkey grin above Sully's head, as his mother's heels clacked into the room.

"Look at him by the fire!" Deirdre shook her raven head, her fashionably flat curls held in place by a pearl headband. "I suppose he thinks he's posing for an oil painting."

Ulysses chuckled lazily. His wife's jokes were so entertaining to him that he turned the radio off or tossed aside his newspaper whenever she came in. Sully found them significantly less thrilling, though his parents usually brought him into their little routine.

"What do you think, Sully?" Ulysses asked, admiring Deirdre as she perched on the arm of his chair, pretending to be indifferent to him and his opulent surroundings. "Do you think Momma regrets the day she let that Foley guy talk her into leaving Ireland?"

"Your father has closed a lot of tougher sales than me, Sully," Deirdre demurred, helping herself to her husband's drink. "I wasn't about to be the first to say no to Ulysses Foley."

"Well, if all my deals were as beautiful as Momma," Ulysses murmured, touching the small of her back, "I would never leave the road."

Sully rolled his eyes, jumping up before his parents made him upchuck. "I'm gonna go meet Wilkie quick!" he called over his shoulder. No one stopped him. His parents were busy creating a human teepee with their touching foreheads.

Sully bolted through the gate separating Foley from Uncle Jack's house. He loved his house; there were so many mysterious spots to explore. His favorites were the shadowy 4th floor, where his Grandma Blaise had lived, and the scary underground tunnel linking his house to Wilkie's.

But these weren't the secret meeting place. They were too dark, and the adults might get mad if they found you in there. For whatever reason, adults got suspicious of dark places. Sully and Wilkie always met behind the stables. If Sully knocked three times on the Walshes back door and ran, Wilkie knew to meet him there within ten minutes. Wilkie's secret signal was to shine his flashlight in Sully's bedroom, or try the playroom. They seldom missed each other, because if they didn't need to meet, they would likely be at each other's house anyway.

"Guess what my daddy says!" Sully said gleefully, as soon as Wilkie's dark crew cut poked around the stable. "That Floyd G and all thum are gonna work for me someday!"

"Work for *us,* ya mean," Wilkie corrected him, eager to share in this vindication.

Sullivan paused. He didn't quite know how it worked, except everyone told him he'd be the boss someday.

"Sure," he agreed, stroking Rushmore's flicking tail. Wilkie would probably do Uncle Jack's job when he retired.

Trying to sneak into the Dixie was Wilkie's second favorite thing to do. His first favorite thing was science experiments.

Aunt Clara was a fantastic cook. Her fridge was always as packed with food as Deirdre's closet was filled with furs and silk-lined stilettos. On Saturday mornings, before the house woke up, Wilkie liked to mix things together from his mother's pantry to see what crazy results they could yield. Usually Sully was there acting as lab assistant.

Wilkie discovered that baking soda, water, lemon, and sugar made homemade Coke that tasted as good as the stuff in the bottle.

They sold two glasses to Samuel as he worked and one to Bridey, netting a profit of twenty-five cents.

Hot water, gelatin, and corn syrup mixed together created fake snot. One morning, the boys had a grand time smearing it all over Kilkenny's face and pillow, shushing his squeals and urging him to play along. Then they ran into Jack and Clara's bedroom, hollering that they needed to come quick, Kilky was sick.

"You faker-bakers," came Clara's gentle chide, hands balled on her hips, when the boys yelps gave way to giggles. Aunt Clara rarely got hollering mad at you.

Jack finished wiping the cream off his face from his wet shave and tossed Clara the towel. She patted Kilkenny's little cheeks clean, cooing like a dove.

"Ya like our science experiment, Uncle Jack?" Sully cheeped, and Wilkie's olive eyes raised hopefully.

"I'll be telling Einstein to watch over his shoulder," Jack murmured, his cool gaze following something outside the window. His rare smile followed.

"Yoo-hoo!" A familiar voice trilled down below. Sully groaned. His mother Deirdre was standing outside, dressed at ten a.m. in a fabulous lamé dress trimmed with sable. The mothers did this at each other's houses about six times a day, called "Yoo-Hoo!" and then waltzed right on in. It had always been this way, since they were girls growing up in Kilkenny City. Neither had a sister who survived infancy, so the cousin in the next alley became her substitute.

"Anyone alive in here?" Deirdre called, clacking through the house in her heels. "Sullivan, are you in there?"

"Aunt Deirdre!" Wilkie called jubilantly as she entered the kitchen, "Look at Kilkenny, he's covered in snot!"

"It's fake, Deedee," Clara called reassuringly. She wiped away the last traces from Kilkenny's tiny face and he squirmed from her grasp. "The twins have been up to their old tricks."

"Lord hear my prayer," Deirdre drawled, swatting Sully's honey-toned head. "All morning, Sully, I've been knocking on your door and talking to you with no idea you weren't there. Hattie probably thinks I'm fit for my bed at the loon asylum."

"He was busy making snot, Deedee" Jack offered, turning the boiler on for tea. A small gold cross lay entangled in the thicket of chest hair that peeped from his wife-beater. Below the hairy epaulettes of his shoulders, Sully and Wilkie noted the gruesome scar carved into Uncle Jack's forearm. It said MCMXVI. He told them that it was for his friend in Ireland, a man named McMaxvi, who was born on Easter.

"*Look!*" Sully crowed, forking a bit of gummy sinew and shoving it under his mother's nose. Deirdre shrieked and recoiled like a schoolgirl.

"Grand!" she plunked down at the table in a huff. "I've fake snot to now add to your long list of shenanigans. I must say, though, you lads showed your hand too soon," she nodded appealingly at Clara, "Think of all the church and school they may have weaseled their way out of, Clairy, had we been none the wiser?"

"Heaven only knows," Aunt Clara crossed herself.

Deirdre shot a kind smile to Wilkie from underneath her fashionable turban hat, "How did you make it, dear?" She always took an extra moment for wee Wilkie. After all, he was her godson.

Wilkie's eyes shifted around as he mumbled his recipe.

"I helped!" Sully horned in.

"They teach you that in school, son?" Jack asked Wilkie curiously, bringing out the tea mugs.

"No," Wilkie shrugged, "It just made sense."

For a moment, the entire party stared at him in faint wonder. Then the kitchen resumed its usual clamor.

"Come along, Sully."

"I want to stay!"

"You'll stay for a cup at least, Deedee."

"I can't, Jackie. I left Lucretia alone in her playpen. Clara, where's the Electrolux? I need it back."

"Oh, is that why you're dressed like Marion Morehouse? To vacuum?"

"Me? There's a laugh. Hattie needs it, we'll be having Colonel Jackson and his wifey over for dinner."

"Sounds like a right bit of craic…"

"Happier times were had at Frognoch, I'm sure Jackie could tell you. But I can probably leave the dry shite convention around 8, so wait up for me, Clara Bow, we'll have a nightcap...come along, Sully—"

"—Mom, you *cussed*!"

"I'll go to Confession. Come, your sister's probably halfway down the road by now..."

"But there's nothing to *do* at home! It's *boring*!"

"Boring, aye? Well the distiller finds work for idle hands. Come with me, lads."

"Bored?!" Uncle Andrew boomed, polishing his gold-rimmed glasses on his Polo shirt, which was emblazoned with the FOLEY emblem and stretched tautly over his big belly. "There's no time to be bored when there's bourbon to be made! Come along now, boys!"

Reluctantly, Sullivan trailed behind his Uncle into the fermenting room, with Wilkie looming behind him. Unlike the forbidden Dixie, there was nothing alluring or mysterious about watching bourbon be made. The fermenting room was filled with big copper sills and smelled like soggy bread. The wooden tubs filled with bourbon mash looked like pudding that someone had upchucked. Uncle Andy treated the stinky stuff like an adored puppy, cooing at it, poking it, watching it raptly with his hands balled up on his hips. He even came to work on Saturdays when he didn't have to.

"...Now when our great-great *great* Granddaddy Angus came over from Ireland, he knew a thing or two about whiskey," Andy crowed, his cheeks pink and his blue eyes wide. "His family had Bunratty Gold, and Angus was taught how to stew the sauce from a young age. Then when some money-bags Scotsman came around and offered to buy the company, the Foleys decided to cash out and make a go of it in the New World..."

Sullivan groaned to himself. It was like hearing in church, *"In the beginning, God created the heaven and the earth..."*

"—Before he came to America," Uncle Andy continued jovially, "Old Angus wasn't using corn in whiskey. But he saw an opportunity here in Kentucky for how fast the dang Injuns were growing all that goddang maize—"

Sullivan glanced at Wilkie in despair, but to his surprise, his cousin was paying fierce attention. There was such a thing as being polite to grownups, but Wilkie was overselling it.

"Uncle Andy?" Sully raised his hand to show that he was polite too. "How long is this lesson going to be?"

"Tell you what," Uncle Andy replied smoothly, "If y'uns stay for half an hour, I'll give you a Chu-ee. If you stay for an hour, I'll take you to the pictures tonight."

"Okay!" Sullivan agreed happily. He looked at the gold-faced watch around his Uncle's furry wrist to mark the time. 12:01. By 1:03, he and Wilkie could be catching minnows at the pond, and by 7:00, they would be at the cinema. All told, it was shaping up to be a pretty good day.

"Andy?" Wilkie peered into the great tub, "Is there corn in there now?"

"Heavens yes, son!" Andy said heartily, "Corn, barley, wheat, all the usual birdseed. Can't tell you the *exact* mash-bill, because that's a *secret* family recipe." He chuckled, wagging his finger.

Sully noticed Wilkie's face jolt up excitedly from the basin. Later, he would have to break it to him that it wasn't the juicy kind of secret.

Andy continued expertly, "You can't see the corn because it's been fermenting for three days now…here, taste it, it ain't too hot." He expertly punched through the thick yellowish skin and slurped the liquid off his fingers. Wilkie and Sully did the same.

"And that's the medicine?" Wilkie said, smacking his lips thoughtfully.

"Sure tastes like medicine," Sully grimaced. He longed to spit out this weird bread juice, but swallowed to be polite. Wilkie helped himself to another taste, looking very annoyingly grownup.

Uncle Andy chuckled. "Bourbon's what we call the Kentucky cure-all, boys. When Aunt Bessie ran away to Florida, my bourbon was my doctor *and* my priest rolled into one…" The boys blinked up at him, and Andrew cleared his throat briskly. "Alright, where were we?

Oh yeah…1792. Kentucky joins the Union and Old Angus buys his first warehouse."

After about 400 sneaked glances at Uncle Andy's watch, Sully finally, at long last, saw the big hand twitch past the little hand at 1.

"—Bourbon isn't *brown* when it's first distilled, it's white," Andy was saying, wagging a finger precisely, "It absorbs the color and flavor of the barrel it's in, you see—"

"Uncle Andy, it's been an hour!" Sully yelped, pointing at his watch.

"Alright boys, you've both been great sports. Here Sully have a Chu-ee. Wilkie, you too."

Wilkie caught the candy, but didn't move. "Can I stay longer?" he asked, deliberately not looking at Sully.

"If you want to, son," Andy chuckled, "But that doesn't mean I'm seeing a double-feature tonight!"

"That's alright," Wilkie shrugged apologetically at Sully, who was full on gaping at him. "I think it's kinda ducky."

Sully watched them on and off all afternoon. Even from the bird's eye view of his bedroom, he could see Wilkie's alertness as he followed Uncle Andrew around. He wasn't being a faker-baker: he really thought Andy's bourbon sermon was better than Clara Bow in heels. Sully didn't get it. He even traipsed outside to make sure he wasn't missing something, but no, it was the same old boring stuff as before. Sully finally had to resign himself to playing with Lucretia and her dumb paper dolls.

Later on at the cinema, Wilkie had the nerve to act mystified when Sully asked why the heck he acted like that all day.

"Like *what*?" Wilkie asked. They were at the concession stand trying to decide between Goobers or Bob Whites.

"Like my Uncle was a swami, and when he said *bourbon,* he put you in a trance," Sully huffed, folding his arms.

Wilkie struggled to explain, "Bourbon's like a big science experiment, except I already know what happens. It helps people, and it makes our family money," he shrugged conclusively, "I like it."

Sullivan finally understood. Wilkie was famous for this three-point logic: if he could find three solid reasons why something worked or made sense, he went with it. With the same inarguable logic, he used his next breath to make a case for Bob Whites as their chosen candy: "They're cheaper, we can each get a penny change, and Uncle Andy doesn't like 'um, so we won't have to share."

From then on, Wilkie helping with the bourbon became just another fact of life. At Foley, there was fish on Fridays, horse-racing on Saturdays, and Wilkie up at five a.m. every day, to help Samuel fire up the sills. Clara fretted over Wilkie's new employ: her favorite worry was that Wilkie wasn't getting enough sleep. Jack pointed out that their paperboy was his age, and up at the same time to hurtle the *Daily News* at their door.

"Every man crusades for his purpose," Jack said, with his face to the fire. "Wilk is fortunate to not have to leave his yard."

In the summertime, Wilkie and Sully had campouts nearly every night. Uncle Jack pitched an A-line tent, making them help him hammer the stakes into the earth with big rocks.

"There's your domatera, lads," Jack muttered, a cigarette clenched between his teeth. He also taught them how to gather sticks to make a campfire. Aunt Clara hustled the boys out sausages to roast, and rose-water marshmallows that she made herself.

One Saturday evening, Ulysses whisked the mothers into Chicago for a show. Sully and Wilkie watched with glazed faces propped up on fists while Clara and Deirdre swished around the parlor in new dresses and velvet hats. They giggled girlishly when Ulysses, all trussed up in his finest haberdashery, sprinkled them with compliments.

"I've got the two most beautiful fillies in Kilkenny or Kentucky as my dates," he boomed to an imaginary comrade, "How lucky can a guy get?"

"I think his eyesight's going, Clara," Deirdre said, blotting her red lips. Seconds later, she left an imprint of motherly love on both Wilkie and Sully's foreheads, instructing them to be good for Bridey. Lucretia came streaking from her bedroom in her nightgown, and Ulysses scooped her in his arms, planting kisses on her head. Bridey, the new maid, watched from the doorway with a slight smile, her expression becoming alert as Deirdre gave a few last-minute commands. (Later on, Deirdre whispered in Clara's ear that she hoped Bridey was writing home to Kilkenny about how comfortable the Sullivan girls' new surroundings were: "We've come a long way from taped-on shoes, Clairy-belle,").

Wilkie and Sully decided to have a campout. They crawled into their tent, holding the lantern up to their faces as they told crazy-true stories. Wilkie told the one about the Irish Crown Jewels, which were stolen from Dublin Castle twenty years ago. His Da had described for him seeing the sparkling badge, necklace, and crown under a MISSING header on the cover of the *Kilkenny Journal* for weeks as a boy delivering papers.

"The thieves," Wilkie said, in mysterious tones, "*Still* haven't been caught to this day. And Ireland is *still* missing her national treasure." The light shone eerily under his eyelids.

"Whoa," Sully breathed. "Where do you think they are?"

"My Da reckons they were sold to an Indian princess for 50 million rupees," Wilkie said expertly.

Sully was becoming increasingly aware of a faint thunder against the earth. He sat up. "Wilkie, do you hear that?"

"Kilky! Go away, we warned you *twice* about the golden jackals—"

"No, it ain't your brother!" Sully peeked out the tent's curtains. There, about fifty feet away and advancing swiftly towards them were a bunch of men on horseback, dressed all in white, some carrying torches. They looked to Sully like evil ghosts because they had white hoods over their faces. The men yodeled some crazy war chant as they charged right for the tent. Frantically, Sully turned off their lantern so they wouldn't be seen, and yelped at Wilkie to take cover. It was too late to escape, the crazy ghost men had them circled…Sully saw the bucking silhouettes of those horses from hell, then the men began to kick the tent…they were going to get stomped to death under those merciless hooves, Sully just knew it. Wilkie was hollering in his ear and Sully hollered to the ghost men, "*GO AWAY! PLEASE STOP!*"

But then, they heard the sound of a car zipping full force towards them. Shots were fired, not just a rifle, but the relentless, hurtling *POW POW POW POW!* of a machine-gun.

"*Wilkie!* Sully!" Uncle Jack's voice sailed clean over the tent. Sully was heartened enough to unfurl himself from Wilkie and poke his head outside. Jack's car sailed straight towards the gang as he fired ceaselessly at them—wildly, Sully noticed that Jack's friend Ernie was driving while Uncle Jack shot his gun.

"Shove over Sully, it's my Da, I wanna see—"

"They're leaving now, let's go on out!"

Horses whinnied in agony; Sully saw that Uncle Jack was shooting them in the rear, making them bolt off into the woods, ignoring their owner's commands to slow down. He and Wilkie watched with savage triumph as one man was thrown from his horse...

Jack watched too, hanging out of his cabriolet with an expression of mild interest on his face. "And here I thought I'd have to quit Protestant hunting when I left Ireland," he remarked to Ernest, who hooted with laughter.

"Da!" Wilkie and Sully ran to him. Wilkie seemed torn between wanting to throw his arms around his father's legs, and acting tough.

Jack stewarded this by patting his son's raven head. "Alright, son?"

"Uncle Jack, why were they attacking us?" Sully asked breathlessly.

"Because we're Irish, because were Catholic, it's the same old story." Moodily, Jack stuck a cigarette in his mouth, groping the pockets of his suspenders for a lighter. "Ernie, will you bring that one over here?" he jutted his chin at a man thrown from his horse and laying in a crumpled pile a few feet away.

"Hang on, I lost my goddamn hat," Ernie grumbled in his Chicago accent, exiting the car and rising to his full 4'11 height. He jammed his fedora on his head, then grabbed the hooded man and dragged him, moaning faintly, by his armpits.

Jack pinched the tip of his white hood and wrangled it off.

"If you're aiming to take a man's life," he sneered down at the writhing pile of robes. "You owe him the respect of your face, maggot."

Sully didn't breath. Even the wind stopped whistling out of shame for Uncle Jack's disgust.

"I wasn't aiming to take any lives!" the man cried from the ground. The moon shone like a spotlight on his sweaty, pained face.

Jack ignored him. "Wilkie, Sully, look at this man." The boys jumped forward eagerly. "His brothers abandoned him, left him for dead. He stands for nothing. He fights for nothing. He *is* nothing. That is why he conceals his face."

The man was crying, whether from pain or molten shame, Sully didn't know. He attempted to sit up, but Jack calmly placed a boot on his chest and restored him to the ground.

"When you set out tonight, soldier, had you any idea whose land you were terrorizing?"

"You're Black-Jack Walsh," the man heaved, and his eyes seemed to dance in a new dimension of horror, "I'm sorry—"

"That's grand, maggot," Uncle Jack spat, his words cold and jagged, "But you'll be doing a lot more penance tonight..."

Ernie stepped forward. "Should I bring the squirts home?" He gestured to Sully and Wilkie with his ringed hands, his fingers short as cigar stubs.

"What? *No!* Uncle Jack, let us stay!" Sully pleaded.

"Da, we can help you!"

"Yes," Jack said, ignoring them. "Bring them over to Foley, will you? Dede's maid Bridey will put them to bed."

Ernie planted a hand firmly on each of their backs, "Your Pop don't need your help on this," he assured them, "He's the toughest guy on two feet." He rang the bell at the back porch and whistled when Bridey came outside in her Victorian-style nightgown.

"Top of the evening to ya, lassie!" Ernie crowed, bowing clumsily and removing his fedora.

"What a holy show!" Bridey fussed, dragging the frightened boys in by the scruff of their necks. She glared at Ernie as he stuck his oily head into the foyer, telling him if he was waiting to be asked in, he should expect to wait until next Christmas.

Wilkie and Sully were both secretly relieved to be rehashing the excitement from the warmth and comfort of their beds. They tried to spy out the window, but Bridey came in and fussed at them to get to sleep, did they want her to be fired and disgraced, on a steamer back to Kilkenny by morning?

The boys pushed the twin beds together and brought the lantern under the quilt with them. Wilkie had changed into Sully's red union suit with the sailboat on the pocket. If it were any boy in his class, Sully would have sulked at the idea of loaning out his nice pajamas, but Wilkie transcended Sully's attachment to his possessions. His cousin would let him finish his oatmeal, use his fishing pole, and take credit in one of his science experiments, all before noon tomorrow. Sully's young soul harmonized this special debt of generosity by sharing with Wilkie anything he had that Wilkie didn't.

"We would have been goners if my Da hadn't shown up," Wilkie uttered, his voice shimmering with pride.

"I had my rifle, I would have shot if I had to!"

"Your rifle only has six or seven bullets, Sully," Wilkie said realistically, "There were at least 30 of 'um guys."

"How ducky was your daddy's gun!" Sully breathed, "Did you see how fast they all ran, lickety-split?" He rolled onto his back, replaying the glorious scene in his mind.

"Do you think he shot any of 'um dead?"

"I saw him only shoot the horse's backsides," Sully recalled juicily, "Maybe he didn't want to kill 'um, 'cause then the cops would come and put him in jail."

"Maybe," Wilkie thought for a moment. "Sully, do you reckon he's gonna kill that one guy?"

"I dunno," Sully said hoarsely, and his heart sped with the thrill of imagining what could be happening out there. The window brought them no clues; the night was as still and dark as the Atlantic when they sailed to Ireland.

But as he tunneled from awake to sleeping, the awful clomping of horse hooves and war chants rose to a crescendo in his head, forcing Sully's eyes open.

"*Wilkie,*" he hissed, and his cousin gave a quarter turn. "Did ya notice how that one man knew your daddy by name? Called him Black-Jack Walsh, like he was some'un famous."

Wilkie fully turned, appearing to ponder this like he did most things. "I think," he began slowly, "That my Da is sorta famous from the Irish army. Like how everyone knows who Padraic Pearse is. And that's why boys at school know my Da, too."

Sully didn't agree. No one at school knew or cared about Padraic Pearse. The only reason he and Wilkie knew about Padraic Pearse was because sometimes Uncle Jack drank bourbon and made them sit and listen to his stories about the Easter Uprising of '16, when Padraic Pearse died for Ireland.

Sullivan's sleep that night was haunted by dreams of big Floyd G on a horse, galloping circles around their tent and singing an endless taunt, *"Black-Jack will cut you from the back! Black-Jack will cut you from the back!"*

But when he woke up, the morning sun poured cheerfully through his bow window. Wilkie's side of the bed was empty. Sully unlatched the window, and his voice carried in a crest of birdsong. Wilk was outside excitedly rehashing the events of last night for Uncle Andy, who listened intently with his foot on an empty barrel.

Sully ran into the kitchen, slathering a piece of bread with a blob of jam in the kitchen and bolted outside in his PJs. He wasn't about to let Wilkie have all the storytelling glory for himself!

Late, sticky August is when the boys learned the truth.

The parents were going down to the Dixie, as was their Saturday night custom. They tossed the kids their usual warnings to be good and piled into the Coupe. Leon zipped them off into the night, against Jack's protests that they should walk.

"Zzyzyx is grand by moonlight," he said softly, pulling a Carroll out from behind his ear.

"What's Zzyzyx, Jackie?" Deirdre chirped, swiping his cigarette and plugging it into her quellazaire. She flashed him a bratty grin, quite uncharacteristic of a bourbon baron's wife.

"T'is Jackie's name for the old state road Dede!" Clara said.

"T'is the ast word in the dictionary and last stop on my anti-Temperance route," Jack added. Though he spoke in an undertone, the women still shushed him, nodding pointedly at the boys, who were listening to their every word, as always.

Hattie bustled around opening up all the windows in the house, but the mugginess only seemed to multiply. Little Lucretia was so hot and miserable in her canopy bed that Bridey patted down her little limbs with a wet towel. Sully and Wilkie were uncomfortably hot too, but their bigger problem was boredom. Thanks to the threat of hooded men on horses, campouts had been recently outlawed.

"What if we sneak into the Dixie tonight?" Sully suggested in a phantom's whisper. They were laying on the sprawling entryway to Foley with their bare bellies pressed into the marble, trying to get cool.

Wilkie raised an eyebrow, alarmed by Sully's stupidity. "Why don't we just ask Bridey if we can touch her girdle?"

"Listen!" Sully said hoarsely, "All of 'um are at the bar tonight, so there's no one to see us sneaking off." He sat up excitedly, rolling his shirt down, "We'll just tell Bridey that we're headed to the stables to give Flying Ebony some water."

"Or, tell her nothing at all," Wilkie said, rubbing his palms together like he did when a movie started getting good.

They decided that, with Bridey settling into Ulysses' armchair with *Ivanhoe*, Option B was probably smarter. Sully estimated that they had 30 minutes before she became suspicious of the quiet, so he brought along his Daddy's gold pocket-watch to keep track of time. They snuck out the backdoor on tiptoe, then sprinted along the picket-fence that divided their two houses, dramatically sucking in their breath as they passed the Foley graveyard.

In Sully's mind, the forbidden Dixie was maybe just a stone-throw past the Walshes house. On foot, in the gaseous swelter of the night, the bar felt much farther. The boys hustled down the poorly paved road, hoping against hope that the bar would soon appear. Wilkie's confidence in their journey plummeted, and he rattled off a bunch of terrifying scenarios…*what if Leon sees us as he drives back? What if my Da walks home early? What if Bridey comes looking for us?*

"Wilkie, this is our *last chance* before school starts to solve the biggest mystery of our lives!" Sully said, halting empathically in his tracks. He checked the pocket-watch, squinting at the numbers around the PALEK logo, "Only seven minutes've passed. I say, if we don't find the bar in five, we turn around."

Wilkie agreed. They roamed a few more yards and suddenly, the box-shaped Dixie came into view, in the light of a warped lamppost. There were no signs of people coming or going, no light or sound exuded from within, but they knew this was all part of the Dixie's mystique. They had studied it for a long time from the 4th floor of

Foley, with late Grandma Blaise's opera glasses. They knew there was about the cellar door entrance around the back, where they had seen guys like Ernie traipsing in and out with mysterious boxes in hand.

Sully pointed to the Bosco doors. *Let's go,* he mouthed to Wilkie.

When they unlatched the doors, an undulation of music and mirth swept over the boys, seeming to beckon them down the dark cellar stairs. Without a word, they automatically grabbed each other's clammy hands, using the other hand to grope the stucco walls so they wouldn't fall. At the last step, they were lowered into what appeared to be a grubby kitchen.

Even in the dark, Sully could see the dirty grout tiling under his feet and make out the outline of a giant rusty sink. He was surprised that his fancy mother would bring her mink and silk around such a place. Then he heard laughter commingled with a piano, coming from just beyond the kitchen.

"It sounds like some kinda party," he whispered to Wilkie, who nodded swiftly. The words had no sooner left Sully's mouth when the double doors swung open. Wilkie and Sully turned to stone, grabbing each other's hands, steeling themselves for a wave of parental fury.

A man stalked into the kitchen, muttering to himself while he rummaged through a broom closet.

"—Can't believe they have Ernie working the door again, that fool would let Coolidge in if he slipped him a dollar—where's the goddamn, oh there it is…"

The man seized a scraggly mop and dragged it noisily from the kitchen, apparently not noticing the two 8-year-olds. When he kicked the doors open again, a gust of party sounds washed in. Sully heard the booming voice of an announcer:

"Next up, the Sullivan sisters will charm you with their Charleston and jig their way straight into your hearts—"

"*Wilkie!*" Sully hissed to his cousin, his curiosity burning stronger than ever. "They're sayin' my name out there!" he dropped down on all fours and crawled to the swinging doors.

"Come *on!*" he urged Wilkie, who was only half stooped over, hesitating. Then his cousin copied Sully, dropping down and skittering beside him in the dark.

"Lord, these floors are musty."

Sully shushed him, his heart going faster than a hummingbird's wings. So excited was he to unveil the big mystery, he didn't even worry that Uncle Jack might be waiting for them on the other side. Sully head-butted the doors apart, and both boys gasped.

It looked like the greatest party Sully had ever seen. The massive, stonewalled room they found themselves in seemed to vibrate with merriment, with throngs of snazzily dressed adults laughing and dancing. The men were dressed like people in a movie, in two-tone gangster shoes and fedora hats like Ernie's. The women were a buffet of beauty, some of them in silk dresses with severe bobs, some of them with jeweled headbands and red lips, some of them with a kiss curl on their dainty foreheads. Sully would have believed that they were all here filming a movie, but for the lack of cameras.

In another corner, a band played 'Willie the Weeper,' a song always on the radio. A man in a bowler hat wailed the words as if in physical pain, "*He winked at Cleopatra, she said "Ain't he a sight! How about a date for next Saturday night?*" Across the floor, barrels of bourbon were employed as cocktail tables, holding several thin-stemmed glasses with amber liquid. Sully noticed a big barrel up towards the front with a line formed behind it.

"What's the hold up?" a man in suspenders hollered while another man knelt before the spigot.

"It's empty!" the second man yelled back, jostling the barrel from side to side.

Sully looked at Wilkie, who was whispering in his know-it-all voice that the barrel was aged four years ("See? You can tell 'cause Andy puts the year it was made on there. *See?*") He glanced at everyone watching this same scene, all the stylish men and women craning their necks and frowning. Sully somehow knew that they were all here for the bourbon, that the music and dancing revolved around the bourbon, that when the bourbon went away, so did the laughter and the ladies in sequined dresses.

The song ended, leaving a load of heated chatter in its wake, and a man with a feather in his fedora jumped behind the microphone.

"We've temporarily run out of bourbon," he announced smoothly. He waved his hands to silence the jeers that followed. Sully sprang onto his knees like a prairie dog; he knew this voice well. It was—

"Samuel!" Wilkie whispered excitedly.

"He's the one who said my name just now!" Sully realized happily. He wondered if Samuel somehow knew he was coming, if he asked the audience to get ready for him.

"—But!" Samuel continued into the microphone, "We happen to be standing a few paces away from the finest whiskey-maker in all of America—"

"—Oh, stop!" Another familiar voice crooned from a table nearby. Uncle Andy sat there in suspenders, flanked by two women in sequined frocks. He didn't appear to be missing Aunt Bessie at all tonight.

"—So while we get another barrel rolled on down here, can y'all please give a warm Dixie Stronghold welcome to the Sullivan girls!"

Sully elbowed Wilk, rising higher on his knees to see what would come next.

Then— *"Wilkie!"* he pointed dead ahead, as a cocktail waitress in a turquoise plume headdress sashayed from view. Wilkie followed his finger, his small face becoming animated with terror.

Jack and Ulysses were sitting comfortably at a barrel table, not ten feet away. The boys tried to flatten themselves against the ground, Wilkie moaning that they hadn't yet been seen, they ought to book it, but Sully stayed stubbornly put. When he dared peek up again, he saw the feather-crowned waitress striding purposefully for their father's table with a tray in hand. Dipping into a graceful plie, she deposited two tumblers full of gleaming amber at their elbows.

"Hey!" called out a guy in line, pointing defiantly at the table. "How come they get drinks? Ain't fair!"

Coolly, the waitress flopped her feather from her eyes, addressing her naysayer. "Because, Mr. *Foley* and Mr. *Walsh* get top priority—if that's all the same to you?"

The line of thirsty onlookers burst into laughter, and the man, hunching his shoulders, muttered a churlish apology to the floor. Jack gruffly offered him his drink.

"Well, now I have to give Jackie mine!" Ulysses said loudly, "No, no, Jack—take it!" he added in a joking voice, "Consider it a thank you for being Employee of the Year since 1921!"

Uproarious laughter swept the crowd, then Sully was aware that the lights were dimming on the floor, and brightening over the bar. He heard the chatter die out and the music crank up, playing a song that was distantly familiar to him…

He peeked again, and from his dark corner, he saw his father's grinning face in a crescent of light. He recognized this look, knew that he could only be laying eyes upon his mother. Not even when Ulysses appraised the waitress in her leotard were his features so awash with pure, adoring admiration.

Sully motioned to Wilkie to follow him back out of the shadows. Wilkie obeyed, frowning at his own father. Sully looked at Jack, shocked to see his smile juxtaposed Ulysses' perfectly. Uncle Jack did not smile, not at the milkman, not at the shop clerk, not at his sons when did something that made the rest of the room titter. Sully always thought it was part of what made him scary. But there Jack was, grinning floppily as though witnessing some great miracle on stage.

Solemnly, Wilkie elbowed him. He needed to see what they couldn't from this angle, what his father was watching with such joy. They crawled across the sticky floor, staying close to the wall to avoid bumping any shins. Settling into a corner with cobwebby velvet ropes, they looked up at the stage, where all the other faces were focused.

There, bathed in light like a holy apparition, were their mothers— but oh, how they'd changed! They were not wearing the clothes they set out in, but slippy lamé dresses cut well above the knee. The mother's legs were dancing furiously—the audience loved it, Sully could tell by the way they whistled and cheered—and with their raven hair styled identically and their dance steps so in sync, Sully could barely tell Mom and Aunt Clara apart. Their dance was one Sully had seen before, many times, usually after the mothers had drank some bourbon and instructed the men to haul the furniture out of the Foleys' parlor. They danced how they did in Ireland, legs chopping the air stiffly, arms glued to their sides. At home, the rigor of their step always gave way to nostalgic laughter—sometimes his mother or Aunt Clara would even cry—talking about the dancehalls of Kilkenny, names Sully didn't know, people from his mother's life before he was born...

"There was Slugger O'Toole who was drunk as a rule, and fighting Bill Tracey from Dover," the singer sang in his corner, his nose two inches from a songbook, while a fiddler played along cheerfully, *"And your man Mick McCann from the banks of the Bann, was the skipper of the Irish Rover..."*

Sully knew this song, and so did Wilkie. Both their mothers had lulled them to sleep this tune, 'the Irish Rover.'

They watched for ten, fifteen more minutes, as their mothers switched to a more fashionable dance, shimmying their shoulders and sashaying their legs. The singer began to scat, and the crowd went bananas.

Afterwards, Samuel returned to the microphone to announce that a new barrel was here. He made a "ta-da!" gesture as two sweating men rolled it through the crowd. Everyone went wild again.

"Let's go, 'fore the lights come on again," Wilkie hissed, with a cautious glance at the stage, where the mothers stood back-to-back, beaming in their spotlight.

Sully agreed. It was one thing to have eluded their father's notice. Only divine intervention would prevent their mothers' from spotting them.

Outside in the heavy black heat, Wilkie was angry. "Samuel *lied* to me!" he stomped his feet into the gritty road, "So did Andy! People don't drink bourbon for health, they drink it so they can get *drunk*."

Sully did not answer right away. They knew what drunks were from funny filmstrips: drunks were bums, stumbling gangsters, people you laughed at and poked at with sticks.

Plus, drinking was illegal, everyone knew that. Miss March taught them about the Twenty-First Amendment in school last year. Anyone caught in possession of alcohol, she warned the class, could go to jail for up to twenty years.

"I guess Floyd G was right," Sully said dolefully, jamming his hands in his pockets. "Our daddies are crooks, Wilk."

"Don't say that," Wilkie urged him, and he walked with a carriage far more daring than he had on the way there. He held his head high, as though steeling himself to an imaginary Floyd G., or anyone else who called his father a crook.

But when school started a few weeks later, Floyd G., who was doing 5th grade again, barely paid them any mind. One day at recess, the boys' friend Joseph whispered to them that it was because Floyd was scared of them now.

"You know what your daddy did, right Wilkie?" Joseph hissed through his chapped lips. His lips were chapped because so many juicy stories passed through them. He knew everything from listening at the heating vent of his mother's bridge games.

Wilkie raised his eyebrows coolly, because he wasn't big on admitting when he didn't know something.

Joseph explained that Floyd's uncle was Jack's unlucky captive on the night of Sully and Wilkie's campout. Apparently, Jack had cut out Floyd's uncle's eyes with his army knife, telling him that the next time he dared try to come on his land, he would recognize him as the eyeless man, even if he wore his white hood.

"He's right scared of you," Joseph hissed, with some kind of awe. "He's afraid Black-Jack's gonna cut out his eyes, too. Isn't that ducky?"

"We don't call him Black-Jack," Sully said, squaring his shoulders.

Wilkie, meanwhile, remained quite serene. "You can call my Da, 'Black-Jack,'" he told Joseph, "As long as you don't call him a crook."

Chicago, 1930

In 1929, Jack was indicted on charges of unlawful possession of a gun. According to Mr. McCracken, the Foley's infallible lawyer, it was a subterfuge for the liquor trafficking arrest that Jack always managed to elude. McCracken had Jack's sentence whittled down from eleven years to eight months, using a snazzy oration designed to fit into newspaper quotes.

"They tried to throw the book at him, but Jackie caught it—and read it," McCracken brayed, to the reporters swarming the courthouse. "My client is a Trinity scholar, he's no criminal."

The case brought Jack a tremendous amount of celebrity. His face was on the front page of every newspaper from Newfoundland to New Mexico. The press didn't trouble itself to get the stories straight. In one rag, they wrote that Jack was arrested for stabbing a man who hummed, "God Save the Queen" at a urinal. Another one trumpeted that Jack had filled the Louisville water tower with bourbon. Of course, it was Jack spinning these tales for any reporter who asked, but he was always surprised to see his fables printed into facts.

Privately, Jack seared with the shame of letting himself get caught. He went to his Commander-in-Chief to issue an apology, fully expecting to be dishonorably discharged.

"Don't worry about that," Ulysses Foley assured him firmly, cupping Jack's drooping cheek the way he would do his son Sullivan's before he left to fight in World War II. "You just take care of yourself in there."

"I knew that the risks were high," Jack told Ulysses, "But the rewards were incalculably higher."

Ulysses repeated these words often while Jack was in jail. "He said he knew the risks were high, but the rewards were incalculably higher," he told the Rockefellers and DuPonts; the rich and curious who went to the cinema to experience such danger and adventure. The words helped to assuage Ulysses' guilt at seeing his best and most loyal manservant go to jail.

After Jack was released from Alcatraz, he wondered if his true punishment would be Foley's tempered faith in him. Ulysses was as jovial and brotherly as ever, but he no longer mentioned Jack owning part of his company. Jack was not miffed from a business standpoint: he was a soldier, not a businessman, and he already had more money than he ever knew existed. But there was the resonant chord of Ulysses' recruitment speech that hummed in his ear, all these years later: *What are we as men if we cannot leave something to our sons?*

Jack lamented to his good friend, Walt Zimmerman, the opportunity he had pissed away like money at a horse-track. The guys all called Walt "Egghead" because he was a whiz with numbers. He even had his own firm, Zimmerman & Co, which helped entrepreneurs like Jack to manage their money. Egghead was a pragmatic Jew who always had a funny comeback when Jack called him Shylock or Christ-killer. His friendship was silver to Ulysses Foley's gold, but it came with fine print and a 10% commission.

"If you're so eager to own American stock," Egghead preached to Jack, "*Now* is the time to buy." They were eating lunch in a diner across the street from Egghead's office in downtown Chicago. "Coca-Cola, General Electric, Colgate-Palmolive, they're all in the toilet right now."

"They could all turn out to be junkers, the way this economy is headed," Jack grumbled into his weak tea. The crash on Wall Street had cast an austere fog over the entire country. It had certainly crippled his business. People weren't going out and drinking as much, and bar-owners weren't buying his barrels.

"What have I been telling you, ya goddamn mick," Egghead mimed throttling his neck, "Those stocks are on the Dow. Steelier than Lady Liberty's tits." He added in a goading singsong, "They're as good as your precious Foley Bourbon, you can believe that."

"*Alright,*" Jack said irritably. Egghead had been after him to buy the feckin' stocks for months. When he came to visit Jack in Alcatraz, Egg gave him this same pitch. ("As if I have any paper in here but the Bible and *Ulysses,*" Jack had muttered. To him, of course, they were interchangeable).

He reached for the chubby billfold in his pocket. He never carried cash, but he had just come from collecting off his bookies at Balmoral Park.

"We'll stick with my $500 ceiling." Jack licked his thumb to begin counting it out.

"$500 each," Egghead said sternly.

"$*500 each*?" Jack echoed in scandalized tones. "T'isn't selling the fecking horse I was today, you know." With stubborn finality, he added, "I can only do one today." Because Egghead was drinking a Coke, he said, "Sign us up for the Coke, will you? All you Americans are determined to rot your teeth on it…"

Jack trusted Egghead. He was the one who encouraged Jack to buy gold and silver, because the value appreciated, while cash just stayed stagnant in a bank slot. Egg also helped him with the gambling algorithms that Jack now used to reign the horse-tracks, boxing rings, and baseball fields of Chicago and Louisville. Because of Egg, Jack now had a flourishing second income to support Clara on, while saving the ample fruits of his bourbon trafficking for his sons: Wilkie, Kilkenny, and the new babe Pearse, who was not yet baptized.

"Now, Coca-Cola comes with quarterly dividends," Egghead told Jack, draping a napkin over the rest of his egg-salad sandwich on rye. "But I advise you to not collect them." He paused, shooting the waitress a slick smile as she cleared his plate. When she left, Egg added, "Let them marinate in that secret vault of yours under the sills of Foley Bourbon."

Jack waggled his brows. Egghead was the only one of his friends who knew that he kept his private treasury at Foley Bourbon, though he didn't tell him exactly where (only Clara knew). Egg always snickered when he overheard Jack tell people that his treasure was hidden in the Caves of Kesh or Hill of Tara. Even Ulysses subscribed to a strain of mythology that Jack was wiring money to a P.O box in Kilkenny City.

"So...$500 gets me how many shares? 14?"

"13."

Jack protested, "They're $30 each, you were raving to me at Alcatraz."

"They are, but you can't forget the Egg Tax," his friend replied with a winning smile.

The waitress swished over to drop the check on them as Jack thumbed out the last of his twenties.

"Can you get this, lad?" Jack said lazily. "You've tapped me out for the day. I may yet have to hitchhike back to Kentucky."

Egg pursed his lips, reaching for his own wallet. "You know, it's the Jew who has the reputation for being cheap, when really it's the Irishman."

"T'is a fact for certain."

Egg ranted, "And the irony is, you're probably the richest man in this town," he glanced amusedly at Jack's feet, "With the shabbiest shoes."

"I like my shoes," Jack said stubbornly. They were the same ones he wore at the mill in Ireland. "Who am I trying to impress? God gives me everything I need."

As if to illustrate his point, Jack reached for his copy of *Ulysses*, automatically checking for his key in the back. It was there when they sat down 30 minutes ago, but he always liked to be sure.

After the christening of Jack and Clara's new son, Pearse Aurelius, (Pearse for Padraic, Aurelius for Jack's love of gold—and for the last good Roman emperor) Wilkie and Sully met their parents in the parlor of Foley, announcing they had something to tell them.

They lads had remained in their suits after church, in hopes of being taken more seriously. After all, they were nine and ten years old, respectively.

"I think that Wilkie should start getting paid to make the bourbon," Sully told the adults. "We think it's only fair."

"Is that so, Wilkie?" Ulysses asked, leaning forward in his armchair.

Wilkie's eyes traveled to the ground, then lifted to Ulysses' midsection. He shuffled his feet.

"Of course!" Sully answered heartily, elbowing his cousin. "We're not asking for him to get the Babe's salary, we just think he should get paid in more than just Chu-ees." He looked to the mothers, his azure eyes glowing dolefully. "Wilkie's giving up his entire childhood to make our bourbon."

The mothers dissolved into dithery sighs.

"Wait a moment," Ulysses leaned forward in his armchair. "I've been told that Wilkie's most ardent passion is bourbon distillation— "

"—it is" Wilkie said, his gaze tearing upward.

"—that he esteems his craft more highly than he does baseball or boxing matches or the fine sport of viewing pictures—"

"—I *do*— "

Ulysses continued, "—but what I'm hearing now is, what I believed to be a fine apprenticeship, and hoped would flourish into a lengthy career at Foley Bourbon, is actually an impingement upon his childhood?" Though his own blue eyes gleamed like a poker tell, his tone was the standard one used during business negotiation. It was more for Sully's education than for Wilkie's. He had taught his son to always ask for the sale, and now he was testing Sully's ability to close.

"Well," Sully replied unhesitatingly, "I think Wilk already *has* a career here, he just isn't getting paid for it." He nodded at Wilkie, who slowly pulled a notepad from his pocket. "For months now, we've been keepin' track of the hours he works, and the tasks he does."

Sully launched into their data, helped along intermittently by Wilkie, who raptly corrected him when Sully misspoke, or rustled through the notepad to find him the exact thing he was looking for.

Sully explained that his cousin worked around 25-30 hours per week, and accomplished as much in that time as any Master Distiller on the Kentucky Bourbon Trail ("including Uncle Andy!" Sully crowed, and the adults laughed). They knew this because they biked around to all the distilleries—Farley Parish, Old Barnaby, Daisy Crown, etc.—and surveyed the owners. True, the sills were closed, with padlocked chains over their warehouses, but their distillers were still happy (albeit wistful) to speak to young Messers Foley and Walsh.

"When they were still makin' bourbon, here's what they paid their Master Distillers." He passed around his little chart.

Ulysses stroked his walrus mustache, his face growing business-like again. "But Sullivan, those men are all out a job right now, so this list is moot."

"Huh?"

Ulysses explained patiently, "You're trying to draw a conclusion from comparative data that has since become obsolete. Our situation is unique, as we're the only folks making bourbon in the country." He sipped his coffee. "When you have a monopoly, like I explained to you Mr. Rockefeller has on the railroads, you get the luxury of setting the terms."

Wilkie was frowning, but Sully's eyes were shining.

"So we can say how much we oughta pay our distillers?"

"If we can decide together on a number that we both agree is fair," Ulysses agreed, his eyes shining in perfect reflection of his son's.

For a moment, they calmly stared each other down, both suppressing smiles. Clara frowned, waving a hand between them.

"Is there a no blink contest on?"

Without breaking eye contact with his father, Sully said reasonably, "Daddy told me to never say a number first!"

Ulysses chuckled. He reached into the breast pocket of his Battistoni and withdrew a pen like a bullet—possibly the same one he had used to draw the state of Kentucky for Jack in the pub ten years ago. He motioned for Sully to bring over his notepad then he carefully wrote a number down for the boys.

"How's that for the wage of Wilkie Walsh?" Ulysses asked kindly.

Wilkie's eyes widened excitedly.

"Would that be weekly or monthly?" Sully asked his father briskly.

"Weekly, Sully."

"And—and, is there taxes on it?"

"Ten year olds don't pay taxes," Ulysses smiled.

"Alright." He looked at Wilkie, who nodded furiously, blushing and looking desperate to have this all over with. "My Master Distiller accepts your offer!"

"Impressive," Jack murmured a few moments later. He was the only adult who stayed behind when the women left to check on the other children, and Uli went outdoors to crow to Andy that he had a new distiller on the payroll.

Wilkie glanced over at his father. He avoided his eyes throughout the negotiation, because he never knew how Da would react. But Jack was regarding him with the same untempered approval as he did when Wilkie read aloud the Proclamation of the Irish Republic at home. Wilkie's small chest thrummed with pride.

"Thanks!" Sully crowed, bopping up and down hyperly. "And I'm Wilkie's agent, so he said he'll give me a percentage of his first *three* paychecks!"

"I think you've earned your tithe, Sully," Jack growled. "I am also inclined to think, Wilkie, that your hard-work in this domain has earned you some restitution." Idly, he lit a match and blew it out. "Have ye heard before, byes, about the concept of restitution?"

"I haven't…" Wilkie said slowly. Sully hadn't either, but he stopped jumping around to pay attention.

"Back pay," Jack explained. He pulled a stamped certificate from his leather wallet. "I have here $250 worth of General Electric stocks, bought from Egghead. You met my friend Egghead earlier."

The boys nodded somberly, thinking of the man in the trench-coat who kept missing all the cues in church to kneel and stand. At the after-party, he pulled coins from their ears and told them his son Walt Jr. was just their age; they ought to come to Chicago and play with him.

"Right. So Wilk, I am giving you the choice," Jack continued stonily, "You can take these shares, which may well be worth millions someday—" he sensed Wilkie's mounting excitement and doused it in cold reality, "—years from now, son, maybe only after you've become a grandfather. Or they may go bankrupt, and serve only as a coaster for your tay…" he shrugged unhelpfully. "Your other choice for restitution is $250 cash. Exactly what I paid for it today."

The boys frantically exchanged a look, as if the right answer to this trick question would be written on the other's face. Wilkie opened and closed his mouth several times in a row.

"Why wouldn't he choose money?" Sully demanded suspiciously. Wilkie silently thanked him for asking the obvious question.

"Why do you think?" Jack replied, as serene as a sphinx.

"One is worth a lot right now" Wilkie said slowly. "One might be worth something, but I have to wait a long time to see…"

"The stocks are more of a gamble," Jack prompted him. "Depends on if you're a gambling man or not."

"Are you a gambling man, Da?"

"Never about war or women."

Wilkie felt like he might burst with the desire to have $250. "Can I have the money, please?" He looked to see if he got the answer right but as always, his father's face was a map with no key.

"You may, son. I'll get it to you once we're home."

Later, as Wilkie stood in his parent's bedroom holding the fat wad of bills in both hands, he had the gnawing feeling that he chose wrong.

"What's wrong, son?"

Wilkie mumbled at his father's knee that he wasn't sure about his decision.

"Fear not, son," Jack pat his head, "The stocks will go towards your inheritance."

"My what?" Wilkie squinted up at him.

"Da has his whole fortune laid aside for you lads," he explained, with all the pride of the Irish Republic gleaming in his voice, "You will inherit my treasure someday, when the time is right."

.

The Home of Seamus and Patrick Walsh
Five Miles from Zzyzyx Road
October 2014

Blaise has given me permission to gloss over Year 23 of her life. It isn't important to our storyline. For readers who desire a more complete chronology, I can tell you briefly what 23 held for her.

After graduating college and seducing Conor Walsh, Blaise left Kentucky. She worked as a sales rep for Foley Bourbon, interestingly choosing the South Bend, Indiana territory. When I asked her why, she told me in a voice of *"isn't it obvious?"* that she hoped to meet a Notre Dame quarterback with the heart of Rudy and the body of Chris Klein.

She did not, but she did have a slew of intrigues with a series of faceless businessmen, always introducing herself as Kelly McCullers. I imagine most of them still daydream about her, their souls entombed in the Hilton room where they saw her freckled sin.

The position only lasted a year. Blaise tells me she missed the creature comforts of life at Foley. I imagine it was difficult for her going from being a mermaid in an enchanted pond to a minnow in a running river. Her official statement is this: "Indiana was just NOTD."

I don't recall seeing her at all during the 2011-2012 season. However, I do remember looking up from the traffic of my life to wonder where the Jag had gone.

Okay, back to our story. We're picking up right after her 24th birthday. You're about to get all the Nicholas Sparks shit and then some. I may need a Pepto Bismal and a few millies of Ativan just to write this...

YEAR 24
Foley Bourbon
Zzyzyx Road
2012-2013
"In Which Patrick and Blaise fall in love...<3"

Chapter 9

Blaise was dying. She might already be dead. If she wasn't dead yet, she wanted her granite mausoleum ordered for a late birthday present, so she could sleep peacefully in the yard with all the other dead Foleys.

The gruel-gray November sky grated through her eyelids, blotting up the last of her birthday dreams. She opened one bloodshot eye and felt a fire-poker spear her temples. She opened the other eye and nausea crested in her stomach. Blaise leaned over the side of her baroque bed and wretched. Nothing but filmy bile came up, but she was suddenly hungry.

"*Hildieee,*" Blaise moaned, crawling out of bed and reaching for her Celine bag. As she grabbed the strap, the contents rained cruelly upon her: bronzer, tampons, flask, Tic Tacs, but of course, no goddamn Ibuprofen.

"HILDIE!" she called louder, staring at her dead girl reflection above the mirror. *What's Courtney Love doing in my room?* Her party makeup from last night was smudged like a painting left out in the rain. Her throat stung, and she remembered, with a groan, how she straddled Chef Juan last night, sucking his tongue while he cooed a Spanish song in her ear.

Blaise buzzed Hildie and George's intercom over and over, a bratty move she hadn't pulled since she had her tonsils out in 8th grade. As she waited for aid, she limply touched the birthday gifts spilled across her dresser: a crisp envelope from her uncle's law firm, endowing her with 1,000 shares to **FOLEY BOURBON;** a kilo of Swiss gold, also from Duffy; a 'HAPPY HALLOWEEN!' card from "Uncle" Jimmy Fleming, stuffed with two wrinkly twenties and some

Lucky 7 lotto tickets; a crocodile flask embossed with the Foley coat-of-arms from Daddy; a $500 Starbucks gift card from McCullers; tickets to see Lorrie Morgan at the Grand Ole Opry from Auntie Cricket; an opal necklace from Aunt Kennedy, which Blaise secretly found hideous, and a python Fendi, also from her dad, which she put on his credit card one night when he was especially drunk.

"Whatsa matter with you, girl?" Hildy grumbled predictably, filling her doorway with a frown.

"I'm *dyinggggg*."

"You hungover," Hildy corrected her, in the pitiless Alabama chaw that Blaise loved. "The way you was carrying on last night, actin' like a college girl on spring break."

Blaise felt this was an insensitive thing to say to an aging sorority queen, especially when she woke up with the worst hangover of her life.

"Thanks Hildy," Blaise dismissed her with an imperial hand, "Now can you send Georgie in please?" Sweet George would bring her an Egg McMuffin, a Venti coffee, and the entire pharmacy of CVS if she asked him to.

"Don't think you're gonna sweet-talk him!" Hildie yowled, "Georgie and me, we takin' Mommy to see Cassie and the baby," she pursed her lips in disapproval, but reflexively reached down to grab Blaise's hamper. "It'll do your poor mama good to get some fresh air."

"Give Mommy a kiss for me," Blaise managed, sounding like a wounded soldier on the battlefield, "I would, but I can't get up."

"Go next door and get Chef Juan to fix you breakfast," Hildy suggested. Then she added smugly, "He seemed pretty sweet on you last night."

Blaise smeared Ivory 10 under her hamburglar eyes and furiously brushed her teeth. She told herself that she looked "Morning After Chic," as though she spent the night before doing wild things on velvet cushions. She *felt* like a lying virgin who looked like a mugshot for a meth arrest.

"Hi boys," Blaise purred, stalking through the kitchen door of Succotash next door. The Latin kitchen boys whistled at her. Their median height was about 5'6, and most of them were married, but they were some of her favorite flirting partners.

"Slash!" Blaise cooed at Cesar.

"Axl Rose!" he whooped, throwing up his fleshy, tattooed arms. Last night, they channeled their inner Guns N' Roses by doing an impassioned duet of 'November Rain' on karaoke.

"Hola baby, how's mami feeling?"

"I feel like caca, papi!" Blaise bawled. "*Donde esta* Juan?"

"He stay home today, princess," Cesar replied, grinning in his peeled Bart Simpson t-shirt and checkered pants. "His little daughter is sick and his wife has work."

Blaise felt a spurt of guilt at the word *wife*. "Cesar, will you make me your *huervos, mi amor*? Please papi, you're the only one who does it the way I like." She lowered her voice, "And, can I buy some Oxy off you? Please, my sweet, handsome Slashy Slash." Cesar worked part-time as an EMT, and had access to any drug from Ativan to Zoloft.

Cesar whooped, "Mami is hungover from last night!" He began speaking rapido Spanish with Francisco, the fry cook, who shook head darkly at Cesar without looking over at her.

"It's not fair to speak that sexy Latin tongue when I can't understand you," Blaise pouted. Male attention was second only to eggs and opioids to getting her on the road to feeling better.

"Listen mami, you want the hangover cure?" Cesar asked bracingly, pointing his spatula at her. "The ultimate hangover cure?"

"*JES!*" Blaise cried. "Jes papi, *jes!*"

"Okay" Cesar said. He took his flip-phone out and instructed her to copy down a number. Then he eyed her shrewdly, "You won't get me in trouble, right baby?"

"For what? Giving me the number to your mechanic?" she winked gloriously at him, then bit her lip. "But I can't get the cure on an empty stomach, right papi?"

"Okay, I make you *huervos rancheros* now, mami, I know how you like them," he grinned floppily, and Blaise skipped out of the kitchen, pleased to have gotten her way, yet again.

(Editor's Note: "Little did I know," Blaise tells me now, "That Cesar was passing me along to a drug about a million times more addictive than any opioid.")

A few miles away, Pat and Seamus were at home slogging through their Saturday morning, impeded by laziness and mild hangovers. *(Editor's Note: I'll continue to refer to myself in the third person.)*

"You're not hungover enough to *deserve* an IV," Pat informed his twin, sounding judicial despite his reindeer pajama pants with the hole near the crotch. He flipped through the TV, landing on *Rudy* with a small *yes!* of triumph.

"Walsh, can I get an IV?" Matt Crummy called from the kitchen, where he was frying up eggs and bacon. "I'm not *that* hungover," he added, "But I feel like my soul drank a Gatorade after I get one."

"I know, but I only have like, ten of the saline bags left," Pat called, craning his neck towards the kitchen. "We have to ration them for serious occasions, like St. Paddy's Day or a bachelor party."

Pat worked as a volunteer EMT. He was inspired to start after Mr. Foley had gone Charleton Heston on his face in '09. The job supplied Pat with tons of gross medical stories, as well as the secret to defeating even the most goliath hangovers: an IV drip of saline.

Pat's old supervisor had gotten himself fired, but before that, he let the guys take whatever supplies they wanted. After months of drinking with superhuman imperviousness, Pat was disappointed to learn that getting more bags wouldn't be so easy. You needed a medical director's license to do it, and there was currently a nationwide shortage on saline. Thus, the track marks in the guy's arms healed, and they were back to grumpily choking down Advil to temper their Saturday morning malaise.

Pat treated those last ten bags like golden eggs. Fielding inquiries from his cousins Eems (who wanted some for the Final Four tournament) and Deebo (for a law school buddy's bachelor party in Vegas) Pat finally decided he would only give an IV to someone willing to pay a premium north of $100 per bag.

Crummy brought breakfast plates out with Pat's dog Shadow bouncing eagerly at his heels. "Rudy!" he whooped, sitting in the green velour recliner, which, like Shadow and the dining room table, were heirlooms from the lax house. "I felt like Rudy last night, all persistently buying Malibu and Diets for that Anna girl."

"Except, you didn't get into Dame," Pat remarked, plating himself the blackest bacon. He squinted thoughtfully at the TV, where Rudy was hitting on his snotty crush in her navy cardigan. "I always wonder...do you think Rudy ever got with that girl?"

Seamus rolled his eyes at Pat's ignorance, "'Course he did. After he won that Georgia Tech game, no co-ed in the Corn Belt was safe."

Pat groaned suddenly, looking down at his phone, "Who the *fuck* is 502-483-1333?"

Crummy paused, a forkful of eggs midway to his mouth, "That actually sounds mad familiar..."

"What do they want?" Seamus droned, with 3% interest.

"They called and then texted—mad aggressive—" Pat read the text aloud in a dopey voice, "*Hey! Cesar just passed your number along to me. He told me you have the ultimate hangover cure!! Are you available?? I literally feel like I'm knocking on death's door haha.*" Again Pat groaned, "How'm I supposed to say no to that?" His voice migrated from grumpy to curious, "It sounds like a girl..."

"Who's *Cesar?*" Seamus demanded, his interest spiking enough to peer over from his tattered armchair.

"He's this little Puerto Rican dude I used to EMT with," Pat explained, half amused, half annoyed. "He gives my number out to a bunch of people, then hits me up asking me for referral fees."

Crummy snickered suddenly, glancing over from his phone. "Walsh you're right, it's a girl. You're *not* gonna wanna say no." The number resounded because he had texted her on Halloween to say Happy Birthday.

Pat snorted dubiously, sinking deeper into his chair. It was a perfect Saturday, (sunny, windbreaker weather) and he woke up with the ideal hangover: the ache at his temples was *just* enough for him to have an excuse not to do yard-work, but not so crippling that he couldn't enjoy the day with his boy Rudy.

"Listen bro, I'm a lazy piece of shit right now." Pat made Shadow sit, then rewarded him with a piece of bacon. "Even if Carrie

Underwood called and told me to meet her at the Brown in 30, I'd probably make her come to me."

"Well, it's the *other* girl of your dreams" Crummy hinted. "Rhymes with Praise Holy."

Pat's hand, now shaking Shadow's paw, dropped with comic aplomb. Crummy and Shay whooped like annoying middle-schoolers, but he ignored them, picturing red tendrils whipping from the window of her Jag.

"*Absolutely! I'm free all day :)*" He answered Blaise Foley.

The guys were all business.

"Okay Walsh, this is your *only* chance to be alone with her," Crummy said, with the stern grizzle of a football coach to his star quarterback. "This is Rudy getting paged to the field."

Pat nodded faintly, looking between the two of them. "So what do I do?" he asked, slightly desperately. *If she sees me coming and drives off*, he thought, *I might have to kill myself.*

As if reading his mind, Crummy advised, "For one, *don't* take your car. She'll recognize it."

"So *not* my Biscayne, either," Seamus said.

"So what am I driving up in?" Pat asked wildly. "A ten-speed?"

"My car," Crummy said smartly, tossing him the keys to his prized Rubicon. "When you're done giving her the IV, tell her she needs to eat *immediately* after. Then, insist on taking her out for lunch."

"And then, I pay—of course" Pat grinned.

Crummy nodded wisely, "Tell her it's a belated birthday present. She'll love that you remembered."

Pat dashed upstairs to shower and put on his best Lacoste. He traipsed downstairs twenty minutes later in a plume of good cologne, a look of apprehension on his handsome face. "Crums, are you *sure* she doesn't have a boyfriend?" he asked. He felt like he was too old and weary to start a new season of the Pining for Foley show.

Crummy dug up his recent conversation with Blaise, reading aloud in imitation of her dramatic, tinsel-y voice, "*I've been well! I just moved home from Indiana, so over it. Ugh, the boys are treating me well...wait, by boys you meant my brother and my dentist—right??*"

"Aw" Pat smiled to himself and zipped his jacket. There was a saline bag peeping out of the pocket.

"Make us proud, son!" Seamus bellowed, giving him a salute. "I can't believe my bro is finally off to penetrate Blaise Foley!"

"If you come back in the next hour," Crummy warned him, "We're not letting you in."

Blaise shivered, despite the heated leather seats of her Dad's Bentley. She decided to drive the Bentley to fetch her drugs, reasoning that if Cesar's friend turned out to be a murderer, he would at least try to command a ransom for her first. She also brought pepper-spray, leftover from the 'Sigma Kappa Kares' event against Student Sexual Assault.

Blaise pulled down the visor to wince at her reflexion. *My hair looks like a sweat-matted merkin*, she thought, fluffing her red-velvet roots. It didn't boost her morale to think that she was parked in a field waiting for a Latin pill pusher. She knew Oxycotin was bad, not a drug to be trifled with, but she was desperate. The only word inside her brain was *death,* and pain and nausea were taking turns erupting inside her body.

Cesar's friend texted to say he'd be at the field in two minutes, with a :). *He's a friendly sort of drug dealer*, she thought. *What's your name by the way?* she asked him. It would make her feel less sketchy if she knew who was meeting her.

"*Pat,*" he replied, surprising her. *It must be short for Patricio,* she thought vaguely, just as a big Jeep-y car cruised down the dirt road towards her. It had to be him. She reached for her new Fendi, which had Uncle Jimmy's birthday twenties inside, along with the pepper spray.

But the Rubicon sidled up to her, the window rolled down, and life plum stopped making sense.

"Hey Blaise, what's up?" Pat Walsh grinned shyly, leaning far over his passenger's seat to see her.

Blaise positively stared at him. "*You're* the Hangover Cure?" she blurted out.

Pat laughed, "I guess that's my unofficial DBA." He motioned for her to get in his car. Numbly, Blaise obeyed, the backs of her bare thighs giving her a tart ouch as they came unstuck from the leather seat.

"You sell *drugs*?" Blaise asked him warily, feeling deceived on two fronts. He always seemed Disney Prince perfect to her.

"What? *Nooo.*" When Pat smiled, dimples poked up below his chiseled cheeks. Blaise peeked at his scar, still pink and whelky as ever, the only ugly spot on his face. "You *buy* drugs?"

Without waiting for her to sputter some kind of horrified, righteous answer, he went on, "Here, hold out your arm."

Blaise clenched her arm to her side protectively. "Why, what are you going to do to it?"

"I'm going to give you a hydration IV," Pat murmured, looking straight into her eyes. "*That's* the hangover cure."

Stubbornly, Blaise kept her arm to herself. "I've never heard of it."

Patiently, Pat explained the process to her, letting her touch his sterilized needle, the catheter, and the saline bag. He assured her that he was a trained EMT, and would not (as she put it) let an air bubble go through her veins and kill her.

"Alright," Blaise said finally, extending her arm with very little confidence. When Pat approached her with the needle, she instinctively recoiled. "I'm sorry!" she bawled into his seatbelt. "I just turned 24, *I don't want to die!*"

"I know, on Halloween…Happy Belated," Pat said, in his quiet voice. He looked somewhat amused. "Listen, if you don't want an IV, you don't *have* to get one. But it *will* make you feel 100 times better, especially if you're, ah, knock-knock-knocking on the Devil's door, or whatever it was you said." His eyes were laughing at her, but not unkindly so, Blaise felt. It didn't even occur to her to warn him that she had pepper-spray.

"If it starts to go wrong, do you promise to take me to the hospital?" she breathed.

"It won't," Pat assured her, "But of course, I swear to God on Black-Jack's grave, no crosses count." He held his hand over the little gator on his breast.

"McCullers and I always used to swear on Black-Jack's grave," Blaise said absently. She looked into his kind, gentle eyes and decided to trust him. Patrick would not try to kill her on purpose.

"So this is an interesting racket that you're in!" Blaise said tensely. The needle was stabbed in her periwinkle vein, and she had to fight all urge to stare at it.

"Yeah," Pat agreed, holding her ivory forearm steady over the armrest. "I just started doing it for my brothers, and they told a few people..." he squinted at her, as she thumbed keys on her phone, "Did you just google, "Can you die from an IV gone wrong?'"

Blaise gave him an arrested look. "I'm sorry! I'm worried about the air bubble!"

Pat began asking her survey questions to distract her. It worked. Plus, now he knew that her favorite flower were sunflowers and her favorite food, Tennessee barbecue.

"Are you feeling any better?" he asked, after the saline bag was almost fully emptied into her vein.

"*Omigod!* Yes!" Blaise exclaimed, finally pausing to notice. "I'm not having those like, contractions of pain and nausea! Wow Pat— thanks!" she gave him a brief smile—the first of his life—and he felt like he just drank a quart of warm broth. *I have nine more, in case you ever need,* he almost blurted out.

"But you *do* need to eat immediately afterwards," Pat said, in a tone of Doctor's Orders. "We can just go to Stella's diner." Casually, he thumbed over his shoulder. "It's only a couple miles down the road."

"Okay," Blaise said hesitatingly, "Are you scared to be seen with me in public?"

"Nope," he smiled. Unconsciously, she fluffed her hair.

"But what if we're spotted?" Blaise asked, in a borderline coquettish voice.

"Well then," Pat winked, "I'd just have to pretend to be Seamus and let him take the heat."

Something about squashing Blaise's hangover had warmed her to him, Pat thought. Instead of sending her usual vibrations of rage and disgust, she was now acting well...normal. The lively spirit he saw in pictures and videos was coming through to him too.

"Can we get a booth alllllll the way in the back?" she asked the elderly host at Stella's, who was still hunched over when he rose from his post. He obligingly led them to what Blaise declared in a whisper was, "the table of Forbidden Friendship."

Pat accepted her frothy apology when they slid in and her naked shins bumped his. He only wished all their limbs were uncovered and pressed against each other.

"I'll bet Captain Scurvy thinks we're having an affair," Pat murmured, jutting his cleft chin at the old maitre d' as he hobbled away.

"Let's just hope he doesn't call TMZ," Blaise raised her eyebrows. Then she smiled very sincerely. "I feel *so* much better, Pat. Honestly, I can't thank you enough."

"Happy to help," Pat replied, all nonchalance. When she cast her eyes on him, he felt the sun come out and touch every part of him.

They ordered, Pat opting for his usual garbage omelet with home fries. Blaise went for a Greek omelet, rattling off six modifications. "And can I get a side of fries with that instead of toast?" she asked the waitress direly, "My body is just *screaming* for starch."

The waitress laughed and nodded, and Blaise thanked her in an automated trill. Pat thought that she seemed very much used to getting what she wanted. He liked it. *I'd give her whatever she wanted.*

"So, how did you get this goddawful hangover?" Pat asked, after the waitress stuck her pen behind her ear and bounced away.

"I wasn't impaled by my own sword, if that's what you're asking," Blaise said. "It was my birthday party last night. I was drinking bourbon, *of course*, but the kitchen boys at Succotash had me doing tequila shots."

"Ouch," Pat gave a low whistle. "Kentucky doesn't border Mexico for a reason."

"Exactly" she smiled, adding Splenda to her coffee.

"I'm a little jealous that my boy Cesar was invited and I wasn't." Pat grasped his chest, pretending to look wounded.

"Well, you tried to crash my 21st," Blaise stirred her coffee with her brows raised. "That didn't turn out so well, now did it?"

"Oh it turned out fine," Pat said dismissively. "I like my scar. I tell people I got it in prison, no one messes with me." As Blaise giggled some more, Pat added while looking away pointedly, "Of course, it would have turned out better if I got in to see you…"

She sobered up at once. *Is he hitting on me?* It was one thing for them to speak *"la lingua de los ojos"* as Juan used to call his and Blaise's unspoken attraction, but it was quite another for him to outright act like they were on some OKCupid date.

"What did you get for your birthday?" Pat asked her.

"Oh, the usual spread," Blaise shrugged casually, "Cash from my so-called Uncle Jimmy Fleming, and a card asking me to dig up the distillery to look for his father's bones—"

Pat raised his eyebrows, "Hey, that's not a bad idea. We can find my great-grandpa's treasure while we're at it and run off to Fiji together."

"—Uh" Blaise chose to breeze over this, "I also got shares to my family's distillery," she shrugged modestly. "But I get those every year."

The waitress returned with their food, cautioning that the plates were very hot.

"Thank you," Pat said. He looked at Blaise, "I've got some shares to Foley Bourbon myself, ya know."

"How could you?" she blurted out. "Foley isn't not a publicly-traded company. There's no way." The only people who had Foley shares were people with the last name Foley. Everyone knew that.

Pat grinned. "Tell that to the hundy thou I've got at home…"

"A hundred thousand shares?" Blaise breathed. "That's 10% of the company." It was more shares than she, *the Foley heiress*, had by her 24th birthday. "Pat, you're kidding…"

"Nope." He was enjoying this. He had actually fantasized about wowing her with this info.

"How is that possible?"

Pat signaled to Blaise to "hold on" while he flagged the waitress down for some hot sauce. This was done just to torment her a bit, and it worked.

"Well," he said finally, gazing into her eager face, "Remember how, after the trial of the century, the Judge awarded my Grandpa Wilkie shares to Foley?"

"I knew he was suing for shares, but I thought he got a cash settlement!"

"He was offered a choice," Pat corrected her, "But the shares were more meaningful to him, so he took those instead. So, when us grandkids came along, he wanted to pass them down to one of us. But he gave us a test to find out which grandson was most worthy." He grinned winningly.

"And you passed?" Blaise whispered.

"Yup. It was May 1994, the day of my First Holy Communion" he sauced his omelet, nodding. "I remember like it was yesterday…"

"Patrick? May I speak with you out back?" Grandpa Wilkie asked.

8-year-old Pat nodded, following Grampy out of the kitchen of his parent's house. Seamus tried to follow them, but Grandpa gently told him to stay behind.

Grandpa took him for a walk around the rickhouses, telling him all about his quarrel with the Foleys. He explained how he made their bourbon from the time he was 7, then left the company when he was 50. He said he fought tooth-and-nail to own a part of Foley, because to say it wasn't his would be like saying his heart didn't belong to him.

That's why I'm not allowed on the field trip to Foley Bourbon, *Pat realized.*

Grandpa was still wearing his Sunday suspenders and jacket, and Pat had on his frilly five-piece suit. The May sun was hot, and both of their dark heads were sweating at the temples by the time they reached Black-Jack and Clara's graves, where the hedges ended. Grandpa paused to touch his parent's headstones and say a silent prayer.

"You've reached the age of reason, Patrick," Grandpa told him. "Do you understand what that means?"

"It means that I'm now morally responsible for my actions," Pat answered readily. "And now I can go to Confession."

"In our faith, that is what it means," Wilkie agreed. "But for me, seven was a significant age, because it was then that I chose my life's path. Now, your parents would argue that you're too young to

make the decision I'm about to present you with, but I believe eight is just old enough. You understand me, Patrick?"

Pat nodded solemnly, though he had no clue what Grampy was going on about.

"I've offered this to your brothers, Killian and Conchobar," Wilkie said to the sky, "And your cousins communioned before you. And now your twin, too." He pulled a money clip from his pocket. "You can either have $250 to do whatever you please, or you can have Grampy's shares to Foley. 10% of the company."

From where they stood, Foley Bourbon was just visible. Pat peered around the hedges, admiring Foley's stately rickhouse and the beautiful castle of a house. Grandpa yanked him back, warning that he was crossing the property line.

"How much are the shares worth?" Pat asked breathlessly. He knew $250 was a lot of money, but it wasn't even close to $1 Million. Foley was everywhere: he saw it on billboards, in grocery stores, and TV commercials. It had to be worth more than a million dollars. Patrick had not learned percentages yet, or times tables, but he understood that a tenth was equal to one finger on both hands. Even one finger's worth of Foley just had to be about the salary of Bill Gates or Michael Jordan for a year.

Wilkie answered, "The shares are all at once priceless and worthless. If we could sell them Pato, they'd be a greater value than your great-grandfather's missing treasure." Respectfully, he inclined his salt-and-pepper head towards his parent's headstones.

Pat gasped. Black-Jack's treasure was like, a million bajillion dollars!

"How could we sell them?" he asked Grampy keenly.

"Patrick, there is a very, very slim chance of that ever happening," Grampy told him sternly, "If the company ever sold, then yes, but that distillery has sat right there," he pointed a gnarled finger down the hill, "Since the year of our Lord 1788. It's the same age of the U.S Constitution. Foleys' don't sell, they survive."

"Oh…" Pat said.

Seeming to sense how excited, then crestfallen, his speech had made Pat, Wilkie added in a more tender voice, "I just want you to be armed with all the facts, Pato." He pointed down below at a pretty, red-haired woman clicking into the house with a toddler in her arms. "Maybe you'll become friends with Sullivan's grandson someday, and he'll agree to buy them off you." Wilkie's face darkened, "But it will never happen while his father John is alive."

From the Walsh side, Pat heard the screen door fling open. His big brother Conor hollered into the yard, "GRAMPY! PATO! Mom said come inside, we're having cake!"

"Start without us!" Grandpa called back, and the door thwacked shut. Then softly, "Take your time, Patrick."

Pat realized he had to decide right then, there in his uncomfortable shoes. This was way harder than picking chocolate or strawberry milk at lunch, which was about the only decision to be made in his 7-year-old life.

"Seamus chose money?" he asked.

"Seamus is now $250 richer," Grandpa Wilkie answered calmly. "And I'm going to give him a keepsake of my father's, like I did for Conchobar."

"Conor has Black-Jack's pistol," Pat breathed at once. Conor kept it in a cigar box and charged kids from school $1 to hold it. It was unloaded, of course, but Conor told everyone it wasn't.

"My father John's pistol, yes," Grampy said primly, as if referring to Jack by his gangster name at his grave was a show of disrespect. "And I gave Killian the recipe to Foley's bourbon, but told him if he shared that with anyone, I would never let him become my Master Distiller."

Pat thought hard. Whatever Seamus bought with his new fortune—a Gameboy, Nintendo—he would share with Pat. He reasoned, someday when I'm grown up and have a job, I will have $250 every week. But I will never, ever again get to own 10% of a huge company who's also my family's enemy.

With one last look of longing at the crisp green bills in Grandpa's hand, Pat said with finality, "I'll take the shares, Grampy. Thank you."

Apparently, this was the right answer, because Grandpa yippie'd and clapped Pat's shoulder so hard his little knees buckled. Wilkie had tears in his eyes, which was embarrassing but not uncommon (at the church ceremony earlier, he had openly bawled into Mrs. Walsh's hankie, who told him afterwards to keep it).

"Do I get something of Black-Jack's too?" Pat asked hopefully. It would be so cool to bring, say, his army knife for show-and-tell.

"The shares are gift enough, Pato," Wilkie said kindly, guiding Pat into the house, where Mrs. Walsh cut them each pieces of the buttercream cross cake.

"Wow," Blaise said, when Pat finished his tale. "I still can't believe it."

"Yeah," Pat recalled vividly how his brother Conor, his older cousins Eems, Slaw Jaw, Deebo, Falco, all of them had sneered at Pat for being so dumb, choosing a piece of old paper over cash. The big boys boasted about all the things they bought with their $250. His Grandpa told him to store the certificate of shares in a safe place, so he kept them hidden in his saxophone case, behind his practice folder. After a few weeks, his family forgot about them, and Pat didn't remind them, but he peeked in on his shares once a week, then once a month, all the way up through last Thursday.

"That's when I started getting obsessed with stocks," Pat chuckled admittedly, "And business. I even had business cards made that said I was a philanthropic capitalist. And for Christmas, I asked my parents for subscriptions to *Fortune* and *Entrepreneur* magazine."

"Wow" Blaise said admiringly. "It sounds like your grandfather really marked you guys."

"Hmm?"

"Well, he gave Killian our mash-bill—which *I* don't even know— and now he's the Master Distiller. He gave Conor"—Blaise shivered in revulsion— "the pistol, now he's a cop. He gave you the shares, and now—don't you work at a Big Four firm?"

"KPMG," Pat threw her a daring wink, "Look at you keeping tabs on me, Foley." Before Blaise could object, he continued thoughtfully, "You're right though, I never thought of it like that. Our Grandpa gave Seamus Black-Jack's copy of *Ulysses*, and Seamus is a writer now. Well," he shrugged, "I mean, he wants to be."

"*Ulysses* with the secret compartment in the back?" Blaise said excitedly. She couldn't stop herself, "I have the key to Black-Jack's treasure!"

"Really?"

"Yeah! It fell out of Jack's pocket the night he was shot. My great-grandma Deirdre picked it up and brought it back to Kentucky."

She could not believe she told Pat this. When Blaise was a teenager, she opposed her dad's habit of taking Jack's key from the safe to show off for his Derby buddies. She feared that word would get out that they had the key, and like Black-Jack and Clara, become a target for robbers. (Plus, she had just read *In Cold Blood* in AP English, and didn't want to go down like Nancy Clutter). Blaise took the key and put it back in Deirdre's jewelry box, (now Blaise's) where it was discovered after Deirdre died in 1990. *The key to Jack's heart*, said the note under it. According to the Foleys, Deirdre had never told anyone that she had Jack's key.

"Don't tell anyone," Blaise added, taking a mousy bite of omelet.

Pat mimed zipping up his lips. "I'd like to see that sometime," he said, eyeing her. "When are you having me over?"

She raised her brows at him sternly. "You and I can call a truce," she said, "But my daddy still doesn't like you, Walshie, so you still can't come over."

In the moment, Pat gave about -5 quintillion fucks about John-boy. "I like when you call me Walshie," he told her, watching her openly with his infinite eyes.

Usually when a boy looked at her like this, Blaise felt power and triumph. In Pat's adoring gaze, she felt like she was struggling against a rising tide.

"My Grandpa still calls you Kelly," Pat told her, looking at the desert cooler. "Or Sullivan's girly. I think he has your birth announcement saved." He was nervous that came out sounding a little too Buffalo Bill, but blessedly, she nodded.

"They were very good friends." Blaise saw in her mind the picture from Sullivan's wedding day at the Brown Hotel, early 50s, the one that lived in an old sewing tin of Nana Sabina's. Her Grandpa Sully, so handsome in his tux, his face alive with laughter, with his arm slung around a gangly Wilkie. Wilkie wore a carnation in the button-hole of his tux, Sullivan had a rocks glass in hand. The two friends weren't looking at the camera, which like so many of their pictures, seemed to Blaise an intrusion. On the back is written in familiar cursive, *Walshie, my Best Man today and every other day.*

Blaise and Pat fell awkwardly silent.

"Uh so," Pat wildly grabbed at something. "Why did you change your name to Blaise from Kelly, anyway?"

"Oh," Blaise laughed, recounting the familiar story. How her daddy nicknamed her 'Blaise' after the another Foley heiress, who was born in the throes of the Civil War. How, even as a preschooler, she had not wanted to learn to write the name Kelly, only BLAISE, over and over in vibrant Crayola. "So, when *I* turned 7," she said proudly, "I took Blaise as my Communion name. Kelly Rhiannon *Blaise* Foley. Never again let anyone call me Kelly."

Pat dribbled some hot sauce on his lap. Smartly, Blaise whipped a few napkins from the dispenser and handed them to him. He thanked her, thinking that his ex Palmer wouldn't have done that on an anniversary dinner.

"Rhiannon's your middle name?" he wiped his jeans, "Where'd they get that?"

"My mom," Blaise sighed wistfully. "She loved Fleetwood. Stevie Nicks wrote the song Rhiannon about the Welsh witch. My mom wanted me to have a witchy name because, ya know," she gestured to the fake cobwebs on the window-sill, "Born on Halloween."

"I like Fleetwood Mac," Pat murmured, "I'll have to look that one up."

"So Pat, weren't you dating someone in my sorority?" Blaise said foggily. "Someone maybe a couple pledge classes ahead of me?" She knew damn well it was Palmer Desjardins, the blonde from Alabama with the Kate Hudson smile.

"I *was*," Pat said ruefully. "Palmer Desjardins," he pronounced her name phonetically, not the French way, which Blaise found funny. "She moved back to Mobile in July."

"Really? I thought she was slated to become the next Mrs. Walsh."

Pat groaned, "That's actually one of the reasons we broke up. She was always on me to propose. But I had signs from pretty early on that she wasn't, you know," he smiled faintly, "my Forever Babe."

Blaise's heart pounded; she craved to know the signs, but then a stronger version of herself came down and ground it out with her heel.

"Do y'uns want your check?" the waitress asked, shuffling over to clear their plates.

"Yeah," Pat forked over his credit card, "Can you put it on this, please?"

"No, Pat!" Blaise pleaded. "You already didn't let me pay for my IV!"

"That's right," He pressed the card firmly in the waitress's hand. "Because, how would Uncle Jimmy feel if he knew that his birthday money was going into a Walsh's pockets?"

She giggled. "But if you're getting my lunch, it's like we're on a date."

Pat unwrapped a peppermint candy with his teeth. Then he gave a lazy, sexy shrug as if to say, *oh well.* Her stomach felt plunged in seltzer.

The waitress returned with his credit card slip, beaming shyly. "Are you Walsh, as in the bourbon?"

"He sure is!" Blaise trumpeted, "Are you a fan?"

The waitress nodded stoutly, announcing that she had just picked up a jug of the straight rye, which she liked to use in hot toddies. She hesitated, then asked, "Did you guys ever find Black-Jack's treasure?"

Pat looked amused and unsurprised. Clearly, he fielded this question often.

"Ma'am, if we had found it, we'd be paying for lunch with silver bullion."

He drove her through the teeny town of Moravia, vaguely pointing out the house where Killian lived, a former church which he had rehabbed himself. Blaise listened, noticing how the browning pastures were suddenly artful instead of ugly. Neither of them would remember in an hour what they talked about.

He drove her down the muddy embankment to Mr. Foley's car and peered her straight in the face. He no longer looked playful.

"It was good to finally hang with you."

Blaise agreed with Foley dignity, "It was better than a hangover."

Pat desperately wanted to kiss her there in the open field, but he didn't want to ruin everything.

"Alright, well, I'm gonna want to see you again. Is that okay?" he asked her.

"It's a strong possibility," she replied, smiling.

The radio played them no songs, but the digital clock reported that three hours had dissolved between their fingers.

Hours later, Pat laid fully-clothed in bed. The day was dimming, but he made no move to turn on his lamp. He wanted the darkness to come and ebb away the seams of his jeans and the lines of his room. He did not need sight right now.

He heard Seamus come home, and willed his twin to leave him alone. Pat felt like he just spent hours walking in nature, his soul humming against the earth's core. Any talking would disrupt this wonderful sense of inner peace.

On his computer, the music stopped. Pat restarted the song, let the haunting opening bars crash over him:

Rhiannon rings like a bell in the night, and wouldn't you love to love her?

In the darkroom of his brain, fresh snapshots of Blaise were forming. He admired them, the powdery blue vein he pricked, her freckles, the sapphire orbs that had widened and smiled for him. He thought of that soft pink mouth, imagining it dissolving hotly into his. Everything below his belly-button was electrocuted with desire.

Predictably, Seamus thundered upstairs. "PATO! You best not be touching your uh-oh spot!" he hurled open Pat's door and dropped his gym bag. He was wearing a green ARMY tee and his Iraq Veteran hat.

"Were you, by any chance, in the military?" Pat said, by way of greeting.

"Why are you just sitting in the dark listening to random-ass music?" Seamus jammed a carrot in his mouth, "What *is* this shit, Linda Rondstat?"

"It's Stevie Nicks" Pat differed, leaning forward and hitting pause. He was in no mood to explain.

"Why, Foley likes her?" Seamus demanded. He was as ravenously curious as Pat was, still viewing her as a Share Girl.

Pat ignored the question, "Shay, do you remember what I said the first night we met her?"

"You said, 'Take me to the ER, I think my jawbone's broke—and for once Crummy's cock isn't to blame.'"

Pat sighed. "No, before her dad shot me," he said patiently, "What did I say about Foley?"

Seamus flopped onto Pat's bed. "I dunno dude, I was going through blunts like concubines that night. I think you said that you'd still rather make love to KPMG, but you *might* let Foley hold your hand."

Pat let the night come back to him. He let himself be 23 again, saw his unscarred face in the bathroom mirror.

I feel like if I don't marry her, I'll kill myself.

Really it had never died, just lain dormant for a while.

"The way I saw it, it was your Black Jack-meets-Clara moment," Seamus offered, sitting up. "Remember what he wrote about seeing her dance?"

Pat said that he did not.

"Well, where's your book?" Seamus scanned his twin's bookshelf for *Kilkenny-Kentucky*. "You have *the Art of the Deal* but you don't have Jack's memoir?"

"Why would I need it," Pat muttered, "You own seventeen copies." He didn't tell Shay about Blaise having Black-Jack's key, because he would probably soil himself from excitement.

Seamus went to his dungeon to fetch one of the copies. He returned and began reading aloud:

"The first night I saw Clara Sullivan dance was my Genesis.
There was a dance recital at Kilcooley School, in our home-town of Kilkenny City. My Mam had sewn Clara's costume herself and

pointed out her to me onstage. She was a true daughter of Hibernia, but with raven hair like mine. She wore the same green regalia as the other dancers, but to me they were wrens swarming a lovely black swan. My Mam whispered that Clara could be my sister, which made my magnetic pull to her feel somewhat illicit. I felt that she was Hera and I, Zeus, a brother and sister and the progenitors of an entire blessed universe.

In matters of war, I valued prudence above bravery, for bravery is often rash behavior which is compensated for with medals. ("SO true" Seamus moaned, and Pat rolled his eyes). At twenty-five, I assumed I would be prudent about choosing my wife. I would seek a pretty, clever girl from a good family and evaluate her with all the sentimentality of choosing a new knife. When I saw my Clara, there was no evaluation. Were she a prostitute or Protestant, nothing could disrupt my belief that she was the best girl in the world. When her eyes found mine, I knew she was the sun, and I would rise by her all the days of my life.

I asked her round for tea, and a while later, I asked her to marry me. She is my lovely, faithful, kind girl, the mother of my sons, and the keeper of my key.

I have advised my boys to not make an offer of marriage until they feel this special way. "Wait until you're 60, if you must," I tell them. For I do believe it is an event that occurs once a lifetime, but only to those who pay attention.

When Seamus finished, Pat was grinning at the ceiling. "Who knew the Irish Ripper was such a romantic?" he said.

Seamus smacked the book closed. "That's *never* happening for me," he complained hotly, "I have *never* looked into a girl's eyes and felt she was the sun."

"Well, stop hanging with old vets and get on OKCupid, man."

Seamus shrugged. "So?" he leered at Pat with savage expectation. "Is Foley your sun, or what?"

Pat hit play on Rhiannon. "James, don't talk, there's a song in progress."

"Stop pussy-dicking around."

Pat sat up. "Of course she's the sun. If she wanted our house, we'd be sleeping in a tent tonight. If I don't marry her, I'll kill myself. *You* know that."

Seamus gave a low whistle. After a respectful moment for Pat's apotheosis, he asked, "*Sooo...*how are you gonna get her?"

"I'm gonna need your help with that," Pat admitted, "But not tonight."

Seamus nodded readily. "We'll go over the Rue St. Dennis playbook. You have to be the best she's ever had." He sprang up, gaining momentum, "Tomorrow, you invite her over, you put some Mornay sauce on her box, and eat it like a champ."

Pat shook his head firmly, "I'm not sending her so much as a wink Emoji at first," he said, "I want to build the trust."

With that, he kicked Seamus out of his room.

The song was finished, so Pat replayed it, laying down and giving himself over to Rhiannon's eerie spell:

Would you stay if she offered you heaven?
Will you ever win?

Texts from Monday

Pat (10:37): Foley
Blaise (10:41): Walshieeee
Pat (10:42): haha how's your Mondee
Blaise (10:45): Just another Manic Monday here on Zzyzyx!! Ugh this fecking rain put the kibosh on my tennis game tho. How's yours!?
Pat (10:46): Oh just slayin' the game here at Klynveld Peat Barwick Goerdeler :-D.
Blaise: (10:49) Oh is that KPMG to us plebs?! hehe
Pat (10:51): Hehe yesss...do you play tennis every day?
Blaise (10:56) Only on days that Karl my instructor can drag me out of bed!!

Blaise (10:57) He's black and German…soo when he's mean to me, I call him Milli-Vanilli.

Pat: (10:59) Haha does he give you commands in German?

Blaise: (11:04) yes! His favorite one "Schell schnell!" It's like living in a Holocaust movie :-D

Pat: (11:06) sounds intimidating!

Blaise: (11:08) Do you want his card? >:-D

Pat: (11:10) I could stand to learn the game of tennis. But would you play against me? Or do you not deal with amateurs?

Blaise: (11:14) Of course I would! :)

Pat: (11:17) Thanksss. I'll teach you lax if you want. It's like Canadian tennis

Blaise: (11:25) HAHA yes! But I hear there are some variations between boys and girl's lacrosse!

Pat: (11:28) Oh no, I would teach you men's lacrosse. You seem like you could body-check someone

Blaise: (11:31) I do!? Why is that!

Pat: (11:33) Because I can tell you're strong. ;)

Blaise: (11:35) Wowww. Very perceptive of you!! :D

Pat: (11:37) Yeah I like it.

Wednesday

Pat: (2:34) Foleyyy

Blaise: (2:40) haha Walshieee

Pat: (2:45) Did I mention you that I like when you call me that? :)

Blaise: (2:53) Yes!! Walsh how do you have all this time to text if you're at a real job?

Pat: (2:58) I'm making time. Plus I'm working from home rn.

Blaise: (3:15) Soo that means you're in your jammies watching *the Price is Right*?

Pat: (3:20) I was but now we're coming up on Dr. Phil hour.

Blaise: (3:24) What do you watch between them? *Guiding Light*?

Pat: (3:27) *Guiding Light, Bold and the Beautiful, Young and the Restless*, I go right on down the line.
Blaise: (3:36) How do you keep track of all the storylines??
Pat: (3:41) I write a recap of each episode in a little notebook. Then I make predictions of how it's all gonna turn out.
Blaise: (3:47) So do you think the baby is Reginald or Stefano's?
Pat: (3:54) I think it is Stefano's identical twin Eugenio's. Which sucks because the paternity test is gonna be inconclusive. :(
Blaise: (3:59) Hahahaha
Blaise: (4:00) Wow I just realized…someday when you have kids, you and Seamus would both pass a paternity test cause you have the same DNA!! That's kinda cool.
Pat: (4:04) Yeah…he'd probably rig his in court so that I end paying his child support lol
Pat: (4:06) Jk, he'll be a great Dad someday

(Pat had to add this last because Seamus, who was receiving regular screenshots, squawked his outrage over such a defamation of character. "*Of course* I'll be a great dad," he said nobly, "I fully plan on getting a female MMA fighter pregnant in the next five years. And then at 50, when I'm living like Salinger in a secluded cabin, I'll get my vasectomy reversed to inseminate my child bride. Did you her that??")

Friday

Pat: (10:06) Foley, did I just see the Jag whip down Zzyzyx?
Blaise: (10:09) Hahaha yesss.
Blaise: (10:10) Don't tell me that Officer Walsh is gonna come ticket me!
Pat: (10:13) He transferred departments. You're safe ;)
Pat: (10:13) Where are you headed?
Blaise: (10:16) Oh that explains why i haven't been pulled over in a minute! i thought that maybe after a year in Indiana, he forgot what my car looked like!

Blaise: (10:18) You're home tonight?? I'm bound for the grocery store!

Pat: (10:20) Yeahh my Mom lured us home for dinner with chuck roast

Pat: (10:21) I need a few provisions myself. Maybe I should join you.

Blaise: (10:25) Haha okay

Pat: (10:28) That alright? I mean, my cupboards are bare, I'm having to forage for food at my parent's...

Blaise: (10:31) Yeah it's good! But it is public domain...maybe you should wear a disguise haha. I would slip into my pink wig, but I already left

Pat: (10:35) Hmm...I have a Joe Dirt wig that I glued into a trucker hat for Halloween. How about that?

Blaise: (10:38) omg yes! Add some sunglasses for good measure! :) HAHA.

Blaise: (10:42) Not that I'd be ashamed to be seen with you, it's just...awkward questions :-X

Pat: (10:44) No I get it. Just hope you're not ashamed to be seen with Joe Dirt in Ray-Bans

Pat: (10:46) You're going to Kroeger, right?

Blaise: (10:48) Yes how did you know!?

Pat: (10:50) Because the other stores are closed and ValuMarket doesn't seem your speed ;)

Pat: (10:52) Be there in 10

Blaise: (10:54) Alright Walsh I'll meet you in the candy aisle

In the desolate parking lot, under the hazy glow of street lamps, with grocery bags looped uncomfortably over his wrists, Pat was fully positioned to kiss her. But then, his nylon wig slipped off, she laughed, the moment skidded forward, and Blaise was flinging a carefree, "Bye Walsh!" from her car.

Her indifference was an illness that kept him up until four a.m. that night. At several points, he thought about driving to his parent's house just to stare up at her bedroom from his yard.

Being in love with Blaise Foley was the worst case of bipolar. Whenever his phone lit up with "Rhiannon," he puffed the opium pipe of euphoria. It was the happiness of a dog laying in the sun, untethered from mind and unaware that it could ever end.

But if Pat texted her something too sweet, Blaise might stop responding cold. Or he would make some hopeful prod at seeing her again, and she would text, "*haha maybe!*" or (ugh) "*yeahh we'll see!!*" Then everything about life felt brittle and senseless.

In moments of sober clarity, Pat realized it was happening again, his old sickness metastasized.

If Blaise didn't like him, that was fine (*no it's not! Ugh Blaise just like me I'll do whatever you want*). But he couldn't spend six months trying to figure it out (*yes, I could. If you told me to call you in five years, I think that even if I were married by then, I still would*). He didn't need Foley fucking Fever to ruin his pursuit of other girls, thanks. (*Foley, I would rather be at the DMV with you than in Aruba with any other girl, except maybe Carrie Underwood, but I would take you to Aruba over her. I could talk to you about mildew, and it would feel so meaningful, I'd swear our souls were fucking in three past lives*). He just needed to know, once and for all, where she stood.

On Thanksgiving, Blaise texted him 'HAPPY THANKSGIVING!!!' by ten a.m., which zapped away his Drinksgiving hangover at once. They exchanged benign, candied details of their Turkey Day plans like strangers on a bus. Pat asked what she was doing later, and she replied that she would stay at her Auntie Cricket's in Nashville, but be back "*Sunday morning!!! :)*"

"Now, why would she tell me that if she didn't want to see me?" he asked Seamus, smug beyond all reason.

"I think, don't ask her out." Seamus said, an unsolicited Mr. Miyagi. "Just…around 7 on Sunday, maybe ask her if she wants to go for a walk."

"A walk?" Pat squawked. Then the quiet intelligence of it sunk in. A walk was low pressure. It would be dark—no one would have to wear a wig.

That Sunday, Pat and Seamus informed their parents they would be coming over for dinner.

"What are we, Italian now?" their father exclaimed, greeting them at the door.

Their mother was in the kitchen taking tinfoil wrapped plates from the fridge.

"Hello dears. Con came round for lunch, cleared us out on most of the leftover turkey," she explained, hugging them with her oven mitts on. "But Shay, there's still the sweet mash with pecans you like. Pato dear, will you bring Dad another drink? He wants the rye…"

Pat saw the lights on in Blaise's room when they came in. He craned his neck over the stern hedges and rickhouses that guarded Blaise like a moat, aching for a sketch of her hair and shoulders. When he imagined her bare feet pressed into the plush carpet, he nearly pitched forward from the shock of desire.

He had a plan.

Foley are you home? he texted her.

Yes Walsh she replied, *Why, do you need to borrow a cup of sugar? :-P*

"Turkey, dear?" his mother passed the platter as they sat down.

"Sure," Pat plated some of the scabby scraps, silently cursing Conor for taking all the dark meat and gravy.

Yeah I do need sugar. Heard you're the girl to go to for that :D, he answered Blaise.

"Don't we have a rule against phones at the table?" his father said, pointing his fork in reproach. "And why're you eating so fast, Pate? *Savor* it."

"Yeah, Pate" Seamus jeered, disemboweling one of Maura's stuffed shells.

"Because, I'm worried Conor's gonna come in and steal the mashed potatoes from my mouth," Pat replied. He had to get outside to do the next part of the plan. In about 13 minutes, he could clear his plate without arousing suspicion, and claim that he was going to get some sour mash from Rickhouse 2.

"Wasn't Fiona a gem on Thanksgiving, making place-cards for everyone?"

"She was—Mom, can I take your plate?" Pat stood up casually.

"Oh, yes dear—thank you."

"Where are you going?" Mr. Walsh asked, folding his arms over his Guinness t-shirt.

Readily, Pat held up an empty glass jug from the kitchen, "I'm gonna go steal some sour mash. Killy said on Thursday that he had a batch ready."

"Oh, alright. Don't forget to cork it when you're done."

Seamus followed him. "Are you gonna go meet up with her?" he hissed.

Pat waved him out the back door. "I want to find out if," he glanced wistfully up at Foley, "If she likes me."

"*How?*"

"Spy on her," Pat explained, pointing limply at their abandoned treehouse. It sounded pathetic as hell, but he knew the handheld telescope was still up there from when they spied on Foley Bourbon as kids.

"Great, let's go!" Seamus agreed exuberantly, clapping him on the back.

"We can't both fit up there."

But his twin was already halfway shimmied up the rusty ladder that was nailed into the tree trunk.

"You're not going first!" Pat grabbed Seamus's ankle. A scuffle ensued that left Seamus's ankle bitten and a Converse star imprint on Pat's forehead.

"I'll let you see what's going on," Pat promised, breathless but victorious on top.

The treehouse was dank and damp, its warped floor littered with artifacts from their childhood. Pat groped around blindly, vetoing a Bugs Bunny pez dispenser, and let out a *yes!* of triumph when his hand fell on the spyglass. Through the crusty lens, Foley Bourbon was every bit the opulent palace he remembered it to be. Pat scanned through rooms of baroque paneling and red leather chairs, looking for the resident Princess. Her room was the one with the curved bow window, he knew. To his slight chagrin, she wasn't sitting bare-legged on the ledge in that window, like he used to spot her reading teen magazines before her breasts came in.

Then, a rosy comet in blue silk came into view. Blaise, padding languidly around her room, talking on the phone. She bent forward to frown in her vanity mirror, kicking one leg back like a flamingo. Pat ogled her bare foot and heard himself groan. He would dive out of the treehouse and scale the walls like Spidey to take that exquisite foot into his mouth…

"Is she naked?" Seamus said eagerly, lunging forward. The floor of the treehouse groaned in protest.

"*No,*" Pat shushed him, kicking him twin back. His heart was going kilo-of-cocaine fast. "I'm gonna ask her on a walk."

He typed, *While I'm here, I'm gonna go see Jack and Clara. Can you meet me there for a walk? :)*

"You asked to be the Jack to her Clara? That's classy," Seamus whispered.

"No, I asked her to *meet* me by Jack and Clara."

"I dunno dude, kinda morbid—"

Pat had the rim of the spyglass pressed so hard to his eye; he could feel it leaving an indent. He saw Blaise pull her phone away to read his message. *Oh God…* If she sneered in disgust or lied ("*haha I wish I could but I've got company here!*") his hopeful heart would turn into pig slop…

But her eyes widened like bluebells to the sun, Pat saw, and her hand clasped over her mouth. She began pacing up her room, speaking to whoever was on the phone with an adorably disheveled smile. He understood then, as well as if he could read her lips: *She's nervous too! She likes me but she's scared!*

Seamus crawled forward on his arms like a soldier in a trench, demanding to know what was going on.

Dazedly, Pat handed him the spyglass, "I think she's asking her friend how to respond."

Again, the soft floor gave an almighty creak underneath them.

"WHAT ARE Y'UNS DOING UP THERE?"

From the base of the old tree, their father's voice thundered in their ears. Maybe it was his guilt of loving the enemy, but Pat scrambled down the tree faster than his mouth could blither excuses.

"I know what y'uns were doing," Sean Walsh glared at his sons. For one horrific moment, Pat thought his father could hear his telltale heart, thrumming loudly for Blaise. "You were going to play one of your pranks on Foley."

"We were not!" Seamus protested, "We were seeing if the treehouse was sturdy enough to be a playhouse for Fiona!"

"Like hell!" their dad bellowed, marching them inside like they were 9. "Listen boys, things have been calm with Foley lately...of course it's never Peaceful Acres, but I haven't heard from him in months." He tipped his rye down his throat, pacing in front of the fireplace. "That's the way we like it. I don't need this one" he gestured vaguely at Seamus, "Shooting paintballs against his ricks, or the other one playing ding-dong-ditch and getting shot at."

Pat touched his scar. "I wasn't playing ding-dong-ditch," he objected quietly, but Dad was on one of his unstoppable tirades.

"—You have to ask if it's worth us losing the house in Kilkenny or getting sued. You'll be 26 in March—"

"27, dear," Mrs. Walsh placidly corrected him, without looking up from her book.

"27, thank you. All the more reason—"

Pat's phone vibrated. He checked it as discretely as he could.

It was Blaise: *I guess a little exercise never hurt anyone. Meet there in 10? :)*

Pat texted back yes, then proceeded to use every desperate second of those ten minutes. Using twin speak, (a series of head jerks and pointed looks) he convinced Shay to distract Dad. This was no easy task, given that he was already suspicious and highly ruffled. Seamus resolved this by hurling his ultimate grenade into the living room:

"I'm thinking about going back to Iraq after I graduate."

Pat heard his mom's book hit the ground as he darted upstairs to spray some cologne and gargle Listerine. *Poor Shay,* he thought gratefully, hearing their mother's bleating brogue collide with their father's furious tenor. After burying Kevin Carr at age 23, it was their worst fear that Seamus would reenlist.

Pat wrenched open the back door, "I'm going for a walk," he muttered, as if to underscore their angst. *IOU,* he texted Shay.

Outside, Pat ran alongside the hedges, thrillingly wondering if the sound of rustling leaves contained her footsteps. The hedges ended at Jack and Clara's graves, a cross and angel headstone respectively, both bearing the Latin phrase, *Quis Separabit?* Pat grazed his palm over the eroded words. The touch calmed him; he knew his great-grandparents were not angry. They had died knowing the Foleys as their most sacred kin and best of friends.

"Hi," Blaise appeared suddenly from out of the chilly darkness, lowering a hood from her head. She had donned leggings and tennis shoes, but he could see the tease of blue slip underneath her jacket.

Pat was startled. "Whoa, I didn't hear you coming!"

She grinned, "I have practice sneaking around these grounds. Hi Jack, hi Clara!" she touched their graves as Pat had, which he liked. "Shall we?" Blaise nodded at the path ahead. Breathlessly, she explained that her dad was singing himself a whiskey lullaby when she left, but it was better to get far out of his sight.

"Absolutely," Pat agreed, as the strawberry silk of her hair brushed his arm. He felt himself go utterly braindead. *Please God, give me something to say.*

"Soo where do *you* think Jack buried the treasure?"

He meant this almost as a rhetorical question, so it surprised him when Blaise rotated her gaze down on their distilleries.

"I have an idea," she said seriously, sweeping a hand over the land. "But we can't look for it, not until my daddy's, well, you know…" Grimly, Blaise circled her hand over the small, gothic cemetery that was nearly obstructed by the hill on which they stood.

Pat nodded, "Because he'd try to keep it for himself?"

"No," Blaise cocked her head thoughtfully, "He would give it back to your family. He loves Black-Jack, thinks he's second only to his daddy as the greatest man who's ever lived. He wouldn't try to steal his treasure. But if he saw me trying to help your family look for it, he'd squash that quick." The moon illuminated her face, and for a second she looked sad, like a beached mermaid. "John-Boy's a deathly stubborn man. He doesn't change his mind." She smiled admittedly, "It's a trait I inherited."

"But *you* change your mind," Pat murmured, feeling the blaze from her arm as it brushed his.

"I actually don't, Walsh." She skipped ahead like a bratty little girl, "I'm always right, so why would I need to change my mind?"

"But you changed your mind about me," he said, running to catch up with her. The tree branches crisscrossed over their heads like an eerie awning. He noticed creepy things all the time now, welcoming them as envoys from her, the girl born on Halloween.

"Oh did I?" Her gaze on his was daring and cocky and tinged with shyness.

"Sure," Pat held her warm arms. "You used to hate me—not like you hate Conor—but like you wished I would just go away forever."

Her head was nodding, more so quivering, her face back to Sad Mermaid. "Well, I guess I knew that if I saw you too much, it would create a problem for me."

"Is it a problem now?" he asked the hot nape of her neck. When she nodded, her ornate trachea vibrated. He ran his thumb over it. Then he pinned her against the tree and pinned his lips against hers. They accepted the acrid films of the enemy bourbon from each other's mouths, passionately, as if it were food after famine.

"This is better than bourbon," Pat said, lips mashed against her ear so his syllables were dulled.

"Maybe better than *your* bourbon, Walsh," Blaise replied playfully, though her teeth were chattering. He offered her his jacket, but she said she wasn't even cold.

They sat at the base of the tree, their legs melded together, and he could freely touch her hair, her neck, with endless greed and gratitude. He was confessing a few things to her in a slight ramble, that he always, *always* liked her, since that first time at the liquor store, (she smiled to herself) and why he risked death to attend her 21st birthday, and how he didn't care about the past, or what her last name was ("Walsh..." she chided him gently, laying a hand on his upper thigh and looking forcefully away). That he thought about her every time he listened to *Rhiannon*, and he'd had *Rhiannon* playing on repeat all this month.

"That's how I have you saved in my phone." He pulled out his cell to show her, then frowned. The screen was littered with texts from Seamus: Apparently their parents hadn't taken to his fake news well. Shay reported that Dad stormed off to go have a drink at McGettigans, and Mom was calling Father Tim over to give him a talking to.

"Um," Pat felt bad, because he had stranded his twin in the foxhole. But how could he leave Blaise and their little passion picnic now?

"I have to bring Seamus home, he's at our parents' with no car. But do you wanna come over?" he gestured vaguely down Zzyzyx. "Our house is like five miles that way. You'll like it," he saw the playful skepticism in her face, "We have Amazon TV." He sighed, "And my dog gets tired of being my cuddle buddy night after night, you could give him a break."

Blaise giggled, "I dunno Walsh, my Nana said to never visit a man at his home unless he's taken you to dinner first."

"Well, we should listen to Nana," Pat agreed seriously, "How about I pick you up at 7 tomorrow?"

"To go to dinner?" Blaise glanced conspiratorially over both shoulders, "But where could we go?"

"We can drive out to Sexy Lexy," Pat said, referring to Lexington. "An hour away is far out enough." He would drive out to Dubuque fucking Iowa if he had to. He didn't care. He'd cross the Mexican border if she wanted. Maybe they'd never come back.

"I know a cute dimly-lit tavern out there," Blaise allowed, smiling demurely. They agreed to meet tomorrow, in the same field where he gave her the hangover IV. When Blaise tried to scamper off in her tennis shoes, it was a very 2 steps forward, 1 step back situation, because he kept needing to kiss her goodbye, again and again. She felt like the first girl he ever kissed. The trees branches were black skeleton fingers and the grass was mottled with decay, but inside him burst the neon newness of spring.

Pat's father Sean had never been the Master Distiller for Walsh. By the time the trial of '68 was over and Walsh Bourbon formed, Sean was a teenager. By Wilkie's harsh standards, he was far too old to learn the sacred alchemy of bourbon. "Maybe your firstborn son will succeed me," Wilkie told Sean at the time. "There are other jobs for you to do in the company."

"I'll tell ya, bourbon distillin' is like training for the Olympics!" Sean would mock huff when he told this story, "If you don't start by age 8, you gotta call the whole thing off!"

When Sean told stories, everyone listened and laughed. Even non-speakers of English would have done the same, for his goodness and humor were universal. He had very white, straight teeth that were impervious to the jaundice of age (Conor called them "Cherokee choppers") and eyes like blue flame in a jar. He had combed, sandy hair, and plenty of it, thank you very much. He wore t-shirts to work every day, making it a known policy to don suits only for weddings and funerals. His mother Kachine was straight-off-the-reservation Cherokee, and anyone who heard this firmly agreed that they could see it in Sean. It wasn't just his broad face with sloping cheekbones, it was his connection to the earth. Sean loved the sun, always finding projects to tinker on outdoors, singing along with classic rock songs on the radio as Father Sun bronzed his hyde. He was a big picture person: if his sons were well, his wife happy, and the family bourbon prospering, then he could die just fine. Of course, all three things never synced up at once, so he agreed to keep on living, his white teeth barred all the while.

Sean headed up the Marketing Department at Walsh. In college, Pat had the idea for Walsh to sell Red Solo Cups with their logo on them. The cups became a bestselling item, much to Sean's delight. He said a few times that Mr. Foley might be leering down his nose at their Red Solos, but they were far outselling the snotty pewter mint julep cups that Foley Bourbon sold.

"Dad, what do you remember about the Foley trial?" Pat asked his father, lounging on the couch at his parent's house. It was a grey Saturday afternoon, a few days after he took the enemy heiress out to dinner. The rugby match they had been watching just ended. The Walshes paid for Irish TV channels so Mrs. Walsh could feel in touch with her homeland. It was far more common for rugby to be droning in the background of their Saturdays than football.

"Very nice, Sligo—huh? *Foley?*" his dad looked from the TV to him, his pleasant expression curdling. "What made you think of it, Shay—uh, Pato?"

Pat sipped his bourbon ale. *Because all I think about is the Foley heiress.* "I dunno, someone asked me about it recently. I'm curious."

"Well," his father turned the volume down, frowning thoughtfully at the ceiling. "It was tough, I remember, 'cause all us kids grew up playing together. John-Boy, Duffy, me, your Uncle Mart, we were all only a year or two apart."

"So, what do you remember them being like?"

"The Foleys?" His dad's frown deepened, as if the task of locating untarnished memories made his head hurt. "Well, I always thought they were a golden crew. Duffy was tall and good at every sport he tried...John-boy was helping my father make the bourbon since, woo boy, maybe from the time we were 8 or 9? And Mr. Foley always had a nice suit on...my father called him the Irish Sinatra. I remember him always leaning over the fence to talk to my father, with a cigar in one hand and a bourbon in the other. Sully loved to fly, he let us kids fly in the cockpit with him. When we shook his hand, he'd leave a fiver in your palm," He grinned, "Little Kennedy came later, she was born the year after JFK was assassinated, so they named her after him."

"Nice," Pat murmured, but his father was smiling full on now, caught up in some reverie.

"And Mrs. Foley, *God* she was beautiful," Sean sighed so wishfully that Pat was glad that his mother wasn't there to raise her eyebrows. "She looked like Ursula Andress, you know, the first Bond girl. Sabina was her name, from Switzerland. She came to the U.S to be a Pan Am stewardess. The story I always heard was she was dating Peter Lawford when she first met Mr. Foley, but he walked into the Sands Hotel one night and wooed her away, all the way back to Kentucky."

"Wow," Pat remarked. He guessed this was the grandmother who advised Blaise against visiting a man's home without being taken to dinner first. "So then, after the trial, you just never saw them again?"

"Hard to see over those hedges," Sean ruefully pointed out the window. "It was tough on my father. You know, he and Sully were as close as you and Seamus are. Sullivan Foley died in, what was it, '76 or '77?" His father cocked his head towards the chandelier, trying to remember, "Well anyway, your Grampy rarely mentions him, but I know he carries a lot of guilt."

"Why? 'Cause he took his best friend to trial?" Pat asked.

"Because all of it," Sean hesitated, trying to think of how to explain. "My father taught John-boy how to make the bourbon. John-boy was so eager, I think he recognized that his brother Duffy was going to be the star, he was the heir, after all, he was going to inherit the trust fund and the shares, so John-boy wanted to stand-out. Grampy Wilkie and John-boy used to be close, he called him his little apprentice. He's always been intense, John-boy, even when we were kids. I think he felt that Wilkie betrayed the family when he took Sully to court. And then after my father burned down his main rickhouse, he hated him forever." Sean shook his head as the TV aired a commercial for Bewley's Irish Breakfast. "I *know* that John-boy thinks that was what killed Sully—you know he died of a heart-attack that same night."

"Shit," Pat said grimly. "But...how do you know he blames Grampy Wilkie for that?"

"He wouldn't let Grampy attend Sullivan's funeral," his father said, bitterly nipping his ale. "We showed up outside the church to pay our respects—I can remember the bagpipers out front playing *Danny Boy,* and John-boy shouting over them for all he was worth. *"Murderer! You might as well have pulled the trigger! Irish nigger! You killed him!* It damn near killed my father. He spent a few weeks in the hospital. 'Course, he was already admitted to the psyche ward after burning up all the Foleys' barrels," Sean gave a rueful chuckle, "But this didn't help anything…"

"So of all the Foleys and Washes, Wilkie and John-boy are the true enemies?"

"I dunno," Sean grinned, "I think your brother Conor and John's daughter could give them a run for their money."

Pat felt his head go fizzy at the mention of her.

Luckily his father plunged on, "So then John-boy went a little crazy after his dad died. He was bitter from having to remake all his bourbon, too. There was a time when, if you stepped a toe over Jack and Clara's graves, you'd feel a bullet whiz past your ear. When Mom and I got married, I didn't think this house was safe to raise kids in, but by then" Sean chuckled, "John-boy was busy courting his Tennessee beauty queen, so he had to act more civilized, or at least pretend to."

"Dru McCullers, Miss America 1981," Pat murmured. Then fearing he sounded too knowledgeable, he added foggily, "Right?"

"She was Irish, Southern, and beautiful, he couldn't-a dreamt up a better wife," he gave a low whistle, "Miss Tennessee's only flaw was that she didn't drink Foley bourbon," Sean grinned appreciatively, "Never switched over from Jack Daniels. We'd see her on Derby Day and she'd run right up with her red hair flying under her big hat and ask us how our distillery was doing—you could see John-boy looking stricken behind her—and she'd have a Tennessee tea they made special for her in her mint julep cup. Sweet as pie, she'd say— "Sean put on a dithery voice that sounded somewhat like Blaise's— "'I like Johnny's bourbon fine, but I'm a Jack girl at heart.' Lord, it probably killed him."

"So she's kind of a spark-plug too, John-boy's wife," Pat summed up.

"Not like him," Sean said, his face darkening, "Dru McCullers was sweet, he's…something else. The daughter, now *she's* a spark-plug," he nodded firmly, recalling all the times he'd been woken up by a shouting match outside between his son Conor and John-boy's daughter. Her eyes unnaturally wide as though possessed, shooting venom and fire that Sean could feel from all the way indoors. Those eyes were exactly like John-boy's on the day of Sullivan Foley's funeral, when he hollered all those soul-sticking curses at Wilkie.

"Who, *Blaise*?" Pat said, with so much adoring coziness that a more suspicious mind than Sean's would have detected it. "Nah…" He let her eyes surface within him, wells of truth and beauty that men crusaded their entire lives to find. Only twenty more minutes until he could see her again.

"She may look like the mother," Sean murmured, draining his ale and standing up, "But she's got the devil of her father in her, believe you me."

Blaise wasn't doing any bourbon tours today. She had already closed the iron gate and hung the sign announcing that Foley was closed for tours. Conor Walsh drove past with his Christmas tree tied to the roof of his car, demanding to know why. ("Gas leak,

Foley? Be sure to stay inside." "Fuck off, Walsh, we're closed to *you* every day.")

Blaise went back inside and expertly turned all the security cameras off. Then she called her Daddy, knowing the Bombardier plane carrying her parents, McCullers, and Hildy was just touching down in Nashville. They were off to see Wilson Fairchild sing at the Opry. Even when flying regionally, the Foleys always took a private jet, because the bullets stuck in her mother's head set off the metal detectors at airports.

"Daddy, I'm not doing any tours today," Blaise simpered, appraising a floor-length leather skirt in her mirror. "Why? *Because*! I'm home alone and don't feel safe allowing strangers on the property. Do you want me to wind up another kidnapped heiress like Patty Hearst?" she rolled her eyes at herself in the mirror. As she spoke, there were at least five maintenance guys crawling the grounds. She also noticed, a tall, hooded figure approaching the back door who hadn't been there a second ago...

"Daddy, I have to go, my pizza's here." Blaise hung up and ran barefoot down the winding marble staircase, her heart beating madly.

"*Walshie!*" She threw open the door, striking a cute hostess pose.

"*Foley!*" He lowered his hood and grinned at her, his dimples deepening irresistibly. He was   the cutest, sweetest boy on the earth, and he was shamelessly crazy about her.

Blaise waved him in, grinning right back. "Bet you never thought you'd be over here, huh?"

"Oh no, I knew it would happen someday." Pat nodded appreciatively at his luxe surroundings, the high ceilings set with angel carvings and gilded Foley crests. "It's nice." He tried to sound nonchalant, "Soo...are we alone?"

Blaise giggled, "*Yes*. George may be around, but he's cool." She wrapped her arms around him. "Don't worry, I won't let you get shot again."

"Well, some things are worth dying for." Pat kissed her, and they didn't break away for a good five minutes. Blaise noticed her great-great-great Uncle Mungo's portrait leering at her, but he was just jealous because he'd been dead for two centuries and forgot how delicious passion like this was.

"C'mon." She seized his hand and led him past the portraiture of dead Foleys. "I'll give you the tour!"

"Whoa! I see Blacko-Jacko made the cut," Pat remarked, giving his great-grandfather's portrait a customary salute. It was a portrait of Jack that he had never seen before, smoking a cigarette on the terrace of Foley Bourbon at twilight. Pat's house was not yet built, and Jack's coolly approving gaze fell upon an empty pasture.

"Spring 1921." Blaise grinned proudly at his elbow. "The eagle had just landed."

Pat and Blaise had tacitly agreed not to drink their bourbon in front of each other. This happened over dinner in Lexington this week, when the chipper waitress in the necktie asked them what they were drinking.

"What kind of bourbon do you have?" they asked her in unison, then exchanged a guilty look in the tea-light glow. Pat and Blaise went back and forth about twenty-five demure rounds of, "Get yours," "No get *yours*!" while the poor waitress stood there, fake-smiling with her pen poised. Finally Blaise explained apologetically, "I'm a Foley, *he's* a Walsh,"

"Aw!" The waitress simpered, "Aw, you guys are like Romeo and Juliet!"

They chanced moony looks at each other, their insides writhing with glee.

"How about we do some good old-fashioned Jam-o?" Blaise suggested, which was what she drank if she found herself at a dive bar without her flask. Pat happily agreed. When the pert waitress brought them over twin Jamesons, they clinked their glasses together and murmured "*Slaánte...*"

That's what Pat brought her today, Jameson purchased that morning at the Liquor Barn. "It's basically the first bottle I've ever bought," he told her in his quiet way.

"Well, thank you much!" Blaise led him into her father's study, an explosion of tartan wallpaper and bear-skin rugs. Mr. Foley's bar was similar to Killian's at home, in that they had nothing but bottles of amber for offer. Like Killian, Mr. Foley's were unlabeled, as he relied on taste to tell them apart. Blaise pointed to a few dusty, untouched bottles in the far corner. "I have some Scotch too, if you're feeling Scottish."

"I'll stick with the Irish, thanks," Pat said, crumbling up the paper bag. He didn't feel perfectly comfortable drinking in her father's lair. The story of him with Grandpa Wilkie was still searingly fresh in his mind.

"So will I," Blaise said sweetly, pouring them both a few inches of Jameson and clinking glasses with him. "*Sláinte.*"

Pat thought how nice it was that she was ignoring her father's bourbon, which had probably won three World Spirits Competitions, in order to drink C-grade whisky with him. *God I like her.* Urgently he gulped his drink, as if to temper the flow of hot gold through his chest. *And how can I touch her feet?*

"You're barefoot," he blurted out.

"Huh?" she wrinkled her cute nose.

"Uh—nothing. Wait, is this your mom?" He picked up the portrait of a young woman in a jeweled tiara off Mr. Foley's desk. Her teased hair was redder than Blaise's.

"Yeah," Blaise admired the picture wistfully, "She was Miss America in 1981," she smiled, "That's how she met my father. He was a judge that year."

"Really?" Pat murmured, as she gently removed the picture from the frame.

"This is the one she signed," Blaise said reverently.

Sure enough, written on the back in ink was:

Dear Johnny,

Thanks for helping me to cinch the big win! We'll see how well you do getting a Tennessee girl to switch over from Jack ;)

XOXO and Best Wishes,

Dru McCullers

"I've watched the clip of her getting crowned more times than anyone's ever watched anything," Blaise admitted, her eyes and voice softening. This wasn't in the gilded script of her famed Foley tour. "If I could get a scene tattooed on my eyelids, that would be it. But it makes me sad, because she was so, *so* lovely Pat…and now she can barely walk or talk."

"What happened?" Pat murmured. He only knew of Dru's accident as Zzyzyx Road lore. He wanted to hear it from Blaise, rather than the crusty chorus of Kilkenny's sons, who viewed any woe that befell the Foleys as some karmic repayment from fifty years ago.

"Well, she loved horseback riding," Blaise began, somewhat unsteadily. "We both did. That was our thing, to go riding together. We both had mares that year. My horse was Dolley Madison…I was in 7th grade…it was November…I had just turned thirteen." She didn't mention that she got her period that month, or had her training bra frozen for being the first one asleep at Jess Zeamer's sleepover. These murky slides from that time in her life rolled through her mind on the same conveyor belt as horse pastures and hospital beds. "One Thursday, I had a tennis match, so my momma took Dolley riding alone. She wasn't wearing her helmet. She rode too close to our old shooting range, which is up there on Van Etten Road."

"Yeah, I know it," Pat said. Blaise was looking determinedly out the window so he wouldn't see her eyes well up. He touched her hand.

"The man who inspected the shooting range after she was shot told us that it shouldn't have been operational at all," Blaise sniffed. "The wooden planks behind the targets were completely warped. There were gaps in them where the bullets passed through. They got her right here," Blaise rapped on her own skull with a watery smile.

"Who shot her?" Pat asked, looking at Dru's lovely picture and wanting to place his blame somewhere. The sincere crinkle in her green eyes made him wish he could somehow warn the young queen to duck.

"Oh no, it was an accident," Blaise firmly shook her head. "Two guys who did mulch for us, they were just shooting after work. They felt terrible about it." She willed away the thought of her perfect mother splayed on the November grass in her riding breeches, her red hair fanned out over a growing pool of crimson.

"Her doctors said it was a miracle she survived," she went on hoarsely. "McCullers and I sat with her every day, from the time we got home from school until it was time for bed." Gently, she knuckled away her tears like her mother did for her crowning moment. "They said we saved her."

"I'm sure you did." Pat wanted to brush away those tears, but he wasn't sure he was allowed.

"I wish you could meet her," Blaise offered a watery smile, "She loves herself a tall, handsome man. Her face would light up like a Christmas tree."

"Oh yeah?" Pat followed her as she padded out of her dad's study. "So I take that to mean you find me handsome?"

"Jesus, Walsh. If you fished any harder, I'd have to get you a bait-and-tackle." Grinning in a restorative way, she led him up the winding marble staircase. "This is the Ulysses room." She gestured to the portrait of President Grant above the fireplace, his bleary gaze and mutton chop beard bearing down on them. "Named so because he stayed here after the Battle of Shiloh."

"While my ancestors were still herding sheep in Kilkenny," Pat saluted Grant's portrait. *(Editor's Note: It's a shame about that lovely portrait, an oil-on-canvas from 1875. Today, Grant's eyes and mouth have been shot out, his mouth an unnatural, gun-smoked smile. I've apologized to Blaise on behalf of my M16, but I do believe all is fair in love and war).*

"Does that mean the Foleys were pro-Union in the Civil War?" he asked.

"The Foleys are pro-Foley Bourbon," Blaise explained. "We sold barrels of bourbon to both the Confederate *and* Union Armies so they could make ammunition." She showed Pat the wall of sketches that seemed to depict a battle outside of this very house. "Kentucky was a big battleground state, as I'm sure you know, and the Union Army was always traipsing through, trying to steal our horses or loot the house. But you can see here." Blaise indicated the throng of men and women too, lined outside of Foley Bourbon with canons raised and guns cocked, against a row of soldiers on horses. "We wouldn't let it happen." She traced her finger along a Latin phrase arched over the battle scene: *Pro cupam primus.* "That means, the whiskey first. The rest of the earth may be torched to dust, the sun may fall out of the sky, but our bourbon *must* live on," she nodded proudly, "Our sills haven't closed one day since 1788. Not even during Prohibition."

"And what does this mean?" Pat asked her, tracing a finger over the Latin phrase written over a scene of Indians being chased away by men on horseback. "Aren't these words carved into your stone out front?"

"*Misercordias Domini Cantabo in Aeternum,*" Blaise grinned at the ever-familiar words. "It's our bourbon motto." She crinkled her nose, "It's Latin for, *Don't Fuck with Foley.* Just don't do it!"

Their tour was impeded by Pat's need to carry Blaise to the elaborate four-poster bed of the Ulysses suite. He particularly enjoyed the stiff red privacy curtains, and firmly closed them in what Blaise called, "Do-Not-Disturb mode."

"Have the sheets been changed since the General's stay?" He murmured into her soft belly, perfect as a glass of creamy milk.

"*Of course,*" Blaise giggled against the vibrations of heat rippling her skin. "Do we look like a one-star inn to you, Walsh?"

He stopped feasting on her long enough to make them a fire. Naturally, Grant's fireplace was no auto-de-feu, so he had to fumble with the logs and summon his Boy Scout training. Outside the window, he noticed his brother Killian across the hedges, talking with his men in his buckskin coat. Pat swore and ducked.

"Do you mind if we close the curtains, Foley?"

"We can," Blaise said placidly, propping herself up on her elbow like a Penthouse Pet. "But don't worry, Walshie, no one can see inside."

He wisely decided not to challenge her point, and set about unfurling the pompous yellow taffeta.

"Can you imagine?" Blaise peddled her feet in the air, "Someday when I publish my memoirs, everyone will just *die* when they read that we had an affair."

Pat grabbed her feet. For the first time, he wasn't peering at her with shy adoration. "No, they won't," he said, his handsome face hard and defiant. "It'll be old news by then, girl."

Her heart was pounding, but she kept her face coy and demure. "Why's that, honey? You think you're gonna make me your girlfriend?"

"Yeah." He wiggled his ears at her, Alfalfa-style. "At least to start."

She wanted to scream. All the bourbon that pulsed in her veins was replaced with hot blood for Patrick Walsh. Blaise wanted to admit to him everything: *I spent twenty minutes yesterday at the store reading all your bourbon labels. Not only do I no longer want to pretend your family doesn't exist, I crave to know your whole story...I looked through your and Palmer's old pictures on Facebook—and she's beautiful and not a Foley, but I swear, I could make you happier...I have you saved in my phone as Peabody Wilton, because I thought an unsexy name might keep my heart from exploding every time you texted me (it didn't)...*

But she was proud, and she had been taught "the Rules" by her prim Aunt Cricket McCullers, so she kept her heart closed in the privacy curtains—for now.

"C'mere, Foley..."

"Where are ya going with those hands, chief?"

"I heard that's where Jack buried the treasure...you're so wet..."

"Don't assume it's for you. It could be for General Grant."

"Leave him outta this."

That evening, they played Operation and ordered Dominos and watched *Home Alone 2* to get in the mood for Christmas, and—

"—No, we didn't have sex!" she shrieked to Elliot the next morning, calling her as she dreamily watched her Patrick disappear around the hedges. She was in the kitchen frothing milk for a second cappuccino. In the sink rested Pat's russet stained cup and saucer. When they woke up, Pat still in his unbuttoned jeans, he said, *"Hi Mrs. Walsh!"* in a playground taunt. She hit him, perfectly stuck between, *"Aw!"* and *"Ew!"*

"El, you'll die, but I didn't even see his shillelagh," Blaise giggled. She chose a gluten-free Danish from the doily tray that Hildy kept for McCullers. "Why? Because I like him! Next time I see him, I will." She plunged the pastry in the hot milk and rammed it down her throat, imagining the next time she saw Pat.

"He kept saying he really loves my feet," Blaise went on hushedly, in case George was in the next room. She sprawled her legs out across the breakfast nook, scrutinizing her size 11 hooves. "He gave me a foot massage. It was kinda, I dunno, erotic." She had a smoldering flashback of them on her bedroom carpet, Pat kneading her feet like a potter sculpting clay, achingly slowly and with great purpose. He gazed into her eyes and said little but winked a few times. *God.* It was more than a little bit erotic.

"'Anyway," Blaise sighed, "Tell me about your night, Ell." And she listened diligently to Elliot's tale of her latest John Deere, a gentleman from Richmond who came into her bar and ordered pickle-back shots and played Paul Anka on the jukebox, drunkenly singing to Elliot for two songs too long.

Conor Walsh was recently married to a hairdresser named Maura Jones. Everyone agreed they were a great match, although you wouldn't necessarily have put them together. Maura was 5'4 and petite to Conor's 6'5 and burly. It was ironic that Conor, who grew up liberally calling his brothers and many male cousins *faggot,* now spent his Saturday nights out to dinner with his wife's salon family, which was steepled with gay men. Both of Maura's brothers were gay, and between them and the salon owners, someone inevitably got tipsy and made a comment about "Daddy's hard pecs" and "strapping physique," (Daddy being Conor). After much time and practice, Conor finally got used to this unwanted attention, and even learned how to bandy it back with quips like, "Sorry Scott, but that's the only hard you're ever gonna see."

Maura considered this to be growth. Privately, she was very proud of her hubby, considering him to be a dying breed of the two-fisted, red-blooded man, like Stanley Kowalski in *A Streetcar Named Desire.* She knew that if Conor were born sixty years earlier, he would have worked in the Lexington coal-mine like her grandfather had, and she liked that.

Working at the salon kept Maura dialed in to the hottest gossip in town. She often came home with stories about affairs, divorces, pregnancies, engagements, estrangements, and other soap opera segments.

For the most part, it was all pleasant white noise to Conor. Then one day, Maura came home with tidings that broke the barriers of sound.

His wife informed him that the Foley Heiress was taken out to dinner last week by a Walsh boy. This, Maura heard from her friend Andrea from high school, who heard it from her cousin Lindsay, who served them at the Blue Tavern.

"Apparently," Maura raised her perfectly penciled brows, "Whoever this Walsh was *refused* to order his own bourbon. He didn't want to disrespect the heiress by drinking it in her presence."

Conor flew into a rage, launching a full investigation. He even made Maura text her friend Andrea asking if the cousin could look possibly up the name on the credit card slip. ("He paid cash!" came cousin Lindsay's reply).

"Very clever," Conor sneered, "I see that Judas *fucking* Walsh took all the proper precautions."

He decided to round up all of his cousins and brothers for a group interrogation. He sent a text out under the guise of doing Secret Santa, so as to not arouse any suspicion.

"Someone'll talk," he ranted, while Maura drank wine and watched *Scandal.* "If not, I'll get Killy to cut off all their bourbon. That's the next best thing to waterboarding. The traitor will *have* to confess."

"Everyone!" Conor Walsh bellowed, straining to be heard over the ruckus that his 15 brothers and cousins were causing. The feeble lighting of McGettigan's bar draped over his flinty face, which was made even more malevolent by the reddish glow of Christmas bulbs. On the XM radio, 'Christmas Don't Be Late' by the Chipmunks was playing, but you could barely hear it over the clinking of glasses and pool balls and general horse-assery in the room.

"*Everyone!*" he cupped a hand over his mouth, "Everyone shut the fuck up!"

"You shut the fuck up!" Eamon hollered, whipping an ice-cube at him from his bourbon.

Conor expertly caught the ice and looked around at his assembly. "Yo, is everyone here? Alright girls, roll call. When I say your name, say *here.* Killy?"

"Here," Killian Walsh chimed, busy sampling the double-oaked he just brought in.

"Here," croaked 63-year-old Kildare, half rotating on his barstool, the light falling on his bulbous, veiny nose. In spirit of the season, he had traded in his usual Vietnam Vet cap for a Santa hat.

Conor rolled his eyes, "I meant *Killian,* Kildare. This is a meeting for *our* generation." He thumbed over his shoulder, "The VFW meeting's next door."

Seamus rocketed to his feet in soldier's posture, "The VFW meeting *never* ends when you're a guardian of freedom and the American way of life," he bellowed, saluting his fellow veteran across the bar. "Right mein Bruder?"

Kildare raised his drink to Seamus in half-hearted cheers.

"Alright, *I'm* here" Conor pounded his chest. "Goldy?"

"Present," Pat said, looking over from the Jenga game he was setting up (Seamus seized the opportunity to knock it over).

"And we know that Private fucking Joker's here," Conor said, jutting his mammoth chin at Seamus, who threw the Nixon double-Vs in the air. "So onto Uncle Mart's kids..." he hollered, "Deebo?"

"Here," Oscar answered, drinking a bourbon ale composedly, his briefcase at his feet. He was the second oldest cousin, born three months after Killian, with matching navy-blue eyes and wavy black hair. They were often mistaken for twins at school, but their similarities ended at their looks and last name. For instance, while Killian was perfectly happy to wear their ratty "SENIORS '99 - Destination: New Millennium" t-shirt to work, Oscar, a lawyer of genteel taste and impeccable grooming, wouldn't wear it unless every stitch of his Brooks Brothers clothing was at the dry cleaners.

Oscar worked with his father, Marty, at a law firm Marty founded specializing in Intellectual Property. When Marty was 21, his father Wilkie gave him the rights to Black-Jack's novel and assorted journals. Marty had Jack's image trademarked, and launched a wonderful career licensing out Black-Jack's image and suing anyone who used it without his permission. Most recently, *the History Channel* was hit by Oscar and Marty for airing a five-part series on Jack's bootlegging route without their okay. The settlement afforded Uncle Mart a Scandinavian cruise with Aunt Jill, and Oscar, a new in-ground pool.

"Slaw?"

"Here" Oscar's brother Callum called, in dirty flannel, because he worked in the distilling room with Killian. He had only been at Walsh Bourbon since he graduated college, a rookie to Killian, but a determined one at that. Everyone called him Slaw, even his girlfriend.

"Longbow's exempt," Conor said, referring to their younger brother Brendan, the black sheep who moved out to Montana after high school. "Where the *fuck's* Baby Mickey at?"

"He just texted me, he's on his way," Slaw reported, glancing at his Droid.

"If he's not here in 10, I'm sending a squad car after him," Conor said ruthlessly, and Slaw rolled his eyes. "Alright, Uncle Avi's kids."

Uncle Avi (Avanoco) was the first blond Walsh born since the Vikings invaded Ireland (at least that's what he said). He averaged about four jokes a minute, six if he was dealing poker. He had four sons, but often acted more like a fifth brother rather than a dad.

"Eems?" Conor barked.

Eamon Walsh, Avi's oldest son, rolled his eyes, "Obviously I'm right fucking here, Stevie Wonder, sitting three feet in front of your face."

Eems was arguably the only one more bullish than Conor. His mother would coo that Eamon's red-head was a prelude to his fiery character. His cousins would say that Eems was an asshole—but he was *their* asshole. Whenever the Walsh Wives played Fuck, Marry, Kill, Eems was often killed for his loud mouth, or fucked for his hard lacrosse body.

"Open your squinty little eyes. *I'm* here. Falco's not," Eamon barreled on, indicating his absent brother who worked in New York. "Kiki's here," he jutted his thumb toward the bar, where blond

Kiernan was whistling while he washed glasses, "He's poured you two drinks already...And Douska's here—" he indicated his blond brother, Aidan, who raised his hand as if they were in homeroom.

"Alright!" Conor cut roughly through him, "You only get to do your own family, so *sit down*. Uncle Shy's kids..."

Uncle Shilah embraced his Native American side far more than his brothers (even Avi, whose salutes to his Native blood were mainly jokes about keeping Aunt Karen as his Indian Captive). Shilah had married a Native woman, Kimama, and their three sons were born and raised on her reservation. His black mane was as long as his wife's, and their middle son, Onacona, also wore his hair shoulder-length and parted (Conor called him "Smoke Signals" during tonight's roll call). Shy's oldest son, Paytah ("Hawkeye") wasn't present because he lived in Montana with cousin Brendan.

"Where the fuck's Hacker?" Conor shouted, scanning the crowd for Shy's youngest son.

"Yo," Hacker (né Manquilla) droned, without lifting his coin-colored eyes from his phone. His shiny black hair was cut short, possibly to keep it out of his eyes so he could see his many screens.

"Looks like we're just waiting on Baby," Conor ascertained, cracking his knuckles impatiently.

"Sorry I'm late!" Mickey panted a moment later, entering the bar with a lopsided grin.

Everyone yelped, "BABY!" like the *Cheers* gang greeting Norm. He was called Baby because he was the youngest of the 15 (and definitely the prettiest).

Thus they were all assembled, the 15 grandsons of Wilkie Walsh, all born one on top of the other from 1981-1991. They were all a quarter Cherokee, with the high cheekbones and formidable jaws to prove it. In tribute to their Native blood, the boys called Killian "Chief," because he was the oldest cousin, and their Master Distiller. The first rule of their charter was, "Thou shall drink NO bourbon but Chief's bourbon." The charter was drunk drivel composed on a bunch of cocktail napkins, but to them it was the Magna Carta. Like the Chief, each of the cousins had a nickname that dated back many moons. Falco earned his nickname at the age of 2, because he played 'Rock Me Amadeus' on his Sesame Street cassette player so many times, his father finally ran it over. Conor was "Maggot," simply because he called everyone Maggot. Oscar was "Deebo" from the movie *Friday*, which he and Killian saw in 9th grade and quoted until the lines became family lexicon. Callum was 'Slaw Jaw' because his jaw flared so widely, his brothers claimed he had a boomerang stuck in there. Manquilla was 'Hacker' because he was a computer genius who could hack into anything: as a gift on the guy's birthdays, he liked to break into their old AIM accounts and read aloud select conversations from their younger days.

"Right," Conor barked, as Mickey helped himself to some of the double-oaked. "I know you all think we're here for Secret Santa, but that's actually not why I called this meeting of our high fraternal order." He took a slow, brooding sip of his drink. "It's come to my attention that one of you is sleeping with the enemy."

"Dammit, Douska!" Seamus screeched, putting Aidan's shaggy blonde head in a chokehold, "I warned you, if you ever brought an Italian home, she wouldn't be welcome under my roof!"

Pat chuckled along with everyone else, but felt his whole body tense up. He touched his phone protectively, a reservoir of Valentines from his Rhiannon.

"Not a mammadelle," Conor sneered, as Aidan wiggled free, coughing. "My *true* enemy. I got a tip that a Walsh was spotted at a restaurant in Lexington, out to dinner with the Foley heiress."

"*WHAT?*" Seamus gasped, with the cartoonish camp of a telenovela actor. Pat fiercely shushed him.

"That's not possible," Killian objected, shaking his head as though someone had just offered him a vodka tonic. "Sorry Maggot. I think someone's messing with you."

Pat guffawed his agreement, but not too loudly. He knew, from years of dodging blame for broken windows and missing iPods, that the loudest denials came from the guiltiest parties. Conor would zero in on him instantly if he made too much of a scene. He prayed for his brother to get laughed off his soap-box before his interrogation could go on any further.

"Chief, I got it from the waitress who served them," Conor fired back, "Maura does her hair."

"Isn't that a HIPPA violation?" Seamus called out.

"Spousal privileges," Conor snapped. "The witness said that, Foley's date, whichever one of you maggots it was," he pointed his finger in 180 degrees of disgust, "Bought her Jameson all night long." He cracked his knuckles loudly, "Apparently, Foley wouldn't let him drink *our* bourbon in *her* presence."

"Oh really?" Killian demanded, turning and facing them all with blazing eyes. "I hope that's not true, guys…"

"After my brother sweats 10 hours a day on our distillery to make your fucker's bourbon—" Conor plowed on.

"My brother, too," Oscar jumped onboard, nodding supportively at Slaw, whose dark freckled face was a grid of shock and rage.

"—He customizes it to your liking for each and *every* birthday, wedding, and christening—"

Pat's neck burned with shame, even though this was a warped Telephone game version of the truth.

"No one better be accusing *me*," Old Kildare gurgled from the bar, breaking the chilly silence that followed. "That little bitch's family had my father killed in cold blood. I wouldn't take her out for all the peaches in Georgia."

"No one's accusing you, Kildare." Conor scowled. If he were paying more attention, he would've noticed that Pat was the only one not snickering into his glass. "I actually think I've got a pretty good lead-in for a prime suspect." Ominously, Metallica's 'Carol of the Bells' pulsed through the bar. Pat clenched his body for Conor's surprise viper attack.

"So Baby, you used to hang out at Foley's sorority house," Conor said, glancing casually at Mickey, "Is that when you first developed a thing for her?"

"*I* used to hang at her house?" Mickey said loudly.

"That's the story I heard," Conor raised his eyebrows at the group.

"What are you picking on Baby for?" Oscar called, coming to his brother's defense.

Mickey looked wildly around the room. "No, the story was, I tried to go to a party at her sorority house *once* when I was a freshman. The SS wouldn't let me in."

"Yo, I was with you, Baby!" Aidan whooped, jumping up from his seat. "I don't think she realized I was a Walsh, so she didn't yell at me." Vaguely, he touched his curly blond mane, which could certainly throw a Foley heiress off the scent of a Walsh. "She's *scary*," he nodded feverishly at the group, "But she's hot. She's scary-hot, like a dominatrix."

"Douska, is this your confession?" asked his brother Eamon lazily, slinging his thick calves onto his chair. "Does the Foley heiress pour hot candle wax on your asshole?"

"Me? *No!*" Aidan shook his head frankly, "I haven't seen her since she graduated."

"Wait, time out." Onacona set down his pool-stick. With his long, dark hair and serene expression, he looked like a formidable hybrid of rock god and Jesus Christ. "She's the girl on all the Foley billboards, right?" A few of his cousins nodded feebly. "Oh. I never met her," he shrugged at Conor. "Plus, I always thought the rule was that we couldn't go within 500 feet of her. How are we gonna take her on a date, Maggot?"

"We're not allowed to cross the property line," Pat volunteered, just to say something.

"Or her asshole dad will shoot us," Killian murmured, nodding sympathetically at Pat, whose stomach was again besieged by hot guilt.

"Yeah!" Aidan said, pointing helpfully at Pat's face, "Look, he already shot Goldy once!"

"My dick can reach 500 feet," Hacker intoned, finally looking up from his phone. "I could take her out."

Everyone laughed, and the atmosphere felt somewhat lighter.

"So," Oscar said to Conor, with the air of one clearing up a matter once and for all, "If we're not legally allowed to go near this girl, Conchobar, how could any of us even ask her on a date?"

"It coulda been a blind date," Onacona said thoughtfully, sending a smattering of striped balls flying towards the table's pockets. "Maybe they met on Plenty of Fish or something, and when they got to the restaurant, they just really liked each other."

"So is that how it happened?" Conor leaned forward, his voice soft and lethal. "Don't lie to your tribal elder, now..."

Onacona shrugged. "Not saying it was me."

"But you're not *not* saying it, either."

"You have to have a profile pic up for Plenty of Fish," Kiki said inconsequentially. "Not for OKCupid, though…"

"Jesus, Conor!" Baby Mickey suddenly burst out, "I guess everyone's a suspect to you."

"Guilty until proven innocent," Conor agreed, folding his arms over his ox-like chest, "That's right."

"Chill, 5-0, I'm married," Oscar held up his ringed hand.

"So am I," Killian muttered, refilling his and Slaw's glasses.

"Conchobar, how do we know it's not *you*?" Eamon said suddenly, "You're the one who's obsessed with her. You're the one who's always telling stories about arresting her and chasing her all the goddamn time." An "*mmm*" of agreement rippled through the room. "You're the only one of us who's even been around her, right?" He looked around for support. Pat nodded untruthfully, guessing the fact that he woke up that morning with the Foley heiress's bare spine pressed into his chest counted for being around her.

"Hey!" Killian stood up, laying a protective hand on Conor's shoulder. "It's called being a cop, Eems. That Foley girl's a spoiled bitch who thinks she can just do 70 in a 45."

"That's right!" Conor bellowed appreciatively. Pat's hackles rose.

"And let the record state," Killian added, nodding around the room with chieftain pride, "That of *all* you guys, only my family can sit here and say that none of us have been in Foley Bourbon, and we grew up right next door." He folded his arms over the Walsh logo on his Polo, "Now how's that for a clean conscience?"

If the outcries hadn't been so loud, ("We *had* to go for a field trip!" moaned Aidan, "You dared me to go over once and ask for some lemonade!" Kiki called out) Killian might have noticed that all three of his brothers fell suspiciously silent at this, with Seamus tossing Pat a smirk.

"Alright then!" Conor shouted, recovering himself. "Let's settle this once and for all. Kiki, get me the Bible."

"Wait, I've got it." Seamus stood at once, rifling through his backpack and producing Black-Jack's biography.

"No," Conor shook his head, "I meant the actual *fucking* Bible. Keeks," he looked at his cousin, "Don't you have it here?"

"Yeah, sure." Obediently, Kiki jogged behind the bar, locating the Bible under the First Aid kit. "Gotta be prepared in case the zombies or ISIS show up."

Pat realized with dread where this was all going.

"I'll go first," Conor had Kiki hold the Bible for him, which he put his palm over like a witness being sworn in. "I swear to God, on the Holy Bible," his green eyes fell on Black-Jack's mugshot beside the dart board, "*And* on Black-Jack and Clara's graves that I didn't take Blaise Foley on a date, nor would I *ever* betray my brethren like that."

"You didn't say *no crosses count!*" Eamon sang. Pat silently cursed him, because he was counting on using this playground wormhole.

"*No crosses count!*" Conor added firmly. "Now, I want you all to do the same. Or your name is as good as dog-shit with me. *And* you'll be voted out of the High Fraternal Order of Black Jack." He looked at Killian, who nodded in support.

"That's right," the Chief agreed, "You can go to Foley to drink." The room met this with loud boos and jeers, which Killian ignored. "*Keeks,*" he called behind the bar to his cousin, "When we find out who our fallen brother is, *don't* serve him until Slaw and I say." He glanced around the assembly with his Stern Dad face on. "We'll still love him, but he'll need to do some penance so he can realize the error of his ways."

Kiki nodded obediently, and no one argued. You didn't challenge the distillers, because they reserved the right to cut you off, and then you'd be fucked—very fucked indeed.

"Right," Conor was looking very pleased with the level of indignation he had drummed up. He held the Bible out to Killian, "My family'll go first."

"Oh, with pleasure!" Killian slammed his hand on the Bible, "I swear to God on Black-Jack *and* Clara's graves that I didn't take Blaise Foley on a date." His blue eyes shone with a rare, savage gleam. "And I additionally swear that if she *ever* told me I couldn't drink our family's bourbon in front of her, I'd go Wilkie on her rickhouses."

The pledge was met with whoops and wild Apache calls.

"Thanks Chief," Conor applauded his big brother, adding in a respectful undertone, "You were never considered a suspect."

"Goldy," Conor held the Bible out to him.

If he were, say, the 6th or 7th one to go, Pat could groan that this whole spectacle was getting ridiculous, and they were all grown men taking oaths that ended in No Crosses Count—wasn't there something wrong with this picture? But the excitement of ceremony was still alive in the room as all the Walsh boys turned to face him. Pat knew from Seamus's grim, bracing look that he fully expected Pat to confess. For all his dermal layers of irreverence and debauchery, his twin was honorable at his core. He would not perjure himself before his band of brothers, no more than he would sleep with any of their wives or girlfriends. Whether you were 5 or 75, you just didn't lie when you swore on Black-Jack and Clara's graves. You just *didn't.*

"Thanks bro, for making me relive my PTSD of getting shot," Pat forced himself to chuckle, laying his clammy hand on the Bible. He hoped like hell that he looked every bit the Golden Boy that everyone was always saying he was, because his insides were a bag of live worms. "I swear to God that I *would* take the Foley heiress on a date, but I can't chew steak anymore, because her dad's bullet took out my goddamn molars."

Everyone laughed, even Conor, who moved on to Seamus without demanding a more complete vow. He couldn't believe his good luck! *Chalk that one up to being born on St. Paddy's Day,* he thought blissfully.

Beside him, his twin loudly swore on his honor as a soldier that he would obey the Constitution of the United States against all enemies, foreign and domestic—

"Wrong vow, Fuck-Fuck," Conor grunted, as laughter rippled through the room. "Just answer, did you take the Foley heiress on a date or not?"

"Sir no, sir!"

As Pat predicted, everyone quickly lost interest in Conor's witch hunt (Hacker was funny: "I swear to God," he uttered, his chubby cheeks still, "In the presence of Black-Jack, that I would never betray my brotherhood by asking out our enemy—why, did she say something?"). By the time it was Baby's turn, the guys were having side conversations and scrolling through their phones. Conor, however, looked more homicidal than ever while he ordered Mickey to swear not only on Black-Jack and Clara's graves, but upon the lives of his parents and brothers that he wasn't the traitor.

"I swear." Mickey's huge eyes looked fit to crack.

"Now say, 'God strike my father down and send me straight to hell if I'm lying—"

"Enough!" Oscar and Slaw both yelled.

"Alright," Conor withdrew the Bible, adding in a scathing undertone, "Just hope Uncle Mart doesn't have a heart-attack tomorrow..." He raised his voice, surveying the group mistrustfully, "I don't know who the Judas is among us—"

"Oh, does that make you Jesus?" Seamus called out.

Conor flipped him off without looking at him, "But I hope you can sleep tonight knowing that you lied on the Bible, *and* Black-Jack and Clara's graves."

Kiki, busy pouring bourbons for a middle-aged couple from Missouri who were doing the Kentucky Bourbon Trail, leaned over the bar and hissed, "Conchobar, take it down a notch. We have *real* customers present."

"I'm not a real customer?" Kildare roared in his Santa hat, rattling his empty glass of ice.

Oscar sighed pityingly at the whole scene, because he was a busy lawyer who only had 1-2 drinks on weeknights, and had a pretty, pastel-wearing wife waiting for him at home. "Guess that's a wrap." He grabbed his briefcase, "If we're not doing Secret Santa, I'm gonna clear out of here."

"We're not doing Secret Santa?" Kiki bawled, forgetting about his real customers and looking crestfallen.

"I wouldn't want to risk Conor getting me," Onacona said darkly, glancing up from the billiards table. "I'll wake up with a horse-head in my bed. '*Merry Christmas!*"

"Yeah, Schneeball's head," Conor sneered. No one but Pat caught the reference, because they were the only two who cared to know the name of Blaise's horse.

In the questionable Safe of the grubby McGettigan's bathroom, he texted his sweet Blaise:

Foleyyyyy :- :-* hi beautiful I can't wait to see you later...haven't been able to get you off my mind all day. When you come over, do you think George could drive you, just so your car doesn't get recognized? :)*

Blaise would understand the need for precaution. After all, sneaking around was half the fun of their forbidden love.

The first time Blaise visited Pat and Seamus's house was by carriage of a taxi, which Pat insisted on paying for, dashing out into the evening drizzle with his wallet. After Blaise admired the house's many rooms (and silently pursed her lips at the Carrie Underwood poster), they fell into their new greeting ritual: first, they kissed for a good ten minutes, letting their hands graze over the other's limbs, as if proving to themselves that they were actually real. Then Pat poured them both Jamesons over two ice cubes, and Blaise assumed her recumbent stance on Pat's velour couch. He removed her heels with the tender wonder of a groom undressing his virginal bride, and Blaise smiled upon him in lazy comfort.

The whiskey traveled swiftly to her brain, applying a Midas-like touch to her many thoughts. She thought how amazing and sweet Pat would be, on top of her, inside her, her inaugural sex and possibly her ultimate. Of course she *wanted* Patrick Alan Walsh, but she was only now coming to truly trust him. After their sexy slumber-party, Blaise stopped telling herself at every turn that all this was a sick bet, and the boys at McGettigan's had pooled their money and wagered that Pat couldn't get the Foley heiress to sleep with him ("I think you've seen *Cruel Intentions* too many times," Elliott told her).

Pat massaged Blaise's feet; his expression thoughtful. She had just asked him how knew that Palmer wasn't, in his words, his "Forever Babe."

"Well, for one, I knew you were still out there," Pat said suavely, and Blaise went "aw!" (she secretly hoped he would say that). "But there were two other big things."

"Tell me," Blaise said, mewing with pleasure as he rubbed the balls of her feet.

Pat explained to Blaise how Palmer rang in 2012 with an ultimatum: propose this year, or they break-up. Pat, ever the reasonable man, spent a good few months evaluating things as they stood. Palmer did so many things well: she attended family weddings and earned rave reviews from the Walsh Wives (and crushes from his little cousins). She drank Walsh bourbon around his family (but sweet chardonnay in private) and made them dinners that she took pictures of and uploaded to Facebook. She gave blowjobs with alacrity—though Pat took note here of an unswerving frequency: it was as though Palmer believed that twice-weekly blowjobs, thrice weekly spinning classes, and a quarterly family wedding was the algorithm that would lead to their own starry engagement.

"Well, I went camping with Crummy..."

"*Crummy!*" Blaise cheered fondly, and Pat grinned.

"We were out by Cumberland Falls, and I was marinating on this decision, ya know, letting the whiskey deforest all the trees in my head," he went on, "And I realized that she couldn't concede me on two important points…"

"Which were?" Blaise playfully rubbed a foot over his chiseled cheekbone. He grabbed her ankle and wetly kissed her painted toes with sudden ferocity. It was sexy and a little scary, that her feet could awaken the beast in him like that.

"Well for one, she would *never* let me do that," Pat said dolefully, "She hated that I was always wanting to play with her feet."

"What? *Why!*" Blaise said, wondering how someone could veto such pleasure. "The way I see it, it's $10 less that I have to pay Mai when I get a pedi!"

"I don't know" Pat replied. "She just thought it was weird. She called it my "little problem."

"She called your foot fetish a *little problem*?"

Pat felt himself go red. He had never actually said the words, "I have a foot fetish" aloud. Only Crummy knew, because he was the type of friend with whom you could share a secret so deeply vaulted, not even your twin knew about it. When they camped,

Crummy, in his infinite wisdom, put it to him in blunt terms. "It's a long haul, Walsh. Do you want a lifetime of jerking it to foot-job vids on PornHub?"

"No," Pat said absolutely. It was a glorious feeling to realize that he was still free to say yes or no.

He told Crummy what he repeated to Blaise now, the other thing that made him feel it wasn't right: Palmer and Seamus had never gotten along. He recalled at a barbecue how Palmer shrugged unapologetically when Pat asked her to stop using the phrase "dead soldiers" for the empty bottles, because it offended Seamus. *Pat, it's a common expression.* And Seamus, hearing her, wearing his Killed in Action bracelet for Kevin Carr, yelled *Have you ever actually seen a dead soldier, Palmer?* He stormed off and Pat called him, concerned, and Palmer cried her old lament, *you always choose him over me. You never defend me.* Later, she made her familiar pitch in tones meant to sooth and tantalize *I think we'd be really happy if we moved home to Mobile. You could still see Seamus every month or two, but I think it's time to cut the cord.*

"That's why" Pat said to Blaise, "If you like me at all..." (Blaise made a 'so-so' gesture and he laughed shyly) "You have to love Shay."

As if on cue, Seamus's Biscayne whizzed down the driveway with the music blasting. Suddenly Blaise was very nervous. Imagine if Seamus just kept jeering and sneering at her like Conor did until her smile grew strained, and she finally snapped?

—Now I have reverted back to the First Person, because saying "*he*" instead of "*me*" in this transformative moment feels all wrong.

I knew she was there. I ordered her there, because I was being eaten alive by curiosity. The goddess with the pickled liver, the girl I wasn't sure existed but for dreams dissolved on your pillow, *Blaise fucking Foley*, had somehow synced up her orbit with my twin brother's. You have to understand, I expected her to sail in on a seashell like Venus.

I could not believe Pat's audacity in telling a story about her, calling her "Blaise" with a familiarity that seemed almost vulgar. How dare he say, "Oh Blaise likes that movie," in the same breath that he talked about his job or garbage night or any of his other daily banalities.

I guess that I wanted to normalize her too, but I thought the best I could hope for was to become a docent in the museum where her portrait hung and attain a master's degree in her mannerisms.

When she watched me clomp through my back door, she did not smile at me, which seared my heart most splendidly. She was studying me over her shoulder, arms folded, tequila sunrise hair tousled down her back. My mind absorbed the lint along her prominent shoulder blade and the purple crescent moons under her eyes (it would soon be rewired with Venus vision, absolutely unseeing of her imperfections).

"Hi," I said stupidly.

"Hi," Blaise replied. Then, quietly, almost shyly, "Are you mean like Conor?"

"*No!*" I couldn't help but laugh. "*Fuck* Conor!"

Pat zipped up his Patagonia, announcing that he was going outside to grill up the steaks. He asked Blaise with the annoying thrill of new intimacy, "How do you like yours cooked?"

"Rare, please!" she answered.

"Me too, bro."

When we were alone again, she gazed at me timidly. I realized that I didn't know what to call her—Foley? Or *Blaise*?

"So you like your steak bloody?" I blurted idiotically.

"Like *Friday the 13th*," she replied, allowing a bite-sized smile. I felt the pegs tightly holding my sinew come unscrewed a few turns.

As we sat at the table, (not in front of the TV) I noticed that Pat was trying to make our isosceles triangle into an equilateral one. Let me explain: in social settings, whenever Pat and I form triads or quartets, there are always things uttered between us that no one else could understand. I can't give examples, because they fade away like scribbles on a shaken Etch-A-Sketch. But it's our movie, really, and we can make everyone else the extras if we want to.

I tried to pull him back to me, but Pat kept bringing her right along. "Oh, Shay was just saying X," "Remember how I told you about Y, Blaise?"

When you're an identical twin, no one, mother or lover, could ever love you (or loathe you) like the other half of your zygote. As certain as the sun sets in the West, I know that I'm the love of Pat's life. When I lived in Iraq, he would set his alarm for three a.m. to call me. If I died in Iraq, half of him would've died with me.

But as we sat there eating steak, (not marinated in Walsh bourbon sauce) I had the feeling that I was losing out to Blaise Foley. If she kept coming around, I would no longer be Pat's #1 Favorite Person Ever. His adoring gaze foretold a prophecy of all of us losing out to her, me and all the guys who grumbled her name at McGettigan's the other night.

All of this might have been alarming, were it not for how she acted towards me. Blaise seemed like she was on a date with both of us. For every irresistible smile she flashed Pat, I got one too. When telling a story, she volleyed her expressive face between both of us. It was flattering, I won't lie. Especially after Palmer, who regarded me like a stepson she couldn't wait to ship off to boarding school.

The three of us spoke a dialect native to the children of Zzyzyx Road. Pat and I teased her for how she pronounced our last name her (*Wash,* no L). She laughed, saying it was an affectation of her father's. She imitated Mr. Foley's crusty bluster: "I *told Wawsh that it's all gonna come out in the wawsh. Then I said, Hildy-baby, do you mind getting my wawsh?"* She told us the stories about Conor, and they were far more vivid and colorful coming from her lips. Interestingly, our brother had failed to mention all the times Blaise Foley beat him when they raced down Zzyzyx.

Blaise charmed and seduced us both, winning the votes for queen of our bicameral court. The element I associated with her before was fire. She was still fire, but now I felt deep warmth from her rather than a scalding burn. She was, to us, the old nursery rhyme about the girl with the curl but in reverse: *when she was bad, she was really, REALLY bad...but when she was good, she was glory.*

"Shay, Blaise has all these old pictures of Black-Jack at her house," Pat told me, tipping more Jameson into my glass.

"Yeah!" Blaise nodded avidly at me, "And postcards! Jack and my great-Grandpa used to go to Cuba together all the time," she giggled, "I found one he sent one to my great-grandma Deirdre: *'Havana great time, but wish the Black Beauty were here.'*"

"Deirdre..." I echoed. How weird to hear about the people whited-out of my family's history.

I knew my brother was eager to get the last 24-year-old virgin in America into his sheets (we went over my Rue St. Dennis playbook this morning) so I decided to leave them alone in bliss and sin. Before I left, we invited Blaise to come along tomorrow to pick out a Christmas tree.

"We can drive out to Sassafras to pick one up," Pat said sportingly, naming a Podunk town three hours west on Route 15. "If we get spotted there too, Shay and I'll just have to say we kidnapped you as ransom for Jack's treasure."

Blaise agreed, sensually rubbing her hand along his cheek. "It's not kidnapping if I go willingly," she purred. He kissed each phalanx of her knuckles, gazing into her eyes. I drained my glass and rose to the warmth spreading down my stomach.

"You don't have to leave," they both said to me placidly. Her legs were slung over his lap.

I told them I was just going to McGettigan's for a nightcap, even though I didn't really want to.

At the bar, I had a drink with my second cousins Kerry and Kildare, and thought of the fourth cousins together just down the road. When I imagined them exploring each other's bodies and kissing so earnestly, I swore I loved them more kindly than their Creator.

Alright, James Branagh out. Back to your regular scheduled programming.

Every spring in Louisville, the dull brown winter was thawed by the excitement of impending the Kentucky Derby, which was held the first Saturday in May since 1875.

In Walsh and Foley World, the months leading up to Derby Day were paved with various bourbon events. In February, the Meet-the-Distiller series took place at the Kentucky Colosseum, a gilded theatre which also hosted the Miss Teen Louisville pageant and the Bluegrass Festival. People paid $50 to mill around the great hall, tasting bourbon and shaking hands with the likes of Messers Foley, Barnaby, and Walsh. Everyone left the event with a bias towards Foley or Walsh, and a six-p.m. hangover.

Killian Walsh enlisted only the best manpower to assist in the Meet-the-Distiller series. Actually, his crew consisted of whichever cousins or brothers happened to be free and not hungover on a Thursday afternoon. This year, the honor fell to his brother Conor, and little cousins, Aidan (Douska) and Manquilla (Hacker). Killian offered the guys each $50 and a t-shirt for their time.

Conor borrowed his cousin Eem's pickup truck to transport the barrel. Then they just had to roll it through the atrium, plug a spigot in, slap up a few placards of Black-Jack, and they were in business.

Inside the gaudy ballroom, other distillers were just starting to set up. The conch-shaped speakers above their heads dimly played bluegrass ("Kentucky muzak," Aidan murmured). The Walsh boys took blatant sips of their bourbon directly from the spigot. Mr. Barnaby hurled them a disgusted look from the next booth over, shaking his white, leonine head. Hacker waved merrily, a trickle of whisky running down his pudgy chin.

"Douska, put out the cups" Conor droned at Aidan. To Hacker, he said, "Fuck-fuck, what the *hell* are you wearing? "

Hacker shrugged. He wore a graphic t-shirt of Chief Sitting Bull standing proudly on the bloody corpse of General Custer, warbow in hand.

"Put this on," Conor barked, hurling a Walsh tee his way. "You gotta represent the brand—" He stopped abruptly, because just then Blaise Foley clacked in the room, trench-coat and red hair flapping behind her.

"Foley!" Conor thundered, his voice reverberating like a fog-horn.

Blaise lowered her sunglasses one inch. "*Walsh!*" she called back in sarcastic
singsong.

Douska and Hacker automatically looked up at the sound of their name, then elbowed each other, smirking. All 15 of Wilkie's grandsons had heard tales of Maggot's flammable rivalry with the Foley heiress. Now they were going to get to witness a live show.

"Saw your new billboard," Conor whooped, referring to the sultry ad of Blaise drinking bourbon in a negligee. "God, are sales so low that the million-dollar-heiress has to resort to stripping?"

"Billion dollar, actually," Blaise said pityingly, taking a few steps closer. "And ew Walsh!" she wrinkled her nose in disgust, "I don't want to hear about how you found a new spot to park your cop car and jerk off."

"Get over yourself," Conor sneered, laying his palms on the stand. "I'm married now, to a girl who's hotter than you." He looked to his little cousins as though expecting them to chorus, "*way* hotter!" but they both stood there frozen. (Plus, as they furtively looked the Foley heiress up and down, they didn't necessarily agree).

Blaise glared at Conor, match in hand. For that rude comment, she was ready to not only burn him, but *cremate* him (after all, he had seen her naked—a girl has her pride).

"You know, Walsh," she clacked closer still, "I heard that you had a little meeting at McGettigan's a few months back." Blaise made her voice drippy with condescension, "You put your little cop hat on and were trying to solve a mystery about just *who* took me on a date!" she smirked and sang her best Mariah Carey, "*Why you so obsessed with me, boy I wanna know…*"

Douska and Hacker came unfrosted, doubling over with laughter. Conor's arm swung out and caught Hacker in his belly.

"Who told you that, Foley?" he seethed, his face burning fuchsia.

"*Obviously* I heard it from the boy I'm seeing—duh" Blaise smirked, "You know him. But he's nicer than you. Cuter, too." With that, she turned triumphantly on her heel.

Conor couldn't let her get last licks. "Yeah, well have fun fucking your cousin, you Kentucky *cousin-fucker!*" he yelled after her.

Blaise halted. She whipped around, and in one second, her face transformed to full-on possessed. "What did you say to me?"

Conor hesitated, but he couldn't back down, not with his little cousins watching. "Well, only pure Kentucky *trash* would fuck their cousin—"

Blaise ran at him full-force, her heels clacking hotly against the linoleum. Douska and Hacker both leapt back, thinking she was going to jump-tackle him. Instead, Blaise reached into her trench coat and, like a cowboy drawing a gun from his holster, ripped out the flask strapped to her leg. She viciously slashed Conor with streams of bourbon, sending him into howls of protest.

"IT'S IN MY MOUTH!" he screamed, sinking to the floor like a soldier hit blasted with mustard gas.

"How's that taste?" Blaise screamed, and she dumped the flask of Foley clean over his block head.

"Miss Foley!" Mr. Barnaby strode out from behind his booth, "What in the name of Seabiscuit's saddle is going on here?"

At once, Blaise woke up from her rage seizure. "I'm sorry, Mr. Barnaby," she breathed, letting her arms go limp. She pat her red hair and face, looking about the room with dawning embarrassment.

"Well you're gonna hafta apologize to your daddy too, for wasting good bourbon like that," Mr. Barnaby tutted. He clutched her elbow paternally and guided her away.

Hacker and Aidan peered down on Conor as he got to his feet, drenched and coughing. Around the ballroom, distillers in khaki pants were staring at them in different degrees of puzzlement and disgust. There were always jokes about not putting the Foleys and Walshes next to each other. Now it would be the talk of the day.

"Are you alright, dude?" Hacker asked tentatively.

Conor ignored him. "This proves it," he fumed, scrubbing his face with a paper towel. "Beyond a shadow of a doubt."

"Proves what?" Douska asked, pushing his glasses up the bridge of his nose.

"Who the real Brutus is among us," Conor spat in his most baleful tone, "Who's sold his soul to Satan." When they continued to look stumped, he scoffed, "*Obviously* she's fucking Mickey."

"But she didn't say anything about Mickey," Douska frowned.

"Not by name but," Conor stared at them as though they were missing the Goodyear blimp in a game of I Spy, "C'mon guys, do you really need to me say it?"

"Say *what*?" Hacker demanded.

"No offense," Conor's serious expression didn't crack, "But Mickey's the only one who's *possibly* cuter than me." His cousins exchanged a look, which Conor misinterpreted as their shared devastation. "Don't look like I said something horrible, ladies—you asked for it."

Blaise called Pat straightaway from the bathroom to explain: she lost her temper on his brother and doused him in bourbon in the middle of the Kentucky Colosseum. Was he mad?

"Of course I'm not mad," Pat murmured, standing in the dim stairwell of his office, high from the warmth of her voice. "He was a *dick*. He totally deserved that. I'm sorry he spoke to you that way, babe." They said their I love yous, a new but giddy policy, and signed off.

Pat was secretly fuming, not at Blaise, but at Conor.

"He can't talk to her that way," he roughly told his tribunal (Crummy and Seamus) over dinner that night.

They were at La Boca Feliz, a shoddy Mexican joint far flung from Zzyzx Road. It was $4 margarita night. Seamus lied to do the waitress, claiming that it was Crummy's fortieth birthday, (he was barely 27) and the mariachi band had come over to play 'Feliz Cumpleanos' three times so far. At least the flan would be free.

"I wanna call him out *so bad*." Pat went on, flexing his fists, "I'd never speak to his girlfriend like that."

"That's a false equivalence," Crummy differed.

Seamus agreed, "To him, Foley isn't your girlfriend, she's the Roadrunner to his Wiley Coyote."

"Fine, but I don't want to be the guy who sits back and does nothing," Pat said, tersely cramming a chip in his mouth. "What's Blaise gonna think?"

Crummy struck a wise pose, drinking his cheap margarita as though it were a cognac by the fire. "I don't think that's the best way for you guys to come out of the closet, man."

"Neither do I," Seamus agreed. "You know he'll campaign hard against you. He'll get Killian worked up over the bourbon thing, you know—" he mimicked Conor's highfalutin voice, *"Pato refuses to drink your bourbon since he got with her!"* And he'll get Dad going on the past, and Jesus—he'll tell Kilkenny's sons that Blaise drinks Irish car-bombs or something. And forget about Uncle Shy's crew," Seamus crunched ominously on a tortilla chip, "All Con has to do is *mention* that Blaise had an uncle named after Andy Jackson..."

"Well, fuck all of 'em, then," Pat said coldly, "If they're not going to accept her."

"Walsh, you don't mean that," Crummy said, in an almost fatherly way. "You *love* the Walsh brotherhood." His looked a bit doleful, "You'll be the best man in my wedding, but I'm not even sure I'll make your groomsmen cut."

"'Course you will," Pat said stoutly. "Whoever heard of the lone horseman of the apocalypse?" ("Ayy" Crummy grinned).

"I think you should stick with the original plan," Seamus opined, draining his rocks glass and snapping his fingers for another.

"St. Paddy's Day Massacre," Pat murmured.

"What's that?" Crummy asked.

"Pato brings Blaise as his date to our family's St. Paddy's Day party," Seamus explained, "Everyone meets her all at once, with a *noiiiiice*, healthy buzz on."

"No one can get *too* mad," Pat added, tapping his temple craftily, "Because it'll be our birthday, too. You can't throw someone outta their own birthday party."

"Pretty goddamn genius," Crummy nodded, looking impressed.

The mariachi band, thinking Seamus had signaled to them, began advancing on their table, belting out a passionate rendition of 'Guantanamera.'

"Jesus," Crummy groaned, barely audible over the trumpet and accordion. "I feel like I'm on Spring Break in Hell."

Pat tossed the band a fiver, politely declining their offer of an encore.

"Okay, so we'll do that plan: keep it under wraps until St. Paddy's Day." He crunched another chip, adding in a more optimistic tone, "Blaise already said she'd go."

"It'll be okay," Crummy said, without much conviction. He knew how intense Pat's family was. He had the bruises and lacerations from their drunken rugby matches to prove it.

The only point that the Foleys would ever concede to the Walshes was the supremacy of their St. Paddy's Day parties. The Foleys, for all their dignified Irish pride (or perhaps because of it) did *not* celebrate the holiday with bright green hullabaloo. Every March 17th, Mr. Foley offered his wife and daughter corsages of green carnations, and the family went to mass at St. Brigid's, where Aunt Lucretia had once served as a nun. At home, the family had a quiet meal of shepherd's pie or wild salmon, their table set for no more than six.

Maybe their St. Paddy's Day was subdued because they knew they couldn't compete with the Walshes' bacchanalia. The Foleys had no shortage of cash or class, but pure fun wasn't something Mr. Foley couldn't brew inside his distilling room. Even if they *tried* to host a competing party, all the bagpipers within a fifty-mile radius went straight to the Walshes' church after the St. Paddy's Day parade. The Dixie Dubliners, a local band who put a bluegrass spin on Irish folk music, came to play every year. Mrs. Walsh hadn't bothered booking them since the mid-90s.

The Walshes' party started at five p.m. in the sprawling gymnasium of their church. It went until five or six a.m., when Father Tierney came downstairs to yell that they were disrupting morning mass. Usually the cops were called at some point in the evening, but they were sweet-talked into taking a shot or doing a jig in the middle of the dance-floor. Now that Conor Walsh was a boy in blue, the cop's arrival was something to be embraced rather than feared.

Their St. Paddy's Day was the best party of the year. Newcomers often said it was the best party of their lives. Veterans of the party knew to take off from work the next day. Walsh grooms idealized the party as a blueprint their own weddings, seeking to match it in levels of fun and memorability.

At three p.m. on March 17th, Mrs. Walsh was starting to get worried. Her husband Sean wasn't back yet from picking up one of the fiddlers in Lexington who had somehow missed the caravan to Louisville.

Her concern wasn't that Sean might drink and drive (he got a DWI the day the twins were born in '86, and would tell you it was a lesson learned), but that she may not have time to talk with him in private.

She had big news, and she needed to give it before the party got underway.

Yesterday, her son Patrick asked her to lunch, picking a lovely restaurant not far from the Daisy Crown distillery. Pat left Seamus at home, an unprecedented move that signaled to her that he had something major to tell her.

At the table, Patrick fidgeted and nodded blindly with the topics she raised, while she silently prayed that he hadn't had a bad bill of health. When she brought up tomorrow's St. Paddy's Day party, his dreamy eyes fell sharply into focus.

"Mom, that's what I wanted to talk to you about." Patrick cleared his throat and sat up in his chair, "I want to bring someone to the party."

"Really, dear?" she murmured, fully steadying herself for a blow. Here it was, the thing she had neglected to see in her brother Alan, the confirmed bachelor who lived in Cork. If any of her sons were to be a puff, she imagined it would've been Killian. He never left her side as a boy.

"Yeah…" Pat continued slowly, "She's someone I've been seeing for a while now—" *She!* "—but I'm worried my family won't accept her."

"Patrick, dear. Is she, you know," Mrs. Walsh delicately mouthed *Jewish* as the server leaned in to refill her teacup. "Because it's different nowadays, dear. You remember your cousin Ailish, she married the banker from London. My sister didn't mind, dear, she just can't phone them on Saturdays."

Patrick's handsome face broke into a chuckle, "No Mom, she's actually Irish-Catholic."

"Well dear, then what's the problem?" Mrs. Walsh laughed, plunging into her tea with such relief that she scalded her tongue. "And what is all this pomp and circumstance about...*of course* your family will accept any girl of yours!"

Patrick chewed his muffaletta sandwich thoughtfully. He seemed to be in a state of hard hesitation. Finally, he swallowed and asked, "Do you just want to meet her?"

Of course, Mrs. Walsh agreed. Ten minutes later, Blaise was standing at the table, shaking her bony hand with a quavering smile.

Seamus predicted that their mother would instantly—and inherently—*love* Blaise. Mrs. Walsh, after all, had an artery of prestige running through her: if speaking of someone who went to Trinity or an Ivy, she managed to work it into conversation. She wasn't overly showy about her crystal, but somehow even little Fiona knew to call her glasses Waterford.

Decades worth of anti-Foley propaganda were not enough to corrupt Mrs. Walsh's knowledge that "Foley" was the most impressive of all the Irish brands that she so cherished and admired. She looked at Blaise, the beautiful, motherless, heiress with old money manners, and saw a lifetime of lunches like this. She saw holiday meals served under heirloom Beleek porcelain; a date to bridal and baby showers, and the effusive female companionship that she, a woman with four sons, so desperately craved.

When Patrick got up to use the bathroom, Blaise's good posture imploded. "I love him," she blurted out, her eyes dancing and desperate. Mrs. Walsh patted the girl's nail-bitten hand and said that this was very dear.

When Blaise took her turn in the bathroom, Patrick swiveled in his seat to watch her go. Mrs. Walsh murmured that she was lovely, and Pat agreed, smiling dazedly.

"I'm in love with her," he said plainly. Mrs. Walsh said again that it was very dear, but as dear as it all was, she knew that the news would not be universally well-received. She believed that her job as matriarch was to smooth over all the hard-lines her men drew. She feared Sean and his brothers might do something rash, like cancel the party, once they heard who Patrick's date was.

"What's a fella to do?" Sean sang merrily to her now, busting into the church hall carrying an amp with a string of musicians trailing behind him. *"When her hair is black and her eyes were blue*?" He had been singing Galway Girl to her for years now. Now he also sang it to little Fiona, who was born with the same china doll coloring.

"Her hair is gray and her eyes are blind," his wife deadpanned, crossing the room in her satin green ballerina flats. "In other news, dear, it might interest you to know that your son is in love."

"Which one?" Sean asked distractedly, unraveling a chunky orange extension cord. "Better be the two already married."

"The one we broke our wedding vows for," Mrs. Walsh said steadily. She wished to God Killian had arrived with the bourbon already. These tidings would go down so much better with a nice whiskey emollient. "Patrick has a glad eye for the girl-next-door."

"What girl-next-door?" Sean asked, frowning. "You mean, a Meg Ryan type?"

"Over the hedges," Mrs. Walsh whispered, and Sean dropped the cord in his hands.

"Foley?" he uttered, conjuring up an image of the red-haired girl fighting with Con outside his window. "No," Sean shook his head firmly, "Pat's too smart to be that stupid."

"She loves him back," Mrs. Walsh said, not without a dash of pride.

"John's *daughter*?" Sean breathed. It was inconceivable, sheer madness what his wife was telling him. *"No…"*

"Come," Mrs. Walsh led her stunned husband down the corridor, into one of the classrooms where Sunday school was taught. Today's lesson, she told him, would be on love and acceptance.

Sean sent his son Patrick a text message asking what time he planned on being there. Pat wrote back, *"Around 6:30. See you soon! :)"* He cursed his son's blithe cheerfulness, but nevertheless at 6:15 herded his present sons, three brothers, and eleven nephews into a vacant classroom for a quick meeting. Some of the Walsh wives watched curiously from across the gym, but none of them seemed to feel it was pressing enough to leave their tight clump to join them.

"Alright, is everyone here?" Sean impatiently addressed the cramped crowd, closing the door so hard the glass pane rattled. "Dad? A moment?" His elderly father Wilkie stood in the center of everyone, blithely gabbing about his new shillelagh stick and how smoothly it fit into the palm of his hand (Shilah's sons were doubled over with silent laughter).

"Dad, what's wrong?" Killian asked, bouncing his toddler son John-Patrick on his hip.

"Well, Mom just told me," Sean looked to his wife, who had a death grip on his hand, like a dog trainer fearing her pitbull might go off the leash, "That we have a guest coming tonight who wouldn't ordinarily be at one of our family functions. Oh, hi Father Tim," he said unenthusiastically, as the meddlesome priest crept in the door behind him, clutching a plate of food and a cigarette.

"Who is it?" one of the boys demanded.

"Well, she's here as someone's date—"

"Is it the Foley heiress?" Kiki called out avidly, his eyes shining behind his horn-rimmed glasses.

"*Yeah!*" his father Avanoca snorted sarcastically, clapping Keeks on the shoulder, "And Carmen Electra's coming around for dessert, son."

When Sean and his wife exchanged an arrested look, Avanoca's jaw dropped incredulously.

"Sean, the Foley heiress?" he called out, "You're not serious—?"

Mrs. Walsh piggybacked off of that, "I've met her," she said, in the same voice she used to coax medicine down her son's throats as children, "Her name is Blaise, and she's absolutely lovely—"

"Wait, John's *daughter*?" Sean's brother Martin roared.

"Sully's grand-daughter?" Wilkie called enchantedly, looking as though life still held surprises for him after all.

"Blaise was the patron saint of knitwear, you know," Father Tim volunteered, affably forking his corned beef. Everyone ignored him except for Mrs. Walsh, who made a polite "*ah?*" sound.

"Uncle Sean, whose date is she coming as?" Oscar piped up, sounding equal parts curious and wary.

"This time no one can accuse me!" Mickey announced, holding his hands high in the air, "I came stag."

"They'll be here soon enough," Sean said, without smiling. "But the point of this meeting is this: it's important to my wife that you act civilly—"

"—Both of us would appreciate it," Mrs. Walsh cut in smoothly, "If you treated our guest as you would treat any other guest. I will be very displeased if I hear any accounts of someone being rude to her. *Especially* my boys." She sternly met Killian's eyes, who looked as though he might cry for maybe the fourth time in his adult life.

"Well, I don't know what she's gonna drink," he burst out roughly, "I didn't make any fuckin' Foley bourbon for her!"

"Daddy, you said the F word!" Fiona cheered, bouncing gleefully at his ankles in her pink tutu.

"Killian," his father said warningly.

"I'll be nice to her, Mommy," Seamus promised, stepping forward to unceremoniously hug his mother. Everyone else was filing out, eager to stand guard for the Foley girl's entrance with her mystery date.

"I know you will, dear," Mrs. Walsh murmured. "And Happy Birthday."

Conor had been sent out to pick up ice by his mother, (perhaps in a tactical maneuver) so he missed the big announcement.

When he came in the side door of Blessed Sacrament church, whistling and swinging the dripping bags, he stopped abruptly in his tracks. There was Blaise Foley, casually sitting there under the display of confirmation class photos. Somehow Conor would have been less surprised if Jesus himself floated down from the ceiling. This was the Walshes' church: a Foley hadn't stepped foot inside since Sully Foley came seeking absolution after a wild Vegas weekend in '57. And she damn well knew it.

"Foley, what the hell are you doing in our church?" Conor bellowed at once. "The priest doesn't do exorcisms after 5."

To his amazement, Foley looked up and smiled broadly. "Hi, Walsh. I'm here for the party."

"*The hell you are!*" he spat, just as his brother Patrick came out of the men's room. "Pat," Conor called, inviting him to share in the audacity of it, "Foley here thinks she's coming to your birthday party."

"She is, Con," Pat said peacefully, as Blaise stood up. They were standing unnaturally close to each other and beaming, but Conor still didn't get it.

"So Conor, I think you've met my girlfriend, Blaise," Pat said finally, through suppressed laughter.

(Editor's Note: "I'll remember the look on Conor's face until my sixty-first birthday" Blaise tee-hees now. "He was just sucker-punched! Hands down the most vindicating moment of my life.")

"Does Seamus know about this?" Conor finally seethed, his eyes ping-ponging between them. As if on cue, Seamus burst from the gym, peals of fiddling Irish music trailing behind him.

"*BLAISE!*" he whooped.

She looked over at him and grinned. "Whose birthday is it?" she cooed, as if asking a dog who's a good boy.

"My birthday!" Seamus cheered, tackling her in one of his 5-year-old-with-ADHD hugs.

Pat rolled his eyes. He couldn't get too annoyed with their corny-ass flirtation, because he had designed it this way. And anything was better than Palmer crying to her sister on the phone that Seamus was being mean to her again.

"Does Shay want his present now?" Blaise simpered. Seamus yipped an enthusiastic yes, so she pulled the metallic blue, fish-shaped flask from her bag. "Fish because you're a Pisces-man," Blaise said expertly, sloshing it around, "I put some Glenlivet aged eighteen years in there." She also bought Seamus a first edition of *Lolita* from a rare book store, because he mentioned that he reread it every year.

"Wow. So glad to have you here for Seamus's birthday," Pat coughed, raising his brows.

Blaise giggled sexily, "You'll get your present later, Patrick."

"Really," he murmured, letting his gaze rove over her leather skirt, thigh-high stockings and delicious heels, which he bought her as a birthday present to himself. He suddenly wished they could skip the next three hours and go right to the Inn next door.

Blaise nodded, then glanced fretfully at the double-doors. "I'm nervy," Blaise whispered into his shoulder, so that Conor (who was still staring with his mouth open) couldn't hear.

"I won't leave your side all night," Pat said loyally, lacing her fingers with his. "If you ever feel uncomfortable, we can leave."

"Yes we can!" Seamus agreed, nipping from his new flask. He coughed; scotch was so much peatier than bourbon. "Next time you get me something aged eighteen years, Foles, I want a freshman tied to my bed."

Mrs. Walsh was waiting for them on the other side of the double-doors.

"So good to see you again, dear," she cooed, kissing Blaise's cheek and elegantly ignoring the fact that everyone from Monsignor Owens down to 2-year-old John-Patrick were staring at them. She kissed Pat's cheek as well, "Happy Birthday, dear." Her clear-polished fingers gripped his shoulder firmly. "You're one of my life's greatest blessings."

"Aw, thanks, Mom. Love you." Pat said warmly. He gave Blaise's hand a squeeze. "What flavor cake do we get tonight?"

"It's your year, Pato, so we have red velvet," Mrs. Walsh reported, and Seamus groaned in disgust. "We had a Baked Alaska last year for you, Shay, because you just had to be weird," she rolled her eyes at Blaise, "One year, he had me looking all over heaven and earth for a pineapple upside-down cake." She told them she was going to find Mr. Walsh, who she knew was just dying to meet Blaise.

"Mom, are Kilkenny's sons...alright?" Pat asked tentatively, nodding across the gym where they stood in a tight horse-shoe, casting unmistakably angry eyes their way.

"Oh, you know them, never the friendliest gang until they've had a few teas," Mrs. Walsh said mildly, then excused herself. Her smile disintegrated as she stalked right up to Kilkenny's sons, clearing her throat in a way that quelled Meath Walsh's jeering rant, which was aimed at Pat, but audible to only his brothers.

"That is the Foley girl, and she's come as Patrick's date," Mrs. Walsh said plainly, letting her eyes rove over each of them. "Let it be stated that, if one account reaches my ears of anyone showing my son or Miss Foley the slightest unkindness, they will never again be invited back to this party." Her hospitable smile resurfaced. "Happy St. Paddy's Day!" she said kindly. "Father Tim said the corned beef is wonderful tonight, so eat up while it lasts."

For a few minutes, Blaise, Pat, and Seamus floated on the gymnasium as their own isle, not invited to annex to anyone else's. Blaise felt the awful stink of unpopularity for the first time in her life, and began wondering if she should just give Pat his present and wait for him at the Inn.

Across the room, Hacker was celebrating a small victory. "*Told ya! Told ya! Told ya!*" he whooped in his cousin's faces as he watched Pat standing protectively beside the Foley heiress. "Douska, you owe me $20."

Conor stormed their path, slinging the bags of ice onto the gift table. "Do you guys see what's going on here?" he demanded, gesturing to the trio that was suddenly the nucleus of the room.

Hacker wasn't listening. "Goldy's *such* a boss," he murmured admiringly. "I knew he could get her." He blinked, adding in a hopeful tone, "D'ya think she'd want to invest in my startup?"

"Dunno," Mickey said. "Let's go say hi."

They shrugged, bravely trooping across the gymnasium. (Aidan was torn for a moment, but the look of mutiny on Conor's face forced him to do a U-turn at the last minute).

"Pate, here comes Hack-Attack and Baby," Seamus murmured, nodding appreciatively at his disembarking cousins.

"Right on. Blaise," Pat lowered his voice swiftly, "Whatever you do, don't say anything about the Indian curse—"

"Hi," Hacker peered at Blaise with his coin-colored eyes. "On behalf of our tribe, we'd like to welcome you here." His earnest gaze flicked over to Seamus and Pat, "Oh, and Happy Birthday, fuckers."

Pat laughed, introducing them to his new girlfriend.

"Nice to meet you," Mickey smiled charmingly at Blaise. Then he directed his attention towards Pat. "Way to make me take the heat, fuck-fuck," he griped, punching his arm, "Sitting there in silence while your brother made me swear on the souls of my brethren that it wasn't me…"

Pat laughed admittedly, putting an arm around Mickey. "I'm buying you dinner, Micks. Wherever you wanna go…"

Blaise found her gaze snagged on Mickey, not only because he was prettier than her, but because he looked very familiar…

"Last time I saw you," Mickey said, addressing her with the same playful accusation, "You were throwing me out of your sorority house by the scruff of my neck."

Their circle hooted with laughter, and the shameful memory came unstuck from Blaise's mind. She remembered a themed party; Mohammed-the-bouncer coming and telling her that a Walsh was outside; her charging outdoors to personally tell him he couldn't allowed. Then Elliot and a few other girls bellowed out the window, *"Oh Mickey, you're so fine, you're so fine you blow my mind, hey Mickey!"*

"I'm sorry Mickey!" Blaise cringed. She draped her arm over his shoulders, "You're welcome at my sorority house whenever you want."

"Really?" Mickey asked keenly, nipping his drink. "I always wanted to go in that 18-person hot-tub."

Blaise grinned. "We can all go there for a soak after-hours tonight, if you want."

The guys whistled.

Pat, perhaps a bit scarred from having to listen to rumors about his dallying with Mickey for weeks, jovially announced "Okay, that's enough!" and broke up their hug.

Conor watched this scene darkly from afar, muttering to himself, "Look at her cozying right up to them all…*Dad!"*

Sean Walsh stood at the bourbon slushie machine, refilling his plastic mug and ducking his wife. He knew she was going to try and introduce him to John's daughter any moment, and he simply could not pantomime happiness to meet her.

"Conor," Sean said in his lowest grizzly-bear growl, "I can't deal with another thing right now." His forehead was unnaturally clammy and his eyes wild. "Unless you're here to tell me I won a cruise that'll take me away from all you kids, I don't want to hear it."

"But, Dad, Blaise *Foley*'s over there—"

"*NOT. Another. WORD—*" Then Sean cursed under his breath, because his wife's eyes locked on his. He had a head-start on escaping, however because she was stuck talking with Mrs. Hagan, the old librarian who was fluent in conversation about her cats and bunions.

Conor yanked the lever of the slushy machine to refill his own mug. Then he tore through the crowd, past his mother and the old librarian, hearing the former bleat desperately, "Conor, dear, have you said hello to Mrs. Hagan?"

"Gotta bring Maura her drink!" Conor boomed, descending upon the tight circle of youngest Walsh wives. He firmly waved his middle finger in the air towards Pat and Seamus. The gesture fell upon Aunt Karen instead, who raised her eyebrows and breathed, "*Oh my...*"

The band concluded the "the Irish Rover," so Maura Walsh lowered her voice. She was surreptitiously eyeing Blaise and trading brutal whispers with Tiffany, Oscar's wife.

"Tiff, look at her shoes," Maura murmured. They eyed Blaise's acid-green heels.

"Are they Loubontons?" Tiffany murmured, casting her keratin-straight blonde locks from her eyes. She smacked her gum disapprovingly, "*Little* much for a family party, don't ya think? I mean, I'm in Keds."

"No, they're Jimmys," Maura hissed expertly, accepting the slushy from Conor with an automatic thanks. "I saw a tan sole. Oh my God," she stared, "Is that a croc Birkin on her arm?"

"*Really?*" Tiffany craned her neck to see. "Oh my Lord, I think it is."

"I guess she thinks she's Kim Kardashian…"

Killian's wife Allie shook her own blonde head. She didn't go to Maura's fabulous salon to get her hair done; her sister touched it up with a Clairol kit. And she didn't know the labels the girls were whispering about, because she happily purchased all her shoes and bags at Target.

All Allie knew was that her daughter Fiona was tugging her sleeve, asking to go see Uncle Pat and the girl with the fancy shoes.

"Is she a princess?" Fiona whispered, perhaps intuiting all the staring and whispering over her.

"Maybe, Fifi," Allie replied, "Let's go and find out!"

"Hi! Hey guys!"

Blaise looked up as a petite girl with a sheet of silvery blonde hair arrived, beaming and passing one-armed hugs around their circle. Her other arm was being used to support a toddler boy on her hip, while a little girl stood timidly beside her. Something about her breezy sunniness reminded Blaise of Elliot, which was very welcome, because she was just wishing her best friend were here.

"Hi Blaise, I'm Allie," she wrapped Blaise into a surprisingly firm hug and beamed ever brighter. "And this is Fiona!" Allie patted the dark head of the little girl, staring up somberly from underneath her bangs. "And John-Patrick," she kissed the equally dark head of the toddler on her hip. The boy regarded Blaise impassively, but smiled when his Uncles Pat and Seamus prodded him, raising his chubby fist to bump theirs. John-Patrick was at the age where he insisted on being around his father all the time. Ordinarily, it was upon Killian's hip he rested, intently caressing his father's stubbly cheek while Killian bounced him. But Allie had smartly wrangled J.P away a few minutes ago, after Blaise arrived with Pat, and Daddy went out back with Slaw to have a cursing fit.

Allie knelt down and cooed to her daughter, "Tell Blaise what you told me. Don't be shy, love-bug."

"I like your shoes," Fiona pointed at Blaise's green heels. She squinted up at her, "Are you Ariel?"

"You mean *the Little Mermaid?*" Blaise smiled, laying a hand on Pat's chest. "Yes! And this is Prince Eric, don't you know?"

"Ooh!" Allie grinned. "I think you guys just found this year's Halloween costume!"

Blaise's smile crumbled a bit, because she could not imagine her daddy allowing Pat to attend her Birthday/Halloween Bash.

"Let's do a shot!" Hacker said, elbowing Mickey sportively. "Chief said he was bringing an entire barrel of Diablo." He nodded at Blaise, "Do *you* want one, Blaise?"

"*Yuck!*" Allie gagged theatrically. "I can't handle that stuff, can you Blaise?" Her expression brightened, "They also have bourbon slushies, which are nice and sweet, not too strong."

"Bourbon slushies?" Blaise echoed, as Pat and Seamus cracked up. They knew that with Blaise's whisky snobbery, a slushy to her was the equivalent of going from fine Camembert to Velveeta cheese. But Blaise's more immediate feeling was one of pride: not only could she "handle" a 110% proof, she could drink up half the barrel and still wake up at six a.m. for tennis. She was Blaise fucking Foley. Didn't they know about her?

She opened her mouth to offer some tactful summary of all this, but Pat was jumping in. "That's alright Hack," he told his cousin confidently, "She doesn't need a shot."

Blaise raised her eyebrows, "Oh I don't, do I?"

Pat blinked at her, then lowered his voice. "Well, we don't have any Jami here, babe. I thought that's why you brought..." And he nodded at the flask of scotch in Seamus's hands.

"I'm no Indian giver," Blaise said haughtily, missing the appalled look on Hacker's face. "Tonight, out of respect to Killian I'll drink his bourbon." She was on his turf, after all. It was only right.

The lead singer boomed pleasantly into the microphone, "This next song is going out to a very special Galway Girl from her Pepaw Sean! Can we get a little lass named Fiona out on the dance floor?"

"Fifi, that's you!" Allie squealed, giving her daughter's tush a little prod towards the stage. To Blaise's surprise, Fiona grabbed her hand and asked Blaise to come dance with her.

"Go, Foley," Pat grinned at her like a monkey.

Blaise kicked off her heels, thinking that she wasn't nearly drunk enough to be dancing centerstage in front of Pat's sprawling clan, most of whom were throwing dubious glances her way.

"And I ask you friends, what's a fella to do," Blaise sang to Fiona, *"If her hair is black and her eyes are blue?"* When the riff came, she grabbed Fiona's tiny, sweaty hands and spun her round and round. Allie came out, and they formed a happy dancing circle. Blaise laughed when she looked over and saw Mrs. Walsh, clutching her linen skirt and doing rapid Irish dance to wolf whistles and applause. She saw Pat's face glowing with admiration on the periphery and felt pride beam through her chest.

Blaise mimed casting a fishing pole out and reeling him in, and Pat jigged over like some freakishly tall leprechaun. She danced around him in some Riverdance routine she half remembered from middle-school, which he interrupted, grabbing her elbows to kiss her.

"Uncle Pat!" Fiona pouted, with something like jealousy. She stared broodingly at Blaise, wanting to be a part of whatever she was seeing. Pat scooped Fiona in his arms, twirling her around, until the little girl giggled, once again feeling special.

"I have to admit, she's a pretty good politician," Maura murmured, watching the scene as Conor scowled at her elbow. Dancing with Fiona, the jewel of the family, (the first Walsh girl born since 1796, according to Wilkie) was a surefire way to win over good public opinion. It didn't look like Pat and Blaise were putting on a show either, it looked like they were so in love they forgot everyone else was watching.

"He's dead to me," Conor said tonelessly. He had already texted Seamus to tell him that he had planned on giving him Black-Jack's pistol as a birthday gift, (a total lie) but had now changed his mind.

"Conor," Maura swatted his arm. "Everyone is having fun but you."

This wasn't completely true. Another one of Pat's brothers was experiencing serious St. Paddy's Day blues.

When the twins bounded up to the bar excitedly calling Killian's name, he could no sooner muster up a smile for them than he could transmute his bourbon into wine. Killian was lurking behind his

Fiona-sized barrel like a besieged crab hides in its shell. Because the arrival of Pat and his guest had thrown the party into a tailspin, Killian's bourbon barrel had been propped up without its usual fanfare, like burgers hustled off the grill during a rainy barbecue. As far as Killian was concerned, this party had been rained out.

"*Killy!*" Pat pounded the bar, his face glazed with sweat from dancing. "Blaise wants to try your bourbon tonight!"

"Who's Blaise?" Killian replied stiffly. He hadn't been introduced to anyone named Blaise. He *saw* from across a gymnasium, his little brother wheeling around a girl known chiefly as the Foley heiress, whose father publicly insulted Killian's bourbon every chance he got. Slaw had left when she made her dramatic entrance, and Conor was fuming, but his brothers had the nerve to bop idiotically around the party like Lords of Never-Neverland.

"The girl who's been dancing with your wife and daughter," Seamus said frankly, as if Killian hadn't been watching. While he watched, he was thinking that if Mr. Foley ever tried to *touch*, let alone approach his girls, he would tell him that he hoped his heart belonged to Jesus, because his ass was about to be his. But Blaise Foley was a girl too, (and somehow—Pat's date?) so Killian could only stand there watching in a state of awful, confused inertia.

"Whew!" Allie came off the dance floor fanning herself. "I'm sweating!"

"Are you ready to go?" Killian asked his wife. He relished the stricken looks on his brother's identical faces.

"Go? It's so early yet!" Allie chugged some water from the big cooler Killian had set up. "Did you meet Blaise yet, boo-boo? She said that out of respect to you, she wanted to drink your bourbon tonight." His wife raised her pale eyebrows.

"*Really?*" Killian snorted, ignoring the twins as they nodded vociferously.

"Yes," Allie insisted, collecting her hair into a ponytail.

"Well, tell her to come get it then," Killian said crabbily. When his brothers bolted off to relay the message, Killian drew himself up, sneakily combed his hair, and threw away the stack of dirty plates on his bar. Not that he remotely cared, he ranted to Allie, but he didn't need for the Foleys' idea of him as a toilet-bowl distiller to further set in.

"Uh-*huh*," Allie smiled knowingly. Then she spotted their son toddling towards the exit and hustled after him, calling, "*Where d'ya think you're headed, JP?*"

A moment later, Patrick reappeared with the Foley girl, both of them wearing smiles—Pat's, tentative; Blaise's, demure, like someone appraising an expensive good they weren't yet sold on. *How weird to see the Foley heiress at close-range*, Killian thought. Somewhere in the primal region of his brain, he registered that she was hot, but he forced himself beyond this. It wasn't purely out of respect to Pat or Allie, but also to himself. He refused to dissolve into a dithering idiot because a hot redhead showed interest in his bourbon.

Especially when that redhead was a Foley.

"Killian, this is Blaise, Blaise this is Killian," Pat said, and they slowly shook hands, sizing each other up like two Great Danes at a dog park. Pat went on that Blaise was his girlfriend, (which was too vast for Killian to compute, so he ignored it for now) and that she was the only person Pat ever met who loved bourbon like Killian did.

"Oh yeah?" Killian challenged. It was a very weighty statement, he thought. If Pat said it about anyone else but Grandpa Wilkie, Killian would snort—loudly.

"Is that so?" Blaise's eyebrows went up, and he realized she thought it was a weighty statement on *her* end. "What have you got in there?" she nodded at his barrel. "The 120-proof?" She didn't call it by its brand-name, Diablo's Death, because that would be too chummy and familiar for them.

"Yeah." Killian nonchalantly told her she could try some, so Blaise did, swirling it around her cup with an ice cube to open up the molecules before tossing it back.

"Nice," Blaise pronounced, in the tonal equivalent of golf claps. "Cinnamon and peppercorn are really coming through for me." She added in her charming way, "I always heard you were bit of a flavor virtuoso."

Killian nodded, then asked, unable to help himself, "How old do you think it is?" He spent a lot of time devising methods of making his bourbon taste older than it was.

"36 months," Blaise said positively.

"Well, 37 and two weeks" Killian said grudgingly, and the corners of Blaise's mouth turned up. "So does it taste thin to you or?—"

"*No!*" Blaise assured him, "I can just tell the age by how the burn hits my throat. But it *tastes* as full as an 8- or 9-Year." Blaise intended this to be a compliment, and Killian received it as such.

For the next hour, they were off, speaking their esoteric language of sills and aging methods and mash-bills. It was as though they finally had permission to show curiosity for the estranged sibling that their parents had told them not to ask about.

Holding court by the barrel, Blaise ended up meeting loads of family members when they came by to get drinks: Pat's Uncle Shilah and his serene wife Kimama, looking like an earthen king and queen with their long black manes; ("We call them Hiawatha and Minnehaha," he told Blaise) Uncle Marty, the lawyer, who nodded curtly when Killian introduced her ("He'll be friendlier once the ambrosia kicks in," Killian assured Blaise); Father Tim, the Dublin priest whose frequent house-calls were Sean's favorite gripe (Sean apparently called the priest "Thornbirds,"); Maura Jones-Walsh's fabulous brother Benjamin, dressed to the nines but without a stitch of green on him.

Finally, Blaise saw the person she had thought about more than any other that night. He was at least fifty years older than any picture she'd seen of him, but she recognized him instantly by his huge Adam's Apple and his gaunt, Abe Lincoln-esque cheeks. Blaise saw the *Sullivan* and *Walsh* coat-of-arms pinned to his green suspenders, and the next moment was surprised to see her vision blurred with tears.

"Grampy, over here!" Killian called out excitedly, explaining to Blaise in an undertone that his grandfather was blind now.

Killian quickly set about fixing Wilkie Walsh a sizable drink and placing it into his gnarled, outstretched hand.

Blaise watched the younger distiller hold his breath as the older distiller tasted, wearing the face of someone trying to bend a spoon with their mind.

"Not bad, Killy," Wilkie pronounced finally, his expression brightening with an affable smack of his lips. His voice had all the quaver of old age, but his mind was obviously sharp.

"I wasn't sure about not chill-filtering it with a double-barrel," Wilkie continued thoughtfully, "But it ended up lending some fine heat." He butted his glass against his cane, "You might want to consider selling it as your small batch this year, but I would age it three or four more months in the second barrel."

Killian nodded reverently.

"Sounds like you know your bourbon," Blaise couldn't help but remark.

Wilkie cast his milky eyes in her direction. "Yes ma'am," he said, with sudden humility. "Bourbon has been my life's work. It is my blood."

"It's my blood, too," Blaise said, swiftly wiping away a tear. "You started making it when you were only 8, right?" This man had taught her father the sacred alchemy of distilling; had lived with her Grandpa Sully on the land that was her most familiar scenery.

"Sounds like you know a thing or two about me," Wilkie mused, sporting a half-smile. "Yes, I started off at another distillery, but," he waved a gnarled hand, "You probably haven't even heard of it."

"Which one was that?" Blaise asked him playfully. She glanced at Killian, who tapped his temple and mouthed *he knows.*

Wilkie didn't answer her, appearing instead to address an imaginary third person, "You know, my grandson Killian always says, at least my maker left my sense of taste when He took my vision." A grin stretched over his withered face, "But I reckon I'd trade my ability to taste for my glims back, just to see how beautiful Sully's granddaughter turned out."

"*Aww,*" Blaise laughed. Wilkie looked very pleased with himself, spinning his trick bowtie around and around.

Sean Walsh stormed over in his green tuxedo t-shirt. "There you are, Dad," he barked, nodding at Killian without looking at Blaise. "My wife made you a plate, come along and eat."

"Did she warm it up?" Wilkie squawked, "The last one she fixed me was cold as ice." He gestured to a spot about six inches to Blaise's left. "Don't you see who I'm talking to here, Seany? Where are your manners!"

"Oh *I* can see alright," Sean grumbled. He gave Blaise a suspicious, sideways glance. "Does your daddy know where you are, little lady?"

"*No,*" Blaise replied admittedly. Nonetheless, she drew herself up and met Sean's eyes, wanting so badly to impress Pat's father. Men his age were her specialty, but she seemed to have left her bag of silky party tricks back at Foley Bourbon.

"*Woo-hoo-hoo,* boy!" Sean cheeped, pouring bourbon into his cup. He gave Killian a cryptic look which Killian returned with a shrug, then Sean grabbed a hold of his father's arm and pulled him away to eat.

Sean's reaction troubled Blaise, so she took another shot with Killian. She was getting to the stage of drunk where she could share intimate truths with strangers—or maybe she felt a bourbon bond with Killian.

"I wouldn't come to your family's party just to stir the pot, Killian," Blaise gurgled earnestly. "I really care for your brother."

Killian nodded with the resignation of a smoker hearing that they needed to quit, or at least switch to vaping. "Well, it seems to me like it's mutual," he murmured. They both watched Pat for a moment as he crawled, sock-footed, into the bounce-house with Fiona. Love for him gushed through Blaise's veins like sap in a maple tree.

"And," Blaise lowered her voice confidentially, "Tonight, to show you all that I come in peace, I'm gonna give Pat an old family heirloom for his birthday," she winked winningly. "I think you know what I mean."

Killian stared at her. "You don't mean, *the* heirloom?" he said, trying not to get too excited. "The treasure?"

"*Shhh*" Blaise put a finger annoyingly to his lips. "If my dad finds out I gave it back to you *Wawshes*, I'll be working at Arby's come Monday—"

"Don't worry, your dad and I don't talk much," Killian muttered. He pressed on eagerly, "But is it—the treasure?"

"It's the *key* to the treasure" Blaise whispered in Killian's ear. "What Clara wore around her neck at the trial, and what Jack kept in the back of *Odysseus,"* she hiccupped, *"Isn't that cool?"*

Killian deflated somewhat, but this *was* still pretty damn cool. Wilkie always told him the key was forever lost after Clara and Jack's murder. "Can I see it?"

Blaise thought about it for a second, then nodded, reaching into her bag. "It's a skeleton key" she whispered. Killian stroked the rusty blade with a breathy little, *"wow."*

"What are you guys doing back there?" Seamus and Pat appeared, their faces sporting matching, Slushie-drunk grins. Pat's was far loopier than Seamus's, because he had also drank up the scotch in Seamus's flask when Seamus was busy flirting with the Maid-of-Erin.

Blaise sprang to her stockinged feet. "I'm showing Killian your birthday present," she taunted Pat, hiding the key behind her back.

"Ooh, what is it," Pat slurred, lumbering behind the bar to frisk her. "Seriously B, what is it?" he wrenched the key away amidst Blaise's squeals of protest, then held it high above his head, frowning blankly.

"The key to Jack's treasure," Seamus said automatically. He recognized it from the Wikipedia page on Black-Jack, more specifically image 2.7 of Clara sitting big-eyed in court with the key around her neck. "Pat, let me see it? It should have a Latin engraving…Let me *see*—" The allure was too much to bear; he grabbed it from Pat's hands and jetted off. Pat let out a yelp and sprinted after his twin.

"Hard to believe they're 27 today," Killian muttered, shaking his head at such Tom Foolery. "It's not too late to change your mind, Blaise."

When Blaise found Pat and Seamus in the dimly lit lobby, they were joined by several male family members—including Conor. They were all peering worshipfully at the key like preteen boys with their first *Playboy.*

"Foley, is this *really* Jack's key?" Conor demanded, when she was still ten yards away. "Why the hell do *you* have it, of all people?"

"It's mine," Blaise smiled at Conor gloatingly. "And now I'm giving it to Pat." She glanced fondly at her man, catching him staring at the red toenails underneath her tights. He was really drunk.

"Hey—I'm sorry," A swarthy, handsome man addressed Blaise, crinkles coming off his navy-blue eyes, "Are you *giving* Pat the treasure? I'm Oscar, by the way," he shook Blaise's hand formally, Walsh cufflinks gleaming in his sleeve.

"He's Mickey's brother," Hacker offered, busy examining the key from every angle.

"Hi, Oscar," Blaise said, wondering if this was the lawyer son of Marty's that Duff often griped about. "No I mean, I have the key, but it's not *my* treasure to give." Blaise explained to their hungry faces that she hadn't found it, but they were welcome to look for it, once she inherited her distillery.

"So," Oscar frowned pensively, "Maybe twenty, twenty-five years from now—?"

"Less than five," Blaise amended, with a pang that her daddy's death knell was so soon to ring. "And I'll rescind the Walsh ban, and you guys are welcome to come look for it. Paddy, Shay," Blaise served them each a gooey smile, "You can come, of *course*," (the twins whooped and slammed their arms around each other) "Hacker, Oscar" she nodded at them, skipping breezily over Conor. "And," she waved back towards the gym, "Killian, Sean, Marty...hell, Wilkie can come, as long as he leaves his matchbook at home—"

"Wait a minute, is someone being left out here?" Hacker crowed, with a pointed glance at Conor, whose face was turning the color of a bad sunburn.

"Uh oh," Oscar smiled knowingly, "Is Conor not allowed, Blaise?"

"Well," she looked appealingly over the group, "Last time I saw him, he called me Kentucky cousin fucking *trash* in front of the entire bourbon community..."

The guys gave a low whistle.

"Uncalled for, Maggot," Oscar shook his head judiciously.

"Deebo, she dumped an entire flask of *her* nasty-ass bourbon over my head!" Conor bellowed. "It actually got in my mouth! I was almost *poisoned!*"

"It was great," Hacker murmured, his shining eyes tilted up.

"Walsh, I already apologized for that!" Blaise bleated, laying a hand over her heart.

"The hell you did!"

"I meant, I apologized to myself, for wasting good bourbon on *you.*"

Conor smirked diabolically, announcing that when it got in his mouth, he swore it tasted like cheap Canadian Mist.

"Please," Blaise examined her nails, looking bored. "You probably rang out your shirt and drank it the whole way home."

"I'd rather get an Italian flag tattooed on my ass."

"Hey guys!" Oscar waved his hands annoyingly between them. "You guys need to *calm down.*"

"Shut up, Deebo, this is how we talk," Conor spat. (Privately, Blaise agreed—she didn't like when anyone but Duffy intervened on their fights.)

Conor looked at Blaise furiously, "So now you're not gonna let me look for treasure on your distillery, Foley?" He seemed to feel like this was a breach of their unspoken rules, the Geneva Conventions that kept them from ever going too far with one another—(I.e., Blaise would never *actually* call the D.A about getting him fired, and Conor would never tell Pat that she used fellatio to get out of a DWI).

"Well, I didn't like that you called me that," Blaise folded her arms stubbornly.

"Yeah!" slurred Pat, staggering forward and slinging his arms around her like a drunk orangutan. "Plus Con, in Kentucky it stops being gross after third cousins."

"*Ugh,* Pat, go home." Conor said in disgust. "Fine Foley, truce" he stared determinedly at the ceiling, "I'll only call you a KFC on special occasions," he smirked, "Like birthdays and Christmas."

"No! *Never!*" she bargained. "And every time you come to my distillery, you have to bring chocolate—otherwise you won't be allowed in."

"Fine. Psycho." Conor rolled his eyes, then reached out to pump her hand once.

"Wait, are you guys making up?" Seamus asked, looking a trifle disappointed.

"*No!*" Blaise shrieked again."*Never!*" (Conor, waiting imperceptibly for her answer, seconded this with a snort of: "It's not *that* Happy of a Birthday, fuck-fuck.")

After a long beat, Oscar said airily to Blaise, "So anyways, it's nice to meet you."

Everyone laughed.

Wilkie emerged from the gym, singing to himself in his moth-eaten voice. His walking stick against the linoleum made a sound like a peg-leg.

"Grampy!" Seamus called, plucking Jack's key from Hacker's grasp. "C'mere, we want you to see something!"

Wilkie rounded his pearly stare on them. "Is that supposed to be some kind of joke?" he asked with mock outrage, and his grandsons chortled appreciatively.

"Are you having fun, Wilkie?" Blaise asked kindly, as he hobbled over.

"My, my!" the old man straightened his trick bowtie and beamed at the sound of her voice, "We meet again, Kelly!" Before she could gently ask him to call her Blaise, Wilkie went on, "So which lucky one of my fifteen grandsons escorted you here tonight, Miss Foley?"

"Which one do you think I'd go for, Mr. Walsh?" she looped her arm through Pat's and winked at the boys.

"Well, there are two I can think of who would be serious retribution," Wilkie mused, his unseeing eyes transmitting wisdom and magic. "My oldest grandson, for one. Imagine, if I spent thirty years schooling my protege, only for Killy to go back over the hedges?"

"Grampy, Killian's married," Conor said impatiently, "Remember, he had you as one of his groomsmen?"

"Oh, yeah, to the lovely Allie!" Wilkie chuckled airily. "Well, the other one I thought of was the one who took my shares to Foley Bourbon, St. Patrick himself," (at this, Oscar gave a slight, regretful groan, rubbing the bridge of his nose, and Conor rolled his eyes huffily.)

Wilkie went on proudly, "Patrick was the only grandson who had the foresight to know, at the age of 7, how valuable those shares were."

Hacker, looking mildly furious, objected: "Hey, don't lump me in with those eejits, Edudu—I wasn't given the choice!"

"Grandpa, it *is* me!" Pat burst out, brazenly kissing Blaise's freckled nose, "Honestly, I didn't even have that in mind when I was chasing her, I just really fucking *liked* her!" He had the same wondrous expression of a trailer park yokel being interviewed on the 6 o'clock news about winning the state lottery. "She could've worked at Manley's Mighty Mart and I'd still be a goner for her."

"Aw," Blaise cooed. She couldn't resist rubbing an appreciative toe up Pat's pant-leg for this.

"Bully for you," Wilkie growled. "Well, Miss Foley, you could have full equity ownership of your distillery again. But I must respectfully caution my grandson to not sell his shares for less than they're worth." He looked suddenly stern, "Patrick knows what they cost me."

"I know, Grampy, I know," Pat tried to match Wilkie's gravitas, but in his drunken state, it came off as looking goofy.

"Alright Grampy, hold out your hand," Seamus ordered suddenly. He placed Jack's key in the old man's palm. "Do you know what this is?"

Wilkie frowned, turning the key over and over. Then comprehension swept his face like dawn over dusk. He ran the pruned pads of his fingers over the Latin engraving, reading not from sight but from memory, "*Contra vim mortis non crescit herba im hortis.*" He gasped.

"You know what it means," Blaise whispered, her eyes lit up mysteriously.

"*No plant grows in the garden against the power of death.*" Wilkie uttered, "It's my father's key." He looked towards her voice, "Where was this, Kelly?"

"My great-grandmother Deirdre had it with her jewelry," Blaise explained, almost apologetically. "And she left her jewelry to me."

"Deirdre!" Wilkie gasped again, and for a moment he seemed lost in a reverie. "Of course, that makes sense!...Aunt Deedee was there when my father died...that's when his key was said to go missing...my brothers and I always thought the murderers stole it...my dear Lord." Perhaps Wilkie could sense that his grandsons' attention was focused entirely on him, because he laughed wildly, "Boys, I have not seen his key since I was twenty-five years old!"

"Holy shit," Hacker murmured, glancing over his grandpa's withered form.

Wilkie continued faintly, "…Even then, Da only let Foley or Kilkenny or me only hold it for a minute…Dear Lord," he repeated, now cupping the key in his trembling hands as though it were a baby chick. "Oh, but Kelly…does this mean you've found my father's lost treasure?"

Blaise gazed into those hopeful white eyes. "Not yet," she said, patting his hand.

"We will, Grampy" Conor barked, in his police commando voice. "Foley told us we can look for it when her dad goes off to that great distillery in the sky. So…" he paused awkwardly, as if trying to think of polite wording, "Don't, uh, go taking any long trips until then…"

"He's ninety-three years old, Maggot!" Pat chuckled, his balance wobbling for a second (Oscar caught him before he fell). "What long trips could he take?"

"Oh my," Wilkie uttered, only half listening to them. "Wait until Pearsy hears that it's found!" He glanced up wildly, "What time is it in Ireland?"

The door to the gymnasium flung open. "Dad," Sean Walsh called, eyeballing their huddle suspiciously. "People want cake. Can you come and say your prayer?"

"Coming, Marty!" Wilkie yapped. He pocketed the key with the deftness of a much younger man.

"Hey, Grampy, don't get too attached to it!" Seamus called after him. "It's *ours,* remember?" Wilkie, however, seemed to be suddenly deaf in addition to blind. "Come along, everyone!" he said loudly, motoring as fast as his shillelagh stick could take him.

Hacker and Blaise followed everyone else as they funneled into the party.

"I've never seen a key like that before." Hacker marveled.

"I know!" Blaise agreed fiercely. "I've spent two weeks combing the internet for a decoy, so my dad won't notice it's gone" she shook her head, "I couldn't find a key that remotely resembled it. *Not a thing*!"

Inside the party, the band stopped playing, and the party chatter came to a simmer. Everyone seemed to be turned expectantly towards the stage. At first, Blaise thought they were eyeing the two gorgeous sheet cakes that had been wheeled out. Then she saw Wilkie laboriously climbing the stage, guided along by a dutiful Killian.

She turned to Pat and Seamus, who were flanking her. "What's he—?"

"Happy St. Paddy's Day, everybody!" Wilkie boomed, the microphone screeching as he bobbed too closely (Killian swiftly adjusted it to be level with Wilkie's chest). The crowd lightly applauded; a few people hooted. "Most of you know that St. Paddy's Day was not always a happy holiday in our family," Wilkie said, his quavering voice suddenly grave, "On this day in 1948, my lovely mother Clara, one of the few angels to ever walk the earth, was laid to rest after her murder.

"My mother," Wilkie continued, his voice becoming stuffy, "Was so proud to be a Grandma to my nephews Kildare and Meath, who were born before she died. She would have been seven times over the moon to meet my brother Kilkenny's younger sons, Derry, Wicklow, Tyrone, Limerick, Dublin, Sligo, and Carlow. The same goes for my brother Pearse's sons, Finlo and Fergus, over in Ireland. My sons, Sean, Martin, Avanoca, and Shilah, would have been blessed to know her. The same goes for my fifteen glorious grandsons." He drew in a deep breath and began ticking them off on his fingers, "Killian, Oscar, Conchobar, Eamon, Callum, Karac, Brendan, Patrick, Seamus, Kiernan, Paytah, Onacona, Manquilla, Aidan, and Mícheál."

"Wow," Blaise murmured, as the crowd applauded his recitation.

"And that was in order," Seamus muttered appreciatively.

Wilkie's torso creaked forward in a bow, then he continued, "You all know that my father, John, departed a few weeks after his Clara. He died trying to protect his wife and Clara's cousin Deirdre, who miraculously survived the attack. I can tell you that your parent's casket is a heavy burden to shoulder. Carrying *both* your parent's caskets, in the span of three weeks' time, with the disquieting knowledge that they did not depart this earth peacefully, was almost unbearable to me." His voice took on a slightly rueful tone, "I was but 27, which is how old Patrick and Seamus are today."

Seamus muttered, "Well *Feliz Cumpleaños* to us…"

Wilkie paused. "I could not have shouldered this burden without my brothers. Pearse, who was barely 18 at the time, and our departed Kilkenny in heaven…And of course, my brother from the bourbon, Sullivan Foley."

The crowd visibly rustled. Blaise felt her cheeks slapped red. Hot emotion, divorced from her embarrassment, surged through her.

"Aw, that's so nice!" Pat said loudly, causing several people nearby to snicker. Mrs. Walsh hinged forward to give him a sharp look.

"Sully was my best friend," Wilkie continued, unseeing of Killian's raised eyebrows beside him.

"Though most of you haven't heard our stories, or seen our pictures. We had fifty years of brotherhood destroyed by *one* argument."

The crowd once again seemed to twitch. Blaise steeled herself for rays of hatred and blame, but what she was picking up on was a whirl of laughter: the Walshes, like her, thought it funny to refer to the Foley-Walsh war as "one argument." Especially since it which spawned a 100 Day Trial, decade's worth of tourism, and their names solidified in American lexicon as a term for bitterly feuding parties.

"It means a lot to me that Sully's granddaughter, Kelly, should come here tonight," Wilkie was saying. He fished Jack's key from his pocket, adding in a voice that throbbed with Irish sentimentality, "And the fact that she has given our family back my father's key, when it has been at Foley Bourbon for nearly sixty years…well, there are simply no words."

Pat apparently disagreed, "Hey Grampy, that's mine!" he slurred, swaying on his heel.

"Oh Patrick, have some coffee," Mrs. Walsh hissed, six people away.

Sean frowned, craning his neck to see. "What'd she give him?" He peeped over at Blaise with mock distrust. Then—a shadow of a wink.

"Now before we sing Happy Birthday to Patrick and Seamus, I'd like to say a prayer for my parents." Wilkie bowed his sterling head, speaking into the mic:

"*O God, who hast commanded us to honor our father and our mother; in Thy mercy have pity on the soul of my mother, and the soul of my father, and forgive them their trespasses; and make me to see them both again in the joy of everlasting brightness. Through Christ our Lord. Amen.*"

"Amen" echoed the room.

Wilkie's face rose to them, continuing in his aerial tone, "May their souls and the souls of all the faithfully departed, through the mercy of God, rest in peace."

Blaise opened her mouth to say Amen, but to her surprise, voices began popping across the room:

"Our mother, Kachine," Sean called out, his eyes closed tight.

"*Kevin Carr!*" Seamus hollered beside her.

"Our father, Kilkenny," roared an older man with eyes like a Siberian husky.

"Sully Foley," Wilkie said softly—and Blaise understood; these were the names of their Dead. Several more names were said, some inaudibly (like a wispy woman in green slacks who Blaise guessed was a widow) some hurled in almost savage remembrance. Blaise and Pat did not have any dead yet, so they merely listened. She felt another stab of pain, thinking that if the curse of sixty-one was truly real, she would be standing here five St. Patrick's Days from now, calling out, "*My Uncle Duffy and my father, John!*"

After a half minute of stoic silence prevailed, Killian stepped forward, smiling awkwardly. "Okay, sooo...cake?"

Everyone laughed, and the party resumed its former clamor. Blaise saw Conor slapping hands with a brigade of policemen filing in the gym. A red-bearded cousin in a kilt was talking animatedly to a ring of lacrosse players in Louisville jerseys.

"Blaise!" she turned towards a lilting brogue. Mrs. Walsh was busy plugging sparklers and candles into the sheet cakes. *Come help?* she mouthed sweetly.

"My father-in-law has taken a shine to you," Mrs. Walsh said happily, ripping the "2" and "7" shaped candles from their packages. "What was that business of him calling you Kelly?" she lowered her voice, "Though at his age, if that's the worst of his senility, we should consider ourselves lucky—"

Blaise explained with a laugh that she was christened Kelly, but went by her communion name of Blaise.

"Well dear, I would agree that Blaise suits you," Mrs. Walsh murmured, and she fleetingly envisioned *Patrick Alan & Kelly Blaise* in Celtic font on creamy wedding invitations. "Now, let's sing Happy Birthday to the byes, shall we?" she lit a few candles with a lighter, passing it to Blaise, and instructed Father Tim to announce into the mic that it was time to sing Happy Birthday.

"Oh now you want me?" the priest muttered, nursing a bourbon slushie. "I'm a man of the cloth, I should be saying the prayer…"

Mrs. Walsh ignored him. "Stay right there, dear," she nodded firmly at Blaise as all her sons closed in. Blaise felt a blush from this acknowledgement, that she was asked to stand in the innermost rung of Pat's life. She recalled seeing a Facebook photo of Palmer from his last birthday, as she held up the Baked Alaska for him to blow out. Now *she* was the one standing beside him.

After the swirls of candle-smoke cleared, Blaise hugged both birthday boys. Unlike at a Foley birthday, where Hildy or Cressida served them slices on doily plates, there were no maids here, so Blaise decided to step up. She fairly cut Shay and Pat slices with a giant icing shamrock and plated a bunch for others, including a queue of little kids led by sweet Fiona.

"Blaise, dear," Mrs. Walsh appeared again at her elbow. "I don't know if you've *properly* met Patrick's father."

Sean Walsh lurked behind his wife, surveying Blaise with a look of comical caution. Her stomach elevatored up and dropped down.

"I know where you were twenty-seven years ago today!" Blaise said, concealing her nerves with good cheer.

"He was in jail," Mrs. Walsh remarked, shooting her husband a severe look.

Sean's smile bloomed. Blaise was charmed by how perfectly white and even his teeth were.

"I got a DWI on my way to the hospital!" he crowed bluntly. "I didn't expect my wife to go into labor on St. Party's Day!"

"And, you didn't know you were having twins—right?" Blaise asked tentatively.

"No!" they exclaimed. (Sean beaming openly, added, "Hell, I thought Mom just needed to lay off the pie!")

The couple told the story of the day Patrick and Seamus were born, alternating verses of it, smiling while the other spoke, but not interrupting to correct each other's details.

Sean said, "Well, see, we thought we were having a girl. Our ultrasound tech told us that it wasn't *a* boy. I guess that was her cute way of telling us we were having two."

Nodding woefully, Mrs. Walsh chimed in, "I thought I was finally getting my girl, dear. We were going to call her Saoirse."

"Yeah!" Sean agreed, "Pat and Shay slept in Saoirse's pink room until they were maybe 10."

On St. Patrick's Day '86, when Sean heard that his mother was bringing Mrs. Walsh to the hospital, he drunkenly set off at once from the party. His errant driving attracted the eyes of a cop, already on the lookout for drunk drivers. When Sean slurred at the cop to fuck off, his wife was in labor, the cop booked him. He used his one phone-call on his brother, Marty. Marty bailed him out, and Sean ran to the hospital, calling for his wife and for Saoirse. The nurses came at him with two blue-wrapped bundles instead.

"I said, oh no, those aren't mine," Sean chuckled.

"As if he ordered Colcannon and they brought him cabbage," Mrs. Walsh shook her head.

"I'd say Pat was the biggest surprise of our lives," Sean murmured. "And Shay's a close second. I don't know girl," he looked at Blaise with raised brows, "You may be gunning for honorable mention."

They all laughed—Blaise very timidly.

At this point in the story, Conor Walsh's face piped in between his parent's. "Oh, you guys are talking about the day that Tweddle-Dee and Tweedle-Dick were born?" he nodded. "*What*, Mom? He likes when I call him that!"

"I remember perfectly," Killian boomed, sweeping in with a tray of Diablo shots and habanero juice chasers. He was in a jolly host mood now; he had not again asked Allie to leave. "Dad brought Con and me to the hospital to meet the babies, then we came back to the party and asked everyone what they thought we should name them."

"Do you really remember that, Killy?" Sean asked, in a tone of surprise.

"Yeah," Killian nodded. "Everyone said one needed to be named Patrick, 'cause he was born on St. Paddy's Day."

Their party glanced with affection at the twins, who were taking turns doing the limbo with Wilkie's shillelagh stick.

The bagpipers arrived, trooping through the gym in a chain of knee-high socks and kilts. A semi-circle formed around them as they began to caterwaul their Irish melodies. Wilkie, repossessed of his shillelagh stick, wobbled his way over to where Sean and Blaise stood.

"Bagpipers!" Wilkie scoffed. "If I am called home to be with my Lord tonight, don't have pipers at my funeral. I won't come."

Blaise couldn't tell if he sensed his son's presence, or if he would freely issue this statement to any partygoer in earshot.

"Don't let the Lord call you home tonight, Dad," Sean said wanly, clapping as the group finished 'Scotland the Brave.' "You'll ruin St. Paddy's for the rest of us."

Blaise touched Wilkie's bony elbow. "Wilkie, I just loved your prayer." She felt her throat closing up again.

"*Kelly*!" Wilkie said delightfully, straightening himself up. "Sean, you have to warn me when there's a lady present!"

Blaise decided this was a good time to bring out the old pictures she brought along, in an optimistic gesture of goodwill.

"Yowza, Dad!" Sean admired the first photo, the one of Wilkie and Grandpa Foley in tuxes on his wedding day. "You were actually handsome!"

"Oh, describe it for me, Seany," his father bleated wistfully, "What I wouldn't give to see…"

"You're with the Irish Sinatra, looking like the dapper duo," Sean reported. "There's a carnation in your button-hole."

"That's Sully's wedding day," Wilkie said at once.

"See what he wrote on the back?" Blaise read it for him. "'Walshie, my Best Man today and every day.'"

Just then, Allie swished over with her rippling blonde hair and clutched Blaise's wrist, burbling that she wanted her to meet Maura.

Sean watched her leave with a small wave, then began to rifle purposefully through the pictures, "Now, where's *Mrs.* Foley?" he murmured, "Talk about what I wouldn't give to see…"

Blaise and Pat were cuddling, telling the story of how they got together to a group of Walsh Wives, which included Maura and Allie. Actually, Pat wasn't so much cuddling Blaise as he was using her to support himself. He had convinced Monsignor Owens to do a few more shots with him, and was now soused beyond all reason.

"So, after he gave me this hangover IV, we started texting all the time," Blaise told the ring of women, whose eyes were lit up as if watching *the Notebook*. "And, even though he'd say flirty things to me, I didn't think he could possibly be hitting on me. I was like," she mimed caressing her chin pensively, "…he's not *that* dumb, is he?"

"I *am* that dumb," Pat brayed proudly, "I *was* hitting on you."

"You could have *any* girl" Blaise plugged on, zoning out in his eyes. "Any other girl wouldn't have to keep you a secret from her family—"

"I don't care," Pat said stubbornly, "You're the only girl I want, Foley," he nuzzled her forehead and wrapped his arms around her.

"Wow!" remarked Aunt Karen, patting her feathery blonde head. She was married to Pat's Uncle Avanoca. Despite his Indian name, Uncle Avi was as flaxen-haired as his wife. "You guys really are a modern Romeo and Juliet story!"

"So, how did Pat get you to give him a chance, Blaise?" Maura Walsh prompted her, her dark eyes glinting. Blaise had been stunned to learn that this normal girl was Conor's wife. She had expected Mrs. Conor Walsh to be a crass female bodybuilder, or some bleached blonde who rode a mechanical bull for fun.

Blaise did not want to commercialize their first kiss, that moment at Jack and Clara's graves when she decided to stop suppressing her feelings. "Oh, you know," she cocked one shoulder demurely. "I don't think any of us here are strong enough to resist a Walsh boy's charm," she grinned around the circle. "Right, ladies?"

The younger wives giggled, caressing their collar bones with ringed hands.

"I guess," Aunt Karen rolled her eyes, as if said charms had worn thin after thirty years of marriage. "Pat, honey, maybe you should have some coffee" she frowned, eyeing him as he wobbled. "Falco just went to the kitchen to put a pot on."

"Okay, Kiki!" Pat dribbled, tripping over his snub-nosed shoe as he left.

"Can you make me one too?" Blaise called after him. "Splenda, babe, not sugar!"

Sean approached to their circle with Marty. "Karen, where's Avi?"

"He's over there—"

"Oh—Avi! Shi!" he waved his two brothers over. "Get a load of these old family photos, guys!" Sean grinned, bopping Blaise over the head with her pictures.

"Wow! Is that Avi?" Karen squinted at a photo of a little blond boy.

"It's all of us," Uncle Marty said in his cool way. "St. Paddy's Day, 1961," he nodded curtly at Blaise.

"Look at Uncle Sully!" Sean whooped jubilantly, holding up a picture of Sullivan Foley in his green suit, holding a little boy in a spaceman costume.

"Is that me he's holding?" Marty growled.

"'Course it's you, Mart! You didn't take off that space costume all year!"

"Pure class," Marty regarded Sully's fedora and pocket square with some kind of wonder. "D'ya reckon Battistoni had a 44-long dyed green just for him?"

"Probably!" boomed Sean.

"Who's this lady?" Maura asked Blaise curiously, brandishing a slide of a leggy blonde dancing with toddler Avanoca on her hip.

"That's my Nana!" Blaise said happily. "Isn't she *fabulous*?"

"Where?" Sean yelped, scrambling forward to see. "Sabina Foley, *aie-yi-ie!* Mart, remember when she'd sun-bathe by the pool in her gingham bikini?" he grinned, "She'd ask us to mow the lawn, and we'd spend our whole Saturday landscaping Foley for her?"

"Oh, if she asked me to kill you, I would have," Marty said tonelessly.

Pat's other Uncles trickled over. Avanoca, Aunt Karen's husband, was bespectacled and blond, with hair like a lion's mane. He was spry in speech but slouchy in green flannel, somehow recalling a younger Wilkie. Uncle Shilah looked at Blaise openly with eyes like jade stones, but did not seem as won over as his son Hacker was.

"Look Shy, it's Mom!" Sean exclaimed, brandishing a snap of Kachine, pregnant in a paisley muumuu. "Is she pregnant with you there?"

"What year is it—'61? Yeah, it's me" Shilah confirmed, in a deeply raspy voice.

"May we keep it?" his wife Kimama asked reverently, laying a hand on Shilah's wrist.

Blaise said sure. She couldn't think of an object less likely to be missed at Foley than a photo of Wilkie's pregnant wife.

"Look! Here we all are!" Sean said, sounding moony. He held up a group shot to their circle, of the Foley and Walsh clans, happy and whole and jumbled together, with Wilkie and Sully in the thick of it.

"Yup," Marty peered gravely over Sean's shoulder, "Before it all went to shit."

"Look, our Uncle Kilkenny's there!" Avanoca exclaimed, pointing to a dark-haired man in glasses and suspenders. "And Aunt Velma! God, they look so young!"

Matt Crummy had arrived at the party forty minutes ago, but he still hadn't found Pat or Blaise. Every time he tried to make some headway through the green crowd, he was delayed by some family member who would snag him, murmuring with raised brows, "Did you hear who Pat brought as his date?"

"I know," Crummy said over and over, "She's my friend."

Locating Pat in the crowd of dark heads and green shirts was a Walsh version of Where's Waldo, but finally he zeroed in on him over by the stage. As he went over, Crummy was besieged by Cousin Kiki, who was apparently still reeling from Pat's bombshell.

"I don't get why he didn't tell *me!*" Kiki bawled, grasping at his *Sinn Féin* t-shirt. "I mean, if all three of his brothers died in a tragic car crash, *I* would be next in line to be his Best Man! No offense, Crumb-cake," he added delicately.

"None taken," Crummy said. "I'm gonna go wish him a Happy Birthday."

As he got closer, Pat's glazed smile came into focus, and he realized that Walsh was drunk. Watching Pat wobble like a newborn colt, Crummy upgraded this to *very* drunk, perhaps at a level unmatched since Spring Break in Acapulco, 2008, when Pat proposed to a prostitute named Cipriana on the beach.

"KEEKS! CRUMMS!" Pat flung his arms dead around Kiki and Crummy, as though they had just cut him down from a crucifix. "I've been looking all over for you gringos!" he mooed senselessly. "I was jus' talkin—*hic!*—to Monsignor Owens here."

They looked at the clergyman, who on closer inspection, appeared to be dabbing at a light brown stain all down his robes.

"Hello," Monsignor Owens smiled at them all with some difficulty, "Patrick here was kind enough to spill his coffee on me."

"S'okay, Monsignor!" Pat brayed, swaying and colliding with a chair. "My cousin Falco went to go find us the Tide thing—the pen. We'll be aw'right." His hiccupped, then grinned at Crummy. "Crummy, what the *hell* are you doing?"

"Just standing here buddy, what are you doing?" Crummy said in amusement. "Happy Birthday. Where's Blaise?" he scanned the gym for her red head, but didn't see it. "Please tell me it went well."

"Yeah, fuka!" Kiki raged indignantly, "Oops—sorry, Monsignor—" he shot Owens a crooked grin, switching back to a comical leer for Pat. "Why didn't you tell me about her? I feel like I don't even know you right now! Do you also have six children you fathered illegitimately and three annulled marriages?"

Pat smiled angelically; the truth was that Kiki, as the McGettigan's bartender, prided himself on being the TMZ of Zzyzx Road. If he had known about Blaise, Pat feared he would have served up the gossip like he served Carlow Walsh his daily three Manhattans with extra cherries.

Thankfully, Pat was spared from having to answer by the arrival of Falco, Kiki's big brother. He was as dark as Kiki was blond, with a saturnine temperament to match. Usually at parties, he and Pat were holed up in a corner discussing their finance jobs. Earlier, when Blaise shook his hand, Falco observed the Patek watch around her wrist and cursed his 8-year-old self for not taking the shares.

"Sorry Monsignor—I couldn't find any Tide stick," Falco reported, giving Crummy a nod of welcome. "My mom said club soda might help." He handed Owens a paper cup and some napkins. "And I got *you* another coffee," he said to Pat.

Pat held his hand up to block it.

"I'm done drinking tonight!" he said nobly, drawing himself up. "I was telling Monsignor over here that I want to be able to perform tonight for Blaise, as a man."

"Oh yeah?" Falco nodded thoughtfully, "I guess, yeah, Monsignor Owens would be the perfect person to tell…"

"He's still a man, Falco," Pat said defensively, clapping the Monsignor on his shoulder, "He's a virgin, not an *alien*." He appeared not to hear their groans of disbelief, for his eyes had found Blaise. "Look at her," he uttered, pointing across the gym, where Blaise was chatting animatedly in a circle. "I want to throw her over my shoulder right now and drag her to bed," Pat groaned, as if the need was causing him great pain. "Do you guys know what I'm talkin' bout?"

"Sure—the savage shillalah dance!" Kiki chirruped.

"Playing Yatzee?" Crummy frowned.

"I think you need to tell her," Falco said, nodding at the others. "Otherwise, how will she know?"

"Yeah, girls like to hear it from ya," Kiki agreed.

"How should I tell her?" Pat whispered, looking around.

Crummy tapped his chest. "Just listen to the song in your heart."

Obediently, Pat placed his hand over his heart, appearing to listen as raptly as a doctor with a stethoscope. Then he looked up. "There really is a song in my heart! I'm gonna go sing to her!"

Falco saluted Pat as he brushed past them. "Sorry Monsignor," he laughed shiftily, "I'll give you his address so you can send him your dry-cleaning bill."

"I've never seen him so hammer-steined," Kiki said in awe, "He should just sleep in one of the classrooms 'till the next AA meeting."

"He was nervous about bringing Blaise" Crummy said loyally. "I don't blame him for having a few." He craned his neck to watch as Pat bobbed along the stage, all the purpose of the world in his expression. "He's not really gonna sing, is he?"

When Blaise finally checked her phone, she had amassed a few texts: one from her dad, dozily reminding her not to drive tonight, one from Lauren, asking "*how's the party going??*" with a trio of nervous emoji, and one from Matt Crummy, demanding "*where are you*" in his no-frills way.

"Oh, is Matt Crummy here?" Blaise said happily, scanning the gym for his tall, lordly frame.

"I think I saw him with my boys," Aunt Karen said, glancing vaguely around. "Falco told me that Pat spilled coffee on the Monsignor, so they were helping him clean up," she grimaced, "Maybe he should be cut off."

"Killian!" Blaise said, as he passed by with another tray of shooters, "Have you seen Pat? Apparently he spilled coffee on the Monsignor."

"He did?" Killian looked amused, then his eyes fell past her to the stage, "As a matter of fact, there's your Romeo now."

Blaise looked over. Pat was onstage, in a tight huddle with the band. He gave a coy little wave to the crowd.

"Top of the evening to ye," Blaise heard a familiar voice say. Matt Crummy appeared at her elbow, looking as though he had just come from work. He still had on his KPMG slacks, but on top he wore a green t-shirt, on loan from Seamus that said, "GIRL ARE YOU IRISH? 'CAUSE MY DICK BE DUBLIN'!" It did not suit him; he kept crossing and recrossing his arms uncomfortably over his chest.

"Crummy!" she hugged him fiercely.

"Yo," Crummy plucked two shots off Killian's tray. "I think I'm gonna need this…" he tossed them back, eyeing Pat warily.

"Good evening, beautiful people!" boomed the singer into the mic, grinning under his plaid newsboy cap. "We are the Craic of Cork. Hope you're all having a great time out there!" A few people applauded lightly. "Now we don't usually do requests and dedications outside the Celtic songbook on St. Paddy's Day, but this young man over here," he gestured showily to Pat, "whose birthday it is today—"

"—WOO!" screamed Seamus; Blaise whipped around to give him a suspicious look.

"—he tells me he would *love* for us to sing a special song to his special girl!" continued the singer, "Fortunately this number is one we know well from weddings—" his tone became business-like, "That's right, if you're looking for a live band for your wedding or anniversary party, just like our Facebook page, the Craic of Cork, you can inbox us about booking—"

The opening chords to a familiar song rang out, and the singer began belting out, "*I've been really tryyyyyin', babe. Tryin' to hold back my feelings for so long…*"

"Oh my God!" Blaise screeched, as Pat jumped off the stage, dancing seductively towards her.

"*And if you feel, like I feeeeel baby, then come on*" wailed the singer.

Blaise looked to the sidelines for help; surely some brotherly hand was going to calmly guide Pat off the floor. But the crowd was laughing as it shrank obligingly against the walls, clearing up a space for Pat—*and her!*—on the dance floor. Blaise heard Seamus's diabolical laughter over the sound of a chair being dragged, then the chair thrust underneath her so she had no choice but to sit. She shook her head in disbelief at the faces encircling her: Conor, whooping as though viewing a striptease; Matt Crummy, chuckling into his face-palm; Seamus, filming the scene with his phone and gayly singing along; and Killian, hunched over with laughter.

"Let's get it on," crooned the band, and Pat mouthed the words along with him, as if doing his best charade of a wolf howling at the moon. *"OHHHHH babe, let's get it on."*

Somewhere in the chaos of her mind, Blaise prayed that Mrs. Walsh had taken this moment to step outside.

"We're all sensitive people," Pat emoted, pointing around the room 360 degrees, *"With so much to give. Understand me sugar?"*

"Walsh, you're never going to be able to run for office after this," Crummy remarked, his droll voice drown out by the singing and the wolf whistles.

"Therrrrre's nothing wrong with me loving youuuuu!" Pat actually sang along now, pointing at himself, then her. *"Annnd giving yourself to me can never be wrong...if the love is true."*

"Oh God!" Blaise laughed. Pat put his hand out to her, smiling invitingly. She took it, having no idea what was coming next. In one swift maneuver, Patrick pulled her to her stockinged feet and slung her over his shoulder. The move wasn't entirely seamless; Blaise shrieked and flattened her skirt with a hand, pretty sure she had just mooned half the room.

The party didn't seem to mind. They clapped and stamped their feet and cheered even harder. Pat walked her towards the door, and she understood with her heart beating between her legs that this was their big exit. She could see, upside-down, the throngs of people in green waving them goodbye.

"Have fun!" a few called suggestively. Through laughter, Blaise tried to decide if this was the sexiest or most embarrassing moment of her life...

"Blaise, your purse!" she saw Maura and Allie's legs dart over, handing Pat her crocodile bag stuffed with the pictures she brought, and her long-lost green heels. Then, a pair of creased brown suspenders and a shillelagh stick came into view.

"Grampy, let me get Jack's key?" Pat slurred.

"Who's that—Shay? Alright," Blaise saw his knobby hand go into his pocket and fish out the key. Without another word, Pat transferred it to his own pocket.

Then the Foley heiress and Walsh heir left, just as clamorously as they had come.

An hour later, the party was still talking about it. They might very well be talking about it for the next ten years.

"That was the opposite of an Irish exit," Uncle Marty said wryly, as Mrs. Walsh bustled around the room, telling various members of the clergy that Pat and Blaise had left,

"*Separately,* of course."

"Well, I want a paternity test!" Sean quacked, tucking into his third slice of shamrock cake. "I think we just found out that my son is actually half black."

In the days and weeks following St. Patrick's Day, Blaise kept expecting her daddy to call her into his office for a stern talk. Something like 125-150 people had witnessed her being dragged out of the Walshes' church, caveman-style, by a lovestruck Pat Walsh—surely it would get back to her father. But John-boy remained blithely ignorant to the affair. When she lied routinely about spending the night at Lauren's apartment, no cold, arresting expression came over his face, he just gibbered, "Okay honey." After Blaise left, he told whatever person or hat-rack was closest that he understood a young woman's need for independence.

"Look at Kennedy!" he might say to his wife, who made for a decent audience (she could not defy his points, but she also couldn't nod her head). "Kenny left Kentucky to go to school in Arizona, and that's where she decided to stay." He sipped and added for his own assurance, "But Blaisey would never go that far."

Perhaps it was evidence of how firmly polarized the Walshes and Foleys were that the news did not leak. John's crew simply did not socialize with anyone in Walsh world, and vice versa. Though the Iron Curtain stayed drawn, there began to come a few curious peeks from behind it.

In April, Uncle Duffy and his law partner were out to lunch at Doc Crows. As usual, when Duffy noticed Marty Walsh eating with his son, he asked the hostess to be seated as far away from them as possible.

"Walsh is here," he muttered to Mr. Van der Vee. "I could smell the poly-blend a mile away."

Both Marty and Duffy had their own boutique law firms. The legal community in Louisville was small and tight, and Marty and Duffy inevitably brushed up against one another from time to time. To minimize contact, the men spoke only via courier. These messages were far from Valentines: every judge in Kentucky had some anecdote about Messers Foley and Walsh's volcanic correspondence. The most recent one came when Marty filed an injunction against the Foley for releasing a small batch of Black-Jack blend, claiming on the label that it had been Jack's favorite nightcap to enjoy with Clara and her sherry. Duffy didn't respond, so Marty filed a citation for contempt, sending the messenger off to Foley's firm with a cookie-tin full of live bait. In turn, the next time Duffy spied Marty and his son eating at Doc Crows, he sent them an anonymous round of Foley 7-Year, instructing the server to tell them that Johnny made it especially for them—but only after their glasses were empty.

That afternoon, Duffy ordered the Baby Back ribs and a glass of the 12-Year neat. When Marty rose to leave, Duffy purposefully leveled his eyes at Van der Vee, pretending as though he were saying something really gripping.

But then, "Howdy, Duff," Marty muttered as he swept past, greeting him for the first time in forty-five years.

Marty's son Oscar, (whose legal briefs had been littering Duffy's desk for a few years now), paused mid-stride, saying awkwardly, "Hi, Mr. Foley." Then he clomped after his father.

Duffy stared after them. "The hell was *that*?" he muttered to his Mr. Van der Vee, who could only shrug. Duffy dipped his fingers into his bourbon and made the sign of the cross.

A few days later, McCullers Foley was at the Red Ranger gas station near home, purchasing gas, a Coke, and some lotto tickets. As he rubbed his Lucky 7s with a quarter, he heard a nasally voice behind him crow, "Kinda funny to see the billionaire bourbon heir playing scratch-offs."

McCullers turned around. Seamus Walsh was smirking there in his black leather Converse and diamond gauges. McCullers didn't know him, but the black hair, blue eyes, and antagonistic grin could only spell one name.

"Eat a dick, Walsh," McCullers snarled. He was pretty sure this Walsh was a brother of that cop who had a full citation book against his sister.

To his surprise, Seamus laughed, elbowing the blond guy with glasses beside him. "Keeks, look. It's Blaise's brother."

"Oh hey man, what's up? McCullers—right?" the blond smiled enthusiastically, dumping an armful of groceries onto the counter. A bag of hot fries skidded to the floor, but he didn't seem to notice. "I'm Kiernan, you can call me Kiki." He extended a hand; which McCullers did not take.

"Do you play poker," Seamus asked, still smirking. "We've having a game tonight. $80 buy in. We'll let you use your EBT card."

"Oh yeah dude!" McCullers trilled sarcastically, backing up towards the door, "Save me a seat with my back to the door, I'll be there!" And he jogged to his car, whipped home, and went straight up to Blaise's room to share this bizarre tale with her.

"Isn't that weird, Bam-Bam?"

Blaise giggled, springing off her bed to close the door. She told her brother she had something to tell him, feeling thankful that his Walsh bias wouldn't be as insurmountable as their father's. McCullers' grudge against the Walshes was like a piece of land that he inherited, never visiting, but paying quarterly taxes on. He hated Conor because of how he treated Blaise, but his dislike for the rest of the clan was a thin blanket order.

"Wow," McCullers gave a low whistle as his sister finished her story. "The only person who's gonna be more heart-broken about this than Dad is LJ."

"Well, let's not tell them yet," Blaise replied steadily, as though she had this whole thing mapped out.

"And when are you going to?"

Blaise replied, "When—I mean, if—things get really serious between us. *Engaged* serious." She could not justify cutting out her daddy's heart and sticking it into a blender with battery acid for anything less than a diamond ring. She didn't see it as a betrayal, but she knew her father would.

"*Engaged*?" McCullers said incredulously, picking up one of Blaise's old Beanie Babies and hurling it across the room. "So what are you gonna do, sneak around for another year or two?"

"Maybe!" Blaise said, with false confidence. "We've gotten away with it for four months now."

McCullers shook his head for a moment, staring at the ceiling. "So John Foley has one kid who can't drink his bourbon, and another who's dating a Walsh." He gave a humorless chuckle,   "Frankly, I dunno what he's gonna talk about anymore."

"Well, I still drink his bourbon—*of course,*" Blaise said haughtily. She didn't mention that the 15 year burned her throat last night, maybe because she had grown accustomed to the far more youthful Jameson. She grinned at McCullers, trying to brighten up, "So why don't you come over to Pat's tonight, meet your new brothers?"

"Well, which one is he?" McCullers said stubbornly, "If it's that cop, I swear to God, I'm gonna have you bound, gagged, and sent to a convent—"

"It's not," she assured him, looking out her bow window. She saw their dad traipsing across the grounds from his distilling cabin, peeling off his leather gloves. "I'll have a quick drinkie-poo with Daddy," Blaise said, "Then we'll go over to Pat's, so you can meet him and Shay."

I'm feeling another need to lapse into First Person here, to describe my impressions of Foley Jr.

When McCullers told me to eat a dick at the gas station, I recall I was wearing my Iraqi Veteran t-shirt. I admit, it takes some sack to leer down a veteran like that (and we who became men under the Mesopotamian sun are a special strain of crazy). I was intrigued by McCullers Foley right away, could tell right away that he was sired from the same fire as his sister. My invitation for him to come to the poker game was sincere.

Believe me, reader, I have pissed away many hours fantasizing about Blaise's phantom little sister. Join me in imagining if, instead of Prince McCullers, the Foleys welcomed another Princess, a second rose-brush for us to watch fructify from our cuckoo's nest. Blaise's sister would not be her perfect clone, because sisters don't bud off each other like bread cells. But their markings would be so aligned that if I crossed my eyes at close range, I could mistake Blaise's sister for her, and vice versa. There might be the same red cape of hair, but Dru's springy green eyes instead of John's blazing blue. Her body might be softer, its edges not as expertly and divinely whittled as Blaise's. She could never challenge Blaise's status as the most sparkling, willowy girl in the room, but she might choose to market herself against that. For every milligram of Adderall that Blaise took, she would roll a fat blunt. For every tennis match Blaise won, her sister would sleep past noon, cocooned in lazy comfort.

I imagined that Blaise's sister would have a trick of seduction that Blaise does not. In my dreams, she's a Comp Lit major, clicking around in a suede skirt and combat boots, nibbling on pencil tips with Blaise's pedal lips. When she lends me her copy of Ovid's *Metamorphoses*, passages are underlined and initialed "J.B. <3." Or maybe she'd be a fencing champ, or a knife thrower. Maybe she'd just have a pair of Venusian breasts for me to rest my head on. (B's B-cup is the only part of her that I could ever find flaw with, and even then I feel like I'm splitting hairs).

Anyway, McCullers Foley is very real, and when he reads what I said about his sister's boobs, he may threaten me with violence. Ever the Irishman, he is quietly devoted to his women. You know this from the way he pushes his mother's wheelchair, nodding stoutly at Dru's every coo. McCullers looks as much like Blaise as a boy can resemble a girl. Hair: strawberry blonde and somewhat fluffy. Eyes: wide and oceanic, but missing a few keys from Blaise's expressive octave. Skin: fair and freckled, his back pocked like quail eggshells from sails on the Barnaby's boat. Build: 6'1 and solid, no pudge to pinch on him.

McCullers often goes running along our family's shared grounds. Sometimes, Conor would tail him in his police car, an idle warm-up for his matches with Blaise. McCullers would sense him creeping, whip around and give him the frosty Foley stare that could make a black bear back down. No fun to be had, Conor would leave his indifferent prey there in the shoulder of Zzyzyx.

I told Blaise once that hanging with McCullers makes me feel like I have Kevin back. Of course, she cried, re-quoted me, and cross-stitched it on her heart forevermore. I didn't mean it so mushily, I just meant that we liked doing the same shit together. I wasn't trying to make a new best bro in adulthood, especially since I have 14 male cousins and brothers buzzing around my head like a goddamned baby mobile. I don't really make new friends. I'm there for my vet buddies, but so many of them are busy now leading underwhelming lives. I see them buying a two-bedroom ranch with their VA loans, or marrying some chubby bride with skunky highlights, and I'll hit the Like button, wondering if death would have them more glorious.

I admit, McCullers had an automatic glory about him. Yes, it was sealed by the Foley crest, but I don't think it's the label that appealed to me as much as the legend. I'm writing an entire book about his sister, and he deserves a small but sturdy monument within it.

When McCullers first came to our house, his grudging, cool countenance melted after about five minutes, and he started asking me all about my time as a sniper in the army. He loves guns too. Imagine my surprise when this red-blooded, Fortunate Son of Kentucky glanced over at Blaise, lilting in perfect French, *"Tu aurais dû choisir l'autre frere, cel qui sait tirer un arme."* ("You should have picked the other twin, the one who knows how to fire a gun.")

Blaise giggled, *"Il parle francais, Seamus, il comprend tout."* ("Seamus speaks French, he can understand you.")

"Ah bon?" McCullers glanced at me, quailing a bit. Everyone but Pat blushed for separate reasons. (Pat guffawed, "Huh?" in a way that made me despise him with the brevity and intensity of my fifteen-year-old orgasm).

Why should I surprised to learn McCullers spoke French? He had the same Martiniquan nanny and Montessori schooling as Blaise did. He looked like old Kentucky money to the soles of his $500 loafers, but his eyes glowed with life outside Louisville. Like the Barnaby boys, his collegiate career was muddled and vague, but unlike them, he hadn't left after a few semesters to "help out with the distillery." He left to work as a ski instructor in Villeneuve, the tiny

Swiss village where he had attended boarding school. He would "probably" go back to school and finish eventually, to "maybe do something useful for the distillery, maybe go to law school," but there was no ticking bomb above his head, (apart from the one counting down to his sixty-first year). He lobbied for gun safety at shooting ranges, using his mother's tragic accident as a cautionary tale. He had already made some money in a real estate scheme with his good friend Loyce Barnaby Jr., the details of which escape me now.

Re: McCullers' rich boy hedonism, I have received a report from Sammie Goldstein, the delectable Jewess whom Blaise has appointed her bridesmaid. You've met Sammie here and there—she's the little mink who wore a bodysuit and cat ears for Halloweens 2009-2012. Sammie looks like a Goya girl, if Goya had infused mischief into his marquessa's dark eyes.

"Let me take you back to Christmas 2007, the first time I met McCullers," Sammie laughed, when I recently got her on the phone at her parent's home in Chicago. "I was spending my first Christmas at the Foleys' ski house in Switzerland."

"I know of it," I murmured, not unwistfully. The Foley's 15 room chateau, seated at the base of the Alps with panoramic, snow-capped views, is where we are supposed to have Pat's bachelor party next month.

"Right," Sammie explained that she and Blaise had just become friends that semester. They were united in their dogma that friends should steer clear of each other's brothers. "Unless, of course, it's true love—in the style of Cher and Josh, or Noah and Allie."

On the private jet to *der Schweiz,* Blaise got drunk and patted Sammie's knee, telling her she loved her so much, she could have her little brother if she wanted.

"So did you guys…?"

"Are you *kidding*?" Sammie chuckled ruefully, explaining that when they got to the house, they found 17-year-old McCullers Foley stretched out by the indoor pool in sunglasses and a Vanderbilt hoodie, and lounging beside him—naked apart from her landing strip—was a 6-foot-tall model named Lilou LePrince. ("Basically the hottest blonde gazelle I've ever seen," quoth Sammie. "And I was in the *hot* sorority.") McCullers was absent-mindedly stroking Lilou between her thighs while reading a magazine (not French *Vogue,* where Lilou was ubiquitous that month). Once or twice, he slipped his juicy fingers into his mouth. When Lilou rose to swan-dive into the pool, McCullers muttered, *"Tu m'as fait mouillé, chérie,"* without glancing up. (I can only imagine Lilou's coquettish reply, *"tu m'as fait pareil."* Then a Serge Gainsbourg song swelled to a crescendo in endorsement of such gallic hedonism).

"He was *17,* Seamus," Sammie said emphatically. "That's the age most American boys are getting laid for the first time!"

"And how old was Lilou?"

"28," Sammie replied. "I follow her on Insta," she added, with a sigh of feminine envy that I would never understand. "She's verified."

McCullers had apparently been a sickly child, in and out of the hospital with unexplained bouts of illnesses which were now known to have been caused by a severe gluten allergy (when he and Blaise got into a fight, he still called her "Smelly Kelly," and she still chased him around the house wielding a slice of bread). According to McCullers, his inability to drink bourbon had caused his father to reject him somewhat, and further esteem Blaise as the prize of his life. He did not tell me this bitterly, but matter-of-factly. Actually, he seemed relieved to be off the hook for a lifetime of making the family sauce.

I recall this one time we were at his shooting range which abuts the woods behind our distilleries. Since Dru McCullers' terrible accident, the range has been made-over in steely penitence, all the rusty framework replaced and the loose back-boards sealed up. McCullers spends a lot of his time there. He even teaches a gun safety course once a week.

"Nice," he said in cool admiration, when I unloaded a full round into the bullseye.

"That's why they call me Deadshot!" said I (Deadshot is my family nickname, in case you were curious—though I'm always Maggot to Conor).

He nodded again, then suggested we roll a spliff. Like Pat and Blaise, our relationship was still in the closet, so we were sure to take cover in case Mr. Foley's Bentley came around the corner.

We were talking about girls and guns and other glories when he asked me outright if Pat wanted to marry his sister.

"Yeah man, I think so."

McCullers nodded his strawberry-blond head in acceptance. He squinted into the setting sun, muttering, "I know Pat's got a good job, but I could share some of my trust with her. Blaise thinks she can make it on love alone, but she's never had to fly coach or drink well whiskey before…"

I wasn't following him, "Why would you have to share your trust with your sister?"

McCullers stared at me as if trying to figure out if I was joking. "Well, my dad is going to cut her off if she marries a Walsh," he said slowly. "And she'll never be able to work at Foley again."

"She thinks your dad loves her enough to accept them," I ventured, thinking, *please don't let him take her away from us.*

"Deadshot," McCullers passed me the spliff unsentimentally, "You don't know John."

"So your dad would want them to break up?"

"I mean...*yeah.*"

"Well, what if they don't wanna?"

"Uh, then she should start looking for jobs with her 2.7 GPA," McCullers said baldly, "Sell her horse for money."

"Well, what do *you* think they should do?" I demanded, feeling my seams of normalcy coming undone. There had to be some union we could appeal to, an injunction we could file to stop him. The thought of Blaise going back over the hedges and taking her red hair with her was too cruel to bear.

McCullers pondered the question. "Well, according to the Indian curse, my dad won't live past sixty-one," he said matter-of-factly. "Could they be undercover lovers for a few more years?"

"Doubtful," I remarked. Sneaking around was already starting to seem like Disney farce. Our family wasn't built for it. There were too many people, too many parties, too many pictures being taken. In Walsh world, Blaise and Pat were on the ascent to full acceptance, even adoration. So when Blaise begged Maura or Tiffany not to tag her in a photo, she was met with quizzical smiles and head tilts.

The day after St. Paddy's Day, our father wanted to call up John-boy and deliver a curdy speech about the kids loving one another, and how they ought to lay aside their differences. Blaise begged Pat to stop him. "It's not the right time!" she insisted.

Our father deferred to her wishes, but he didn't like it. "The longer we put it off," he said ominously to our mother, "The harder it'll be in the end."

At the time, we all wondered how much longer she could straddle both worlds.

YEAR 25
Halloween 2013-Spring 2014
Zzyzyx Road/Brown Hotel/Duffy Foley's home
'The Plottings of Lord Pluto'

Chapter 10

In the end, Duffy was the one who discovered Pat and Blaise. It happened on the night Blaise turned twenty-five, Halloween 2013, which also happened to be the eve of Duffy's 60th (and final) birthday.

As a man, Duffy Foley was sterling and distinguished. When the Kentucky sun struck his tawny head, it shone like a puddle of smelted dimes. His mother Sabina was Swiss-French, described as a stick of plutonium stuck in the body of a Bond girl (in true Oedipal form, Duffy only slept with French women his entire life). With his untelling eyes and mountain froideur, his Swiss alleles may have been stronger than the Irish ones. Duffy had a reputation for being the most vengeful Foley. He had no wife and children, and therefore had ample time in his evenings to marinate on his trespasses and decide upon recourses. A litigious man, all of Duffy's passions were expressed through the law.

He was also a billionaire, the heir to the Foleys' eleven-digit trust fund. The question of who he was going to leave it to after his sixty-first birthday was a topic of great speculation. My father and Uncle Marty often discussed it on barstools in low voices.

"Imagine if he left it to Blaise?" my father said, leaning back and letting the picture be painted. "Boy, she'd be set. Wouldn't have to worry about another thing."

"But what if he leaves it to Johnny?" Uncle Mart growled. "The asshole'd probably have our whole distillery plowed away."

It was a sobering thought, but it was never discussed sober. After all, we didn't really believe in the curse of sixty-one, not then. For us, it was fun barroom banter, like talking about where Jack's treasure was buried, or who would win in a fight, Eems or Conor.

Duffy was the first person to visit Blaise after she was born, turning 35 at midnight in the maternity ward, long after the other uncles went home. While Dru slept deservedly in her hospital bed and John commanded congratulations from the pay-phone, Duffy cradled the soft pink bundle in his arms. The rise and fall of Kelly's tiny chest seemed to depend entirely on him.

John-boy returned, motioning eagerly for his daughter. Duffy could tell his brother was already head-over-heels. In a moony voice, Johnny fed Baby Kelly all his lovestruck honey, about how amazing she was, the heiress to America's blood, and how all the amber and honor and sills and stories would one day be hers, all hers. "I'll teach you everything I know, baby girl," he promised, kissing her fuzzy red head.

Duffy half-listened to his brother's speech, making his own silent pledge. *I will always protect you, Kelly-girl.* A psalm came to his mind, the one about walking through the valley of death with no fear, because Thou art with me.

Duffy would become his niece's Thou.

Blaise's twenty-fifth birthday took place in the Foley's ballroom with all the usual fanfare. She and her sororal squad spent the day decorating the room to look like something out of Bram Stoker's nightmare. The only source of light was the many skeletal candelabras planted along the buffet tables. Their pearly wax dripped eerily onto scarlet velvet tablecloths, and more than once Hildy had to change out hot brown tartlets caught under the drizzle.

By 9:30, the dim room was crawling with grand dames and Kentucky Colonels. In one corner, Blaise earnestly told the Governor that she was experiencing no quarter-life crisis, ("Wait until you turn 50," he said dismally, tossing bourbon down his bolted neck—he was Frankenstein for the night).

In another corner, Aunt Kennedy nagged at her surly brothers to snap a picture with her. For Halloween, John-boy had donned a pirate's patch, but couldn't be bothered to change out of his corduroys and loafers. No fewer than three guests asked if he had recently had Lasik surgery.

Willie Cooper and Ace Barnaby, Loyce's little brother, were discussing Willie's golden days training racehorses. ('We almost had the Triple Crown in '83 with Obsidian Dream," sighed Mr. Cooper, "But we ran her too hard and she placed third at Belmont...")

Blaise's friends were languishing in their kittenish costumes, paying lazy attention to whatever came to visit them (i.e., a tray of orange petit-fours, or one of the hopeful Barnaby brothers).

Duffy Foley watched his niece as she crossed the room. She was maturing, he could tell. Her hostess gestures tonight reminded him achingly of a younger Dru. His mother told him once that a true woman feels responsible for the comfort of an entire room, but can tend to each person with such grace, you would never suspect you weren't her only one. That was how Duffy viewed his niece now, as she touched the elbows of her guests and renewed her lovely smile for each one. She brimmed with a woman's knowing kindness.

Lately, he had wondered about Kelly-girl. She was twenty-five now, approaching the age when girls began to get engaged. Kelly-girl had always been embarrassingly candid about matters of the heart (how many stories had he been forced to listen to about that damn Jake Abramo?). But since him, there had been no mention of another leading man. It surprised Duffy: by now, he imagined his zealous niece would have converted a Rothschild to Catholicism and married him at Foley Bourbon in a full, swanky ceremony. Duffy wondered (not without pride) if his niece had, like him, sworn off marriage, recognizing it for the unnecessary entanglement that it was. With the leviathan empire she stood to inherit, he would be relieved to think Kel had outwitted any predatory suitors...

"*Duff!*" Blaise whinnied, wobbling up to him now in her spike leopard heels. Though her leopard tube dress rode up and she sloshed milk punch as she walked, Blaise managed to appear composed, thanks to her smile and deft self-correction. "Duffy baby, we may not make it 'till midnight." She nodded towards her pile of friends, "We have another house to go haunt."

Duffy nodded, swooping in to accept Kel's emphatic cheek-kiss. "Happy Birthday, *60,*" she growled, so that only he could hear. She held his gaze firmly. "It's not your last. You're gonna lick the curse, I know it."

Duffy nodded dispassionately, "Happy Birthday to *you*, Kelly-girl. You okay to drive?"

"Of course!" Blaise yelped, clumsily adjusting her cat ears. "Love you, Duffaluffacus Rex. See you for dinner tomorrow." She pointed at him warningly, "*Your* ass is getting sung to, not mine!"

Duffy smiled knowingly. Kelly-girl always threatened to make sure his name alone was on their shared birthday cake at dinner at the Brown Hotel. In truth, it was all for her.

He seized his topcoat with the Persian lamb collar from the coatroom. He decided to leave too, but first he went out onto the terrace for a solitary cigarette. As was his custom, Duffy said goodbye to no one as he left, unless you counted his father's portrait hanging in the sunroom.

As he quietly mounted his Aston Martin, he watched Blaise lean out the window of her car to thumb the key-pad. Her voice carried back to him, a wordless timbre of vaudevillian pomp and self-depreciation, designed to make her worshipful friends laugh. The iron gate creaked painfully open, and the carful of girls peeled off into the smoky night.

Duffy cranked his ignition, reflecting upon his niece's wobbly walk. *She's too drunk to drive*, he decided. There was bound to be a DWI checkpoint tonight, on account of Halloween. And that godawful Walsh cop was always around.

Duffy decided to follow Blaise, just to make sure she was alright. That was his job, after all.

As he drove a surreptitious 500 yards behind her, Duffy reflected on the time he overheard Kelly-girl cheerfully tell her friends that if she accidentally killed Jake Abramo during a lover's quarrel, she would dial Duffy instead of 911. She was kidding, but she happened to be right: Duffy would have the boy's teeth dissolved in a barrel of lye before his parents even knew he was missing. The truth was, the meaning of his life was to erase the bad from hers. Duffy was an impressive piece of architecture that people could admire, but only his nieces dwelled within.

To his surprise, Kelly did not take the state road towards town. She traveled instead for several miles along back roads, finally funneling into a residential area with houses he knew were built in the early 2000s. Duffy did not recognize this neighborhood. Everyone in their crowd lived in sprawling estates on land so old, the deed had been traded with gold and buffalo meat, and sealed with a handshake from the Indian chief.

Duffy's curiosity now overshadowed his concern. He crept behind Kel as she rounded a hill spiked with an old timey sign that said Crabtree Drive. He was careful to lurk several paces behind. His caution was wasted; the girls did not spare him a single glance as they exited Kelly's car, a happy clamor of heels and chatter. Over his odometer, Duffy watched his niece as she rapped on the front door, smiling at whoever answered. A disembodied hand welcomed the girls in.

Duffy lurched closer. The house was a huge, a white colonial with black shutters and a tire-swing hanging in the front yard. It looked like the kind of home which had a 7-foot high tree at Christmas. *Probably passed out king size Hershey bars to the trick-or-treaters earlier,* he thought.

Shame yanked at his guts. What the hell was he doing here? *Thank God Kel didn't see me.* Duffy imagined his niece spotting him, her face flashing from surprise to disgust. There would have been a tremor of betrayal between them, a suggestion of voyeurism that perverted their steely bond.

The uncle put the car in drive. His niece was safe from the slings and arrows of a breathalyzer tonight. He yawned, his mind drifting to a nightcap, maybe a call to Sophie in Paris—

But then, his gaze snagged on something in the lawn more horrifying than anything Halloween could bring.

There, staked beside the tire-swing, stood the sign of satan as Duffy knew it:

*"The Walshes
Est. 1983"*

There was no doubt about it. Kelly was behind enemy lines.

Duffy's first instinct was to rescue her. He actually unbuckled his seatbelt and reached for the door. Then he stopped. Kelly-girl went into that house willingly. He had seen her smile under the porch light.

The knowledge that she was at Marty Walsh's home popped like a swamp bubble in his brain. From the wispiest, carbon copy receipt of memory, Duffy recalled an article in the paper from years ago, *Martin Walsh of Crabtree Drive*...Maybe one of his kids had been photographed for the sport's page...

Duffy lit a cigarette. Everything leaping inside him a moment ago was now icy and still. He littered his cig pointedly on the sidewalk, hoping Kelly would recognize the golden cuff of his Nat Turner when she left. A crashing bang of anxiety was her due, he thought, with spite that seared from within his Foley chromosomes...

Another bubble swelled in him, popping heavy blobs of swamp everywhere. This was a memory of he and Marty laying on their bellies as kids, spying on their parents in the parlor at Foley. His mother Sabina, her Barbie doll blonde hair swept up like a conch-shell, dancing in a pink swing dress; Marty's mother Kachine, her black hair flowing like her muumuu, warming the halls with her throaty laughter. The fathers, ignoring their wives' levity, talking seriously around highball glasses. Burt Bacharach or Dusty Springfield crooned from the record-player; the room gauzy with cigarette smoke. The wives always looked like they were having a blast, but it was their fathers whom Duffy and Marty came to spy on...

Duffy stuffed this back into his cabinet of unexamined things. He drove onwards from all that he did not understand.

"It's a little late for trick-or-treaters," Marty Walsh said to the quartet of girls on his porch. He wore no costume, but managed to look both distinguished and rumpled in his argyle vest and pilly bedroom slippers.

"Happy Halloween, Uncle Mart!" Blaise replied, in the elvish tone made for disarming even the most hard-ass of men (which Marty was reputed to be).

Sure enough, Marty waved the girls into his foyer, commenting wryly that their number was convenient: "I happen to have four sons." He gestured to a gilded frame above a shoe-tree, which the girls glanced at with careless intrigue. It was a caricateur drawing of four black-haired cherubs above the words: **For us there could be no greater joy, than having four beautiful, wonderful boys: Oscar, Callum, Brendan, Micheál.**

"Hey baby," Pat came grinning around the corner to enfold Blaise in his arms. When he invited her to a Halloween/Birthday party earlier, she foolishly thought at first that his Uncle Marty was throwing her one. It turned out Marty's son Callum also happened to be born on Halloween, one full term of Reagan's presidency ahead of her.

Blaise's friends chided Pat for his lack of a costume, and he shrugged adorably. All the girls, (Sammi, Elliot, Lauren) were currently single, and eager to mix with Pat's tribe of tall, strong-jawed cousins. Blaise hoped to afford them an opportunity tonight to do just that. That Kiki was fun and frenetic, a lighter shade of Seamus. And there was dreamy Mickey, a baby to the Walshes but a man to them.

But to Blaise's surprise and the girl's chagrin, Mickey wasn't there, nor was the birthday boy, nor *any* boy other than Oscar in his Brooks Brothers blazer, his strapping looks and yuppy charms rendered moot by the ring on his finger (and the wife sitting beside him).

"You just missed Callie," said Marty's wife, Jill. She offered the girls slices of his half-eaten birthday cake, a carrot cake with an icing pumpkin in the middle. Like her husband, Jill looked like she was slowly coming undressed from work. She had on a navy pencil skirt and pantyhose with a University of Chicago Law School sweatshirt. She and Marty had matching raven hair and striking blue eyes. Something about Jill's enunciated cheekbones and smiley formality reminded Blaise of Maria Shriver. When Elliott called her, "Mrs. Walsh," Jill told her that she never changed her name from McGuinness. ("I never felt the need to," she added frankly).

"Where are all your other boys?" Elliott asked, eyeing their four tuxedoed senior portraits on the wall appreciatively.

"Brendan lives in Montana," Marty said, accepting the china cup of coffee his wife passed him with a nod of thanks. "And Mick had some party he wanted to get to with Aidan," he sipped and raised his brows at the girls. "They'll be sorry he missed you."

"It's *really* a pity we missed Callum," Blaise said dramatically, eyeing the birthday boy's senior portrait. Callum "Slaw Jaw" Walsh wasn't as obviously handsome as his brothers, but he was very striking: his jaw flared so widely that he almost looked like he just had his wisdom teeth pulled, and his indigo eyes conveyed a certain depth, even at 17. She wondered if her coming tonight had anything to do with his leaving. Seamus had told her that he left the St. Paddy's Day party in protest when she arrived. Secretly, she empathized with him: before Pat, if her cousin Zabana showed up to a family party with a Walsh boy on her arm, Blaise would have burned the whole goddamn thing to the ground. When she learned that Slaw Jaw shared her macabre birthday, she decided to give him an olive branch of a gift. He was a distiller, so he would appreciate it.

It was his grandfather's bourbon, barreled in 1944, Wilkie's last act before shipping off to war. This, he had written on the barrel, (which was collecting cobwebs in one of the Foleys' Lexington warehouses) along with his stout will:

"If I die at war, Sully knows the mash-bill and Pearsey and Kilky can split my share of Da's treasure.
-Wilkie Daedalus Walsh, 1944."

Though 95% of the bourbon had evaporated from the barrel, Blaise was able to fill up half a crystal decanter when she went to the rickhouse earlier that day.

All the men plus Blaise got glasses to taste. It was true tarantula juice, leaving their throats blistered raw. Tears streamed down Oscar, Pat, and Uncle Marty's cheeks, but not Blaise's. Even 70-year-old bourbon couldn't make her cry.

"Tiff, do you want to taste?" Marty croaked at his daughter-in-law, Tiffany, an Atlanta girl with Budweiser model looks and debutante manners.

"No thanks," Tiffany sniffed primly into her Diet Coke. She told all the girls in a voice of Venetian lace that she wasn't drinking because she and Oscar were "trying."

"Trying what?" Elliot gobbled, busy pitching candy-corns into Sammi's cleavage, which protruded from her leather catsuit like Pillsbury rolls. They were bored because the boys they were promised weren't here.

Blaise was nowhere near bored. With Pat massaging her shoulders, she excitedly gabbed to Marty and Oscar about Wilkie's 70-year-old bourbon. "How lucky that we still had it!" she said. "It may just be the world's oldest spirit."

She stopped herself from correcting her own fib: this couldn't be the world's oldest bourbon, because she found something older than Wilkie Walsh himself in the warehouse: it was a secret shelf of Foley bottled in 1920, and if she was right, it was a very lethal blend indeed. Her Daddy had told her all about Uncle Andy's "special sauce," claiming he used to serve thallium-laced bourbon to Prohibition Agents who raided their distillery. Apparently, Andy knew it was the poison only by a certain Latin engraving on the bottle. Blaise always believed this to be Foley mythology, but today, she unearthed these bottles with the *exact* Latin that her father described. For ten minutes, Blaise had stood in the damp, dim space, holding the grimy bottle longingly. Finally, she forced herself to put it down. She couldn't guarantee that the poison wouldn't wind up in her daddy's nightcap some night, after one of their stormier fights...

Marty yowled something about being sure that Callie would appreciate it.

He fucking better. "Yeah," Blaise nodded, laughing. "He's lucky—I was thinking about giving it to my Uncle Duffy."

"Duffy?" Marty said with sudden sharpness.

"Yeah" Blaise pretended not to notice Marty's change in tone. "It's his birthday too. Actually—is it midnight yet? I'd better text him."

Blaise dug out her phone from her bag (catching Tiffany craning her neck to peep the label). To her surprise, she saw Duffy had messaged her:

Guess you took Mark 12:31 a little too close to heart, Kelly Rhiannon...

What the hell's 12:31 in the Bible? she thought, posing the question to Google. Up came some Christian Message Board with a fish symbol over a quote index.

"12:31 : Love your neighbor as yourself.' There is no commandment greater than this."

Her blood turned to blue slushie. *Duffy knows!* For all Blaise knew, he could have been quietly sitting on it for a month and decided, out of spite, to detonate the bomb on her birthday. You never knew with him.

"I suggest you meet me at the Brown tomorrow an hour before dinner starts." Her uncle wrote. She could hear his tone through the text, cooler than railroad tracks in January.

Blaise hesitated, staring at Pat's chiseled profile, which suddenly seemed like a beautiful view on the last day of vacation.

Blaise tried to play dumb with her Uncle, *"Whatever do you mean?"*

Duffy ignored this. *"I already called the bar to make sure they have a 25-Year in stock... assuming you still drink your family's bourbon..."*

She bristled. Here was Duffy's famous stinger she had always heard about. Well, he should just watch himself. She could morph from mermaid to stingray in under ten seconds.

Let's give ourselves a good hour and a half, Blaise answered. *And nothing could keep me from my daddy's ambrosia. You know that.*

Her Uncle didn't respond.

Blaise supposed getting caught red-handed was the easiest way. In recent months, she had tried to find peaceful allies in the Foley-Walsh war, looking to the women in her family for help. Though Aunt Kennedy and Nana Sabina had both departed Foley Bourbon decades ago, their presence was still abundantly felt through its opulent halls. Kennedy's grinning, sixteen-year-old portrait with her tawny horse, Versailles, greeted you from the third-floor landing. Nana's legacy of good taste was preserved in several of Foley's 29 rooms, which she had decorated in mid-century mod as her pet project in the 50s.

But when she finally told Nana Sabina about Pat, Blaise was surprised and disappointed by her reaction.

"Oh dolly, I'm sorry—you know I love you, but you *can't!*" simpered Nana over the phone in her throaty Swiss accent. "*C'est pas possible!* Those Walsh boys spell nothing but trouble for you." A glass clinked on her end. Sully had converted her from champagne to bourbon circa 1952, and to this day, Sabina drank nothing but her Johnny's ambrosia mixed with branch. Blaise pictured her grandmother sprawled on her sleigh bed at her palatial Malibu home, twirling the cord of her antique phone with a red polished finger.

Blaise clinked her own glass furiously. "That's unkind, Nanny-boo. I'll have you know that Sean and Marty Walsh both think of you as their first love. *And* more beautiful than the first Bond Girl."

Her grandmother scoffed stubbornly. "Those boys were *born* with that wild look in their eye." She swigged her drink. "No wonder they were such animals to my poor Duffy and Johnny. The way they carried on in that courtroom..."

Aunt Kennedy had similar objections. "You *really* shouldn't go there, Bam Bam," she sighed, when Blaise called her at home in Tucson. After Kennedy's trust fund kicked in at twenty-five, she had a southwestern version of Foley Bourbon built in the desert.

Blaise pictured her aunt out there now, watching the sunset with her bare feet plunged in the pool, riding breeches rolled up, possibly smoking a joint if her kids weren't around. Unlike her glamour-puss mother, Kennedy's style favored fishermen sweaters and men's Polos. She had her mother's siren power over men, a fact which majorly exasperated her big brothers growing up.

"I know how hard it is," Kennedy went on in her placid contralto voice. "Good lord, my bedroom had a perfect view of the Walshes' house growing up! Imagine seeing Shilah on his motorcycle in his muscle shirt each day with that sexy ponytail of his..." she giggled.

"Ooh," Blaise purred, and for a brief second she forgot her own all-consuming drama. "Listen to you, Kennykins. You guys would've been a cute couple. Coulda made some cute little Irish-Indians together…"

Kennedy told her to hush. She sobered Blaise right up with her next caveat: "Johnny's already shot your boy once. Don't gamble with his life now, honey."

Now Duffy apparently knew the truth. She did not tell Pat—*for now*. The dynamics in Pat's family were different, and love for them was louder with lower stakes. If the Walshes had rejected Pat's love of Blaise, he might've been run off the road by a hot-headed cousin. If Blaise was rejected, she could be stripped of her title, her shares—everything that made her somebody in this world.

Nevertheless, Blaise felt hopeful the next evening. Her Uncle had always been her get out of jail free card. Maybe he would once again produce a magical solution that would help them all live Happily Ever After.

Casually, she fibbed to Daddy about needing to leave early to buy Duff a birthday gift, and set off to meet him.

Her Uncle arrived at 6, exactly an hour before dinner. Blaise glared at Duffy as he greeted Vance the bartender, requesting a double of the 25-Year, neat.

"Didn't we say an hour and a half before dinner?" Blaise demanded. Her cocktail napkin was littered with cherry stems gnawed thin with nerves over the past 32 minutes.

"*You* said an hour and a half before," Duffy responded coolly, sidling out of his coat to reveal one of his father's impeccable suits. "I only had an hour."

"Hmm," Blaise recognized this as her uncle's way of setting the terms of their meeting. "Well, Happy Birthday."

"Happy doesn't even begin to describe it," Duffy said dryly, raising his glass to Vance. For a moment, uncle and niece sipped their drinks in chilly silence.

"So, what the hell do you think you're doing, Kelly?" Duffy said finally. He gave her the sideways glance that courtroom artists had nicknamed the Snake Eyes.

Blaise tried her best to look aghast. "*Excuse* me? You'll have to fill me in, Duff," she sipped delicately. "You texted me a random biblical verse last night. I'm completely lost."

"Cut the shit, Kel," Duffy growled. He had never cursed at her. "You know what I'm talking about."

"I do?" Blaise breathed, deciding to go full steam ahead with this tactic. "Why don't you enlighten me? *Seriously.*"

Duffy considered his niece, lithe and steely at once in her black cocktail dress. He recalled how he always told Kel to never admit to anything, that a good defense team could explain away the sun. He now empathized with the plight of Dr. Frankenstein.

"So how's Marty Walsh lately?" Duffy asked finally, signaling to Vance for another drink.

Blaise's stomach imploded, but she kept her face a mask of tranquility. "I would think you'd know better than I would," she cheeped. "You're both officers of the court, are you not?"

Duffy sighed, staring out the window above her head. The sun was setting, and the familiar Louisville skyline was becoming illuminated in blue and white lights. Soon, the old Aegion building would be red-and-green for Christmas. Carols would start warbling over the radio, and holiday tins of bourbon balls would crop up at his office. His last Christmas.

His last birthday with Kel...

"Kelly-girl," Duffy peeped his father's golden pocket-watch. 6:35— they were wasting time. "Whatever's going on, you *want* to tell me. If I'm reading the situation right, you're gonna need an ally here."

Blaise felt something slacken in her. "And...how are you reading the situation?" she asked carefully.

Duffy swiveled on his bar stool to face her. "Something going on between you and a Walsh boy?" he asked, in his lowest voice yet.

Blaise kept her chin high, though her lip quivered treacherously. "I'm scared," she admitted.

"Don't be scared,"' Duffy advised. "Be *honest*." His old instinct to protect her soared above his desire to win his case. "Have I ever let you down before?"

"Never," Blaise said unhesitatingly. She decided to go on trusting him.

"The thing is, Duff, if his last name were anything else, we'd walk through that door together in about 15 minutes," she nodded miserably towards the marble lobby, "Then he'd keep his arm around me all through dinner, and talk to you and my daddy both with the utmost respect, and by the time the night was over, you'd *completely* understand why I love him."

Duffy drummed his fingers on the bar contemplatively. His wedding finger was bare, but on his pinkie was the gold ring set with the Foley logo. He knew it would be on his nephew's hand by this time next year.

"It's not Marty's son the lawyer, is it?" Duffy asked scathingly.

"*Oscar?*" Blaise gave a laugh like a hiccup. "God, no. He's *married.*"

It pained Duffy to hear her speak the enemy's name with a splash of fondness, even intimacy.   "Well, which one is it?" he insisted. "The one that was always in the newspaper for track and field?"

Blaise laughed, stalling. "I feel like we're playing *Guess Who: Walsh Edition.*"

"Kelly," Duffy said warningly. He imagined the shame if Vance overheard. Walsh wasn't even on the menu here, because the Brown Hotel was firmly in Foley camp.

Just then, the sound of John-boy's laughter whooshed in from the lobby. Blaise saw her father wiping off his penny-strap loafers, cawing loudly, "I'm not gonna need my iron supplement for a week after the steak I'm havin'!" Aunt Kennedy clicked in the revolving door behind him in a black dress and fur shawl, fussing at Jericho's sport-jacket. Zabana came next, looking statuesque in a red Galliano dress on loan from Blaise's closet. McCullers followed, diligently pushing his mother's wheelchair through the handicapped entrance. Dru wore the green chiffon gown that Blaise selected for her earlier.

The maitre d' swept out to greet the Foleys all at half court. He didn't bring menus because the chef, Gustave, always prepared a special tasting menu just for them.

"All the Walshes know about us," Blaise said hastily, watching her father as he pompously shook the maitre d's white-gloved hand. "And *they* accept *me*. Even McCullers knows about us. He's met him—he *likes* him." She squeezed the next bit from the last air in her diaphragm, because their family was coming through the bar area now. "But I decided that I won't tell my father about him unless he proposes."

"Yoo-hoo!" Kennedy tinkered, kissing Duffy's whiskered cheek. "Look at my two lushes sitting here at the bar! Happy Birthday, big bro!"

"Thanks, Kenny," Duffy said, rising elegantly to kiss her back. "Nothing wrong with having a preprandial tonic with the best birthday gift God ever gave me." He gestured to Blaise, who felt the flush of guilt that Duffy intended her to.

"Aw!" Kennedy flashed her pearly smile.

"60, woo boy!" Johnny hooted, thumping Duffy on the back. "Don't be surprised if Elvira pops out your cake later." He nipped his brother's drink and gave a peppery cough, "The 25-Year, Duff? Jesus, did we elect a new pope?"

"Blaisey?" Dru breathed, gazing up from the wheelchair with her vacant green eyes. The names of her loved ones were among the only words Dru could still speak.

"Hi, Momma" Blaise answered vaguely, pitching forward to kiss Dru's soft cherry hair.

As they were ushered to their table in the private back room, she tried to catch Duffy's eye, but he seemed to have steeled himself to her. He ignored her throughout dinner, chatting with his nephews and Zabana instead. When Blaise asked, "Duff, how's the foie gras?" he gave her only his snake eyes and a cold nod.

Do you hate me now? I thought I was your Kelly-girl. She wanted to throw her drink in his face but also to crawl into his lap, a feeling her father so often inspired in her. Blaise picked at her sea-urchin custard, her anger fraying into gloom. She wished that all those people who squealed about how sweet her and Pat were could know how it really felt. Here she was, eating a Michelin-star meal, in the VIP room of a hotel whose concierge would probably bring over a kilo of cocaine if she asked for it, but if the boy she loved wasn't sitting beside her, it was all just cardboard scenery.

At the head of the table, Dru's mouth hung dazedly open, dribbling pureed carrot onto her lovely dress. No one noticed but

Blaise. A lump came to her throat. The whole world was a sad, godless sham indeed. No one was really looking out for any of them. She dunked her napkin in her water and dabbed at the carrot before the waitress could notice, and tell all the Brown staff what a shame it was about poor Mrs. Foley: a queen reduced to a vegetable.

"Kel," she felt Duffy's hand on her shoulder. "Let's go outside to see Orion's belt."

This was his code for having a cig. Blaise quietly acquiesced, wiping Dru's face first, which lit up like a baby seeing its mommy. "*Blaisey*," she breathed. "*Blaisey...*"

"Duff," Blaise said, once they were all lit up outside. "Do you need me to give you the whole speech about how I didn't do this to hurt you guys?"

"It concerns a Walsh," Duffy said, "I wouldn't expect the Gettysburg Address." Catching the look on Blaise's face, he sighed tiredly. "Go on and tell me whose boy he is."

"He's Sean's" Blaise said tentatively. "His name is Patrick."

"An Irishman named Patrick. Someone call Heraldo."

"He's so smart, and so *kind*. And he has his MBA," she added hopefully, "He could help me with the business." Duffy was looking disgusted and bored, so Blaise reached for her ace card. "He's the one who took Wilkie's shares to our distillery."

Duffy stared at her behind his stylish frames. "He has the missing 100,000 shares?"

"*Yes*," Blaise breathed. "Wilkie offered them to each of his *fifteen* grandsons at their First Holy Communion, the shares or $250 cash. Pat was the only one smart enough to say yes."

Her uncle's face was inscrutable. He puffed in thick silence for a minute, then from the corner of his mouth, he asked:

"Does anyone in our family know?"

"No, no one—"

"Never on your life," Duffy uttered, "Tell anyone what you just told me, Kelly. You hear me? *No one.*"

"Why not?" she asked pointlessly, for he just shook his silvery head.

"Fine," Blaise raised her eyebrows, "Don't worry, Duffy baby—I can play Crypt-Keeper Kelly for as long as I need to. But what about you? Can *you* keep secrets?"

Although Duffy appeared to ponder the question for a good 30 seconds, he did not answer it. "Well, your instincts were right on one thing," he said, stubbing his cigarette out on his loafer. "Unless that boy asks to marry you, we don't breathe a *word* of this to Johnny." He motioned for her to follow him, calling briskly, "Come along now, they'll be wanting us for cake."

Blaise followed her Uncle. As they crossed the threshold of the party room, they both snapped automatically into charming Foley mode, easily bluffing about the smoke they just had, and the birthday cake they were about to enjoy.

"Where is the Mistress of Darkness?" Duffy chuckled. "I was told she'd be popping out of my cake."

"No way!" Blaise joined in the jovial routine, "I want Ryan Gosling instead!"

The server dimmed the lights and wheeled out an exquisite, barrel-shaped cake with brown sugar fondant, and the FOLEY logo as perfectly printed as it was on the label. In gilded icing, the words were written:

Happy Birthday, Duffy and Blaise - aged 60 and 25 years to perfection!

Duffy put his arm around her as the room sang Happy Birthday, and they blew out their sparkler candles together, wishing for exactly the same thing.

Please let her come to her senses...
Please let him...

Last night, when the party sang to her, Blaise used that wish on him too:

Please let this birthday not be Duffy's last.

For weeks, Pat agonized over what song he should go with to propose. Not that he really wanted to do it, but tradition was tradition...

The 15 grandsons of Wilkie Walsh (aka, the High Fraternal Order of Black-Jack) had a secret charter that they all were all answerable to. There were several sub-groups within the High Fraternal Order, and each one had its own unique customs.

The four oldest, Killian, (Chief) Oscar, (Deebo) Conor, (Maggot) and Eamon, (Eems) fancied themselves "the Elders," and gave themselves the power to amend the charter that governed the High Fraternal Order of Black-Jack (though they could be vetoed by sneers and jeers from their younger compatriots).

The three youngest, Aidan, (Douska) Hacker, and Mickey, (Baby) called themselves '09, because that was the year they graduated high school. In 7th grade, they made a sworn pact to never ask out Bebe Fiorina, the girl they all had a crush on, for fear of ruining their brotherhood (secretly, Aidan still planned on making her his wife someday--her or Elliott Appleton).

Pat and Seamus were in '86, along with Brendan (Longbow) and Kiernan (Kiki). School was a barrel of monkeys for them and hell for their teachers, because no matter what they did, they couldn't split up the wild Walshes. Growing up shoulder-to-shoulder like that meant that '86 were the closest cousins. They governed themselves with a private charter, and the smug presumption that *every* Walshman wished he could be in '86.

"Slaw and Falco would give up a lifetime supply of bourbon *and* pussy for membership to '86" Seamus was fond of crowing, to be met with death stares from the former and latter, (both born in '84).

"Imagine when '84 circle-jerks" Kiki would pipe in, "There's only two of them, so it's actually more like Pong."

'86 never actually circle-jerked, but it had its stout customs. In honor of their fallen brother Kevin Carr, with whom they had all grown up, '86 played hooky on the anniversary of his death in July to watch *Tommy Boy* and drink Diablo's Death—Kevin's favorites. They also agreed to propose to their wife with a song, as Kevin had before shipping off to Iraq ('Leaving on a Jet Plane' was his song for Katrina).

Selecting the right song was no easy task.

"If your girl's name happens to be a song, then you're fine," Kiki opined. His engagement to Sarah had soured, but he had proposed to her with the Fleetwood Mac song of the same name. *(Editor's Note: this song has since been removed from the McGettigan's jukebox, as has 'Sara' by Jefferson Starship).*

"Speaking of Fleetwood..." Pat told '86 about Rhiannon, thinking it would be a sound choice, but the guys threw cold water on it.

"That song's about a witch, dude."

"It doesn't have the right tone."

In the end, Kiki thought of Blaise's song. It derived from a faded picture that Blaise kept on her dresser at Foley, of Dru McCullers pregnant and beaming in denim and flannel.

"Is that you in there, Foles?" Pat had asked, and she beamed like her mother, showing Pat what was written on the back in cursive: *Waiting for October!!*

Kiki intuited another meaning from the words.

"That's a *Polaris* song!" he said excitedly. He explained that *Polaris* was the band who provided the soundtrack to *Pete & Pete*, the cult Nickelodeon classic that Kiki often had projecting on the wall at McGettigan's as he bartended.

Pat listened to 'Waiting for October,' and instantly knew it was the song he wanted to propose to Blaise with.

He would do it at Proof on Main, on Valentine's Day, with Seamus on backup vocals and Kiki on guitar. They decided that Pat would get up from the table during dinner, and return with '86 to serenade Blaise.

Pat asked his brother Killian to siphon off a flask of Best-Man-Blend, and eight flasks of Diablo. This was another Walsh tradition: immediately after proposing to your girl, you appointed your groomsmen by summoning them to McGettigan's and making them chug an entire flask on the spot.

"So, who are these for?" Killian asked avidly. "I better be getting one." Though he admitted it to no one, Killian had grown to really like Blaise. Any grumbling about her in McGettigan's, he silenced by telling Meath or Kildare, or even Conor, that they would be drinking vodka if they kept it up.

"You'll see," Pat said gloomily. He was so nervous that he couldn't eat or sleep, though his bourbon thirst was at an all-time high. "Unless she says no, then they're all for me."

"She won't say no," Killian trumpeted, "She loves you. She told me so the first night I met her."

Killian was right: Blaise said yes to Pat on Valentine's Day, to a ring that far more modest than any former Mrs. Foley had ever worn before, which Pat knew, and felt a need to apologize for.

"I know it's not the Hope diamond," he said sheepishly, as Blaise held her bejeweled hand up to the light. "But it's the best a guy can do when he's madly in love on a $90K salary."

"Hush," Blaise purred, putting her fingers over his lips. "I absolutely love it. I've already decided I want to be buried with it."

"So...is that a yes?" Pat laughed, trying to ignore the fact that the entire restaurant, including Shay and Kiki, were watching them and awaiting her answer.

"Yes!" she squealed. They kissed, and the dining room burst into applause. Blaise allowed herself to enjoy it for a wonderful 45 seconds, before turning to a fresh worry:

How high will Daddy's BAC need to be for him to accept this?

In the end, Mr. Foley learned about the engagement, not from Blaise, but from Jake Abramo. Yes, Jake Abramo, the basketball champion of ULou, and Blaise's red herring for true love. Unlike Pat, Abramo had always been a welcome guest at Foley Bourbon. He and John-boy enjoyed a playful, sitcom-level rapport in which Jake asked Mr. Foley questions like, "Yo, Mr. F., if I marry Blaise, we're changing the Foley logo to an Italian horn—that cool with you?" Mr. Foley would comically blunder his objection, and then the two would have a fireside talk about Louisville basketball.

According to Sammi G., who still keeps time with him, when Abramo heard the news of Blaise and Pat's engagement via the aqueduct of sorority gossip, he drank up a quart of vodka and listened to *the Bronx Tale* soundtrack, sitting stoically in his parent's den for hours. Then he sent a few incendiary texts that he falsely believed to be poetic.

To Blaise, Abramo said: *Haha I remember you used to not let me kiss you if I drank walsh at a party. But congrats i guess…love u xoxo.*

To Mr. Foley he wrote: *yo Mr. F…I know this isn't easy for either of us but I had to say that im sure our girl is doing what she thinks is rite. She never even used to let me drink walsh at parties, always kept it brand loyal…idk what happened. Hope u find peace…love u man…don't wanna break ur heart even further but vodka sponsored this message…haha…all love to my Kentucky pops…*

Mr. Foley, enjoying a bourbon by his fire, impatiently replied: *What in the name of Custer's saddle are you babbling about, boy?*

Duffy called Blaise. "Shit's hitting the fan," he muttered, turning off his auto-de-feu and sliding into his loafers.

Blaise was at McGettigan's for an impromptu engagement party. Fretfully, she turned away from the pack of Walsh Wives admiring her ring. "Does my daddy know we're engaged?"

"Yup," Duffy said bleakly. "You better get on home. Bring the boy with you. I'll meet you there now."

"McCULLERS!" Blaise screamed, tugging a reluctant Pat by his wrist through the backdoor of Foley.

McCullers appeared in the kitchen in a Vanderbilt sweatshirt, looking even more reluctant than Pat. "Why do *I* have to be here for this? I was having fun at the party."

"Well, the party's over Cully," Blaise said gravely, reaching for the closest bottle on the wet bar and shakily pouring herself an inch. "And I *need* your support." She dipped her fingers in the whiskey and made the sign of the cross. "Where's Daddy?"

"KEL-EH!" John's voice sounded from his study with impressive rancor.

"He called you Kelly," McCullers said with relish. He reached for a bag of gluten-free pretzels in the cabinet, his big eyes getting bigger. *"Uh oh."*

"What does that mean?" Pat asked Blaise.

"It means," Blaise whispered, leading the boys up the winding marble staircase. "That I may get sent to bed without dessert."

The Foleys were assembled in her father's study: John and Duffy, drinking silently and standing on opposite hemispheres of the room, and Dru, sitting placidly in her wheelchair. She smiled a dreamy echo of her beauty queen beam when her kids entered the room. "That's my momma," Blaise whispered, and Pat waved at her. For some reason, he thought of a monarch butterfly caught in a spider's web.

Hildy stood behind Dru, fussing with her cherry hair and murmuring inaudibly. She pursed her lips sassily at Pat and Blaise, as if to say, *I hope what you two know what you're doing.*

"Hi, Momma," McCullers drawled, padding over in his socks to kiss her.

"*Cully!*" she breathed in delight.

Duffy gave Pat an apathetic once-over, then glanced at his niece's tiny new ring. His apathy twitched to revulsion. Fortunately, Pat missed the expression.

Hildy, in a seeming attempt to conjure up some normalcy, clicked her tongue at McCullers' pretzel crunching. "Now Mc-Cuh-luhs, you know Missy vacuumed the entire house today. Why you hafta go droppin' crumbs all over the place?" she rolled her eyes at Mr. John, but he only had eyes for his daughter.

"So Kelly, aren't you going introduce us to your guest?" John-boy asked, in a deceptively jolly voice.

"This is Patrick," Blaise trilled, also sounding like the Mayor of Pleasantville.

"Patrick *what*?" McCullers chimed innocently.

Blaise gave her brother a look of death, adding lightly, "McCullers has already met him."

"I met him," McCullers confirmed, plopping by the fireplace to scratch Mingus's belly. "He's coo."

"Oh so McCullers, *you've* met him?" John growled, rounding on his son.

"Yeah, now you have too," McCullers said baldly. "John, meet Patrick. Patrick, John." He looked between them and shrugged. "Meeting adjourned."

"Oh, so your brother's known about this," John roared, ignoring Pat as he stepped forward and proffered a timid handshake. "Everyone's been picking daisies with the devil behind my back. What about you, Hildy," he pitched a look of blame her way, "Did you realize what was going on?"

Hildy looked aghast. "Now Mr. John, this girl is full grown. What she does in her private time is no concern of mine—"

"Don't blame Hildy!" Blaise shrieked, feeling guilty for the 100 times she had modeled outfits for her before George chauffeured her to Pat's.

"And Duffy, you knew—" John snarled.

"Well, that depends on your definition of *knowing*," Duffy said, in his maddening, lawyerly way, "I may have become aware, around a time in the recent past, that Kel might have become involved with Sean's son—"

"Sean's son?" Mr. Foley gasped, laying a hand over his chest as though the shock of it was on par with the shock that stopped his father's heart. "My neighbor from hell? The one who has bagpipers waking me up at six a.m., and fed Ex-Lax to my poor dog...and *vandalized my rickhouse with a giant John Thomas?*"

There was a heavy pause in which the Foley brothers cast reproving eyes at Pat. McCullers, meanwhile, was suppressing his snickers over the "giant John Thomas,"

"Mr. Foley," Pat stepped forward earnestly, "I'd like to apologize for my family's behavior over the years. We've pulled a lot of stupid pranks that I see now weren't funny at all."

"No, they weren't," Mr. Foley said snippily. "You've got no future in comedy, boy." He chose a crystal decanter off his bar-cart and freshened Duffy's glass, who inclined his silver head in thanks.

"Now Mc-Cuh-luhs, I know you can't have any ambrosia with your, ah, *delicate condition*," Mr. Foley affected a lisp, as though his son's gluten intolerance was one with homosexuality. "But I wonder if my daughter and her new squeeze will join me in a drink." Challengingly, he added, "That is, if she'll *condescend* to drink my ambrosia..."

"Of course!" Blaise said haughtily, snatching up a julep cup and thrusting it forward. She elbowed Pat to do the same, who obeyed so quickly that he tripped over his feet. Hildy strode forward, muttering something about finding some vodka for McCullers.

"*Slaite,*" Pat murmured, clinking his glass against theirs. "Wow, Mr. Foley, that's really good," he said hopefully, as father and daughter leered each other down with identical beams of venom. "Uh, how long did you age that for?" He looked helplessly to the sidelines, where Duffy watched them intently, and McCullers, still reeling from his father's remark, wore an expression of mutiny in a junior league of his sister's.

"Now Kelly," Mr. Foley simpered, ignoring Pat. "Once you're married to your young man here, how d'you plan on supporting yourself?"

Pat misunderstood this to be the Father-of-the-Bride talk, a rite of passage that older Walsh boys had prepped him on.

"I'll support her, Mr. Foley." He drew himself up nobly, prepared to deliver his LinkedIn bio, sprinkled with assurances of Catholicism and boy scout badges. "I have a good job at KPMG. I have a house nearby where we can live—"

Disgustedly, Mr. Foley's eyes twitched one centimeter towards Pat, then refocused on his daughter. "And where will *you* work, Blaisey?" he asked mildly, as though making small talk at a party.

Blaise felt something volcanic ripple through her. "Well, I thought I would keep working here," she said, imitating her father's crazy calm. "Considering that you've trained me for it since birth, and I have equity stake in the company…"

"But Walshes aren't allowed on *my* property, angel," Mr. Foley reminded her, in a voice of honey and poison. "And not even in my most cruelest nightmare would I allow a Walsh to keep *shares* to my company."

From the corner of his eye, Pat noticed Duffy stir, but when he turned his head, the Uncle was motionless with the same intent look on his face.

"Mr. Foley," Pat said tentatively, "We can keep my and Blaise's assets separate. I'll do a prenup—that's fine by me." He wasn't sure if they were listening to him, because they were locking eyes as though determined to telepathically set the other on fire. "I'm not interested in Blaise's money, she knows that—"

"If you *touch* even one of my shares," Blaise seethed to her father, "I'll burn this whole place to the ground."

Mr. Foley slugged his bourbon. "Like his grandfather burned up my best bourbon," he said readily, the honey in his voice turned to vinegar. "Broke my father's heart. Might as well have pulled the trigger on him."

"That was forty years ago, Daddy. We *have* to get over it."

"Get over losing my father?" Mr. Foley said, in a slow, drawn-out way, glancing incredulously at Duffy. "That's not something to *get over*, Kelly Rhiannon." He sipped and met her eyes, "If you want to find out for yourself, just stay with this boy."

Hildy returned just then, clutching a frosted bottle of Grey Goose. She gave a small yelp as Blaise hurled her julep cup against the wall, splashing her with flecks of bourbon.

"*Jesus*," McCullers muttered. "Are you okay, Hildy?"

Duffy crossed the room to gallantly offer her his pocket square.

Blaise did not notice anything in her line of fire but her father: her vision was too blurry. John's eyes, too, were pink and watery.

"You're breaking my heart," he whispered.

"*You're* breaking your own heart, Daddy," Blaise quavered. "My Uncle supports me—" John shot Duffy a dangerous look. "My brother supports me—"

"I support my sister," McCullers repeated baldly, raising his hand.

"—the Walshes have been nothing but nice to me—they treat me like their *daughter*—"

"Oh, and why wouldn't they!" John roared, revving back up to 60. Rage wasn't enough to fully annul the Foley decorum sewn into his cells, and since Pat was standing right there, he could not speak freely. So he switched into French, his mother Sabina's language, and the Foleys' secret tongue of harsh truths. "*Tu es beaucoup plus haute que lui.*" He took a scathing swill of his bourbon, "*Sa famille est poubelle. Tu le sais.*"

"They are not!" Blaise screamed, stamping her foot (Pat grimly recalled from Mlle Joubert's class the words for *family* and *garbage*). "We owe the Walshes a lot, Daddy. For eighty years, we've built our empire on their backs!" She glanced fleetingly at Pat, warmed by the respect and adoration glowing in his eyes. "Our sills would have closed if it weren't for Black-Jack...and Wilkie made our bourbon for forty years, and helped make our bourbon *known to everyone in the world!*"

"*DON'T SAY THAT MAN'S NAME TO ME!*"

"I will!" Blaise shouted, "He's a part of it, we're connected to them—you can't deny it. Why do you think people come from across the country to visit us!"

"—to taste good bourbon—"

"That's not all! Believe me, Daddy, *I'm* the one giving the tours!" Blaise insisted. "They want to hear about us and the family next-door." She imitated all the questions she was asked every weekend, "*Are you still fighting with the Walshes...? How did that whole thing get started...?*"

"People seem to like our Romeo and Juliet thing even better," Pat chimed in, nodding supportively. "I dunno, they'd probably like that the story has a happy ending." He draped his arm over Blaise's shoulders.

Mr. Foley leered. Blaise could tell he despised them touching. The heat of betrayal radiating from John burned her for treason and infidelity. Her instinct was to restore herself to the high noon of his heart, but she didn't know how to take Pat along with her. *You can't,* whispered an inner voice scathingly. *You're gonna have to pick one or the other.*

Her daddy affirmed this with his next words: "Well, a story like that has no room on my bourbon tours." He drained his drink, smacking his lips with satisfied finality.

Blaise bawled, "You don't care about me!" She hated her father to see her crying now, so she strode forward and seized the arms of Dru's wheelchair.

"Where are you going with Momma?"

"Taking her to bed. Excuse me, everyone." Blaise glanced at Pat and mouthed something he couldn't make out, then wheeled her mother from the room.

"*Woo,* boy," Hildy sighed, using Duffy's square to dab the beads of sweat on her forehead.

Mr. Foley finally looked at Pat.

"You better get the hell off my property now," he said in a low voice, his blue eyes like radioactive warning signs.

For one wild moment, Pat thought Mr. Foley was advancing towards him, but he made for his bar instead.

"If you're not gone by the time I turn around," Mr. Foley said over his shoulder. "The story's going to take a *really* bad turn. I promise you that."

McCullers and Duffy both threw him urging looks, but Pat hesitated. What kind of a man left his fiancé in the snake pit like that? He tried to think of what Conor would do, but McCullers was mouthing *GO!* in a way that he had no trouble interpreting.

Pat said unsurely, "Well, it was nice to finally meet you, sir."

John snapped, "Boy, you'll be meeting St. Peter if you don't get out of my sight right now."

Pat slowly backed out of his study.

"Blaise?" Pat whispered into the burgundy abyss. No answer. He followed the sound of her sniffles down the shadowy corridor, and into a thickly carpeted bedroom. The room was dark, but he could see the metallic gleam from her mother's wheelchair reflected in a floor-length window. For a disorienting moment, Pat couldn't make sense of the quivering mass of red hair and limbs. Then he realized that Blaise was laying across her mother's lap, sobbing, her face buried in Dru's stiff neck. Dru was crying too, softly, unable to move her arms or offer her daughter any comfort.

"Blaisey...Blaisey..."

He observed Blaise's beautiful bare feet, spot lit by the moonbeam. For once, he felt the thrilling crackle of desire subdued by gloom.

"Excuse me."

Pat whipped around. Blaise's Uncle Duffy stood there, looking about as friendly as a three-headed dog.

"I'm afraid you must be going now," the uncle stated, his gray eyes narrowed beneath his scholarly specs. "Thank you for coming by."

Pat lingered in the doorway, willing Blaise to jerk upright and overrule her Uncle.

"Please leave," Duffy insisted, stepping forward. "My brother has reached his limit for tonight." He tapped his cheekbone, adding wryly, "You'll recall the last time you saw his limit."

Pat touched his scar, bristling. He flung another look of longing at Blaise, unable to tell if she knew he was there or not. *Bye baby,* he thought helplessly, trudging past Duffy to leave. He couldn't think of what else to do.

On his way downstairs, he braced himself for Mr. Foley to jump out with his shotgun and march him off the property, but the entire palace was suddenly still. No one would ever have guessed that 30 minutes ago, the heiress and Master Distiller were screaming at each other loudly enough to awaken their dead relatives in the cemetery out back.

At home, Pat replied with feeble gratitude to the texts of congratulations rolling in. He whistled for Shadow to join him in bed, and began tapping a message to Blaise:

hey baby...I'm sorry I left, but your Uncle asked me to go. Let me know if you want me to come back and get you :)...also i'm sorry tonight didn't go better. I don't mean to cause friction between you and your Dad. I think with time he'll see that my intentions are honorable, for the most part at least :-P. I love you Foley, there's no girl for me but you. I'll do whatever you need me to do so we can be together.

He waited for Blaise to respond, laying in his flannel sheets that and fighting waves of fatigue.

By one a.m., he still had no reply.

Seamus woke up the next morning to a dull pounding sound. He had a hangover from being urged to drink his Best Man flask last night by three generations of Walsh men (including his grandfather, who pounded his shillelagh stick in tandem with the chant of *"CHUG! CHUG! CHUG!"*).

Seamus discerned that the sound was not, indeed, coming from his head, but from his basement window. He wrangled on a sweater and clomped out back in his Adidas sandals to investigate.

"Jaysus," he griped, finding his twin banging a lacrosse ball against the garage. "I thought I was back in Iraq for a minute."

Pat turned, twirling his lacrosse stick between his big hands. His cheeks were red and streaked with tears. "Foley's gonna break up with me," he croaked, wiping his face on his sleeve. The ball dropped from his net and bounced at their feet.

"How do you know?" Seamus demanded, grabbing his shoulders.

"Here," Pat said miserably, pulling out his phone. He watched Shay's face as he skimmed Blaise's toneless response to his mushy monologue: *Can I come over this morning? We have to talk.*

"Well, I dunno," Shay said reasonably, rubbing his temples. "It doesn't necessarily mean she's gonna break up with you."

"*'We need to talk'* is the universal code for breaking up, dingus."

"Really?" Seamus shrugged uselessly, "I wouldn't know. No one's ever broken up with me before." He added with a note of curiosity, "What happened last night with her dad?"

Pat sighed, "He threatened to cut her off, and threw me out of the house."

Seamus gave a low whistle. "Tough break, dude."

They had to shelf the discussion, because Foley texted that she would be arriving in a few. Pat went inside to shower and Vizine his eyes. When he emerged from the bathroom, his fiance was sitting at the breakfast bar, legs dangling in tan equestrian boots. She smiled at him, and his heart burst like a supernova.

"Pate, I was just asking Foles if she's gonna break up with us," Seamus announced, crunching indignantly on a mouthful of almonds.

"*Never!*" Blaise breathed with kittenish outrage. Pat was barely heartened by this, because she would've said this about anyone. She would still flirt with Caesar-the-fry-cook if he was on his way in to be fired, out of pure boredom and the love of attention.

Blaise looked at him from under her swollen, pink eyelids. Excessive crying had lent a wizened look to her lively eyes, which

Pat tried not to read as resignation. "Do you want to go upstairs for a minute?" she asked him softly.

"Okay," Pat agreed, letting her lead the way to his room. He noticed with a surge of hope that she was still wearing the ring he gave her yesterday.

"Want me to take your boots off?" he asked gruffly.

"Sure," Blaise smiled, unfolding her graceful legs onto his bed. Pat felt the swooping salvation of a man pardoned from Death Row, because he knew she would've denied him this exquisite pleasure if about to break up with him.

They gazed into each other's red-rimmed eyes. Blaise cupped Pat's scarred cheek and he kissed her sacred little palm. He rubbed the balls of her feet in their socks, marveling at how joyous it felt to have a terminal diagnosis overturned.

"Did you *really* think I was going to break up with you, Walshie?" she purred accusingly, her tired eyes twinkling.

"You said, we need to talk," he said grudgingly, tapping her nose. "You're *not* allowed to break up with me, Foley, and you're *never* allowed to die." He kissed her. As always, it was like biting into juicy pink fruit.

"Well, we *do* need to talk," Blaise murmured, laying a halting hand on Pat's wrist as he began unbuttoning her shirt. "We need to make a plan." She looked him somberly in the face and whispered, "*I want you to kill my father.*"

"Really," Pat gurgled. His head was still on an aerial plane, and from up here it didn't sound like a terrible plan.

Blaise giggled, "No, not really. I just wanted to see what you'd say. *Walsh!*" she scolded him, as he tried peeling off her socks, "Focus!"

"I can't!" he groaned. Nevertheless, he slung her feet out of his lap and got into listening position.

Blaise began briskly, "I can't let my dad take my shares back. I *cannot*. It would murder my soul. I *earned* them. I mean, who the *hell* does he think he is?" she folded her arms fiercely. "John-boy's built his empire on *my* back too, you know. Having me do all his tours and tastings and billboards," she sniffed, "By the time I was 12, I could name every blend in his rickhouse blindfolded. I was the face of his whole goddamned brand!"

"You're 100% right, babe," Pat said loyally.

"When you said last night that you were willing to do anything for us to be together," Blaise asked throatily, "Did you mean it?"

Pat blinked. "You do want me to kill him, don't you?"

"Not physically, just emotionally," she said. "Just think, together you and I own 20% of Foley Bourbon. What if we found some outside investor to buy our shares?" she nodded avidly, her eyes popping out from their pillowy curtains. "We could take that money and—bear with me—found our own company! You could leave KPMG babe, you could help me run it—you'd be so good." She stroked his cheek, "I could have my own bourbon line like I always wanted—Killy would help me, he and I have talked about it—we have our names behind us, and a hell of a story. If there's one thing this industry has taught me, it's the value of a good story. *Trust me*," she finished, nodding with the promise of all the glory in the world.

He did trust her, as purely as he loved her. For a moment, he took her hand and joined her in the glowing Utopia she described.

Then his practical brain began to look for holes.

"Selling shares of a private company is hard, babe," Pat admitted, taking her hand. "I'm not entirely sure how it works in the private-securities market."

Blaise shook her head. "I know a lot of wealthy people," she said confidently. "And I know how to bend men to my will." She wagged her eyebrows and began toeing his thigh, as if to prove her point.

"Mata Hari Foley," Pat uttered. He grabbed her foot in utter worship, and kissed the warm, pungent cotton of her sock.

Gently, Blaise pulled her foot away. "But would you be down, babe? To sell our shares?"

"Sure," Pat shrugged, waving towards his saxophone case. "You know where Walsh's treasure's buried." He got a sudden, searing flashback of last night, and the way Mr. Foley's eyes had spelled REDRUM. "Your dad's gonna be furious, isn't he?"

Blaise sniffed primly, her whole carriage going erect. "He can either read about it with the rest of America, or he can walk me down the aisle at our wedding. *His* choice." Her eyes were going a little REDRUM too. "If he truly loves me, then he'll accept us. If not, then his love was always conditional—and I no longer agree to his conditions."

"Whoa," Pat said. He couldn't help feeling thrilled to be a part of her bottom line.

They touched their foreheads together like fawns in the woods.

"Let's make a pact to stay together, no matter what," Blaise purred.

"I'm with it," Pat grinned. "That's what the ring's for, girl."

He began to unbutton her shirt again. This time she didn't stop him.

Five miles down Zzyzyx Road, John Foley was giving a similar speech about Blaise to his
sister Kennedy.

In lieu of having a mother to talk feminine sense into Blaise, Mr. Foley relied on his little sister, Kennedy. She lived 1700 miles away in Tucson, Arizona, but one of the Foleys' planes resided in a nearby airfield, in case Kennedy needed to jet home and referee a fight.

When Johnny called his little sister that morning, he said conversationally that he was going to have the locks changed on Blaise, and could Kenny let him know when she was coming home next? "I want to be sure I have a new copy ready for you, baby."

"Dearie me," Kennedy dithered over the phone, "Please don't do anything, Johnny. I'll be there ASAP."

Blaise went home, her emotional hangover cancelled out by postcoital bliss. *Oxytocin is even stronger than OxyContin,* she mused, inhaling Pat's cologne on her neck and sighing. *I should Tweet that.*

She was surprised to find Aunt Kennedy sitting at the dining room table in a yellow Norwegian sweater, her copper hair spilling over a Sudoko puzzle.

"Hey little rebel," Kennedy jumped up and enfolded her in a hug that felt like a golden robe.

At least one person in this family isn't mad at me, Blaise thought.

Her aunt admired Blaise's ring, grinning, "Well I see you followed my advice to a T."

Kennedy had a rebellious nature herself. Her nickname growing up was the Louisville Lolita, because she was caught a few times in compromising positions with men twice her age. In an effort to rehabilitate Kennedy's wild streak, her mother sent her away to boarding school in Switzerland. There, she was expelled for having an affair with the 47-year-old headmaster. During Kennedy's senior year at University of Arizona, she had a pow-wow with her married Native American studies professor and got pregnant with Blaise's cousin Zabana. Blaise's friends thought Aunt Kennedy was impossibly cool, never marrying but accruing a trove of adventures and misshapen valentines. John and Duffy called her their little hippy.

"Z went to get takeout from Gralehaus," Kennedy explained now, "We ordered you a chicken sandy with fries." In a more austere tone, she said that Johnny went skeet-shooting with Mr. Barnaby, and shouldn't be expected home until tomorrow.

"*Good,*" Blaise said savagely. "Did he ask you to come here?"

Kennedy sighed deeply. Blaise took this as a yes.

"I'm *very* happy for you, Bam-Bam," she began, in her stoned preschool-teacher voice. "I trust you when you say Pat's your true love. But I do think you owe your father a little space to get used to all this change," she touched her ringed hand. "You're his *pride and joy.* It wouldn't have been easy for him to see you married off to any man. But he still has a lot of pain in his heart to heal as far as the Walshes are concerned. I think it would be very gracious of you to give him that time."

Blaise felt herself demilitarizing. "What do you suggest I do?" she asked grumpily.

"Well," Kennedy cocked her penny head. "Maybe you should come back to Arizona with us for a little while."

Blaise scoffed. "You know how that desert sun is hell on my ivory complexion, Kenny."

"It's March, honey. It won't get above 70."

"Yeah but..." Pat's face surfaced in her mind. "How could I leave my man?" Blaise said, in a comic wail.

"Aw!" Kennedy pushed her chair back and held out her arms. Blaise went grudgingly to her lap, something she hadn't done since she was a teenager. "I know, honey," her Aunt cooed.

"Arizona's a tough sell when you're in love."

"Yes it is," Blaise sniffed.

Kennedy pat her head. "You can meet Agnessa," she sing-songed, "She's visiting this week."

"Who the *fuck* is Agnessa," Blaise muttered, though she knew perfectly well Agnessa was that bougie Eastern-European girl whom Zabana had met skiing in Jackson Hole over New Years, and been enchanted with ever since.

"You'll love her," Kennedy said breezily. "We told her all about you. And Coco's there, he'd love to see you," she sensed from Blaise's bored expression that she needed to sweeten the pot. "How 'bout this, Bam: if you come with us, I'll tell you something I never told anyone else before," she leaned back and grinned. "And I suspect you'll be very interested to hear."

Blaise perked up. "Is it something scandalous?" she asked avidly. "From your wild-child days?"

"Maybe," her Aunt said coyly. "But please come. I think it's a good idea."

Blaise slid off her lap, thinking. She didn't think she could share a roof with her father now that the Walsh bomb had detonated. And she knew that if she camped out at Pat's, it would further infuriate Daddy.

"Alright" Blaise rolled her eyes. "I'll come—just for a few days."

"*Yay!*" Kennedy clapped giddily.

"Your story better be good, Miss," Blaise said sternly, "I'm leaving a beautiful Irishman behind for this."

Aunt Kennedy's house had once been described by *Town and Country* magazine as a "Southwestern safari...a luxury oasis in the middle of the desert." She lived on ten acres of rocky desert with only her horses as neighbors. Kennedy loved her house; every year she added more onto it. The backyard was the focal point, where the family lounged and ate and entertained guests, usually in the big sun gazebo with the sliding doors open. Her son Jericho had built her a bike-rack from adobe clay for last Mother's Day, which Zabana decorated with Grecian blue tile. The walkway to the house was paved with white stones, and led to Kennedy's colorful cactus garden. The pool gleamed like a sapphire mirage in the middle of the oasis. In winter months, they slipped fisherman's sweaters over their bathing suits, huddling around the fire-pit with damp heads.

"I want you to meet Nessa," 27-year-old Zabana Foley said, leading Blaise by her limp wrist to the sun-drenched pool area. She murmured in Blaise's ear, "She's always sunbathing topless by the pool. Try not to blush."

Blaise was impressed, but hid it with a shrug. "Well, that *is* the European way, Z." She was glad she spent the last twenty minutes of the flight to Tucson quelling her red, puffy eyes with cucumber serum and mascara.

Immediately, Blaise noticed a pair of tan legs in the lounge-chair by the pool. Her eyes slid up a supple torso, Playmate-style breasts, and the blinding gleam of ice on her left hand.

"*Nice boobies!*" Zabana called, flinging open the gate and grinning. The girl gave an oddly throaty shriek, springing from the lounge-chair to hug Zabana, a cape of blonde hair dancing behind her. She didn't bother refastening her bikini top, letting the triangles dangle over her enhanced breasts like a bib. She had a gymnast body like Elliot's, though she was a few inches taller and even more in shape. Blaise noticed a thick, veiny scar running down the entire length of Agnessa's left arm.

"I missed you, Zaza," she purred. Her accent was so thick it bordered on burlesque. "I may never go back to New York."

Zabana giggled, "My little brother would love if you stayed." She touched Blaise's shoulder, "Nessa, this is my cousin Blaise."

Agnessa raised her oversized sunglasses. Blaise gasped again. The girl was even more beautiful sans filter. She had a diamond-shaped face, flawless skin, and lips like a French courtesan. It wasn't just the lips that made Agnessa look seductive—her brows had the Baltic arch that meant gypsy or temptress on a cartoon. Her eyes were blue crystal, with a daring look about them, as though someone had just bet her to do something that she was absolutely going to do, and collect $100 on.

"So you are engaged to bad boy next door, honey?" Agnessa said, making a tutting sound. "I hear all about it. Let's see how he do." She grabbed Blaise's wrist and held the ring up to the sky. "Not bad," she hummed.

Blaise looked at Zabana, who shrugged and giggled. "Nessa is a professional gemologist. She just got engaged herself."

"That is right," Agnessa whooped, doing a little dance-step. "Get that ice or else no dice, girls!"

"Congratulations," Blaise said slowly. "Who's the lucky man?"

"Ali," Agnessa sighed. She jutted out her own ringed hand for the girls without being asked.

"52 karats. He buy it off some Bollywood actress when she get divorced."

"Wow," murmured Blaise, raising her brows at Zabana. Even the Foley girls were impressed by a rock of this size. The code of old money prevented them from discussing their own assets, which made bougieness like Agnessa's very intriguing. It was like being a preacher's daughter and giggling in the back pew with the naughty kids.

"But you're marrying for love, right Nessa?" Zabana winked at Blaise. "Not money?"

"Well both, Zaza." Agnessa replied, "I love Ali *and* his money!" She grinned with her tongue between her teeth, tying her bikini top. From the corner of her eye, Blaise saw her 23-year-old cousin Jericho duck from his bedroom window. He must have been spying on Agnessa as she sunbathed. *The little perv…*

The girls migrated to the sun gazebo, kicking off their shoes and resting their bare feet on the fire-pit. Agnessa's toes shimmied into a gauzy black bolero that covered her big scar. Her toes were painted acid-green.

Kennedy flung open her bedroom window and waved down at them. "Hi chickies!"

"I feed your horses an hour ago, Kenushka," Agnessa called up at her. "Don't worry for tonight."

"Anyone for bubbly?" Zabana pulled a bottle of Prosecco from the cooler and poured them three flutes. Being from Arizona, she wasn't as evangelical about the bourbon.

"Cheers ladies."

"Cheers," Blaise felt scalded that her cousin didn't propose a toast to her and Pat. To prevent herself from saying something bitchy, she turned to Agnessa.

"So where's this Prince Ali of yours?"

"He in his own desert," Agnessa replied, flicking her hand dismissively. "Saudi Arabia. I have to move there after we marry," her tone deflated ever so slightly. "But Ali promise he gonna buy me house on the Albanian Riviera!"

Blaise gulped her champagne. "*I'll* buy you a house of the Riviera, honey," she trumpeted, emboldened by Agnessa's spirit of luxury.

"Ooooh, really?" Agnessa purred, raising her sunglasses.

"Not if you get cut off from your trust-fund, you won't," Zabana said pointedly.

Blaise rolled her eyes at Agnessa, who looked unfazed.

"Don't worry, Blaise," she said, "If Tatu try and take your trust fund away, I go talk to him." She smooshed her boobs together and shimmied her shoulders. The girls cracked up.

Blaise pictured her daddy, seduced into reason by Nessa, walking her stiffly down the aisle to Pat, eyes swirling with hypnosis. She felt her dread of the future flutter away, because life suddenly felt that simple.

Over the next few days, Blaise gobbled Agnessa up. When Pat called her, she locked herself in her room to tell him that she had met the most fabulous girl in the world. ("*You're* the most fabulous girl in the world, Foley," Pat said sulkily, "When are you coming home?")

"The girl has $400 sunglasses on, Pat," Blaise laughed, glancing out the window at the pool, where Agnessa was furiously reading the Koran, topless. "But she walks around the house turning off all the lights, because she says grew up under Communism. She also uses the same paper-towel eight times before throwing it away—

she actually hangs it on the window-sill to dry. I feel like we're in a Soviet version of *the Waltons.*"

Agnessa's creaky European values gave her a searingly unsentimental view of love. One time the girls were sunbathing (Agnessa, topless, Blaise, sweating painfully through her SPF 85) when Jericho trotted outside.

"Nessa," Blaise elbowed her, "My cousin's outside."

"So he is," Agnessa murmured, appraising him as he laid shrimp skewers on the grill, whistling to himself.

"Don't you want to cover up?"

"Let him look," she shrugged brazenly. "If this thing with Ali fall apart, I need Plan B, girl."

Before Agnessa began selling million-dollar condos in NYC, she worked as a dominatrix. She told the Foley girls all about her clients, mainly businessmen whose wives believed they were playing squash after work. ("They *were,*" she smirked, showing the girls a picture of herself all done up in spike boots. "It was not a lie.")

She revealed that while Zabana and Kennedy were off fetching Blaise, she started a fun game of Slave and Mistress with Santiago, Jericho's 19-year-old nephew.

"I yell at him in Russian to bring me a drink," she explained. "And when he don't understand, I say he gonna get punished." Now, Santiago kept hanging around her, innocently asking when his punishments were happening.

"You are questioning Mistress? That's five more lashings," Agnessa said lazily from her pool chair. "Now bring Mistress a Diet Coke, slave-boy."

And, to the girl's amusement, Santiago scampered off in his red Nike Xs, bleating, *"Yes mistress!"*

In a series of private talks in the gazebo, Agnessa heard Blaise's tale of forbidden love. She admired her quiveringly earnest eyes, listening to her sigh Pat's name five times a minute. She decided what the girl needed was more of an education. Let the engagement be postponed for a year, give Tatu a chance to calm down. Let Blaise come back to NYC with her, or even Saudi Arabia. Her fiancé Ali had four other brothers, two of which weren't total idiots. They would go gaga for Blaise's milk-and-cinnamon coloring, her delightful Kentucky drawl. Who needed Tatu's money when there was oil money?

On Agnessa's last day in Arizona, she made her proposal: "Come back to NYC with me, Vlashi."

Blaise was helping her pack. Moreover, she was watching Agnessa roll her silk panties into tight blintzes and line them up in her leopard suitcase.

"I can't do that,'" Blaise breathed theatrically. "I have a fiance who is firmly planted in Kentucky."

Agnessa raised one highly arched eyebrow. "But Tatu throw you out of the house," she reminded her baldly. "So why not come on holiday with your Auntie Nessa?"

"Tatu didn't throw me out of the house," Blaise said with dignity, though that wasn't completely true. Daddy's texts to her over the past few days were totally bipolar, ranging from a heart Emoji to a surly refrain of their fight. An hour ago, he randomly texted to say that until Pat's ring was off her finger, she shouldn't bother coming home. Blaise all but had to break her fingers to keep from replying, *Cool, call me when your sales drop!! :-D*

"Vlashi," Agnessa held her arm in a sisterly way. "Don't go to Tula with your own samovar."

"What's a samovar?"

"Don't make your beautiful life hard, love! I haff hard life before." Agnessa touched her scarred arm absent-mindedly. "Trust your Auntie Nessa when she say, good life is *better.*" She clapped her hands giddily. "*And* Ali is gonna be in Saudi Arabia for a month, so you can stay in the penthouse with me."

Blaise felt the hum of inspiration in her chest. She knew this wonderful, bougie girl had entered her life for a reason. Now, she realized that Agnessa could help link her to a buyer for her and Pat's shares. Plus, she had seen the penthouse; knew it wasn't bad at all for a temporarily residence. Agnessa gave the girls a 360-degree video-tour, pointing out on the waterfall shower and Carrara marble kitchen; the incredible views of Central Park from her floor-to-ceiling windows.

"I could say the desert sun was wreaking havoc on my skin," Blaise said quietly. "And that I wanted to stay with my new friend Nessa instead."

Agnessa clapped her hands again. "I can have Slave Boy pack your bag for you."

It was settled. When the Foleys' plane took off bearing Agnessa, (the "PJ" she kept calling it) Blaise would be onboard.

Blaise's father didn't love the idea, but Kennedy talked him into it. Blaise eavesdropped sullenly from her room, hearing her Aunt coo, *"I know,"* and *"I completely understand, Johnny."*

Kennedy was a masterful diplomat when it came to her big brothers. She got to enjoy her freedom, and the golden apples of the Foley fortune while living 1000 miles out from under their thumb, and no one ever said boo. Someday, Blaise hoped to learn her magic.

Pat openly detested the idea of Blaise going to New York.

"For how long?" he asked churlishly.

"Maybe a month," Blaise replied gently. "*Two* max." She was watching Santiago pack her suitcase while Agnessa swatted him with a frayed leather rope.

"Are you kidding me Blaise?"'

"I know, baby," she cooed, tiptoeing into the bathroom and turning on the sink. She didn't want Slave-Boy and Mistress to overhear this. "But I think it's the best move for us." Her voice lowered to a whisper, "And I think Agnessa knows people who could help us with our plan."

About a week after Blaise left for NYC, Pat was awakening to his own functioning misery.

His alarm went off at 6:01 every morning, but there wasn't that divine pile of warmth beside him, squawking about the noise. Every bar or restaurant he was in, he looked up whenever the door opened, like he used to when Seamus was in Iraq. *Idiot,* he chided himself each time. Still, his mind looked for his girl to be there, bringing the sun.

When he felt gloomy, he listened to *Everywhere* by Polaris. It was the song Kiki sang for Brendan when he was away at rehab:

I put your photograph away
I can't look at you today
I put your letters upstairs
But it's no good because you're everywhere…

When Blaise's FaceTime call came in, Pat's gloom evaporated, giving way to a relief that was almost giddy. There was not a mite of distance between them, and it was all working out for the best. *My fiancé is in New York for work,* he found himself saying to Raj at the gas station, the female admins at KPMG. They all nodded and asked how she was doing, and Pat felt like this weird limbo they found themselves in had a sort of functioning normality to it.

One night as Pat walked to his car after work, a pair of headlights flashed him. Once, then twice.

Pat squinted across the dim parking garage, momentarily blinded as the car hit its high-beams again. His confusion switch to awe as he registered that it was a jet-black Aston Martin. It looked like the Batmobile. The driver's hand reached out the window and nimbly waved Pat over. Automatically, he went.

"Come have a seat," Duffy Foley said as a greeting, bowing his silvery blond head to look Pat in the eye.

Pat did as he was told, shifting his brief bag to his feet. The car smelled of crisp leather and cigars. He wondered how Blaise's uncle found him at work.

"How are you, Mr. Foley?" Pat said, then cursed himself for sounding so earnest.

Duffy didn't answer. His eyes were on Pat's bag. "Is that J.W Hulme?" he asked admiringly, and Pat nodded. Gift from my niece?"

Pat nodded again.

"Huh," Duffy turned the radio dial off. "She got me one too, for Christmas. Even had it monogrammed. Right thoughtful of her."

"Yeah, it was," Pat felt relaxed enough to laugh. "I love mine."

Duffy didn't laugh. Actually, he looked deathly serious. "You're not surprised I wanted to speak to you, are you?"

"No," Pat said untruthfully. He ventured a joke, "Though the car garage threw me off a bit."

"Well, Kelly doesn't know I'm here," Duffy said, his grey eyes sweeping the rearview mirror as though checking for a tail. "If I invited you out to say, Doc Crows, the word could get back to her. You know how this town talks."

"Sure do," Pat agreed.

Duffy still didn't smile. "She doesn't know I'm here," he repeated slowly. "And I will be *extremely* disappointed if she somehow finds out about this meeting." His eyes rested intently on Pat behind his sterling frames. "You understand, Pat?"

He met Duffy's gaze and felt something contractual pass between them.

"Understood."

Duffy pulled a slim cigar box from his center console. He lit a cigarillo, then offered the box to Pat, who declined politely. "You millennials don't smoke," Duffy observed, "I'll bet you'd say yes to an eCigarette, though." He shook the box at Pat, "Have one."

"Alright…"

"Now you know," Duffy went on, once Pat was all lit up with his zippo, "My niece Zabana just brought those back for me from Chile. That means they're special to me. You have to stay here and savor it to the end. Even if you don't like what I have to say."

"Okay…" Pat replied warily. He inhaled through pinched lips and suppressed a cough.

"This business between you and my little niece isn't good right now," Duffy said matter-of-factly. "You know that."

Pat wished he could affect Seamus's crazy leer and say, *I don't know that, actually.* But since he was Nice Guy Pat, he took a small hit of cigar and waited.

"There are a few ways, however," Duffy continued, ashing out the window, "To make all this unpleasantness be done with."

"Like what?" Pat asked at once.

Duffy reached into his breast pocket and withdrew a little piece of paper. He handed it to Pat.

"Okay," Pat said blankly when he unfolded it. Handwritten there in ink was a seven-digit figure.

"Is this your bank statement, sir?"

Duffy finally laughed. "Yeah—maybe after the crash of '29," he said wryly. "No Patrick, it's an offer for you."

"Money?" Pat croaked. "To do what?"

"To walk," Duffy said simply, and Pat felt as though his guts were suddenly filled with a big, maggoty steak. "Break it off with her. Blame it on the family, blame it on cold feet. We'll have this money wired directly into your bank account." He waved his hand with the cigar like a music conductor. "She'll never know what *really* happened."

Pat dropped his cigar out the window.

"You didn't finish that."

"I didn't like it," Pat replied, his voice sounding like it came from inside a knotted hose. Seamus would have stubbed the cigar out in Duffy's dashboard and told the Uncle to go fuck himself. Or maybe not. His twin had never been in love, couldn't know how it made you shut up and endure gruesome things.

"Patrick," Duffy said paternally, as Pat wrenched his car door open. "Don't make any rash decisions, now. *Sleep on it."* His voice behind the gauzy blue smoke was disturbingly serene. "I'll check back with you in a few days. Don't forget this." He passed him the little piece of paper with his offer on it.

Pat blinked at him from outside the car. Duffy waved, ever the mannerly gentleman, and the black Aston Martin backed out, zigzagging neatly through the garage, and disappearing into the camouflage of night.

Every night for the next week, Pat kicked through the double-doors after work and looked for the Aston Martin, ready with the lines he spent hours rehearsing at work. After a few days of no shows, it all began to seem like a bizarre hoax. If he didn't have the paper slip with the seven digits in his wallet, Pat might have believed he took an accidental swig of moon juice and hallucinated the entire scene.

I'll give him another week, Pat decided. *Then I'm gonna tell Blaise.* She deserved to know the measures her family was willing to take to keep them apart.

Maybe it would change her mind about some things.

That Sunday night, Pat was in his room watching *American Pie 2* when a blocked number called him.

"Are you alone," came a voice tersely from the other end.

"Yes baby," Pat said lazily, thinking it was Kiki or Eems pranking him. "Want me to tell you how big my cock is?"

"That won't be necessary, Patrick."

Pat sat up. His brethren would never call him by his Christian name. "Mr. Foley, uh is that you?"

"Indeed it is."

"I'm sorry sir," he clutched his forehead, mortified. "Your number came up blocked, I thought maybe it was a prank-call— "

"So you *are* alone."

Pat's heart thumped irrationally. He got out of bed and padded over to the window, half-expecting to see the Aston Martin parked under the dimmest street-lamp.

"My twin brother's home, but he's in his room downstairs."

Duffy made an *Mmm* sound of acknowledgement. Then he asked briskly, "So have you thought about the offer?"

"I didn't need to think about it," Pat said readily. "I respectfully decline." These were the words he had scripted, but the tone was feebler than the resounding tenor in his head.

"Hmm," Duffy replied, in a thoughtful, almost pleased sort of way. "Imagine that."

"Yeah," Pat shrugged at his faint reflection in the window pane. "She's, you know, the girl I want to marry, and I—uh—love her, you know, and I think that if her father gave me a chance, I could explain that to him…"

Duffy let him bramble on for a few more breaths. When Pat was done, Duffy sat silently on the other end for so long, Pat thought they got disconnected. Then Duffy said, "If all that is true, then I'll need you to come by my place tonight."

"Uh," Pat replied, feeling surprised and a little miffed. He glanced at his warm bed with Shadow in a cuddly ball and his computer paused on Stiffler's face. *Who's this uncle to order me anywhere?*

As if reading his mind, Duffy added, "It's vitally important, or I wouldn't ask. I can help you, but we don't have a lot of time." He paused. "Do you have a pen ready? I'll give you my address..."

Duffy lived 30 minutes away, in a handsome Tudor house about 1/8 the size of Foley Bourbon. The property was fenced in, with pearly white rocks encircling the whole house, reminding Pat of a castle moat. The pine trees flanking Duffy's home shrouded it protectively with their branches.

The Uncle opened the door as soon as Pat pulled up, watching him fixedly behind sterling frames that glinted in his porch-light. He shook Pat's hand, looking him straight in the eye, and thanked him sincerely for driving out all this way.

He's got B's good manners, Pat thought, letting his irritation fizzle into curiosity.

Duffy led Pat through a house that seemed more like an immaculate museum. Classical music followed them from room to room, playing from disembodied speakers. In a proud voice that a father might use to identify his kids in pictures, Duffy named his artwork— "Here's Dr. Gauchet's portrait, of course,'" "Oh, here's my Chagall, it just came in from Oslo." In the dining room, the Uncle gestured to a bust of a woman in yellowing marble, saying, "That's Diana from around the time of Augustus's reign."

Pat didn't know the first thing about art, but he could guess that none of these fancy pieces were knock-offs.

He followed the Uncle over heated stone floors, past a bronze piano with lion's paws and a grandfather clock taller than himself.

Arriving at a set of rustic barn doors, Duffy turned halfway, saying, "Oh, there's something that I would like you to see," and slid the doors open. Into a gigantic library they walked, with sky-high bookcases lined with books. Rows of their spines were uniform in color, suggesting legal volumes or encyclopedias.

Lounging on a burgundy chaise and reading by light of candelabra was a long-haired brunette.

"Sophie, *cherie,*" Duffy said to a woman lounging on a burgundy chaise. She sat up, placing her book and wine-glass on the floor. "This is Patrick, the young man to whom our Blaise is betrothed."

"Ah!" Sophie exclaimed, sweeping forward to kiss Pat's cheeks. Pat registered that she was older but incredibly beautiful, with creamy skin and lips like ripened raspberries.

Duffy and Sophie began speaking rapid French. Pat pretended to be fascinated by the books. He had a hunch from the way Sophie glanced at him that they were speaking of him.

"*D'accord. On descend la, cherie.*" Duffy kissed her and waved Pat purposefully towards the bookshelf. He ran a hand over the many spines, murmuring, "Let's see…we're looking for *Kentucky Records, Early Wills, and Marriages*, 1929…"

Pat helped him look, wondering what the hell use such a book could have. "Uh, Mr. Foley, is this book going to help Blaise and me?" he blurted out. He imagined some crazy loophole, some record that showed Blaise's great-grandpa Ulysses had willed the family estate to the Foley heiress in the rare event that she married Black-Jack's great-grandson.

"I suspect only the Good Book could help you two now," Duffy murmured. His hand stopped at a dusty tome, which he pulled with a soft "*Ah!*" of triumph. In the next moment, the bookcase began to move like something out of *Clue*, whirling around to reveal a whole secret chamber in the walls.

"Whoa," Pat breathed, glancing back at Sophie. She winked prettily from her chaise.

"Yup," Duffy waved Pat into the secret room. "Inspired by Foley Bourbon, which has two hidden passageways—that we know of," he raised his eyebrows mysteriously, pressing some button on the wall to close them in.

Pat saw that this dimly-lit room also contained a trove of priceless paintings and sculptures. Some were hung up and illuminated under picture lights. Others rested against the wall over a blue tarp on the ground, as though awaiting their time on display.

Pat made his way over to a white guitar hanging on the wall.

"This isn't whose I think it is…?" he asked in awe, reading the autograph scrawled there in marker.

"Oh, the Stratocaster," Duffy nodded. "Yeah, he played that at Woodstock in '69. I had to have it. 'All Along the Watchtower' saved my life in 'Nam." He gestured to the opposite wall, "But *this* is what I wanted to show you." His voice gleamed with sterling pride as he led Pat to the frame on the wall. "It's the crown jewel of my collection."

Pat gasped. He was looking at a blown up, black-and-white photo of Black-Jack, outside his country house in Kilkenny. Jack appeared older and craggier than his 1929 mugshot, though his expression was keenly alive—euphoric, even—as he ran towards a dark-haired man in an army uniform with his arm outstretched. Laughing in surprise, Pat recognized the soldier as a young Grandpa Wilkie. Even from the side, Pat could tell his young grandfather was grinning, thrilled to be received by his father with such joy.

"Is this from the day my grandfather got back from war?" Pat asked, noting the duffel bag at his feet. Under Wilkie's boots, someone had written in cursive, *Who could separate us?*

"Yes," Duffy said softly. He pointed to another, light-eyed man, beaming as he watched the scene from his car. "That's my father, Sullivan." He indicated a laughing dark-haired woman in the background, who struck a fancy appearance with her swank dress and sparkling jewelry, "My grandmother, Deirdre." His finger traveled to another dark-haired woman, frozen as she ran excitedly from the house. "*Your* grandmother, Clara...and I believe that's your great Uncle Kilkenny." Duffy flicked his hand carelessly at a bespectacled man watching the scene below from a window.

"So this was after Jack and Clara moved back to Ireland," Pat murmured. "It's funny, but I've never seen it before."

"Well, no one has."

"Really?" Pat asked, "Could I take a picture for my twin brother? He's actually a veteran so he'll appreciate it —"

"No,'" Duffy said sharply.

"Oh," Pat said. "Are you worried about the flash—?"

"It came to me years ago, via my grandmother." Duffy nodded at Deirdre. "She made me swear on my sister's life that I wouldn't let it get out." He fixed Pat with his Snake-Eyed expression. "Take another *good look* at that photo, Patrick. Tell me if you notice anything special about it."

Pat studied it. The picture in itself was special—iconic, even—but there was nothing flagrantly odd about it, no bomb in the sky or gold-bar poking from Jack's pocket.

"I dunno, sir." He glanced at Duffy. The uncle was busy pulling open a trapdoor in the floor, which Pat was only mildly astonished to see led to a narrow, winding staircase.

"Never mind," Duffy said coolly; apparently Pat's time was up. "Let's not forget the reason you're here, which is Kelly."

Pat nodded, then glanced back at Black-Jack and young Wilkie. He itched to know the big mystery.

"Who *took* the picture?" Pat asked. To his surprise, Duffy paused thoughtfully at the top step.

"No idea," he mused, stroking his whiskered chin. "But whoever they are, they have a PhD in keeping their mouth shut."

Downstairs was where Duffy kept his wine. He flicked the lights on, leading Pat into an arched, cave-like structure, explaining that the subterranean coolness was good for wine storage.

"Sophie got me into it," Duffy explained pleasantly, selecting a bottle off the vast shelf. "This is from her father's winery in Saint Emillion. Do you ever drink wine, Patrick?"

"Sometimes…" Pat hedged. The only time he ever tried wine was when he brought a bottle to the lake-house where he took Blaise's virginity, thinking it might be romantic. They had not thought to bring a wine-opener, however, so Pat watched a YouTube video on how to saber the bottle open, using a butcher's knife and spraying purple all over the deck. Drinking in bed out of stained coffee mugs, he and Blaise grimaced and agreed that wine tasted like ink. He volunteered none of this information to Uncle Duffy.

"Care to join me in a glass now?" Duffy asked, inviting him to sit at a little table with oak chairs.

Pat said yes, watching the Uncle uncork his bottle. Shay had cautioned him not to drink anything Duffy gave him, saying that the Foleys had a reputation for poisoning their enemy's bourbon with thallium. *That's how they used to get rid of the Prohibition Agents,* he warned, his eyes glinting conspiratorially.

"And here I thought you might try to get me to drink your brother's bourbon," Pat chuckled in a hearty tone, as though they were good enough friends now to laugh about their differences.

"*Sláinte*," Duffy murmured, handing Pat his glass and bumping it against his own. He rubbed his stubbly grey chin and said obliquely, "My brother Johnny was never part of the plan."

"Oh..." Pat took a sportsmanlike sip of the stuff. *Still tastes like ink.*

Duffy sipped too, relaxing into his chair. "I'll admit, I'm happy to be drinking wine right now instead of writing you a check."

Pat was surprised to hear Duffy bring up his offer. He had guessed that the subject would be shelved by their mutual Irish reserve. "I couldn't do that," he said, shaking his dark head.

"Good man," Duffy said wisely. "That would have crushed Kelly."

Pat blinked, feeling a quake of indignation. "I'm sorry sir, but was meant to be a test?"

"Well if it was, then you passed."

"Did Blaise's father ask you to do it?"

"My brother was never a part of the plan," Duffy said again. In a vague, conversational tone, he added, "I actually saw my little brother today. Went over to Foley for breakfast." He reached into the breast pocket of his blazer and pulled out a small tape-recorder.

"Johnny didn't realize I was recording him," Duffy explained matter-of-factly, completely unbothered by the fact that Pat was staring at him. He pressed the red PLAY button.

Instantly, Duffy's voice came through, just as cool and stately over the recorder. "Kelly seems like she's doing well in New York," he said. There was a pause, something like a sigh, then John Foley's voice came on, unmistakable in his blistery drawl.

"Yeah, at least she's not as scorching mad at me as she was before," Johnny said. There was a pause, then he added in a moony tone, "She called last night to tell me she loved me. I know my girl. She's coming around."

Pat felt dread tiptoeing up his spine. Duffy listened intently with a hand over his mouth, his leg crossed over his knee.

"What are we doing about that, by the way?" asked Duffy on tape. "I mean, if she decides to go forward with her...plans?"

"Exactly what I told you yesterday," Johnny said, all mush zapped from his voice. "Call Tuttle and have her shares cancelled...we'll have her thrown off the trust too. Got to be cruel to be kind, Duff."

"And what's the timeline on that?" came Duffy's low voice.

"We've given her *more* than enough time to come to her senses," her father said ruthlessly. "I say, she gets one final warning, then I'm calling Tuttle myself. No daughter of mine is marrying a Walsh." Then in a fervent murmur, "I can't have it, Duff. I just *can't have it.*"

There was a pause, then Duffy changed the subject, commenting on how he wasn't sure if the new landscaper was working out because he had noticed a few patches of crabgrass growing out back.

Duffy leaned forward and pressed STOP.

Pat shoved his glass of wine away. He felt like he had been given the poison through his brain rather than his mouth.

"Mr. Foley, I don't understand." He tried to swallow to ease his clenched throat, but his mouth was too dry. "You said on the phone that you could *help* us."

Duffy drained his own wine, looking more composed than ever. "I can," he said calmly. "But like I said..." he stared Pat in the eyes, who was surprised to see a glint of daring ignited in the grey.

"My brother isn't a part of this plan."

Editor's Note: I followed my twin to Uncle Duffy's Cabin that night. I had to make sure he wasn't going to kill him

I found Pat's Jeep parked right outside the address he texted me as a precautionary measure. Carefully, I lurched several paces behind him, cutting my lights off and hunkering down behind the wheel. Duffy left the porch light on—rookie mistake—but the trees fencing his house like goddamn Trojan soldiers blocked my view. Of course, my M14 lay in the backseat with my night vision goggles, but that was a precautionary measure (so far).

I texted Pato asking his status, reminding him to not drink the bourbon. Then I sat in darkness for 20, 30 minutes, a sniper conserving his blinks and breaths. The front door to Duffy's house flung open, but it turned out to be a decoy in the form of an attractive older woman, whistling and calling in French for her cat. After a moment, Frenchie gave up on Léon and went back inside.

Pat still hadn't responded. I prodded him, Respond ASAP or silence will be read as request for support to Location. *Surely, Duffy wouldn't kill Pat with the Frenchie in the next room.*

The red minute hand twitched forward on my dashboard. 10:25…10:30. Still no word. My innards coiled tighter as I slipped into machine mode. At 10:35, I'll make my move.

At 10:33, my phone buzzed. It was Pat, turd-firing me with texts. He texted like a bad poem, but in that moment he was William fucking Wordsworth:

Jesus please don't come here.
It's fine!
He didn't even give me bourbon
he gave me wine
Poured from the same bottle
We talkin

"Wine?" I laughed out loud. Bourbon heirs don't drink wine. My brother was in the jaw of King Claudius, but he was safe tonight.

I drove away, and I didn't think about the night again for months.

"I know you have the missing shares" Duffy told Pat calmly, swirling the maroon sediment of his wine around the glass. "Kelly told me a while back," he added, addressing the look of surprise on Pat's face. "But my brother doesn't know."

"Well, I'm certainly not gonna tell him," Pat laughed in a dogged way. He waited with dread for Uncle Duffy to reveal matter-of-factly that he knew his and Blaise's plan to sell their shares and launch their own empire.

Instead, the Uncle crossed his shin over his knee, looking pensive. "Do you know about the Foley curse, Patrick?"

"I'm sorry?" Pat said blankly. "Oh, where you guys think you die at sixty-one?"

Duffy blinked, then continued patiently, "It's an Indian curse. I used to not believe in it either. Then in 1984, I saw my Aunt Lucretia die at on the morning of her sixty-first birthday. She was a nun—the kindest woman I ever knew. She donated almost every cent of her trust fund to helping the poor. She adopted a little orphan girl from Zaire." Duffy's eyes grew unfocused on a point above Pat's shoulder.

"I remember the night before her last birthday. She was very peaceful, even more so than usual. She wanted her family all around her. We assured her that she would be fine. Even if there was some curse on our heads, surely God would spare an angel like Aunt Lucy." Duffy tilted his head back, remembering. "The next morning, we were all nervous to knock on her bedroom door. My little sister Kennedy did it. Then she ran into the kitchen calling to us, 'Hey y'all—Aunt Lucy's fine! She asked us to bring her some birthday tea!' So we crowded in the doorway to her room with a tray. But," Duffy smiled ruefully, "She had passed by then. We found her with her rosary in her hands. One slipper on."

"Wow," Pat murmured in awe. "But, I mean, how did she—"

"Well, the coroner said it was natural causes," Duffy said, "But we knew better." He rotated his foot in a circle, revealing taupe socks with a red diamond pattern. "I'll be sixty-one in November," he added pointedly.

"I'm sure you'll be fine," Pat said, rather clumsily. "Maybe just, you know, stay home on your birthday."

Duffy waved a dismissive hand. "Nevertheless, I'm in the process of tying up all my loose ends right now."

"Loose ends?" Pat said blankly. "I'm sorry, sir, are you sick?"

"Not *yet* I'm not. But I won't live a day past Halloween this year." This he stated as plainly as if reading from a legal deposition.

Pat struggled to think of what to say. He didn't want to be insensitive to Duffy's plight, but he also didn't believe the healthy, upstanding esquire before him was going to be taken down in six months by an apache death curse.

Duffy went on. "You know, you earned my trust by refusing that money, Patrick. I think my instincts are correct in trusting you. I don't have a lot of time here."

"You can trust me," Pat said, leaning forward in his chair. He didn't know what he was leaning towards. Foley approval? Avuncular respect? *Old family secrets and lost treasure?*

The uncle considered him for a long moment, stroking his neat beard stubble. Then he continued steadily, "When Kelly sees what I'm leaving her...well, it's going to be a lot. But if my name ever comes up—ten years from now, twenty years from now—I'd really appreciate it if you reminded her that..." he turned his steely gaze to the ceiling. "I saw the best versions of myself in her eyes. And whatever the worst version is, I hope she can learn to forgive me."

Pat wasn't sure he believed Duffy Foley would die in the next six months, but he agreed anyway. "I will, Mr. Foley."

Then he sat back and waited to hear what Mr. Foley willed to Blaise.

Seamus: an Afterword
April 2015

There was so much that I didn't know then.

Blaise never really told me much about her time in NYC. Every time I asked, she talked about what fun she and Agnessa would have clicking around the city streets. ("I would go to her open houses and pretend to be an all cash buyer," she said dreamily, "Then we would go eat lobster risotto at the St. Regis.")

She remained tight-lipped on any information that could've explained why Pat had paused the engagement and fled Zzyzyx Road. I'll admit, I didn't press her. I was scared she might blow up and shut down and deny me the privilege of finishing her story.

I thought I knew how her story was going to end. I've never been so wrong.

As I write, it's spring of 2015. Nearly a year has passed since Pat met Duffy in his wine cave. A lot has changed on Zzyzyx Road. Not to give away spoilers, but there are two less Foleys on the trust fund.

I can tell you now that Duffy didn't leave Blaise his money. He left every cent of it to someone else. By the time my book comes out, you will probably have read the *Forbes* article on them, or even seen their Lamborghini Veneno zooming around, if you spend much time in Louisville.

To Blaise, he left something else.

Pat did not tell me about it at the time. The Will of Duffy Foley was one of two secrets my twin ever kept from me. Talk about having a PhD in keeping one's mouth shut.

I have to admit, once the smoke cleared, I was pretty impressed by Pat's vow of silence.

I think the best way of explaining this part is via a short story I wrote about my twin's experiences after he left Louisville in August. I enclose that story here.

(Editor's Note: Pat used to tell me that I was one of three people who had the number to his new track phone. I never thought to ask him who the other two were)

Pat went to Iowa for a song he heard once, years ago.

It was back when he was still dating his ex-girlfriend, Palmer Desjardin. She brought him along as a very reluctant date to a banquet dinner for her sister's softball team. Pat was visiting Mobile for a long weekend, and hadn't brought along a tie for the event. Palmer's father lent Pat one of his ties from a broad collection of silks and stripes. Pat remembered scraping a bit of crust off the bottom, guessing that Mr. Desjardin had probably let it drag in his soup.

Pat was bored sitting in his chair while Palmer worked the room, the apples of her cheeks blooming with her smile. She knew everyone, and wanted to know them better. He knew no one, and wanted to keep it that way. These people would only ask the question that he and Palmer had been fighting about for months: *so when are you two getting engaged?* He tried to enjoy the luster of her blonde hair, the red crepe dress billowing out around her ankles, but it just made him tired. He hadn't told her he loved her in weeks.

Pat asked the server what they had in the way of bourbon. The server checked, said the bar had only Foley.

"He's a Walsh," Palmer answered for him primly, "So that's a *no.*"

Pat tried to nip from his flask, but Palmer swatted his wrist with a look of warning. Now he had to suffer through this night sober. Hopefully, this bought him a good three days of not having to see her when they got back to Kentucky.

Pat was all set to tune out the student acapella group who appeared on-stage. But then, their voices came, spooling golden notes into the air and using their mouths as percussion. He remembered two girls stepping forward to do their solos:

"I have never had a way with women, the hills of Iowa make me wish that I could…I have never had a way to say I love you, but if the chance came by, oh I, I would…"

Pat suddenly wished he could live inside that song. He didn't feel like a bad actor in a shitty show after that song. He felt that it raised him and this entire room up, way up. He told Mr. Desjardins that he didn't get a program, could he have his?

"Aww," Palmer cooed, stroking Pat's arm, thinking this somehow had to do with her.

"I really like that song," Pat told her defiantly, "I want to know what it was." 'Iowa,' it was called.

"No wonder," Mr. Desjardins mused across the table. "Isn't bourbon half corn? Corn comes from Iowa."

"Bourbon's 51% corn," Pat said, to no end. Because Palmer's father was right. The song wasn't just objectively pretty. It made the DNA in his cells vibrate, the way that Irish music or the National Anthem did. He saw the corn fields when the girls sang, pictured a truck delivering burlap sacks to the distillery, saw his brother Killian's filthy hands unloading the kernels into his cookers.

Later, Pat found the song on YouTube. The original version by Dar Williams was more reflective and mournful. He liked that one too, but it was for a different mood: *You were wandering along the hills of Iowa, and you were not thinking of me...*

When Pat and Blaise put their engagement on pause, he did not immediately think to go to Iowa. He drove up through Indiana, asking every gas station he stopped at what town he was in.

"French Lick."

"Rocky Ripple."

"Falcon Landing."

"You're in Churubusco, son. Where are you trying to get to?"

Pat couldn't begin to know how to answer that. He saw a sign for in a town called Shamrock Lanes, deciding to stop for the name alone. At the run-down gas station, he noticed a display of faded Iowa atlases. He bought one, taking it as a sign that the heart of the corn belt was his final destination.

Then he thought, *I need a job.*

In the Craig's List ad, they said that drivers who lived along Interstate 80 by Cedar Rapids would be preferable. Pat wanted to be preferable, so he found a month-to-month townhouse nearby. They also said that applicants needed a clean driving record. Unlike his flawed fiancé, *"Foley, how the hell do you get 15 points on your license?" he rubbing a lock of her hair as they drove in afternoon rain,* Pat's driving record was perfect. He was hired. His job was to haul fertilizer and minerals from Cedar Rapids to Omaha, Nebraska, in a hopper with rusty hinges. Then he could drive back.

"Local work," explained the guy, Ted, on the phone. Pat pictured him in a room with drop ceilings and fluorescent lights, a cellophane-wrapped sandwich on his desk. "You get paid $90 per load. You'll be home every night. It's perfect work for a family man."

"I don't have a family," Pat said.

Iowa was flat and Iowa was corny. He had heard many people complain about driving through the Midwest, but what they called monotony, Pat called consistency. There were certain things that he considered beautiful, and the sun hoisted above quivering planes of corn was one of them. The sky changed from stark and blue to orange and mottled, but the cornstalks remained like a patient, protective army. Pat thanked them for keeping him fenced in. If Shadow licked his face while he drove and Louis C.K was funny on tape, he could even smile.

His soundtrack to the flat roads was whatever the radio gave him. He had no smart-phone anymore, so no iTunes, no Iowa song.

This is freedom, he reminded himself firmly. If he had an i-Phone, he would stare at Blaise's Instagram, plunging deeper into a lake of longing.

After his sixth or so trip into Nebraska, an old woman began to surface in Pat's mind. He didn't know her, but read an article about her months ago. Details of the article returned to him now with surprising clarity. The old woman lived in a minuscule town in Nebraska as the sole resident, acting as mayor and paying her own taxes. According to the article, she saw her town population dwindle from 150 down to 2, then her husband died, leaving her all alone.

Pat wondered how she could stand it. *Doesn't she get lonely? What if some murderer came after her?* He felt a pull towards the old woman that he saw as a responsibility to check up on her. *Someone should.* It was the nice guy thing to do, and he was a nice guy.

At a diner near Omaha, Pat asked his waitress if he could use her smart-phone. He Googled, "Town in Nebraska, Population 1," and discovered it was called Meeteetse. Meeteetse, Nebraska was reachable in 2 hours and 47 minutes by way of I-129 West. If he drove three miles further, he would hit the South Dakota border.

Pat wrote the directions down on a cocktail napkin, then, heeling to his innate practicality, looked up the number of the town's one bar (called "the Bar," according to Google). He called on his new flip-phone.

"Hello?" a woman answered plainly. It had to be her.

Pat didn't know what to say.

"Uh, hi there. Was just calling to check your hours today?"

"Oh, should be here until about nine p.m.," the woman answered comfortably.

"Great," Pat's watch said 11:19. "I'll be coming by this afternoon."

"Great," she agreed.

Pat craved more of a preview. *If I didn't stop by, would you just be sitting there alone all day?* "I guess you don't have a full bar there, huh?"

"I have a full bar," she answered, somewhat defensively. "What do you like?"

"I like bourbon," Pat told her. "But if you don't have it, it's okay."

"I don't," she replied. "I have whiskey?"

"Close enough," Pat assured her.

"Let's see what I've got here..." her voice quavered with hostess anxiety. Fleetingly, Pat thought of his mother, felt a pang. "What kind of whisky do you like?"

"Uh" Pat didn't want to name one she didn't have. "I, anything really, Jameson, Tullamore Dew..."

"I've got a half-bottle of Old Osterhaut."

"Sounds like a party" Pat smiled.

A Town Where No Letters Are Delivered

Patrick began his descent off the highway, onto a series of spindly back-roads with grass bursting through their cracks. He felt a dawning sense of familiarity that was neither friend nor foe to him.

He and Seamus drove through a series of Midwestern ghost-towns like Meeteestee in the summer of 2005, weeks before Shay left for Iraq. They were en route to visit their cousins Brendan ("Longbow") and Paytah ("Hawkeye") in Montana, but took so many detours along the way, Longbow called and threatened to disinvite them.

Seamus loved cruising through decaying hamlets of middle America. When it was his turn to drive, he got off the highway to take the back-roads, ignoring Pat's clucks about wasting time. "Let's look at the towns where no letters can be delivered," he would say. "I think it's romantic." Shay found the acreage of blight invigorating. There was no one around in to snap pictures of them underneath water-towers with squat rusty legs, or the churches that slanted like piles of wet cardboard.

Pat recalled one shady night when he and Shay stopped in a tavern with an elk's head mounted on the wall (was it in South Dakota?). They played Billy Idol songs on the jukebox and harassed the poor bartender about not having Walsh to drink.

An older woman in a strappy red dress giggled at their shenanigans until Seamus slunk over to announce that he was an undercover cop here to bust underage drinkers, and could he see her ID, please?

"But I'm 42!" she simpered.

"*What!*" Seamus mouth fell open in cartoonish shock. For hours, the twins flirted with her and   bought her a pile of white zin spritzers. While Seamus did a body shot of Jameson off her neck, she grinned and stroked Pat's wrist, as though to include him.

At one point, Shay leaned in and muttered in his ear, "She *wants* us. We should go for it."

"You're sick, bro!" Pat exclaimed, but he only drew in closer.

"I know what you're thinking," Shay murmured in the woman's ear, adopting his idea of a sultry gaze. "Have we ever made love to the same woman at once?" he tossed out "make love" because he guessed it was what older people said. "We always said we would, but only if we found the right one…"

She invited them to her apartment upstairs, where another elk's head sat on the kitchen wall. Pat remembered that she made a "cootchy-coo" gesture under both their chins, shimmying out of her heels, swearing, "You boys are only staying for a night-cap…"

The next morning, the twins woke up in their car outside the tavern with throbbing heads. As they drove onwards, Pat had a searing flashback of him on his knees, sucking the woman's toes while Seamus ravaged her boobs, which looked like globs of melting ice cream.

"Let's never speak of last night again," Pat grunted, and Seamus bobbed his head mechanically.

But their vow of omertà was weak. Within two months, Pat's lacrosse team, Seamus's army unit, and of course, the High Fraternal Order of Black-Jack, all knew about the menage-à-trois.

Pat saw the exit sign for Meeteestee, 1. (*Is that 1 for miles or population?* he thought) He veered left down a narrow, cracked road until a sign said, '***Welcome to Meeteestee!***' in sun-bleached, 70s-style cursive.

His first impression was that Meeteestee would make a great set for a zombie apocalypse movie. A line of white houses, each rotting through their roof, sat along the main drag. Beyond them sat silos, reddened with rust and tilted at funny angles. The sky was grey, but made steelier somehow by the all-enveloping stillness. Somewhere beyond the brown pastures, Pat heard the forlorn wail of a train.

In spite of his bleak surroundings, Pat felt a thrill knowing that his being here doubled the town's population.

He spotted the bar right away, a white box with light glowing in the block windows. It had to be the bar; it was the only sign of life around. He locked his Jeep, leaving Shadow asleep in the backseat.

Inside, the bar had a dingy, cozy feel. It was decorated for Halloween, with various gourds and tiny pumpkins scattered across the bar and patio tables. The entire back wall was plastered with pictures of smiling people and colorful postcards. And there, behind the bar, stood the old woman in a red flannel shirt, watching a small television. She looked exactly like her picture, with curly, snow-white hair and a face like a happy otter.

"Oh hello," she looked over and smiled faintly.

"Hello," Pat said back, wiping muck off his boots onto a bristly welcome mat.

She returned her shy smile to her program, *Gunsmoke,* that 1960s Western show that Grandpa Wilkie often had droning on at home. Feeling clumsier than he ever could around a girl his age, Pat chose a bar-stool.

"I would take some of the Old Osterhaut," he said. "Please and thank you."

"You're the bourbon drinker" the old woman replied warmly. For a second, he thought she had witchy powers, but then she prompted him, "Well, it *was* you called earlier to check our hours, right?"

"Oh! Yes." Pat laughed, finding her *our* funny. He saw the rotary phone tacked to the wall above an old cash-register. A Pepsi logo clock with no numbers and dull wattage told him the time—4:15. There was nothing to suggest that he hadn't traveled in time back to 1987. Kelly Foley might not even be born yet. He felt something briny drip-drop into his stomach.

"*Sláinte,*" he said, raising his spotty glass to her and gulping Foley away. "Thank you."

"It's my pleasure," said she.

Pat noticed that he was hungry. He glanced at the menu propped up behind the bar, which headlined fried chicken gizzards for $3.25. He asked her for two cheeseburgers, one for him, one for his dog. The old woman said she didn't mind having a dog in here, so he brought Shadow in.

"As long as it's okay with the mayor," he winked from the doorway. She laughed as though admitting something, slapping two frozen patties on the grill.

"So...you're the only person in this town?" Pat asked, as Shadow licked his plastic plate clean.

The old woman returned Pat's wink. "Not right now, I'm not."

He grinned. "'Do you pay municipal taxes to yourself?"

"Oh yes, something to the tune of $500 a year," she replied mildly. "That's enough to power my three streetlights, and keep my water running." She poured him a water without being asked. "I also write my own liquor license as the village secretary, and sign it as the village clerk. I vote myself in for all these positions each year."

There was pride in her voice as she told him all this. Pat guessed that she was used to fielding people's curiosity. Maybe people drove from all over to see her, as he had. *Maybe she's a Mecca for lost souls of the Midwest.*

"You're doing a good job," Pat gave her a thumbs up. "I'm thinking I should just buy one of the houses here, fix it on up."

"You certainly can," she said readily, surprising him. "I keep a record of all the available lots, in case anyone wants to join me."

"Would you need any help running the bar?"

He was basically kidding, but she surveyed him solemnly behind her glasses.

"I would be happy to have you, but Meeteestee isn't a good place for a young man to start his life." She gestured to his bare wedding finger. "I'm afraid there aren't any nice girls around here for you."

"I'm engaged," belched from Pat's mouth. It was his first time telling someone since he left Kentucky.

"Oh, that's wonderful!"

"Thanks. It's supposed to be a Christmas wedding," Pat said, in a tone that was more funerary. "December 22nd." He sipped and added in an undertone, "We haven't seen each other in a while, though."

"Well, Christmas comes before you know it." She folded a dish-towel into neat quarters, smiling serenely. "I always say it comes quicker each year."

Pat was suddenly annoyed with her Midwestern simplicity, her inability to hear what he was telling her.

"Her dad doesn't like me," he said roughly. "I don't really know how any of it is going to pan out."

The old woman's mouth thinned. He saw there a resolve to not meddle, to deal only in the currency of happy babies and confirmed weddings. The Iowa song came to him, in the key of melancholy:

Way back where I come from, we never mean to bother, we don't like to make our passions other people's concerns…

"Our families are old rivals," Pat plowed on. "Back home in Kentucky."

The old woman chuckled. "Kentucky rivals. So you two are kind of like Foley and that old bootlegger Black-Jack?"

"Kind of," Pat smiled to himself. "But Black-Jack and Ulysses weren't rivals. It was Jack's son, Wilkie, and Sullivan Foley who had the dispute over shares…"

Instead of numbing him, the Old Osterhaut awakened all of the feelings from which he drove. He allowed Blaise to surface inside him, felt her oblong feet rubbing against his turgid crotch. *How does that feel, Walshie?* Her eyes and her smile were delicious devastation. Gently, the whisky led him back to the lake-house, where he took her virginity almost two years ago. *When you whispered in my ear that you wanted me inside you, Foley, my desire was no less primal than the wolves' in the forest. I'll bet when I'm an old man, that feeling will come back to me like it does now, strong enough to beat back death…*

"I like your pin," Pat groaned, suddenly noticing the jack-o-lantern on the old woman's collar.

"Thank you," she smiled. "I'm getting into the Halloween spirit."

"That's my fiancé's birthday," he told her. "Halloween. She'll be 26."

"26!" the old woman laughed in wonder. "My, you two have your whole lives ahead of you!"

"We do, huh?" Pat sat up, rising to the warmth spreading through his chest.

"Maybe you should go and see her for her birthday," the old woman suggested, in a voice as delicate as eggs. "Just my two cents."

Pat drained his whiskey. "Are you my guardian angel?" he asked, drunk and sincere.

"Who knows?" she laughed, and she turned to make a burger for herself. "Could be."

Crazy

Walsh Bourbon hadn't made its way out to Iowa yet, so Pat was careful to ration his and Shay's private collection. The next Saturday, however, he was dismayed to realize he was running out. The only bourbon left was a jug with brown floaters that tasted seriously funky. He wanted to text a picture to Killian and say, *did Slaw make during his internship?* But of course, he wasn't in contact with his big brother.

Nevertheless, Pat took a few shots from the questionable jug. "It's my day off," he told Shadow, as the dog peeped him in disapproval.

His flip-phone informed him that he had no missed calls or texts (not surprising, as only Seamus, the trucking company, and one other person had his number—but not uplifting either). The date on his phone said **10/21** in blockish, pixely letters.

Ten days until Foley's birthday.

Peter Pan Diner, 12:30 p.m.

Pat ate his usual garbage omelet in his usual booth. His mood was the color of mop water, and he didn't know why. He drank bourbon to immunize himself against the blueness, but it only grew inside him like an expandable water toy. If there were a cemetery outside the diner instead of a highway, he would go for a walk in it.

"Excuse me?"

Pat jolted to attention. At his side was a youngish girl with a pile of mussy black hair. She had mascara smudged underneath her spearing eyes, but her white sneakers were sparkling clean. Pat noticed her bare midriff, pale as milk, with hip-bones jutting out of her skirt. He felt a deep zing in his crotch.

"Do you have a phone?" the girl asked him. Her eyes fixed on his, the color of a licked chocolate Tootsie pop. "Mine's dead."

Pat glanced around to see where she came from. He sure as hell hadn't noticed a dark, scantily-clad girl when he came in.

"I left my charger on the bus," the girl laughed, clutching her somewhat bulbous forehead. "Silly me. And I'm traveling, I don't live here." She kicked the flight-attendant sized suitcase at her feet, a little too roughly. "So I'm fucked. And I need you to *un*-fuck me." She made a pleading, puppy-eyed face. "Can I *please* use your phone?"

"Sure," Pat offered his flip-phone. *I need you to un-fuck me* reverberated in his head.

The girl looked down in disgust.

"You don't have a smart-phone? I need to look up my bus schedule."

"I don't, I'm sorry."

"How do you *not* have an *iPhone*? It's 2014."

"I don't know," Pat said, nettling somewhat. "Maybe I'm going as Fred Flintstone for Halloween and getting into character."

The girl gave a screechy laugh, her nostrils flaring open like gun barrels. Two older men at the counter looked over from the football game on TV.

"You're funny," she chirped decidedly, plunking down across from him. "What's your name?"

"Pat," he answered, then instantly regretting it. He should have said Matt Crummy. "What's yours?"

"Oh my *God,* let's play the Rumpelstilkin game!" she shrieked, "Try and guess my name."

Pat guessed the second girl's name that came to his mind. "Rhiannon?"

The girl slammed her palms on the table, causing the Heinz bottle to go timber.

"YOU GUESSED IT!" she hollered. "*On your first try, too!* Hi, I'm Rhiannon," her voice dropped to a professional purr as she thrust a cool, dry hand into Pat's. Her fingernails were five shields of perfect black.

"Nice to meet you, Pat. Is that short for Patrick?"

"No, it's short for Patches O'Houlian." Pat grinned. He couldn't help but feel like the sun was coming out. "Rhiannon, huh? So, are you a Welsh witch like in the song?"

The girl blinked. *"Exactly"* she gushed, although Pat could tell she didn't catch the Fleetwood Mac reference. "See, it's like you know me already!"

"I don't know if I believe you're *really* Rhiannon" Pat said with mock skepticism. "Maybe you should show me some ID to prove it."

"I can't!" Rhiannon wailed, "My wallet got stolen earlier today, when my bus stopped at the gas station!" She unceremoniously dumped the contents of her small purse all the table. A penny and stick of Trident gum flew into Pat's uneaten home-fries. He averted his eyes from the condom that skidded near his elbow.

"So now," Rhiannon plowed on, "I have no phone and *no wallet.* I have a bus ticket, but it's for tomorrow."

"Whoa, I'm so sorry," Pat said, and he meant it. He recalled the time his lax buddy Jimmy Bones lost his wallet and passport on the last day of Spring Break in Cabo. Pat stayed behind with Bonesy to go to the U.S Embassy and vouch for his identity so he could have a temporary passport issued. "I wish I could do something to help."

"I have just enough for some Apple Jacks," Rhiannon mewed pitifully. She smoothed out a wrinkled bill, rubbing it sensually with her fingertips. Pat felt another shameful stir. "I was going to sleep at the bus station tonight."

"Hmm." Pat frowned as he always did when faced with nonsense. Misfortunes didn't just stack up to the ceiling like this. "You don't know anyone in this area that you could stay with?"

"Here?" Rhiannon squawked, glancing out the window at the bisque planes with supreme disgust, "No, I'm like you. I'm not from around here."

"How do you know *I'm* not from here?" Pat said challengingly.

"You," Rhiannon began chewing an imaginary cud, imitating his accent, "Are from one of the Confederate States of America. Arkan*saw* or Ala-*bama* or TeneSSAY. Ain't ya?"

"D, none of the above" Pat said with slight triumph. If she had guessed Kentucky, he might start to get weirded out.

The waitress came and ripped Pat's check off her notepad, flashing her jaundiced smile. "All set over here?"

"Not yet, dear," Rhiannon adopted an angelic face. "Pat, can I get two mini boxes of Apple Jacks with 2% milk?"

"Uh," Pat shrugged helplessly at the waitress, who nodded and bustled off.

Rhiannon flashed her pink gums, looking pleased. "She probably thinks we're boyfriend-girlfriend."

"I have a girlfriend.'"

"No, you don't."

"Actually, you're right. I have a fiancé."

"Who?" Rhiannon demanded, her gummy smile dissolving into a snarl.

Pat nearly groused that Rhiannon wouldn't know her, but his indignant pride took over.

"Well…" And he pointed out the window, to the reason he chose this particular booth each time.

Sharply, Rhiannon followed Pat's finger, glowering at the bluish billboard for FOLEY arched above the highway. Blaise Foley posed like a water nymph with a bottle of bourbon between her pearly shins. Her sapphire eyes looked so forlorn, Pat wanted to grab her shoulders and say, *Yes, I'm here!*

"She's your fiancé?" Rhiannon said, flicking her angry eyes between the billboard and Pat with a snort. "Well, I guess that makes sense…"

"What does?"

Rhiannon leaned in so closely he could smell her tangy breath. "I can tell you haven't been laid in a while."

Pat's cheeks burned.

The waitress glided over to drop off Rhiannon's Apple Jacks and hand Pat his revised check.

"A few months, at least," Rhiannon said, ignoring the waitress and nodding seriously.

3 months and 10 days since I last peeled Foley's panties off, but who's counting? "Well, nice to meet you, Ree," Pat said, making his voice as flat as the Iowa interstate. "And good luck getting on your bus tomorrow."

"Wait!" Rhiannon yelped, tucking her poodle hair behind her ears. "I'm sorry, that was rude. *I'm* rude. It's been a day from hell for me." She smiled at him as though posing for a picture. "Do you think you could give me a ride somewhere? It could possibly save my life, and wind up winning you a medal-of-honor."

Pat stared past her, still blistering with embarrassment. "I already have my bobcat badge from Cub Scouts…I'm not looking for any further glory."

He stood up to pay their check. But when Rhiannon ran after him in the parking lot, yelping at him to please not abandon her, Pat grudgingly let her into the Jeep.

She made him stop at the Kum & Go station to purchase a new phone-charger, begging him to pay for it, swearing she'd pay him back. After all, she informed him, she was going to be famous someday. "Even more famous than your billboard model, I'm sorry to say."

"Alright. Then I'm dropping you off at the bus station."

But at the Greyhound station, all the outlets were burnt out. From his Jeep, Pat watched her sprint from wall to wall, holding one finger up in the window to signal that he should wait. Finally, she trotted out to the parking lot with the charger dangling umbilically from her phone.

"Can I just charge up at your house, Pat?" Rhiannon simpered, hopping in the Jeep and buckling up. "I promise, you'll still be a virgin by the time I'm through."

"Alright," Pat said, sighing with far more reluctance than he felt. "But no funny business."

She made a string of kissy noises about two centimeters from his ear. Her hot breath on his neck made something jerk forward within him, something he was strangling to shut-up.

"You wish."

Pat had never cheated on Blaise, not in the three months and 10 days since he last saw her, not ever. He had a very stalwart definition of cheating that derived from the code of Black-Jack, which every Walsh man tried to hold himself to. *The cardinal sin to me is infidelity to one's wife.* He liked the moral absolutism of it, placing cheating into a category of things he simply would never do.

His father wouldn't cheat on his mother, would simply not put himself in a situation where it could happen.

He pictured his father shaking his head if he could see Pat driving alone with a girl who wasn't Blaise.

Sean wouldn't approve, even if the engagement was on pause.

Despite crunching on Apple Jacks the entire way home, Rhiannon announced that she was hungry as soon as she got to Pat's house. She was also thirsty, had to pee, needed to know the WiFi, and found his house to be freezing.

"Maybe you should have more clothes on," Pat said pointedly, cranking up the thermostat.

"You love it," she yawned, absorbed in her phone.

He took a few more shots of bourbon to emolliate his shot nerves, and boiled enough rigatoni for two. His plan was to give her dinner and drive her back to the bus station, possibly leaving her with a few bills.

But then Rhiannon violated the House Rule without realizing it. Or maybe she *did* know—she seemed to be the type of *diabla* born with a sensor for dirty secrets.

When he brought her bowl of pasta into the den, she was barefoot. He froze; she may as well have been naked. Blaise knew not to go barefoot in the house, only their bedroom. If she walked around shoeless, Pat wouldn't be able to focus on anything else. With the open lust of abstinence, he stared at Rhiannon's dainty feet.

"So Rhiannon," he handed her the pasta. "Why don't you tell me what you're going to be famous for?"

"Hmm," she was sprawled out on his couch in a possessive sort of way, her bare feet sliding up and down the arm. *God I want them sliding up and down my cock,* Pat thought, and he sank deeply into his chaise, imagining himself sinking into her.

"Are you sure you don't want some bourbon?"

"Do I look like Clint Eastwood to you? No thanks." She shook her can of Coke Zero in the air, "But you can add some Malibu or vodka to this, if you have it."

"I don't. Bourbon heirs don't drink that shit." Pat was half-quoting Shay or Blaise, and it made him smile.

Rhiannon smiled back wider. Pat noticed that she didn't ask for clarity on things that she didn't understand, just steered him right back into her dangerous little world.

"Why don't you *guess* what I'm going to be famous for, Pat."

"Hmm," Pat pretended to ponder it, "You're going to be an actress?"

Rhiannon didn't say yes or no. She pressed the heavenly pads of her toes into the couch, moving them in sexual strokes. He felt the invisible pulley tugging at his shillelagh. Sometimes if he and Blaise were at a party, she liked to torment Pat by stacking her naked feet on top of one another, rubbing her pedicured toes over her ornate shin.

It was too much to bear. His mouth was a hot deluge of saliva.

"Rhiannon?" Pat's voice was a mask of fatherly reproach, "You really should stop doing that with your feet."

She lifted her soles off the couch, a look of defiance in her eyes. "They're not *dirty*. Are you weird about feet or something?"

"I'm not weird about feet" Pat said quickly. "I mean, there's *nothing* weird about feet, right?" He stood up, crossing the invisible partition that he had set between them. "In fact, a lot of women enjoy getting foot massages. My fiancé loves them."

"Really?" Rhiannon murmured. From her eyes, you would think she was seeing a display of designer bags that she wanted but couldn't afford. Slowly, she folded her waifish legs so that Pat could sit there and massage her, out of—he knew—some deranged jealousy for Blaise.

"You have nice feet," Pat murmured, hooking his thumbs under her toes.

"Really?" she giggled shyly. Girls were so cute.

"*Beautiful.*" Pat could tell she hadn't had a pedicure in a while by her eroded pink polish and the calcification ringing her heels. Pat did not mind. He could worship the hooves of this dark fawn, relish the clamminess they left on his hands. *Hands only,* commanded a voice from the outrances of his brain, *keep it in your pants.* But this old voice, dispatched from his core of steely goodness, was becoming garbled by an incoming static...

Oh—Pat gently flexed her feet, his nauseous lust quelling somewhat when he saw how dull Rhiannon's arches were. She would not give nearly as good of a foot job as Blaise. Blaise's long feet were so curvy, she could not flex them *en pointe* without howling about a Charlie horse. His fiancé's feet were idyllic, the silhouette of a cello, hand-carved by God for Patrick with love. When he kneaded Blaise's soles and she exhaled in pleasure, Pat felt as though they were feeding each other a meal of great nourishment. *"How is it that the girl of my dreams has the feet of my dreams?"* he would always say.

Rhiannon made a lascivious *"mmm"* sound. "Wow, you're really good at that."

"I've had some practice" Pat murmured. In his mind, he was on his couch at home, tasting Blaise's feet for only the second time and praying Seamus didn't walk in. As he touched her, he watched the last ounce of reserve vanquish from her eyes, replaced by a deepening reservoir of love and trust.

Shit.

Roughly, Pat pushed her feet from his lap.

"Pat? What's wrong?" Rhiannon asked, staring at him as he jumped up.

"I have to let my dog out" he answered mechanically, whistling at the snoozing ball on the floor that was Shadow. When he returned, Rhiannon lay in full recumberence, her feet propped up on the couch as though the royal cobbler was coming in to size her. Pat looked away.

"Can I just spend the night here, Pat?" Rhiannon simpered. "I don't want to go back to that nasty-ass bus station," she pouted, "What if someone tries to rape me?"

Pat unlatched the back door and whistled for Shadow, but his dog was still scampering through the patchy yard. "How do you know that *I'm* not a rapist?" he asked reasonably, "You only met me like, five hours ago."

She cackled loudly, "*You?* You're a Mr. Nice Guy. Trust me, I know people."

Pat stared at the library of Jazzercise DVDs, determined to avoid her feet. He wondered again how old Rhiannon was; where she was from. He did not however, want to learn her real name.

"Okay, I'll make up the couch for you." Pat decided finally.

Rhiannon flashed her pink gums. "Too bad. I thought your fiancé left a vacancy in your bed."

Pat blushed, but rebounded more easily this time. "I sleep with her portrait every night I'm on the road, though."

"Hmm. Don't crush her in your sleep. Those shards of glass could be deadly."

"Thanks for the sound advice," Pat replied, trusting himself to glance over. A shadow had fallen over her dusky eyes.

He went upstairs to get a sheet and pillow to make up the bed on the couch for her, paused with his fingertips on the raggedy linens.

Rhiannon, you are very sexy. You may be the first runner-up to the original Mata Hari of my life.

The digital clock on Pat's nightstand said 3:09 a.m.

Rhiannon stood in the doorway to Pat's room, watching the periwinkle moonlight drape his face. He was sleeping alright, with the fitfulness of an inviolate heart. She guessed that touching her tonight was the first pock upon his clean, Catholic soul.

Rhiannon sat on the edge of Pat's bed and ran her palm down his chest.

He made an *Mmm* sound. She smiled and rubbed his firm pecs, his sunken six pack.

He put his hand on hers, clumsily, like an injured soldier to a nurse. "*Blaise*"

"There is no Blaise" Rhiannon whispered soothingly. "You made her up."

"*Blaise,*" Pat insisted, his eyes shut tight.

Rhiannon picked up the bulging leather wallet on his nightstand. One of the folds contained a fan of crisp twenties. The slits held credit-cards stamped with his name, *Patrick A. Walsh*. He was who he said he was, and exactly who he appeared to be. She opened his nightstand drawer. There was a curiously thick 8X10 envelope with some kind of stock certificate inside. Under the header were a few lines certifying that Patrick Alan Walsh was the recipient of 100,000 shares of Foley Bourbon, from Wilkie Walsh, signed this day, May 30, 1994.

Behind *that* was another certificate, this one with an elegant border and regal header—FOLEY BOURBON—beside a shamrock set in a horse-shoe. This one was older—it decreed that on this, the 17h day of August, in the year of our Lord 1968, Sullivan Ulysses Foley hereby granted 100,000 shares of Foley Bourbon to Wilkie Daedalus Walsh.

Rhiannon read aloud the note, written in tight cursive. "*Walshie— you said at the start that you wouldn't pay for the shares. Well, you have—it cost you 48 years of friendship. Hope it was worth it. — Foley.*"

"Put it down" Pat whispered, suddenly wide awake.

"Oooh, look who's up, Mr. Sleepyhead—"

"Put it down," Pat got out of bed. Challengingly, Rhiannon held the shares above her head.

Pat overpowered her like he never had a girl before. Their bodies fused together, Rhiannon sending vibrations of fury through his skin. He wrenched the papers away from her and shoved her into the door, which she clung to like a raft on a stormy sea.

"You were gonna steal from me," Pat seethed, "*Get out.*"

Rhiannon's dark eyes were now black holes behind which a succubus popped. "I feel bad for you, Pat" she screeched in his face, "You're in love with a girl who isn't even *real.*"

"Of course she's *real,*" Pat thundered. "You're *crazy,* I should never have—"

"You can't prove it though, can you?" Rhiannon cocked her head curiously. Not caring that he was indulging a madwoman, Pat opened his nightstand to reach for the sexy pictures Blaise gave him before she left for NYC.

They were gone.

"You took her pictures," his face was contorted with blame and hatred.

Rhiannon held up her empty hands, looking amused. "I didn't take anything, Pat. You invented Blaise, and now you're waking up from your lie."

He threw her out of his bedroom and locked the door. She kicked it and slammed her palms against it for a good ten minutes, until Pat shouted that he would call the police if she didn't go away.

"Of course she's *real*," Pat muttered, reaching for his phone and dialing Seamus. His twin would laugh at his stupidity, letting a sexy psychopath spend the night. *Did you fuck her? I wouldn't tell Foles.* And Pat would laugh in exasperated *No,* as if the thought hadn't even occurred to him.

The phone rang and rang, never breaking to his voicemail.

Pat hesitated, then with his heart socking the back of his throat, he dialed Blaise's number: 502-483-1333. He would open with, *hi baby…I'm sorry I've been so stupid…*But he only got a bizarre stock voicemail in a clipped British accent, *"this uh-sah does not subscribe to voicemail…this uh-sah does not subscribe to voicemail…"*

Pat awoke to the droning sound his neighbor's leaf-blower, white sun filtering through his blinds. Downstairs, Shadow was barking furiously for his breakfast. Pat looked at his track phone. 10:17 a.m.

Would it have killed Rhiannon to feed my dog? he thought irritably, slogging downstairs. His head felt woozy, which was weird because he only had a two-bourbon night. Maybe it was a hangover from the three-a.m. drama.

"Rhiannon," Pat called sharply, rubbing Shadow's nuzzle as the dog joyfully greeted him on his hind legs. The house was still and the couch empty and neat.

She left? Pat fixed Shadow half a bowl of Alpo and dry kibble. He wondered how she left, if she allegedly only had $5 yesterday for Apple Jacks. Pat made himself coffee and eggs. The more awake he became, the more uneasy he felt.

"Rhiannon?" he called again, looking in the TV room. None of the raggedy bedding he put out for her was there. *Did she steal that too?* But something close to fear was setting in on him.

In the sink, there was only *his* bowl from last night. Pat tore the garbage apart, looking for Rhiannon's empty Diet Coke can, but it wasn't there. He tried calling up Seamus, but his twin texted back to say that he had been dragged to church, lured by the promise of brunch afterwards and, *No, you didn't call me last nite at 3 am! Da fuq*

Now Pat sat at the kitchen table, grasping it like it was only thing anchoring him to the earth. When he thought about last night, the contours of the scenes were weirdly blurred, like a drunken memory from college.

He was spooked. Rhiannon was creepy to begin with, and now she had vanished without a trace. It occurred to him that he had no other witnesses to her. *What if she was never here, and I'm going schizo?*

His eyes clicked on the jug of bourbon on the counter. This time, suspicion jolted him, directing his attention to the weird sediment clods at the bottom. Pat flipped it upside-down and noticed the tape label, Killian's writing, a warning in smudged ink with a little skull-and-crossbones, *MOON JUICE! DO NOT DRINK ALONE!*

"I drank fucking *moon juice*?" Pat yelped. Moon juice was supposedly what Grampy Wilkie drank the night he burned down the Foleys' big rickhouse years ago. It caused hallucinations, or in Grampy's case, an apparition of his dead brother telling him that the Foleys had him whacked.

Does this mean I hallucinated Rhiannon?

Now Pat was obsessed. He needed one person to tell him if they had seen him with Rhiannon or not. He got in his Jeep and drove to the Peter Pan diner without even brushing his teeth. His yellow-toothed waitress from yesterday wasn't working, but said Jeanette would be happy to take care of him.

Pat sat in the parking lot for ten minutes, paralyzed. Then he frisked his pockets for yesterday's check. He found it in the center console and smoothed it over his thigh. Written there in loopy cursive was the tab for "1 Garbage omelet with no sausage and a cup of coffee with cream for $8.95."

No Apple Jacks.

Rhiannon was a head trip.

Pat drove away, feeling rather sheepish as the entire drama of yesterday fizzled into farce.

Wait until he told Seamus—his twin would never let him live it down.

And Blaise. He imagined them naked and lazy in bed, with Blaise rubbing her heavenly toes against his cheek. He would purr into her rosy skin, *you know I was almost unfaithful to you, Rhiannon.* She would pretend to be scandalized in her adorable way. A blush of warmth and comfort surged over him.

Even if he hadn't seen her in months, Blaise Foley was still real.

But a little later, Pat was feeling lonely and horny, and he so often was here in Iowa. He realized he wanted Rhiannon to come back. After berating himself for being so pathetic, thinking, *a blow-up doll would be less sad,* Pat willfully took a few more shots of moon juice. *It's not cheating, it's a head trip,* he reasoned.

He allowed the bourbon buzz to enfold him. Then he turned on the TV, eagerly awaiting the return of his dark mistress.

After a few minutes, the lacrosse game he was watching on ESPN cut off, and the words "SPECIAL BROADCAST," flashed across the screen in big yellow letters.

Then Mr. Foley came on screen.

Pat yelped. The set of a home shopping show formed around John-boy, complete with a cheery countdown timer in the corner. Mr. Foley was explaining to a perky blonde hostess in a gingham apron that he was here today to sell his mint julep cups, for the low, low price of $39.95.

"These can be used all year round, not just on Derby Day," he trumpeted in his bourbon-tour voice. "As long as you're drinkin' my ambrosia from 'em, that is!" The hostess laughed gayly, holding a cup up to the light.

Pat groaned and changed the channel, but Blaise's father was everywhere. On MTV, he winked cornily at the screen. On MSNBC, he was giving out his recipe for the world's meanest mint julep.

He heard someone banging around the kitchen and jumped up to investigate, thinking giddily of Rhiannon and a symphony of toe taps.

Instead, he found Duffy Foley standing there in his three-piece suit, looking dapper as ever and very much undead.

He faced Pat, surveying him with familiar insouciance. "No luck getting my little brother to shut up, huh?"

"Not this time," Pat replied, chuckling in welcome surprise. He didn't mind that the Uncle was here, nor did he wonder how he got in, nor bother with the fact that he was dead. Duffy was a man of unfathomable mystery.

"Care to join me in a glass of wine?" Duffy asked amicably. Pat watched in awe as the Uncle turned on the sink and red wine came gushing out.

"That's a pretty nice trick, Mr. Foley," Pat said, whistling. "Are you actually Jesus in disguise?"

"No," Duffy shook his silvery blond head. "I died for no one's sins but my own,"

They plunked down at the kitchen table and knocked their wine-glasses together in cheers. Pat took a pinched sip, then gulped happily. It tasted like delicious grape juice! *Why don't I drink wine all the time*, he wondered. *Maybe now that I have a wine sink, I'll start.*

"One thing I was always curious about," Duffy said after a sip. "How did you, at the age of 7, know that you should take my father's shares?"

Pat sipped and shrugged. "Honestly, I feel like I get too much credit for that. I don't know, maybe I just wanted something of my own." He shrugged again. "But when I saw how my older cousins were reacting—calling me an idiot, telling me I'd been cheated out of 250 bucks—then I *knew* I had done something smart."

Duffy nodded wisely. "The more afraid someone is, the louder they get."

John-Boy's voice wafted in from the den, dripping with infomercial cheese— *"And I'll tell ya, these cups ain't gonna develop a patina, no matter how many times you wash 'em. Unless you put vodka in 'em, then they'll go straight to black!"*

"Now can I ask *you* something?" Pat ventured. The question was right in front of his brain, as usual. "What was so mysterious about that picture of Black-Jack and Wilkie you showed me?"

"Is it driving you crazy?" Duffy asked, in dry pity. When Pat nodded, the Uncle said pleasantly,

"Good. Now I have some company for madness."

"Does that mean you don't know either?" Pat asked, feeling a little desperate.

"Well, just because I'm *dead* doesn't mean I know *everything*," Duffy said, swirling his wine pedantically. "You'll have to figure some things out for yourself."

"Are you really dead," Pat asked abruptly. "Why do I feel like you're just a dream?"

"I'm not really dead," the Uncle reassured him calmly. "Death is a construct of the mind, Patrick." He glanced out the window above Pat's sink, where the setting sun was mottled with pink and purple. "We Foleys understand this better than most. We see where we have been, and understand where we're going. We have all signed this sacred contract together." He focused his gaze on Pat, his tone sharpening.

"You need to go back to Kentucky."

Pat bowed his head and nodded. "I know."

"I fear that—"

"You don't have to worry," Pat cut through him firmly. "I haven't forgotten."

"Good," Duffy muttered. "Because the hard part's about to come."

"This isn't the hard part?" Pat laughed humorlessly.

"For her," Duffy added sternly. "Remember, I'm leaving her a lot."

Pat nodded like one does when agreeing to a stranger's small talk, letting the bird seed scatter at his feet.

Duffy refilled their wine glasses. Pat noticed that he no longer heard John-boy's voice in the background, but the mellifluous flow of classical music.

"Vivaldi," Duffy said, closing his eyes.

Pat closed his eyes too, letting the red warmth consume him, letting himself be carried away by its gripping tide…

He woke up at the kitchen table in a puddle of his own drool, his scar throbbing against the imitation oak. The overhead light spiked his temples, a cruel and counterfeit sun. Duffy was gone. His track phone told him it was nearly midnight. He had one missed call.

Patrick groaned, turning on both the sink and the TV to test his woozy brain for psychedelic effects. ESPN displayed a grainy biography of Joe Namath. The sink gushed water. He couldn't help but feel a little deflated.

Pat dialed up his missed call. It was one of the three numbers he had saved, apart from Seamus's and the trucking company.

"*Hello*," answered the familiar voice, as delectable as an ice-cream sandwich in July. Instantly, Pat felt his cheek pain dull, and a huge grin took over his face.

"Hey Foley," Pat crooned at his fiancé.

"Hey yourself," Blaise said in her flirty lilt. "I called earlier, Walsh. Where the hell were you? Out wandering a corn maze?"

Pat laughed with deep tenderness. His entire time in Iowa, whenever Shay wasn't around and Blaise could give him a secret call, she always imagined him in creative corn scenes: corn husking, cornholing. She still couldn't believe he chose Iowa for his hideaway spot. ("Personally, I would've gone somewhere warm where the natives speak French," Blaise had opined. "Yeah, but I couldn't risk not being on the same time zone as you, Foley,").

"I actually fell asleep," Pat admitted now, deciding to omit his Duffy dream sequence. "Sorry babe. Where are you?"

"At home," Blaise replied softly. "It's safe."

"Safe" to them meant that John-boy and McCullers were out of earshot. The Foleys believed, like the Walshes did, that Pat and Blaise had flatlined as a couple, and their December wedding was probably off. In reality, the lovers had never gone more than three hours without talking, not one day during this entire season of discontent. Often, they marveled at their ability to pull off the biggest hoax that Zzyzyx Road had ever seen.

"Where in Foley are you?" Pat asked. He loved visuals. He missed having FaceTime.

"In bed," Blaise whispered.

Pat pictured her bony knees drawn to her chest, sitting on that poofy bed like a sexy cake topper. "I wish you were in my bed."

"*Walsh!*" she gasped, pretending to be scandalized. "Look who dialed 1-900-KELLY from Iowa."

"It's *true*."

"Just a few more days," Blaise cooed, and both their minds tiptoed giddily towards Halloween.

"I can't wait, baby." She sighed, "I know, it's been *so* hard."

His entire heart leapt with the creed of her cult. "It's been harder for *you*," he said emphatically. "You're in Kentucky, getting asked prying questions."

"No *way*," Foley murmured. "I've been keeping a low profile. Have hardly seen anyone, except my dad and Shay."

"I can't believe he hasn't figured it out," Pat murmured, rubbing Shay's dog-tag around his neck. The idea that Pat could quit Blaise Foley's opiate love cold-turkey and seek salvation in Iowa was such a sloppy lie, he was almost offended that Seamus believed it.

Sometimes Pat felt bad about lying to his twin, but mainly he felt pretty smug. Shay fancied himself the globe-trotter, the gunslinger, the unpredictable one with all the tattoos and adventures. He had moved to France and then enlisted in the Iraq War without bothering to tell Pat first.

Pat *probably* could've told his twin what he and Blaise were scheming, but there was a sweet sort of vindication in pulling the wool over his eyes. For the rest of their lives, his twin's absolute assertion of what Pat would or wouldn't do would be felled with a question mark.

This was also why he never told Shay about his foot fetish. Some things were just sacred to the self.

Pat thought back to the night, months ago, when Duffy Foley invited him over, telling him that he had earned his trust. Duffy wanted to share his plans for his Last Will and Testament, at least the parts that concerned Blaise.

They went upstairs to call Blaise in New York (the wine cave had no reception). She answered, hurtling from breathless to confused as she realized Uncle Duffy and Pat were together.

"I invited Patrick here tonight," Duffy said mildly. "I'm going to help you, Kelly."

"Thank *God!*" Blaise hollered on speakerphone. "Now can you *please* tell my father that unless he wizens up, he's not gonna walk his *only* daughter down the aisle at her wedding—"

"Kel, you know there's no talking to Johnny," Duffy cut calmly through her. "That's why *we're* going to talk."

Pat interjected, "I think we're talking about going behind your dad's back, babe," he glanced tentatively at Duffy, "Is that right?"

"Yes," the Uncle said quietly.

The pause from the female Foley was so lengthy, Pat worried they had scared her off. But then—

"Count me in," she said, her voice low and resolute.

"You sure, Kel?" Duffy murmured. "Because we can't uncross the Rubicon."

"I am!" Blaise sniffed. "That asshole won't even let me back into my own house. *FUCK HIM!*"

Duffy nodded grimly, "*Alea iacta est.*"

The Uncle's plan was so cut-throat and diabolical, Pat thought it could serve as the illustration for the family motto, "Don't fuck with Foley." In a matter-of-fact voice, Duffy outlined his little brother's demise for them as if reading from a legal deposition.

Upon their father's death in 1977, Duffy inherited 90% of Foley Bourbon (minus the 10% that Wilkie had), and become sole trustee to the family's storied eleven-digit wealth. Just shy of twenty-four-years-old at the time, Duffy had absolute power to spend the money as he saw fit, allocate his sibling's trust funds, and make all the major decisions about Foley Bourbon. Johnny was unhappy with the arrangement—and vocally so. Sullivan Foley died before he could arrange his will, so his estate automatically went to Duffy. Johnny thought it unfair, opining that their father would have wanted Johnny to have a slice of the pie. He was, after all, the Master Distiller.

Johnny proposed that Duffy keep the trust. "But how about giving your little brother equity in Foley Bourbon?"

Duffy agreed. Over the years, he transferred more and more of the shares to Johnny. It seemed to create an equilibrium at Foley. Duffy liked his money, and Johnny liked his bourbon. Duffy took African safaris, bought luxury real estate off the Sotheby's lot, and made his home a museum of priceless art. Meanwhile, Johnny held court in Kentucky, wielding his power through the production of bourbon barrels. Gradually, all decisions about the Foley brand were left to him.

He could even decide to fire his daughter if he wanted, canceling her shares and leaving her a hapless nobody.

"What Johnny did not realize, and still does not," Duffy informed Pat and Blaise. "Is that I have the power to cancel all his shares, and reissue them to another."

Blaise gasped on the phone. "But Duff, would you do that?"

"Not only would I do it, Kel," the Uncle replied, folding his hands serenely. "But I'm actively planning on it."

The Uncle reminded them his death was eminent (Blaise validated this with a wail of despair), and he was putting together a will to be activated on his sixty-first birthday, November 1st of that year. Duffy would cancel all of Johnny's shares and make Blaise the majority shareholder of Foley Bourbon: 75% to be exact.

"So together, Pat and I own *85 percent* of Foley Bourbon?" Blaise breathed, high off the promise of such power.

"Not yet," Duffy said delicately.

He explained that Johnny was on a tear about canceling Blaise's shares. He feared that as the wedding approached, Johnny could have Mr. Tuttle look into the matter, and discover Duffy's secret plans.

"My brother would go nuclear," Duffy explained flatly. "He would probably burn his own barrels up out of spite."

Feverishly, Blaise seconded this. "I know he would, because that's what I would do."

"The *only* way our plan will work," Duffy said, leaning forward on his forearms, "Is if Johnny thinks that you two have broken off the engagement."

"So we tell him we called it off?" Blaise asked.

"Not just him," Duffy said calmly. "*Everyone.*" Behind him, the grandfather clock struck midnight with a chain of ominous gongs. "How suspicious is it going to look to Johnny when he calls Sean up to gloat, and Pat's father hasn't heard a thing about it?"

At first, Pat and Blaise were united in their hesitation, wondering how they could pull off such a hoax.

"What will I tell my bridesmaids?" Blaise fretted.

"Yeah, I can't imagine lying to my brothers," Pat said.

But Duffy made it clear that fickle hearts were not welcome here in the Valley of Death.

"I can't allow myself to depart this earth with uncertainty for the future of Foley," he said, his voice crackling with rare heat. "This is the oldest empire in America, and it's not crumbling under me." He examined his nails, adding sleekly, "If you don't think you can do it, Kel, I'm sure I could leave Zabana the shares—"

"NO!" Blaise shouted on the phone, so loudly that Sophie filled the doorway, looking startled. "I want them! We'll do it, won't we Walsh?"

Duffy smiled as if to say, *That's my girl.*

"Plus," he said, "You know what *else* the majority shareholder of Foley gets."

"The house," Blaise breathed.

"That's right," Duffy said, "You'll get the deed to our beloved Foley Bourbon."

Pat felt reluctance gnawing at him as he listened. Unlike Blaise and Duffy, he did not believe in the curse of sixty-one. He would do whatever Blaise wanted in order to keep her (and her feet) happy, but he could not trick his mind. Whenever Blaise discussed the plan, he imagined them hurtling towards a dead end on very little gas.

As fate would have it, both Patrick and Duffy were wrong: the uncle did not die on his sixty-first birthday, but a few months before. He was diagnosed with stage four pancreatic cancer in June, telling no one but Sophie, and died at home three weeks later. On his nightstand, they found an empty bottle of liquid morphine, an empty flagon of Foley, (aged twenty-five years) and interestingly, a copy of *Crime and Punishment.*

"My poor big brother, suffering in silence like he did!" Mr. John Foley was overheard bawling when he arrived at the scene. "I guess if you have to go, the 25-Year is the best chariot home."

Blaise and her father got into a screaming match about Pat attending the funeral. It escalated to the point of Mr. Foley calling up Father Moony at the rectory to cancel the service, amidst the hysterical protests of Aunt Kennedy, Blaise, Nana Sabina, and Zabana. (McCullers sucked on the end of his tie, rolling his eyes and calling out a general, annoyed, "*Stoppp*")

Blaise gave in to her father's tyranny, vowing it was the last time. After the burial, she went straight to Pat's house in her black dress, asking him if he was ready to put Duffy's plan in motion.

Pat saw her face set for war, felt the flame radiating from her milky skin. He keenly understood that Blaise was going to have those shares, and there was no earthly force that could stop her.

"I am, babe," he assured his fiancé. He had one request: they wait until Seamus returned from his France trip. Then Pat would skip town, leaving a mysterious story in his wake, and ditch his smartphone. There was no way he could pull off a fake break-up while still in touch with Zzyzyx Road.

The night of Duffy's funeral, Blaise tiptoed into her father's study. She climbed into his lap, issuing an apology for her unruly behavior earlier.

"I know it wasn't right to try and invite Walsh today, Daddy," she managed to purr, though the words puckered her mouth like pickle juice.

With a great sigh, (and a glibly low level of surprise) John pardoned his daughter. "You see how that boy comes between us?" he whispered into her hair. "And I thought nothing ever could."

"Me too," Blaise said, wishing the Academy could see her performance.

John gazed into her eyes. "Maybe you're ready to come home to me, baby," he said quietly.

"Remembered where your loyalties lay."

Blaise nodded, pressing the false seeds of discontent into the earth. "I have some thinking to do, Daddy."

Some thinking about what Walsh and I are gonna call my new bourbon line.

As Halloween drew nearer, Blaise and Pat spent a lot of time envisioning the future. Though the forecast for the few months was hazy, the mist could not fully obstruct the bourbon Camelot within their sight.

Pat did wonderful thinking as he drove. His musings through Dubuque to Des Moines had given him the idea for a Foley-Walsh merger. He was sure that he could convince the shareholders of Walsh—Wilkie's nephews, sons, and 14 other grandsons—to get onboard. ("It's too bad that Kiki sold his during a bad gambling run," Pat lamented. "We'd have to buy him some more before the IPO.")

Blaise listened quietly at first, but had now effusively warmed to the idea. She figured they could time the release of Seamus's big book with the company going public. Then they would be laying the bricks in a new, behemoth bourbon empire that had 90% market share, especially in the millennial sector. She hoped people would read their Romeo-Juliet story and buy the bourbon, and vice versa.

"And if my daddy doesn't like it, he doesn't have to be a part of it," she ranted imperiously. "But I'm not going to fire him—he'd have to quit." She sighed, her tone softening grudgingly, as John's often did for her. "I honestly can't see him not making the bourbon, though. And I can't imagine him not walking me down the aisle at our wedding…I know I sound like a Hallmark channel bitch, but I really feel like John-boy is going to do the right thing in the end."

Whenever Blaise said this, Pat's guts squirmed unpleasantly. He was reminded of the last words he ever exchanged with Duffy Foley.

It was that night at his house, after they hung up with Blaise, as the Uncle escorted him to the door.

"Oh, my brother won't be walking Kelly down the aisle," Duffy informed Pat, as though remembering an important detail to tell his house-sitter before setting off on a trip. "Maybe your father can, or my nephew."

"You really don't think Mr. Foley will do it?" Pat asked, frowning.

Duffy stared at him. There in the foyer, the ashen shadows of the trees eclipsed his face, giving him the look of Lord Pluto himself. A wall of power radiated from the uncle that so often brought him to his knees for Blaise.

"Johnny won't be able to make the wedding," Duffy said finally, without offering an explanation.

Pat had never shared this with Blaise.

"So, I think I should go see your mom in the next few days," Blaise said presently, "And heavily hint that we're working through our problems."

"That's good," Pat agreed. "She'll be so happy."

"You think?"

"Of course, babe," Pat said, "You're the daughter she always wanted."

"Aw, thanks love," Blaise cooed, "Yeah, I've intentionally not seen much of your parents, or Killy. It pains me to lie to them."

"But not Shay?" Pat laughed.

"For some reason, not as painful," Blaise said admittedly. "His writing is better for it."

"I can't wait to read this book."

"I can't wait for our lives to begin!" Blaise squealed. She lowered her voice, and Pat heard her open a door, probably checking if the coast was clear. "I'm cleaning out a room for you on the 3rd floor," she murmured. "Where you can put all your lax gear and skis, if you want." She added nonchalantly, "It also has an ensuite bathroom."

Pat laughed, "I see what you're driving at, Foley. You hate sharing a bathroom with me."

"What?" Blaise said innocently, "Nana Sabina says the key to a successful marriage is separate bathrooms. She should know, she's had four."

"You're tryna keep me and my bottle of Dove Men's body wash out of your marble fortress, I get it."

They chatted and talked for a good hour. When they signed off, they excitedly repeated, *"Nine days!"* to each other.

"I love you, Wawshie," Blaise sighed, "After all this time, you're still the best flirt of my life."

He fell asleep thinking; *I could live the rest of my life on those words.*

In the shadow of the Sun King...

7:00 am

Killian Walsh stood in his parent's yard with a steaming hot mug of tea, admiring his distillery against the apricot sky. The love reflected in his eyes was the same as when he watched his children sleep, or saw their heartbeats on a sonogram.

Killian frequently got to work before all his employees, in order to enjoy Walsh Bourbon in this sacred stillness. It was a sort of morning meditation for the chief. Today, on the last day of October, he was in particularly good spirits.

Moments ago, as his mother brewed their Bewley's, she revealed that Blaise and Pat were on the mend. Apparently, Blaise stopped by last night to share the good tidings with his parents.

"Now we mustn't tell anyone, dear," Mrs. Walsh whispered, sloshing milk as she stirred the Irish Breakfast. "Today's her birthday, so be sure to text her, but don't say anything about the wedding, dear, because we don't want to rock the boat."

"I knew it!" Killian grinned. "Don't worry Mam, I've had a barrel of Wedding Blend cooking this entire time."

As he slipped outside, he overheard his mother on the phone to her sister in Ireland, "Oona, dear, start pressing your dress—there's going to be a wedding after all!"

So much for silence, Killian chuckled to himself.

Before his Grandpa Wilkie retired, his morning ritual was to say a prayer at his parent's graves. As a boy, Killian sometimes accompanied him. He imitated Grampy's way of bowing his salt-and-pepper head, furrowing up his brows in a show of great reverence.

Lately, Killian had thought of adopting his grandpa's ritual. Today was Halloween, what better day to start?

He marched up the dewy embankment, absently running a palm over the Foleys' hedges, which were wildly shaggy, at least on their side (*well, we weren't the ones who wanted them,* he thought).

As Killian reached Jack and Clara's graves, he knelt down, running his fingers over the Latin engraving on their tombstones. He tried to drum up some feeling, some suitable prayer from the scion of a bourbon dynasty to its paterfamilias.

You should come to my Grandpa in a dream and tell him where your treasure is buried, Killian thought. Then he added penitently, *thank you, Jack, for leaving behind a legacy that gives me and my entire family a job.*

Killian heard a whistle from the Foleys' side. From the clearing that began at Jack and Clara's graves, he saw a fluffy dog trot into view, followed by a pair of man's pinstriped pajamas. Mr. Foley knelt down to scratch the dog's head as he squatted, but didn't bother picking up his poop. *I guess that's someone else's job,* Killian thought.

The chief spat on the ground. He had no doubt that Mr. Foley had driven the wedge between Pat and Blaise; refused to listen to any other conspiracy theories that often circulated at McGettigan's.

"HEY!" he hollered at Mr. Foley.

Mr. Foley glanced over in surprise. His expression switched to snide amusement when he saw that it was Killian. "Hi Jack, howdy Clara," he chimed, tipping an imaginary hat to their tombstones.

"So," Killian snarled, "Did you hear the good news about Pat and Blaise?"

At the sound of his daughter's name, Mr. Foley's whole comportment changed.

"You don't need to concern yourself with my daughter," he said slowly. "She's none of y'all's business."

"She's gonna be our business when she's my sister-in-law," Killian said savagely. "And I'm pretty sure her being Pat's *wife* qualifies her as his business."

Mr. Foley bristled, and he took two full steps towards Killian. "My daughter," he said, "Has nothing to do with your family."

"Careful not to cross our property line," Killian said coolly. "Look, you can believe whatever you want to believe, but Pat and Blaise are getting married. If you don't like it, my parents can take it from here," he thumbed towards his house. "Trust me, they always wanted a girl—you'd be doing them a favor. But your acting like a horse's ass isn't gonna make her come running back to you. You're only pushing her away."

Mr. Foley leered him down with such fury that Killian steeled himself for a blow. Instead, the elder distiller shook his head vigorously, turning on his heel.

"Load of horse-shit," he muttered to himself. "Blaise knows I would never allow it. C'mon Mingus…"

Mr. Foley disappeared into his hedges, his dog trotting at his feet.

Killian had only ever crossed the property line once. It was in 1st grade, when Oscar dared him to retrieve a whiffle-ball they hit out of bounds. But now, on the heels of such inspiring anger, Killian jumped onto the Foleys' neat grass.

"*Hey!*" he bellowed. "I have a daughter too, man. There's nothing she could do to make me turn my back on her," his heart pounded madly. "That's not what a father does."

Mingus turned to look back at him, cocking his teddy-bear head. Then, "MINGUS!" his owner's voice pierced the morning solitude, and the dog bounded after him.

1:30 pm

I asked Blaise to meet me downtown at my favorite coffee shop, Please and Thank You, so I could give her my birthday present. Recently, I had been coming here a lot to write. I loved the crispy chocolate chip cookies and the record store in the back. They hadn't decorated for Halloween, unless you counted the abundant eyeliner on the baristas.

Foley showed up 12 minutes late with her phone pressed to her ear, waving like a harried celebrity at me and the busboy. My heart swelled with profound gratitude that she had been born.

I couldn't be offended that I wasn't invited to her Halloween Birthday Bash, because it wasn't being held this year. Foley

Bourbon was still mourning the loss of King Duffy, so Blaise and her father had decided to have just a quiet dinner at home tonight.

"Thanks Aunt Cricket!" she trilled into the phone. "Yes, I *promise* I'll start moisturizing this year. Love you!" she hung up, raising her sunglasses to her crown, and rested her big eyes on me. "Sorry doll...hi, Happy Halloween!"

"Likewise," I grinned as she sat down across from me, her crimson hair fanning out like an Indian tapestry. "And Happy Birthday. You get *two* presents from me today, Foles. I emailed you the first one."

It was the first half of *Misercordias*. Of course, I would have preferred handing her a hard copy, but my printer was out of ink.

"Yay!" my muse clapped her hands giddily. "I can't wait to see how it all flows together."

"With any hope, like the Euphrates into the Tigris."

Before I could reveal my other present, Blaise leaned forward, confessing that she had a *big* favor to ask.

"I'm inclined to give my muse whatever she wants," I said humbly, "Especially on her birthday."

"Thanks," she said swiftly, "Can you accompany me to Mr. Van der Vee's office, ASAP?"

"Who the *fuck* is Mr. Van der Vee?" I replied in puzzlement.

"You know who Mr. *Van der Vee* is," Blaise answered. "You wrote about him! He was Duffy's law partner."

"Oh yeah." Vaguely, I thought of the scene at Doc Crows, conjuring up a middle-aged lawyer without a face. Blaise hadn't spent a lot of time describing him ("he wears a lot of olive-colored suits and doesn't drink").

"He's in charge of Duffy's will," she whispered conspiratorially. "It goes into effect tomorrow."

"I'm confused...didn't your Uncle die in July?"

"*Yes*, but Duff knew he would pass away by his sixty-first birthday, so he just arranged his will for November 1," Blaise said smartly. "Mr. Van der Vee just called me and told me I could get my portion early, you know, as my birthday present." She grinned, wagging her sunglasses up and down. Then a frown rippled her visage. "The bizarre thing is, he wants Pat to be there with me when I get it."

"Pat's coming home tonight," I blurted out with ejaculatory grace. This was my other birthday gift to her.

"I know," Blaise said, smiling at her lap. I noticed that she was wearing her ring.

"How do you *know,*" I asked, mildly deflated.

"Women know," she replied, in an ethereal tone.

"Are you guys talking?" I demanded, stirring the straw in my cold brew like a crank. "I'm the Best Man, I need to know if there's going to be a wedding or a wake here."

"But since Pat isn't back yet," Blaise said, politely ignoring my questions. "I need you to come with me to Mr. V's to get the will." She winked, "No one does a better Patrick Alan Walsh impression better than you."

I opened my mouth, but my curiosity was carried away by a new breeze. This was the first mention I had heard of any will. When especially drunk, Blaise sometimes rambled about her "inheritance," in a voice of gypsy foreboding (i.e., "Just wait until my inheritance comes in—then he'll see…"). I had always assumed she was talking about the famed Foley trust-fund, but didn't realize there was an exact date attached to it.

"Is this your inheritance we're talkin' bout?" I asked.

Her eyes glinted alluringly, "Sure is."

"Do you know what he left you?" I asked eagerly, sliding on my jacket. Duffy Foley was a man of continental luxury. He probably kept a jar of Grey Poupon on his nightstand table. I pictured us riding his Aston Martin into the sunset...me finishing my novel at his Swiss chalet. Of course I would go with her to get the will.

"So many questions!" Blaise tapped my nose playfully. "All I can say, honey, is if you thought the first part of Misercordias was good, you better buckle your seatbelt. We're only at the intermission."

The law offices of Van der Vee and Foley were located in a brick building twenty minutes outside of town, down a dusty road that overlooked a horse pasture. The blinds were closed, perhaps as a nod of respect for the departed Mr. Foley.

We were greeted at the water cooler by Mr. Van der Vee, a soda cracker of a man in an olive suit.

Blaise touched my shoulder and introduced me as, "My fiancé, Patrick." I delivered a perfect impression of my twin, making my face all annoyingly earnest and keeping my tattoos covered up.

The efforts were wasted on Mr. Van der Vee, who spared me only a curt nod. He was a balding man of about 60, and from what I could tell, his last name wasn't a precursor to any quirkiness of spirit. He did have a look of fatherly concern for Blaise as she spoke, and for this I liked him.

Van der Vee went to his office and returned with a big security deposit box.

"Is it in there, Mr. V?" Blaise asked. Her tone was as aristocratic as ever, but her eyes were goose-eggs of greed.

"Yes," Mr. V confirmed. He seemed to hesitate, for reasons I couldn't quite judge. Maybe to delay the moment when this strawberry strudel would leave his office.

"Now Ms. Foley, you may need my help with all this," the lawyer said, placing the box slowly in her outstretched arms. "Anything you need at all, just call me. Any time, any day."

"Thanks, Mr. V!" Blaise chirped. From her carefree hair toss, I could tell she didn't plan on calling him until the next time Conor slapped her with a ticket.

"Be careful," Van der Vee said, pumping my hand in farewell. "And Happy Birthday, Miss Foley."

In the car, Blaise rolled down her window and cranked some girly song, singing along with reckless euphoria.

"Happy Birthday, Kelly!" she sang over the whipping wind. She grinned at me, "I'm sorry I couldn't tell you about this before, Shay," she passed me the box, *"This* is how our book is going to end!"

I was barely listening. My eyes snagged on a Post-It note stuck on the beige joints: *Don't let Kel read alone.*

I won't, I silently vowed to Duffy. I didn't know her uncle's handwriting, but I knew he was the only soul allowed to call her Kelly.

"Well Foles, if this box contains spoilers to our happy ending," I murmured, "Then I insist on being there when it's opened."

At my house, Blaise sat caressing the box as though it contained Marcellus Wallace's soul.

"Did you think Mr. Van der Vee seemed a little, I don't know, somber?" she asked, her features rearranging into a vexed expression. "I think he really misses my uncle."

"Maybe," I said, joining her at the dining room table. Frankly, I had already let the lawyer fall through the oubliette of my brain. I was becoming more obsessed by the minute about the contents of the box. *Maybe it holds a map to Jack's treasure,* I thought wildly. Pat had told me about some mysterious picture of Black-Jack and Wilkie that Duffy had on display at his house. He was sure it held a clue to a big family secret, possible even the treasure.

"Are we gonna open this box?"

She grinned, "You're right, let's have at it. I think you should have the honor of reading."

"Thanks!" I said, thoroughly pleased. "You've got me stoked, Foles. Are we expecting Jack's treasure levels of greatness?"

"*At least,*" Blaise grinned.

Inside, there was a pile of papers clipped together, with a wax-sealed envelope on top. With a nod of permission from Blaise, I broke through the red Foley horseshoe seal and began reading aloud a handwritten letter:

My Dearest Kelly,

Writing you this letter is the hardest thing I've ever done, which is why you are reading it posthumously. Some would call that cowardice. The truth according to me is that I couldn't stand to see you hurt. I preferred our finite time to be spent sharing happy moments, and for you to feel insulated against the harsher realities of life. You called me your protector, and it's a title I would have been honored to put on my tombstone. Please believe me when I say that I always tried to live up to it. There isn't a thing I wouldn't have done for you.

The shares to our family's distillery are all yours, Kelly-girl. Consider them a birthday present for all the Halloweens that I will

*miss. I warn you; they aren't tax free. If you want to know what I
mean, please read on. The caveat is that life as you know it will
never be the same. The reward is that you will finally have the truth.
I believe you deserve the truth. I also believe you can handle it.
Through honesty, a new reality can be reborn at Foley, where we
reclaim the integrity and humanity we have lost.*

I glanced up at Blaise. Judging by her wide eyes, this letter wasn't
at all what she expected. "Do you want me to read on?"
She nodded silently.

I continued:

*"Your mother and I were at Vanderbilt at the same time, as you
well know. I was in my last year of law school when Dru was a
sophomore. I had been hearing about this beauty queen for what
seemed like forever. Ever since Johnny came across her Miss
Tennessee poster in a record store, he was a man obsessed. He
was going to meet Dru McCullers, come hell or high water. He
decided that the best way to meet her would be to act as judge at
the Miss America pageant. To this day, I'm not quite sure how he
pulled it off. I think many barrels of well-aged ambrosia were sent to
the executive offices of ABC. I tuned in to watch the show and
couldn't help but smile as Johnny gave Miss Tennessee perfect
scores in every category. He wasn't sucking up—to him, she was
truly perfect.*

*I first met Dru in May of 1981. It was a hot day in Nashville, and
she was laying barefoot underneath a tree, studying for finals. She
was fresh off her national tour, and everyone on campus knew her. I
watched as person after person called her name and waved. No
matter how many times she was interrupted, Dru beamed and
waved right back.*

*Kel, I could sense your mother's goodness right away. It was like
there was a beam of light radiating off her. I understood in a glance
what my brother was crusading for (beyond the prized beauty, of
course). He wanted her light to elevate his darkness. I do believe
every human is born with angel and devil in them. Johnny's devil,*

which you're well acquainted with, had been taking the reins for some time, strengthened by all his anger after our father died. Being close to Dru brought out the angel in him.

Kel, I have devil in me too. I believed there was no problem bigger than me, no situation I couldn't control. Just as I would do anything for you, I would do anything for my little brother. And I have.

One afternoon in 2001, my brother came to my office very upset. I was in the middle of recording my notes for a case, and did not turn off the tape-recorder. Had I not, I may have been able to convince myself of the lie we told everyone else.

My brother confessed that he had just shot his wife. He shot her in the head, so we cannot pretend he didn't aim to kill. He shot her as she rode on horseback past the old shooting range, so we cannot pretend it wasn't premeditated. He wanted it to look like an accident, and it did.

"Why, Johnny?" was all I could ask.

He told me, through gasps for breath, that Dru planned on leaving him. She told him she wanted to get custody of the kids and move back to Tennessee. He couldn't abide that.

I told him to calm down, that I would help him. The lawyer in me took over. I asked him how many times he shot her, and told him to bring me the gun. By that time, George was calling my office looking for Johnny, saying that Mrs. Foley had a terrible fall and her horse was running pell-mell all over Foley Bourbon.

I don't think Johnny planned on Dru surviving the attack, but the outcome wound up better than he dreamed. His beauty queen was paralyzed, so now she couldn't leave him.

Here are the facts: I served as my brother's alibi for the time of the shooting. I hid his rifle. When you and McCullers went to the hospital, I found the two shell-cases and hid them too. Contrary to what Johnny asked me to do, I did not dispose of the evidence.

As misguided as it may seem, I acted on an instinct to protect you and your little brother. I did not want ours to be a family where Daddy kills Mommy, so I tried to erase the truth.

I understand now that truth is ineradicable. The proof of that is sitting in Mr. Van der Vee's office. I have left him all the evidence— including the tape recording of Johnny's confession. If you wish him to, Mr. Van der Vee will help prosecute your father to the full extent of the law. If you don't, he will never speak of it again.

I remain, your uncle in life and in death,

Duffy Foley

"Wow," I uttered, as the story slid over our heads, exhaling with the very breath of sweat.

"Blaise, did you have any idea?"

She did not reply. I saw from her stricken face that she had no idea, and knew I was witnessing the death of a lifelong fairy tale, her greatest bourbon story blown into bits. For a long moment, Blaise seemed to be paralyzed in her chair like her mother, the beauty queen posture intact.

"Blaise?" I ventured, reaching out clumsily to touch her. "You alright?"

As my hand grazed her elbow, Blaise sprang out of stillness, jumping up and running for the bathroom. Though she slammed the door shut, it did nothing to muffle her blood-curdling scream.

"B?" I followed her, rapping feebly on the door.

I heard the tap running, then the door burst open. Blaise clawed at me, not for comfort, but to move me of her way. I wasn't sure if she knew it was me, or just dimly recognized a shape blocking her path.

"Where are you going?" I called after her.

She turned around, looking through me with the chilling artifice of calm. I have spent many hours, perhaps days, choosing words to describe Blaise Foley's thrilling eyes. This was my first time seeing her fury in person. Out of the bulging, febrile blue, the words *demonic possession* came to me.

"I'm going to kill my father," she hissed.

"What? *No!*"

But her riding boots had already clicked out my back door.

I tore after her into the cold boreal forest with no time to grab my jacket, or my phone.

"HEY!"

Her Jag was making its haphazard peel down our driveway. I grabbed for the passenger's

side door, but it was locked, so I pounded fiercely on the window.

"What?" Blaise rolled it down about three inches, looking severely harassed. "Don't you try and stop me!"

"I won't!" I rattled the door-handle. "Just let me in!"

She complied, giving me a nanosecond to squeeze in before rocketing down the driveway.

"I—"

"If you talk, I'll have to drop you off," Blaise intoned, hunkering over the wheel.

"Absolutely," I said, with the feigned Zen of a hostage negotiator. "But how will you do it? Don't you need a gun?" If I persuaded her to go back and get mine, I could put a blood choke on her, rendering her unconscious until I could think of a new plan.

"I don't need a gun," she said flatly.

As we zipped down Zzyzyx, my heart's percussion became a John Bonham solo. I prayed that my brother Conor would stop us in his prowler, then I prayed he wouldn't. I waited for a window to open and for a new current to blow in, but it didn't.

Foley and Walsh Bourbon appeared on the horizon. I leaned back as though bracing myself for a crash, but to my astonishment, she barreled right on by.

"Foley, uh, you just passed your house..."

"I'm going to Lexington first," she fired back, without lifting her eyes from the road. "I need to get some of my Uncle Andy's *special blend* from the warehouse."

"What's that, the 70-year?" I asked wildly.

"Older than that, honey. It's what we used to give the Prohibition Agents." Blaise lowered her sunglasses and sped up. "Thallium's the secret spice. It doesn't leave a trace."

"You're going to poison your dad?"

"Yep" she said readily. *"Tonight."* She sped up even more, "That asshole's about to learn the true meaning of 'Don't fuck with Foley.'"

"Jesus..." I muttered, irrationally choosing that moment to buckle up.

Blaise side-glanced at me. "Do you want to get out?"

I answered truthfully that it hadn't occurred to me.

Now I had about 160 miles round-trip to either talk her off the ledge, or get on board with her plan.

The next time I looked over, tears ran from her sunglasses. Her shoulders quaked in a way that made her look feeble to me for the very first time.

Across town, Mr. Van der Vee was getting impressively drunk at his desk. Usually, he wasn't a big drinker—his stomach ulcer didn't allow it—but today he needed a potion stronger than Milk of Magnesia.

His wife had called to ask when he was coming home (they were starting to get trick-or-treaters), but he told her frankly he wasn't sure. On Duffy's orders, he was staying at work to await a call from Miss Foley. Duffy had said that upon reading his will, she would immediately want her father arrested, and call him about fetching the evidence.

Around five p.m., his secretary poked her gray bob into his office. "I've got Foley on line 1 for you," she announced, eyeing the uncorked bottle of bourbon curiously.

"Thank you, Joyce," Mr. Van der Vee exhaled, reaching for his phone with a mixture of relief and dread. "Hi again, Miss Foley," he said at once. "Please let me start by saying how sorry I am that you had to learn such terrible news on your birthday."

There was a lengthy pause, then a male voice replied suspiciously, "Mr. Van der Vee? This is John Foley...were you expecting my daughter?"

"No sir," the lawyer replied too quickly. *Goddammit.* "I must have gotten myself confused there." He cleared his throat, lamely deciding to start over. "How can I help you, Mr. Foley?"

After another brooding pause, Foley continued slowly, "I wanted to make sure you're still available at ten a.m. tomorrow to go over my brother's will."

"Ten a.m.," Mr. Van der Vee echoed. Of course, he never bothered to write down the appointment, because he expected Foley would be hauled off to jail by then. "I—of course, John."

"Mr. Van der Vee" said Foley, his voice dropping lower than a dragging muffler. "I have to ask you, what terrible news did my daughter learn on her birthday?"

"I—" Mr. Van der Vee fumbled. "I really couldn't say, John."

"You can't plead the fifth, Van der Vee" Foley growled. "Not where my daughter is concerned."

"If you're concerned about your daughter's wellbeing, I suggest you give her a call—"

"Don't give me the slippery eel routine," Foley snapped. "Now, I'm gonna give you one more chance, then I'm gonna start getting angry. *What bad news did she get?*"

Van der Vee nettled. *Why the hell am I ducking and weaving him?* John-boy was a terrible brute, and he was about to get what he deserved. There was no need to keep up the charade anymore. *The Walsh boy will protect Miss Foley until the cops get him.* From this, Van der Vee drew courage.

"How about you take my last chance and shove it up your ass?" he suggested lightly.

"*Excuse me?*" Foley breathed.

"You're excused, Foley," Mr. Van der Vee said. "By the way, your daughter got to the will first."

"What does that mean?"

"It means that Duffy left her every one of your shares, *and* your filthy little secret about her poor momma.*"* He drained his drink with a satisfied smack of the lips, "So, if I were you, I wouldn't buy any green bananas."

The lawyer leaned back in his chair, anticipating the bourbon-maker's response.

A dial tone filled his ear.

Though John felt as though his chest was hit with a canon, he resolved to stay calm. He hung up the phone and left his office in search of his wife.

He found his beauty queen out on the ballroom terrace. Someone, probably Hildy, had wheeled her out to enjoy the sunset and left her there.

Well, that ain't safe, John thought critically. He went up behind her and laid a hand on Dru's bony shoulder, feeling a shiver through her cashmere cardigan.

"You cold, baby?" he murmured.

Dru drummed her polished fingers on her armrest, her sign for *No.*

"Okay. You can set here a little." John drooped down and kissed her cherry head. "Can you believe you gave birth twenty-six years ago today?" He didn't expect an answer, and Dru didn't sign one. "I just texted our baby asking if she was still coming for dinner. Let's see if she wrote back."

He checked his phone and saw Blaise responded 10 minutes ago. *"Absolutely, Daddy! Wouldn't miss it for all the gold in Jack's treasure :)"*

John couldn't help but chuckle. "She really is my daughter," he remarked, not without pride. He stroked Dru's head like a cherished pet. "Our baby's mad at me, Mommy," he whispered in her ear. "She knows about the fight we had all those years ago."

Dru tried to make a sound, but the noise faltered in her rusty throat.

John leaned in closer still. "When she comes over," he uttered. "I'll have to set her straight. Don't be scared, Mommy." His lips mashed hotly against her ear, "Daddy'll handle everything just fine."

Dru's fingers began to fly, but John didn't notice. In a swift, practiced motion, he tilted Dru's chair back and wheeled her from the edge of the balcony. Then he climbed upstairs and expertly unlocked the third door on the left, where his guns lived. With the same tenderness he showed his wife, John ran his fingers over his collection of rifles.

Can't wait to see you angel :), he texted his Blaise, pulling the glossy handle of his Remington 870 and frowning appraisingly. *You're the best thing that ever happened to me.* He considered his Beretta, which he used to shoot Walsh, but it wouldn't do—he needed something fully automatic.

On the balcony, Dru sat under the purpling sky. Her tremulous hands signaled *No, no, no,* but there was no one around to see.

COMING SOON: Domini (Book 2)

Follow @MisercordiasBook on Instagram, for more buried treasure!!

Like what you just read? Please, drop me an Amazon review! You have no idea how much you are appreciated. <3

Character Index (because there are a lot of Foleys and Walshes to keep tabs on)

Foley Camp:

Blaise Foley: (b. October 31, 1988) Heroine of *Misercordias.* Heiress to the Foley estate, including 75% ownership of Foley Bourbon. **Personal Quote:** "in any other state, they would probably call me an alcoholic. That's why I'll never live anywhere but Kentucky." Fiancée of Patrick Walsh. **Favorite Movies:** *Clueless, Mean Girls, Bring it On, Cruel Intentions, the Rules of Attraction, Goodfellas, Silence of the Lambs, Titanic, Sophie's Choice, the Remains of the Day.*

John Foley: (b. July 28, 1955) Father of Blaise and McCullers Foley, son of Sullivan and Sabina, brother to Kennedy and Duffy. Master Distiller of Foley Bourbon (1977-?) Husband to Dru McCullers (m. 1986) **Personal Quote:** "bourbon is the blood in my veins, and my heart beats fully at 5 pm."

McCullers Foley: (b. June 7, 1990) Brother to Blaise, son of Dru and John. Francophone, Germanophone, celiac, skier, shooter, hedonist. **Personal Quotes:** "is this gluten-free?" "I'm flying out to Switzerland tomorrow, with a possible stopover in Montecarlo. No, I don't have to be back for work." **Favorite Movie:** *the Talented Mr. Ripley.*

Dru McCullers: (b. November 26, 1960) Mother to Blaise and McCullers Foley, wife of John (m. 1986). Miss America 1981, former equestrian, natural red-head. **Personal Quote:** "I'm a true Tennessee girl. I may have married John, but I never switched over from Jack."

Kennedy Foley: (b. February 14, 1964) mother to Zabana and Jericho Foley, aunt to Blaise and McCullers, sister to John and Duffy, daughter of Sullivan and Sabina. Heiress to Foley Bourbon, philanthropic millionaire, humanitarian, equestrian, life-long Madonna fan. **Education:** University of Arizona, BA, Native American Studies, 1986. **Nicknames:** Louisville Lolita, Copper-Top. **Favorite Movies:** *Fast Times at Ridgemont High, Desperately Seeking Susan, the Labyrinth*

Jericho Foley: (b. June 29, 1991) son of Kennedy Foley, sister to Zabana. Heir to Foley Bourbon. Half-Irish, half-Mayan, budding humanitarian. **Personal Goal:** to build as many Adobe homes for native families in need as possible. **Claim to Fame:** lost virginity in his cousin Blaise's sorority house at age fifteen.

Zabana Foley: (b. June 25, 1986) daughter of Kennedy Foley, sister to Jericho. Heiress to Foley Trust (2014-?) **Cars:** Lambourghini Veneno, Lambourghini Murcielago, Lykan HyperSport, Chevy Corsica 1998. **Residences:** Tucson, Arizona: Lloret de Mar, Spain; Foley Bourbon. **Favorite Book:** *Call of the Wild*. **Favorite Movies**: *Back to the Future, Stepmom, Ferris Bueller's Day Off, the Wedding Singer, Saturday Night Fever*. **Walsh Crush:** No Comment.

Duffy Foley: (1953-2014) Uncle to Blaise, Zabana, McCullers, and Jericho, brother to John and Kennedy, son of Sullivan and Sabina. Sole Heir to Foley Trust (1977-2014) **Education:** Vanderbilt Law, J.D., 1982. **Profession:** Lawyer, art collector, appreciator of French women. USMC: 1971-73. **Personal Quote:** "when you know from birth that you're going to die at 61, you get really good at savoring the good stuff." **Favorite Movies:** *Godfather, Part II, Platoon, Full Metal Jacket, Shawshank Redemption*.

Sullivan Foley: (1920-1977) father to Duffy, John, and Kennedy, son of Ulysses and Deirdre, brother to Lucretia. Sole Heir to Foley Trust and Estate (1944-1977) World War II veteran, wearer of fine suits. **Personal Quote:** "Daddy taught me to always ask for the sale, never ask about the blind tigers, put the bourbon on par with God and the sun, and always seal the deal with a smile."

Lucretia Foley: (1923-1984) sister to Sullivan, daughter of Ulysses and Deirdre, aunt to Duffy, Johnny, and Kennedy. **Vocations:** Mother Superior, Registered Nurse. **Personal Quotes:** "The Lord is my shepherd, I shall not want." **Claim to Fame:** tended to Black-Jack in the two weeks he lay dying of gun-shot wounds (1948).

Ulysses Foley: (1882-1943) father of Sullivan and Lucretia, son of Blaise (1863-1924), brother to Andrew. **Nickname:** the Silver-Tongued Salesman. Credited with getting Foley Bourbon into Europe, Cuba, and South America. **Life Regrets:** never discovering his father's identity; not living to see his adoptive son Jack become a published author.

Deirdre Foley: (*née Sullivan*...1896-1990) mother of Sullivan and Lucretia, daughter of Tommy and Kathleen Sullivan. **Nickname:** Black Beauty. **Claims to Fame:** named "the toast of the Abbey!" by the *Daily Dubliner,* 1916; appeared on Harper Bazaar's "Best Dressed" list in 1929, 1934, 1937, 1951, and 1969. Self-professed muse of Abbey playwright, Ossain L. Banister. **Personal Quote:** "I was born a Kilkenny sewer-rat, and became the wife of one of the wealthiest men in America. Every ounce of that is owed to how I carried myself. If you believe you're a queen, they'll all believe it, too."

Walsh Camp:

Jack "Black-Jack" Walsh: (1893-1948) father of Wilkie, Kilkenny, and Pearse, husband of Clara (Sullivan) Walsh. **Claims to Fame:** most successful bootlegger in American history, prominent figure in the Irish War of Independence, first person to know the last words of James Joyce's *Ulysses;* holds posthumous record for most posters ever sold. **Personal Quotes:** "I knew the risks were high, but the rewards were incalculably higher," "writing and fighting, that's all I ever wanted to do," "God hang the Queen," "a man does not become a man until he stands up for his country." **Favorite Writers:** Marcus Aurelius, Cicero, Lucretius, Lady Gregory, James Joyce. **Life Regrets:** None.

Clara (Sullivan) Walsh: (1901-1948) mother of Wilkie, Kilkenny, and Pearse, wife of Jack. **Nickname:** the Stepdance Queen of Kilkenny. **Claim to Fame:** knitted blankets for the fatherless babies born to ladies of Jack's brothels.

Wilkie Walsh: (born December 27, 1920) son of Jack and Clara, father to Sean, Martin, Avanoco, and Shilah, husband of Kachine, grandfather to Killian, Oscar, Conor, Eamon, Callum, Falco, Brendan, Patrick, Seamus, Kiernan, Paytah, Onacona, Manquilla, Aidan, and Micháel. **Employer:** Foley Bourbon (1928-1968) Walsh Bourbon (1968-2007). **Retirement Activities:** drinking with Killian, learning to read in Braille, listening to *Gunsmoke,* flirting with 65-year-old Jamaican nurse. **Personal Quotes:** "I may not know much about women. But I had three brothers, four sons, eleven nephews, and fifteen grandsons, so I understand something of men." "I have no intention of dying until my father's treasure is found. Even if I outlive my sons." "There is no force on earth to rival the will of an Irishman."

Sean Walsh: (born December 12, 1954) son of Wilkie and Kachine, father to Killian, Conor, Patrick, and Seamus), brother to Marty, Avanoco, and Shilah. **Sexual Awakening:** seeing Mrs. Foley sunbathing in her gingham bikini on the piazza of Foley Bourbon, a moment on par with watching Ursula Andress emerge from the sea in *Dr. No.* **Best Friend:** his brother Marty (but for God's sake, don't tell him). **Personal Style:** "if I'm in a tuxedo, someone's either dead or getting married. Basically the same sacrament." **Personal Quotes:** "I went to university in Ireland. I knew the way to a girl's heart was to utter those three little words: 'I'm Jack's grandson.'"

Martin Walsh: (born December 11, 1955) son of Wilkie and Kachine, father to Oscar, Callum, Brendan, and Mickey, brother to Sean, Avanoco, and Shilah. **Arch Nemesis:** Duffy Foley. **Education:** University of Chicago, J.D., 1983. **Personal Quotes:** "I specialize in Intellectual Property law. I recall that Jonas Salk, the inventor of the polio vaccine, argued against patenting it. 'Could you patent the sun?' he asked. I would have told him yes, then had his syringes *and* the rays trademarked." **Advice to his Sons:** "do the right thing, at least 80% of the time."

Avanoco Walsh (Avi): (born June 3, 1959) son of Wilkie and Kachine, father to Eamon, Kiernan, Falco, and Aidan. **Nicknames:** Sharky, Avi. **FICO credit score:** don't ask. **Affiliations and Memberships:** Mensa, Gambler's Anonymous (joined in 1985, left, rejoined in 2015), CDIB— Cherokee Nation. **Titles:** Class Valedictorian, 1977, owner of McGettigan's Pub (since 1981). **Life Regret:** never saw Zeppelin in concert.

Shilah Walsh: (born August 16, 1961) son of Wilkie and Kachine, father to Paytah, Onacona, Manquilla. **Education:** Cornell University, BS, 1983. **Favorite Nephew:** Killian or Kiernan, **Nickname:** Hiawatha. **Trademark:** deeply raspy voice (from having his tonsils out at 15, then singing his lungs out at a Todd Rundgren concert), and his long, black mane. **Best Friend:** his brother, Avi. **Favorite Quotes:** "when it comes down to making out, whenever possible, put on side one 1 of Led Zeppelin IV." "I got this one rule. I never go out with girls who say, 'Bitchin'.'"

Wilkie's Grandsons: (in birth order)

Killian Walsh: (born July 4, 1981) son of Sean and Dervorguilla Walsh, brother to Conor, Patrick, and Seamus. **Nickname:** Chief. **Religion:** Bourbon (and part-time Irish-Catholic). **Occupation:** Master Distiller, Walsh Bourbon (2007-?) **Class Notable:** Best All-Around. **Karaoke Song:** 'Red Solo Cup.' **Affiliations:** High Fraternal Order of Black-Jack (Chief, Elder), Louisville Distiller's Association, Democratic Party ("but I'm fiscally conservative.") **If I Weren't a Bourbon Distiller, I'd Be:** "dunno, I never thought of it." **Favorite Ice Cream Flavor:** soft-serve vanilla cone with chocolate sprinkles, ("it reminds me of July"). **Role Model:** "W fucking W."

Oscar Walsh: (born October 15, 1981) son of Marty Walsh and Julianne (Jill) McGuinness, brother to Callum, Brendan, and Mickey. **Nickname:** Debo. **Education:** University of Georgia, J.D, 2009 ("that's where Tiff and I met,"). **Class Notable:** Most Attractive. **Personal Style:** Brooks Brothers meets *American Psycho*. **Personal Quotes:** "I've been meaning to get back into golf," "Growing up with three little brothers and eleven little cousins has made me into the diplomat I am." **Affiliations:** Phi Alpha Delta, Sigma Alpha Epsilon, Louisville Squash Club, High Fraternal Order of Black Jack (Elder).

Conor Walsh: (born March 31, 1983) son of Sean and Dervorguilla Walsh, brother to Killian, Patrick, and Seamus. **Nickname:** Maggot. **Education:** Louisville Metro Police Department Academy. **Class Notable:** Most Athletic. **Arch Nemesis:** Blaise Foley. **Foley Crush:** (*see above*) **Secret Ambition:** "after we find Jack's treasure, the wife and I'll probably move to some tropical island. I can shoot at jelly fish." **Affiliations and Memberships:** Planet Fitness.

Eamon Walsh: (born May 10, 1983) son of Karen and Avanoco Walsh, brother to Falco, Kiernan (Kiki), and Aidan (Douska) **Nickname:** Eems. **Class Notable:** Biggest Ego. **Karaoke Song:** 'Greatest Love of All.' **Trademark:** Bright Orange Hair. **Occupation:** Lacrosse Coach, University of Louisville. **Foley Crush:** "Zabana Foley. What a babe. And she's *rich!* Did she say anything about me?" **Personal Achievement:** Division I All-American Lacrosse,

Notre Dame. *Notes:* according to Falco, he will be the one to find Jack's lost treasure (*see:* Book 2, *Domini*).

Callum Walsh: (born October 31, 1984) son of Marty Walsh and Jill McGuinness, brother to Oscar, Brendan, and Mickey. **Favorite Holiday:** Trick-or-treat. **Nickname:** Slaw Jaw (for both his impressively wide mandible and his lurid AIM screen-name: SLaW on yer jAw 84) **Employer:** Walsh Bourbon, (2007-present) **Karaoke Song:** "I don't sing karaoke." **Secret Ambitions:** to completely outlaw the prescription of all opiates in the United States, and get really good at making bourbon. **Ninja Turtle:** Donatello. **Worst Fear:** that Brendan would start using again. **Secret Crush:** no fucking comment. "What's with all these personal questions? Do you work for the NSA?"

Falco Walsh: (born December 27, 1984) son of Karen and Avanoco Walsh, brother to Eamon, Kiernan (Kiki) and Aidan (Douska). **Nicknames:** Falco; (*prefers actual name be withheld*) "the Dark Prince." **Education:** Cornell University, BS, 2007, NYU, Stern School of Business, MBA, 2010. **Desired Salary:** "double what my brother Eamon makes." **He Feels Most in Touch with his Native Blood When:** applying to college. **FICO credit score:** 740. **Title:** Salutatorian, class of '03. **Membership:** Cornell Club NYC, High Fraternal Order of Black-Jack. **Favorite Comedian:** Andy Kauffman. **Current Address:** "four stops off the Brooklyn L." **Secret Talent:** soothsaying

Brendan Walsh: (born February 10, 1986) son of Marty Walsh and Jill McGuinness, brother to Oscar, Callum, and Mickey. **Nickname:** Longbow. **Current Residence:** 20 acres of land in west central Montana. **Personal Achievement:** four years sober from heroin, as of press time. **Creative Soulmate:** Kiernan "Kiki" Walsh. **Roommate:** Paytah "Hawkeye" Walsh. **Musical Instrument:** bass guitar **Groups/Affiliations:** STBS, (Society of Third Born Sons) a band formed with cousins Kiki and Seamus in 8th grade; High Fraternal Order of Black-Jack ('86). **Favorite Movie:** *Into the Wild.*

Seamus Walsh: (born March 17, 1986) son of Sean and Dervourgilla Walsh, brother to Killian, Conor, and Patrick. **Nickname:** Deadshot. **Musical Talent:** drummer for STBS. **Worst Fear:** Johnny Got His Gun. **Tattoos:** several. **Ninja Turtle:** Rafael.

Patrick Walsh: (born March 17, 1986) son of Sean and Dervourgilla Walsh, brother to Killian, Conor, and Patrick. **Nicknames:** Pato; Golden Boy. **Distinguishing Marks:** prominent scar on cheek from Mr. Foley's bullet. **Personal Achievements:** high honor roll every marking period from 6-12th grade, 93% on CPA scores, got Blaise Foley to agree to marry him. **Favorite Movies:** *Rudy, American Pie 1 & 2, Catch Me if You Can, Brian's Song, Varsity Blues, the Departed, Gangs of New York, Toy Story.* **Personal Quotes:** "I like a girl who can put her best foot forward." **Employer:** KPMG (2010-2014)

Kiernan Walsh: (born June 11, 1986) son of Avanoco and Karen Walsh, brother to Eamon, Falco, and Aidan **Nickname:** Kiki. **Class Notable(s):** Most Musical and Class Clown **Education:** "to be perfectly honest, I'm a few credits shy of my degree, but I believe life is our greatest teacher." **Best Band Ever:** "in terms of career longevity without compromising their artistry, I might have to go with Weezer." **Personal Legend:** believed by Brendan to be the reincarnation of Jimi Hendrix. **Favorite Albums:** *Almost Stoked; Adelaide and Oxana Take Berlin; the Song of the Last Thing You Said* (all by STBS)

Paytah Walsh: (born July 12, 1987) son of Shilah and Kimama Walsh, brother to Onacona and Manquilla. **Nickname:** Hawkeye; the Shaman. **Roommate:** Brendan Walsh. **Instrument:** bow and arrow. **Favorite Book:** *Call of the Wild.* **Spirit Animal:** eagle. **Hobbies:** earthing, archery, wood-whittling, wood-working, hunting, gathering, healing. **Personal Quote:** "somedays, I just want to crawl back into Kim's womb." **Personal Achievements:** revered by Brendan as the only Walsh who could wake up in 1787 and be absolutely fine; once delivered a baby on a nearby reservation.

Onacona Walsh: (born November 22, 1988) son of Shilah and Kimama Walsh, brother to Onacona and Manila. **Nickname:** Hoha; Smoke Signals. **Roommate:** Kiki Walsh. **Trademark:** long, black mane. **Artistic Talent:** silk-screening Native American chiefs on t-shirts in dramatic victory scenes. **Ninja Turtle:** Michelangelo

Manquilla Walsh: (born November 24, 1990) son of Shilah and Kimama Walsh, brother to Paytah and Onacona. **Nickname:** Hacker. **Education:** MIT drop-out. **Personal Achievement:** built his own computer in 4th grade. **Role Model:** Evan Spiegel.

Aidan Walsh: (born August 30, 1991) son of Avanoco and Karen Walsh, brother to Eamon, Kiki, and Falco. **Nickname:** Douska. **Signature Look:** gold-rimmed Warby Parker glasses, multiple layers of Patagonia, a sensible pair of Sperry's. **Titles:** Valedictorian, class of 2009. **Class Notable:** Teacher's Pet. **Best Friends:** "honestly, probably my parents. I'm not ashamed to admit it." **Groups/Affiliations:** Physics Club, Mathletes, Honor Society, High Fraternal Order of Black-Jack ('09). **Foley Crush:** "Does Elliott Appleton count?"

Micheál Walsh: (born October 19, 1991) son of Marty Walsh and Jill McGuinness, brother to Oscar, Callum, and Brendan. **Nicknames:** Baby; Mickey; Pretty Mickey. **Education:** University of Louisville, BA, Theatre Arts, 2013. **Secret Ambition:** to play Black-Jack in the movie version of *Misercordias.* **Personal Legend:** according to Granny McGuinness, it's a crying shame to waste that face on a boy. **Favorite Food:** Italian.

Acknowledgments

Misercordias is a love story, but the true love of my life has been my friends and my family. Every one of my characters has the soul of someone I love. As I send the book into the world, I would like to pause and thank a few souls who made the odyssey so much sweeter:

Cody: I must have been Mother Teresa in my past life to deserve a friendship like yours. Throughout all my personal dramas, you never once let me forget that I was an author in the making. If everyone had a friend like you, dreams would never die and laughter would never end. I love you.

Lila: The fact that you're one of three people on earth who knows where Black-Jack's treasure is buried says it all. You know all my secrets because you ask and you care, and you give your love more selflessly than anyone I know. I think there's no problem your mind cannot solve, and I'm so indebted to you for applying your infallible logic to my books' cartography. Your sisterly love is the ink of my pages. I love you.

Farrell, you are truly the Pat to my Seamus. You are my moon, and Mom is my sun. I worship you both. (PS: Mom, thank you for always paying for my writing classes!) Nicole, you are our rock. And I would like to thank the universe for sending me a real life fairy godmother in the form of Elizabeth Hughes, who simply refused to accept my excuses for not writing. You have shown me unconditional love since I was your Redhead Roundhead. And a big shout out to my rockstar Aunties: Monica, Julie, and Pat. Julie, your heart is oceanic, and our bond is eternal. Pat, you have too much grace, poise, and big-heartedness to not wind up a character (see if you can spot yourself!) Monica, I looked to your Scorpio stinger for inspiration when writing Blaise. You know from my mushy cards how I feel about you, and now the world knows how much I admire your scrappiness.

And to my lawyer, Kelly Fischer: you've been the deus ex machina of my life. I couldn't afford your legal counsel, so my soul harmonized this debt by making you into the most wonderful character. You're my Duffy (minus the curse of 61).

Made in the
USA
Middletown, DE